THE LIGHT TOWER

The Light Tower

By Laurie Lisa

© 2021 by Laurie Lisa

All rights reserved. This book or any portion thereof may not be reproduced or used in any manner whatsoever without the express written permission of the publisher except for the use of brief quotations in a book review.

ISBN: 9798646940569

PROLOGUE

MARCH 22, 1982

As Detective Conrad would later recount to the reporters, his fellow officers, the people in the coffee shop the next morning (and many mornings after that), and his wife over and over again until she tearfully begged him to stop, it was the most *bizarre* thing he had ever seen. "I have been in the department for fifteen years, and I've seen plenty of strange cases, plenty of gruesome cases—I'm not going to go into any of them right now because that would be entirely inappropriate—but I've never seen anything like this. I've helped deliver two babies in taxi cabs, and I've been called to investigate suicide cases that were stranger than fiction, but this?" He would always shake his head at this point in the story. "The woman was *nine months pregnant!*"

Detective Conrad was not the only one talking about the event. Not hardly. The whole town of Bridgeview, Illinois, was talking about the story. Especially the women. The mayor's wife, getting her hair done at Flora's Beauty Shop on Main Street the following Monday morning, said to her captive audience (since she was the mayor's wife, everyone always listened to her, or at least she thought they were supposed to): "I don't know if I'm allowed to say this yet, you know, because of the ongoing investigation." She waited to make sure she had everyone's full attention, and even Flora stopped the mayor's wife's comb-out, the poised comb midair.

The women leaned forward expectantly.

"But the chief of police told my husband that the woman thought her baby was *dead.*"

There was a collective gasp.

"That's right," the mayor's wife continued. "She checked into the maternity ward at St. Matthew Hospital early Sunday morning, and she was convinced that the baby was dead. Even though the doctors let her listen to the baby's heartbeat through their stethoscopes, she still did not believe them."

"No!" the women said.

"Yes." The mayor's wife nodded and then paused, waiting to play her trump card. "And the woman was a nurse!"

"Unbelievable," the women said.

"It is truly unbelievable," the mayor's wife agreed.

"But how did she get out of the hospital and to the abandoned railroad yard?" one woman asked.

"And where was her husband?" another one added.

The mayor's wife, to her dismay, did not know the answer to these questions. "It is an ongoing investigation," she reminded them. "This is all hush-hush."

"Of course," the women said. "Unbelievable."

Police Officer Greg Simpson was not so anxious to speak to anyone about anything. He knew he would never get the image out of his mind. Never. (And he was correct. He would dream about what he had seen on and off for the rest of his life.) His soon-to-be-ex-wife, unlike Detective Conrad's wife, wanted to know every detail, every particular. "But how could she have climbed up that tower if she was *nine months pregnant?*"

He wouldn't have believed it either if he hadn't seen it with his own disbelieving eyes.

"How did she do that, Greg? How did she do it? How could she physically climb up that tower with a bulging belly?"

If he had been inclined to give her an answer, and he was not so inclined, he would have said this: Sheer will. The woman, Melody Arnold (he fervently wished that he had never known her name), had climbed up that tower through the force of *sheer will.*

"I mean, was she having contractions? There is no way in hell that a woman having contractions could climb up that tower. No way in hell."

He shrugged. Whether or not Melody Arnold was having contractions when she climbed up the ladder attached to the side of the light tower was now beside the point. So many useless inanities that spewed from his soon-to-be ex-wife's mouth were utterly beside the point.

"How tall is that light tower anyway? Like fifty feet?"

"Something like that." The light tower was one hundred feet tall. One hundred unbelievable feet.

"Why would a woman do such a terrible thing? I mean, she's going to go to hell, obviously. It's a mortal sin to commit suicide, but when you're nine months pregnant, well, that would also be murder, right?"

Dear God, the woman never shut up. It was the number one reason why she was a soon-to-be ex-wife. "I'm going to take a shower," he said.

In the bathroom, he locked the door to keep out his soon-to-be ex-wife and turned on the water. He turned it as high as it would go. Scalding. He wanted it to be burning, blistering hot. He wanted to feel pain.

Greg Simpson had not done enough to save Melody Arnold. Perhaps no one could have saved her. He knew that, of course. If a woman in her condition had enough *sheer will* to escape from the maternity ward in a hospital, somehow get to the abandoned railroad yard (his department didn't know how she had gotten there yet; they were interviewing cab drivers), and scale a hundred-foot light tower, it was very possible that no one could have stopped her. Yet he felt that he had not done enough to save Melody Arnold.

He was the first officer on the scene, siren blaring, responding to a call that someone—not yet male or female—was climbing up the light tower in the old abandoned railroad yard at 96th Avenue and Blue Line Road. He'd spent the entirety of his twenty-two years in this town, and the railroad yard had been abandoned for as long as he could remember. He and his buddies used to take their dads' guns and shoot at beer bottles on the south side of the yard. Even then, it had been a depressing place, and he had not gone near it in years. When he pulled up to the scene, he found that the old railroad cars were rustier, the yard more overgrown, the whole place more despondent.

But he had no time to dwell on those facts. His concentration was riveted on one fact. A figure was indeed climbing up the scaffolding and was almost to the top. He drove over rusted tracks and toppled gasoline drums until he was as close as he could get to the tower, about forty yards or so. He radioed for an ambulance, jumped out of his car, and ran to the tower.

He waved his arms frantically. "Hey, you! You!" he shouted.

The figure kept climbing, methodically, hand, hand to the next rung and foot, foot to the next rung.

"You!" he shouted, and looking up, even though the figure was tiny, he was pretty sure it was a woman. "Lady, stop!"

There was no sun to impair his vision as he looked skyward. The calendar might have said it was springtime, but it was still dreary, cold, and a gusty wind blew out of the north in Chicagoland. He called to the woman again.

She kept going methodically, hand, hand to the next rung and foot, foot to the next rung.

Stupid, stupid, he chastised himself as he ran back to the squad car. Even if she could have heard him over the wind, she couldn't hear him over his blaring siren. He turned it off and could make out another siren approaching from the north. The ambulance, he thought, or maybe it was his backup. He willed them to hurry as he ran back to the tower.

The woman was now squatting atop the 100-foot-tall light tower.

Adrenaline laced with panic surged through his veins. He'd been on the force for less than a year, and he'd never been in this kind of situation before. In his peripheral vision, he could see a gray overnight bag at the base of the tower. Had the woman been planning a trip? Running away? "Lady, just stay there!" he yelled over the wind. "Help is on the way. Do not move! I'm coming up to get you!"

Before he started up the tower, he wanted to make sure that she understood. She might not be able to see him from her vantage point. He jogged a few steps toward his squad car. He made a megaphone with his hands. "I'm coming up!" he shouted with all his might.

The woman stood up calmly. And jumped.

"No!" he screamed as he stood paralyzed, mesmerized with shock and fear. His mind refused to believe what was happening before his eyes. Her fall was so fast, and yet it seemed to the young officer that it took a lifetime for her to finish the soundless, wordless journey. Her coat flung open mid-fall, and that was when Greg Simpson realized that the woman was pregnant. It was impossible to miss the enormously rounded belly.

"Jesus Christ," he said aloud to the howling, indifferent wind. She was trying to kill herself *and* her baby. This wasn't a run-of-the-mill suicide (as if there were such a thing, he fleetingly thought). This was a fucking *tragedy*.

He closed his eyes and covered his ears, not wanting to see or hear the impact of her body on the still-frozen ground. He was never, ever going to get the image of the pregnant woman's free fall out of his memory. He knew this. He also knew that he should have found some way—he should have used *sheer will*—to help this lost woman and her baby.

Tanner Delaney and Mario Capino arrived approximately two minutes after the woman jumped from the 100-foot-tall light tower. A badly shaken young police officer was on his radio, and Delaney and Capino moved right in. "We'll take it from here," Delaney said to the poor kid. He was as white as a ghost.

They were seasoned professionals, veterans of the mangled and macabre things that could happen, or be done, to the human body. Delaney had been an EMT for ten years, Capino for seven. Really, they thought that they had pretty much seen it all. In their profession, they were practically the granddads of the team. (In their profession, a person could burn out fast. It was a fact. A soul could only witness so much damage and distress.)

"This kind of thing, always bad news," Capino said as they knelt by the body, which had landed face-down. "It's like a dog chasing its tail in your brain, a rabid dog, poor thing."

"Should have gotten the dog a rabies shot," Delaney said. Sure, he was sympathetic to the plight of these poor saps who could see no other way out but to kill themselves—not as sympathetic as Capino, obviously. Sure, Delaney was. Maybe he was. But when you got right down to it, it was a fucking waste of human life.

"No pulse," Capino said.

"A lot of distance to the ground," Delaney said. "Let's turn her over." They gently turned over the body.

"Jesus, Mary, and Joseph," Capino gasped.

No, Delaney and Capino had not seen it all.

They were not looking at the condition of the victim's face, the damage that had been inflicted on this pretty young woman's face when she landed face-down after a 100-foot leap. They were not looking at that at all. What they now knew was that the woman had been pregnant when she jumped; Delaney guessed near to full-term. But this was the thing: Was she still pregnant? A baby's legs protruded from the woman's stomach, which had apparently ruptured during the fall. But this was the most astounding thing: The baby's legs were *twitching*.

"Jesus, Mary, and Joseph," Capino gasped again.

Delaney could not have agreed more. "We've got to get this baby out."

They worked quickly, performing a crude kind of C-section. "Dear God, let this baby live," Capino said. "Say it, Delaney, if this ain't the time to get religion, I don't know what is."

Capino, for once, was right, Delaney thought. Even though he'd left the Catholic Church years ago, a little help from God would come in handy right about now. "Dear God, let this baby live," he said, and they repeated it until they gave the final tug and pulled the baby free of its dead mother.

The baby started to cry, and the two men looked at each other in teary disbelief. They were tough men—no one could doubt that—but no one would ever fault them for welling up at this moment. The baby, against insurmountable odds, had survived a 100-foot jump from a light tower. The baby was *alive*.

"It's a godsend," Capino choked out.

Delaney cradled the soft round head in his large hand and tucked the baby under his coat. "It's a girl," he said.

Doctor Desoto at Mercy Hospital thought it would be a good idea to hold a press conference after the baby was brought in. It was bad enough that his usually professional and stoic staff was swirling around rumors after the two burly EMTs brought in the baby and described the circumstances of her birth. Oh, the outpouring of sympathy, especially from the nurses, quickly escalated into a geyser of misplaced maternal longing.

"Oh, the poor little lamb," they said.

"She's a miracle baby," they said.

"If she were my baby, I'd name her Angel," a young Candy Striper said.

Dr. Desoto, as close as he was to retirement, had not grown more mellow. He *detested* Candy Stripers, could never see rhyme, reason, or purpose for them in his hospital. "She's not your baby," he had snapped. The Candy Striper, naturally, had cried.

The gossip mill churned out even more rumors when the staff discovered who the baby's mother was, and Dr. Desoto could do nothing to stem the tide as nurse after nurse, her colleagues, murmured in disbelief in the hallway.

"How could she have done such a thing?" they asked.

"She was such a good nurse," they said.

"I worked in the ER with her the last day before she took her maternity leave," one said. "She seemed in good spirits."

"We should have thrown her a baby shower," they said.

Dr. Desoto sighed. His nurses were such an emotional lot. However, he was perplexed, too. The woman had been a competent, caring nurse, and if he remembered correctly—really, he should have retired five years before; the memory was starting to slip a little—she had a level head on her shoulders. He could not say that for most of his nurses.

The unforgivable fact that his nurses were gossiping in the hallways and ignoring their patients was the straw that broke the camel's back. He called the local paper, and the newsmen swooped in like vultures. (Dr. Desoto detested newsmen even more than he disliked the Candy Stripers.) He had the staff set up a podium in the nurses' lounge. He put on a clean, white lab coat, wrapped a stethoscope around his neck, combed his still-thick silver hair, and made his entrance.

"This will be brief," he said, "and I would appreciate one question at a time." There was no need for the vultures to caw over each other until he couldn't hear a thing. His hearing, too, was starting to slip a little.

"How did the baby survive the fall?" was the first question.

That, he could answer. "I speculate that because the mother's amniotic sac was still intact when she jumped off the light tower, the amniotic sac may have acted as a cushion and ensured the baby's survival."

"How can that happen?" a young red-headed woman asked.

"Evidently, it can." He smiled at her. He had always had a fondness for redheads.

"What is the baby's physical condition?" the next asked.

"The baby has been checked for internal injuries, of which there are none. However, she does have a broken left leg. She is currently in an incubator and on oxygen."

The questions continued, factual questions that he factually answered until someone got to the question he had dreaded. "I understand the woman," the newsman looked down at his notes, "this Melody Arnold was an ER nurse at this hospital."

"That is correct," he said.

"Was Mrs. Arnold in any way mentally unstable during the last few months?"

Dr. Desoto cleared his throat. "Not that I am aware of. I am not a psychiatrist. I am an internist."

"When did Mrs. Arnold check into the maternity ward?"

"Nurse Arnold was not a patient at this hospital."

It was then that the vultures ceased being polite and started peppering him with questions: Why did she not check into this hospital, where she worked? Where was the baby's father? What were the odds of surviving a fall from a 100-foot light tower?

Dr. Desoto became confused. This press conference had been a mistake. So many questions, and he didn't have an answer for any of them. "I'm not sure … No comment." The room was hot, and it started to spin.

A nurse, who had been standing at the back of the crowd, pushed her way through the newsmen and came to the podium and the rescue of the old doctor. She took his arm and set him down firmly—almost roughly—on a nearby metal folding chair. Even with her platinum blonde hair up and pinned under her standard white hat, she was a handsome woman. Not conventionally pretty, but *handsome*, with high cheekbones, a broad forehead, and full lipstick-red lips.

"My name is Sylvia Hammond, and I am—was—a friend of Melody Arnold."

The noise of the crowd escalated. The loudest voice called out: "Why did she do it?"

"I can't answer that question." Under the calm veneer of her contralto voice, an astute reporter would be able to detect a slight wavering tremor.

"Can't or won't?" called out the same cawing voice.

Sylvia Hammond ignored the question. "I can't tell you the actual odds of surviving a fall from that light tower. I am not a mathematician. I am an ER nurse, the same as Melody Arnold. But I have been out to that light tower, and I urge you to do the same. It's *one hundred feet tall*. Do you know how tall that is? Go out and look up at that tower, and you won't believe this whole thing. You won't believe that a woman who was nine months pregnant climbed up that ladder. You won't believe that a baby survived that fall. There's only one explanation, just one."

The crowd, silent now, waited, their pens poised above their notepads for the answer.

"It's a miracle," Sylvia Hammond said. "It's a *miracle*."

1

MARCH 2012

Kat Flowers was flying, soaring through the air, as majestic as an eagle in the cloudless blue sky. This had been a dream of hers for as long as she could remember, this effortless flight. Kat wanted the feeling of weightlessness to go on forever. She wanted to fly into eternity.

"Ma'am, are you going to jump or not?" The skydiving instructor was standing next to her in the open door of the plane.

Kat opened her eyes. "It's *Miss*," she said. Two days after she turned thirty, and it was like the whole world knew that she was no longer a twenty-something, allowed to fuck up and laugh it off with a, "You know, I'm still very young. I'm practically a *baby*." Nope. In the two days since her birthday, she had been called *Ma'am* three times. The first was the pimply check-out boy in the grocery store, the second a wretchedly young female teller at the bank (who had snottily told her that having checks left in her checkbook did not guarantee that she had money in her account), and now this. And this guy with his soul patch and crinkled eyes had to be older than her. (Maybe it was the helmet? If he could see her long reddish-blonde hair, and if she put it in her usual ponytail, maybe he would realize his mistake. She didn't look anywhere near the *Ma'am* status quo.)

"*Miss*, are you going to jump or not?" He didn't succeed in keeping the exasperation out of his voice.

"Just give me a second, okay?" She was all right if she looked straight out the open door. It was if she looked down at the shifting ground far, far away that she felt nauseated.

"We're over our mark," he said.

She didn't give a rat's ass if they were over their stupid mark. She wasn't ready to jump yet. She could do this; she knew she could. Just not yet.

"Breathe," he instructed.

"I am breathing." She wanted to point out to him that it wasn't her lungs causing the problem. It was the *terror* that glued her boots to the floor of the plane, the terror that would not let her lift her left leg to take that first and only irreversible step out of the damn plane.

"I'll be right with you."

"Good to know," Kat said. What if her chute didn't open, and then by some terrible twist of fate, his didn't open, and then they would be plummeting to the earth, helpless against the inescapable pull of gravity? She would die mangled in a mangled stranger's arms. And she didn't even like him much, the skydiving instructor with the stupid soul patch.

He sighed. "Circle back one more time," he yelled to the pilot.

This would be the third time they had *circled back*. Kat wanted to say to him, "Look, buddy, I paid for this lesson. It's my dime, and you should really show me some consideration." Instead, she said, "Am I going to have to pay for the extra gasoline?"

He actually smiled. "No, it's already worked into the price of the lesson." He patted Kat's shoulder. "This happens all the time."

"Really?" Kat felt a little better.

"Sure. People think they want to skydive, but it's a whole different ballgame when they physically get up here. When push comes to shove, they can't do it."

"You're not going to shove me out of the plane, are you?" Kat said, alarmed.

"Not unless you ask me to."

"Believe me, that's the *last* thing I would ask you to do." She'd rather ask him to sleep with her. And she didn't even like him much, the skydiving instructor with the stupid soul patch. What in the world was a soul patch for? It was an obnoxious nub of hair below the lower lip that, honestly, looked like the guy had missed a spot shaving.

"Close your eyes and visualize the jump," Soul Patch said.

"All right." But she couldn't visualize the jump. Instead, she was visualizing what Soul Patch would look like naked. He had a good body, tall and lean, and she had to admit to herself that she had slept with worse guys before, back in the days when she was slightly slutty, back in her twenties when she had been young and foolish. Now she was thirty, and she was *not* going to sleep with Soul Patch.

Besides, she had a live-in boyfriend, Benson. Benson O'Shea, a part-time model, a part-time golf pro, and a full-time trust fund baby. But because the trust fund distributions were not large, Benson always had some scheme going, some get-rich-quick plan that would raise some fast cash to pay for his manicures, pedicures, waxing, and the occasional Botox injection. And the pot. Benson loved his pot. And she loved Benson O'Shea (most of the time, some of the time—well, maybe not too much). He was her personal B.O.

"We're almost to our mark," Soul Patch said.

"Okay." She could do this; she knew she could. It was a beautiful early spring day. The sky was blue, cloudless, like the backdrop in a movie set. She had dreamed about this moment for so long, and in her dreams, the weightless flight gave her a feeling of peace, an inner serenity that she did not have in real life.

"Are you going to jump, Miss?"

Why did Soul Patch keep asking her that? She had paid for and taken the lesson, hadn't she? She was in this damn plane, wasn't she? "Kat," she said.

"Cat?" He peered down at the ground. "Do you see a bobcat or something?"

No, she was definitely not going to sleep with him. He wasn't very bright. Although this, too, had never stopped her before. She had slept with a lot of stupid boy-men in her slightly slutty twenties. "My name is Kat, with a K," she explained patiently.

Soul Patch still looked confused.

"Kat. Short for Katrina."

"Like the New Orleans hurricane," he said.

"I was named *before* the hurricane that hit New Orleans." Before the devastating hurricane that hit New Orleans in 2005, she had liked her name. But after that horrible storm, it became a burden to have a name that everyone associated with disaster. Katrina equaled flooding, displacement, and a foul-smelling Superdome. It was better to be called Kat.

"Are you going to jump, Kat?"

"Yes, I am." But she was still holding—clutching—the side of the door.

"On the count of three?" Soul Patch asked.

"Absolutely."

"One."

Kat took a deep breath. One step. That's all it was. One step. And then she would be flying.

"Two."

"Is this your real job, or is it like a part-time thing?" Kat needed to distract him. Her heart had started to pound painfully in her chest, and her lungs were definitely not working now. It hurt to breathe.

Soul Patch grabbed her hand, ready to buckle them together. "Two and a half ..."

"It's been nice knowing you," Kat said.

"Three!"

Kat wrenched her hand from Soul Patch's just as he leaped from the plane. "I'll see you on the ground," she called after his falling form. "Adios, amigo!"

Kat did what she always did when she needed to lick her wounds, devour a tube of cookie dough, or slug down a shot of single malt scotch. She went to Granny Nanny's. Technically, Nancy Tebrow was not a grandmother. Technically, Nancy Tebrow was not Kat's grandmother.

Technically, Nancy Tebrow was not related by blood to Kat at all. That didn't matter. Ever since Kat, at age sixteen, had found her way to Arizona and fallen (literally, miraculously) into the comforting arms of Nancy Tebrow, they had become a family of two, a duo of unconditional love. They were related in a way that was stronger than blood. They were related by choice.

Over the years, Granny Nanny had embellished the story more than a little. "I had just dropped off my friend Verna, who was going to visit her nephew in Boise. Then I saw you sitting on that hard, cold bench in the smelly bus station—and it was smelly because some drunk had just thrown up in the wastebasket in the corner—and I just knew we were supposed to be a family," she always said. (It wasn't a drunk who had just thrown up in the wastebasket. It was Kat herself. After not eating during the entire bus ride to Arizona, she had unwisely bought an egg salad sandwich from the vending machine. A big mistake and a lesson learned. Egg salad sandwiches of indeterminate age *did not belong* in unrefrigerated vending machines.)

"You looked so lost, just sitting there with a crust of bread in your hands and your battered suitcase at your feet," Granny Nanny would continue. (Kat had not had a crust of bread in her hands. She had already thrown up the entire rotten egg salad sandwich, and she didn't have a battered suitcase. She had only brought a backpack.)

"I walked over to you and said, 'Honey, are you lost?' And then you burst into tears." (That part was true.)

"And then you looked at me with those darling blue eyes of yours and said, 'I am lost and homeless.'"

That was so not true. What Kat had said was, "I think I'm going to throw up again."

Granny Nanny always got a tear in her eye at this point in the embellished narrative. "And then you told me the entire story about how your mean father had kicked you out of your house because you were disrespectful to your atrocious stepmother, who totally deserved to be disrespected, and how you had no place to go."

So not true. Not even close. Kat had told her only the bare facts. She'd run away from home because her father, who was not mean but who was certainly distant, had said to her that she was not allowed to see Bobby Baker anymore. Bobby Baker, according to her father, was a low-life juvenile delinquent. According to her father, Bobby Baker was a rebel without a cause—no, he was too *stupid* to even know what a *cause* meant—and he was a bad influence. (She would never admit it to anyone, but her father had been right about that one. Years later, when she googled Bobby Baker, she found out that he served time in prison for mail fraud. Kat would have been more impressed if he served time for kidnapping or something like that, but no. It was just a boring crime.)

"And then you collapsed, *sobbing*, into my arms. You poor helpless thing. You were so desperately, *utterly* alone."

Kat had been too naïve to realize that she was desperately, utterly alone. No, in her recollection, she was crying because somehow she had misplaced forty dollars in the distance from Carbondale to Phoenix. Her plan all along had been to stop in Phoenix and change buses, just in case her father was following, which of course he wasn't. It was then on to San Diego, where Bobby had said he would be waiting for her. (She would never know whether Bobby Baker had really gone to California, but she would bet thousands of dollars—if she had it—that he had not.)

"And then I took your hand and led you gently out of that dreadful bus station, and I said to you—I remember this like it was yesterday—'This is the beginning of a beautiful friendship.'"

Complete and total bullshit. Granny Nanny had actually said, "We better call your parents and let them know you're okay."

But what did the facts of the story really matter? The point of the story was that Kat and Granny Nanny had found each other. It took very little persuasion to convince her father that his only daughter should be allowed to live with a total stranger thousands of miles away from her home. It was downright shocking how little persuasion it took for him and his wife, Missy, to let her go. It was a crying shame that her dad didn't get on the next plane to Phoenix and fetch her back home, scolding her all the way for being so irresponsible, for causing so much worry and heartache. It was *fucking unbelievable* that her father, Marcus Flowers, would basically say: "You want to finish raising my kid? Be my guest. Drop me a line every now and then, let bygones be bygones, and so on and so forth. *Sayonara, kiddo!*"

Well, maybe it wasn't so fucking unbelievable when you knew the whole story.

Kat pulled up to Granny Nanny's cozy little bungalow in south Scottsdale, noticing again that the small house needed a coat of paint. It was starting to look a little sad. She walked up the bougainvillea-edged path and let herself in the front screen door. "Honey, I'm home!" she called out.

"In here," Granny Nanny called from the kitchen in the back.

The house smelled like a stink bomb. "What are you making? It smells awful."

"Hello to you, too," Gran said.

"Seriously, Gran, what are you making?" Kat tried to breathe through her mouth, but she could practically taste the offending odor.

Granny Nanny continued stirring the enormous pot on the stove. "A little of this, a little of that. I had a head of cabbage that was going bad, and then I noticed that I had a lonely potato in the back of the vegetable drawer. And then I noticed that I had a couple of cans of beans that were pretty dusty from their long shelf life, and then I noticed that my cumin expired last year, for heaven's sake, and then I decided—what the hell— let's just throw in that tilapia filet I've been meaning to eat for lunch for the past week. And then a little of this and a little of that. I'm calling it ghoulish goulash."

"Don't plan on me staying for dinner." Kat hugged her short Granny from behind. Kat could easily lift the tiny woman if she wanted to.

"Now, my dear Katrina, you don't want to go and hurt an old lady's feelings, do you? And I was planning on bringing out the good china." Granny Nanny turned around. Her lips twitched in an effort not to smile. Her long greyish-white hair was tucked into its usual braided bun, and her blue eyes sparkled in her smooth face.

It was impossible to tell how old Nancy Tebrow was. When Kat was sixteen and meeting her for the first time, she thought Nancy Tebrow had been ancient. However, she still looked exactly the same. She could have been sixty-five, or she could have been eighty-five. It was downright eerie when Kat thought about it. Her skin was smoothly pink and had few wrinkles. "How do you get your skin to look like that?" Kat had often asked when she was younger and thought she could wear Granny Nanny down (*never* going to happen). "Noxzema cold cream," Granny Nanny always said. "I've been using it all my life, and when I find something that works, I stick with it. I'm a one-product kind of gal."

Of course, Kat had asked Granny Nanny numerous times how old she was, and all the conversations followed roughly the same pattern. "So, Gran, how old are you really?"

"Age is only a number," Granny Nanny would say. At that point, she would either pick up her knitting and start clicking needles or pick up her Ruger Lightweight Compact Revolver and start polishing—whichever was closer.

"Sure, age is only a number, but I want to know what your number is. I swear I won't tell anyone. Cross my heart and hope to die." Kat would make the X across her heart.

"I have often wondered where that expression came from. It's absolutely horrible. Who in his right mind would hope to die?" Granny Nanny would sorrowfully shake her head as she started to knit one, pearl two, or as she dismantled the cartridge from the pistol.

"Just give me a hint. How many wars have you lived through of the following: WWI, WWII, Korea, Vietnam?"

"I have not *personally* been in any war, not a WAC or a Rosie the Riveter or a bandage roller or a USO girl. But thanks for asking."

"I'm only asking for you to put me in the general ballpark, Nanny. Throw me a crumb. Give me a lousy decade."

"I like the one I'm in. I always like the one I am currently living in the best. They just keep getting better and better."

An eighteen-year-old Kat would then say, "You think I can't find out? One of these days, when you're not looking, I'll check your driver's license." That was easier said than done. For unknown reasons, Granny Nanny practically slept with her purse. "You snooze off once during the day, old lady, you take a quick cat nap and bam! I'm on it like a fly on shit."

Granny Nanny would give her a loving smile and say, "You do that, dear."

"I will. I swear, I will."

Still smiling, Granny Nanny would say, "You do that, dear, and I will be on *you* like a fly on shit."

So, of course, Kat never looked at Granny Nanny's license. What was the point? It took some time before the full enormity of the realization struck. She was never, ever going to wear Granny Nanny down. Never. Ever. And she could respect that.

Now, in the foul-smelling kitchen, Kat hugged her gran far longer than was strictly necessary. "I thought you pawned the good china to buy the new flat-screen TV."

"Oh, you're right, dear. I get much more use out of that TV than I ever did out of that china." She stepped back from the hug and looked at Kat closely. "How was the skydiving?"

Without waiting for an answer, she moved to the cabinet. "I'll get down the scotch."

Kat slumped into a kitchen chair. "Still on the bucket list." She had thought she could do it; she really did. After the plane landed and she made her way back into the hangar, she quickly changed out of the gear. But alas, she ran into Soul Patch anyway. "Better luck next time, Kat." Without his helmet, he wasn't appealing at all, with a balding circle on the top of his head. She was never going to sleep with him. And for some reason—and it made her feel a little better—she felt like she had dodged a bullet.

Granny Nanny poured two slugs. They clinked glasses and downed them. "Next time, Katrina. You will do it next time."

Katrina poured two more shots. "Yes."

"One of the things I've always loved about you, dear, is that you're a dreamer. You have plenty of time to accomplish your goals."

"I'm fucking thirty, Granny Nanny. *Thirty.*" The second slug of scotch burned even more on the way down.

"Age is only a number, dear."

What the hell. Kat would ask one more time. "How old are you, Gran?"

"It does stink in here, doesn't it? Let me see if I have some candles." She got up to rummage through a drawer.

Kat sighed. Still not going to happen. "Can I throw out the ghoulish goulash?"

"You haven't even tasted it yet."

"That's not going to happen. I could call the HazMat team. That would be a better plan."

Granny Nanny, not finding any candles, had moved to the stove. She stirred and tentatively took a sip. "Or poison control. This is truly dreadful. Well, *say la vie*! Some experiments work and some flop. The ghoulish goulash is a total flop."

Kat smiled. She did feel better. Granny Nanny could always be counted on for raising her spirits. So what if she hadn't jumped? So what if she had not yet soared through the air? As Granny Nanny said, some experiments worked, and some flopped. Her phone vibrated, and she took it out of her pocket. "It's Benson."

"How is Benson, dear?" Even though Kat had been with Benson O'Shea for almost a year, Granny Nanny still wasn't convinced of his character. As she put it, "The jury is still out on that young man. It is very hard to trust a pretty man, Katrina, and that man is pretty. He's as pretty as a girl."

"A little of this, and a little of that," Kat said.

"I should ask him where he gets his nails done," Granny Nanny said nonchalantly.

"You've never in your life had a manicure," Kat pointed out. She grinned. She knew what Granny Nanny wanted.

"Well, Katrina, there is a first time for everything."

"I'll bring some over the next time I come," Kat said, still grinning.

"If it's not too much trouble."

Kat stood up to leave. "No problem, Gran."

"You are such a dear, Katrina, such a blessing to me." She hugged her. "Now, don't forget, okay?"

"I won't."

It would be very hard for Kat to forget that Granny Nanny had taken a fancy, as she put it, to pretty boy Benson's pot.

When Kat got home to the second-story condo at Gainey Ranch that she shared with pretty boy Benson, he wasn't there. Where in the hell was he? She'd rushed home—well, maybe not *rushed*; she had stopped at Home Depot to buy light bulbs—when he'd texted her at Granny Nanny's that he was waiting for her. They were going to celebrate her birthday properly tonight, Saturday, since she had worked the previous two nights. Benson, of course, had not worked at all this week. The one person—an older, society-type woman—he had scheduled a golf lesson with had canceled. All Benson's clients were older, society-type women.

She had a good idea where he was, though. She walked through the startlingly, blindingly white condo to the small terrace off the living room. Even after almost a year of living there, the whiteness of the place still unsettled her. The walls were white, the furniture was white, the floor was off-white travertine, the linens were white. White, white, white, white. In the beginning, Kat had said to Benson when she first moved in, "This condo is absolutely *racist*. God forbid if even a black potholder would walk in here. The KKK décor would lynch it before it dared to jump into a kitchen drawer."

"Yeah," Benson agreed, looking around as if he had noticed the non-color for the first time. "It was the first place my mom decorated, and I guess she thought that if everything was white, she couldn't mess anything up." Benson's mom, Carmella, fancied herself to be some kind of interior designer extraordinaire. But as far as Kat could see, Carmella mostly went out to lunch with her friends and would then take them to an exorbitantly priced furniture store and help them pick out a lamp or an accent table that they really didn't need.

"You can move your stuff in, Kat, you know, change things around a little," Benson graciously offered.

Kat had only brought with her two suitcases of clothes and a box of her precious junk: old journals, some pictures, a few books, her favorite CDs. Since she moved here from Granny Nanny's, she didn't yet have any furniture or sheets or towels. "Maybe we could throw a few serapes around, liven the place up a little. They sell them cheap at the flea market." Kat thought that wouldn't be too drastic.

But Benson's face went as white as the walls. "Um, I think that might be going a little too far. Well, um, actually, I think that might push Mother over the edge, decoratively speaking. I don't think that *serape* is in her vocabulary. Decoratively speaking."

Now that Kat had been exposed to Carmella O'Shea, she knew that *serape* was not in her vocabulary. Period. Still, for a time after she moved in, Kat had thought that she might run over to the mall and buy some flaming red throw pillows or a bold geometric rug or a framed poster that had some color in it. But she kept putting it off, and off, and off, and now it was a year later, and she lived in a racist condo with a pretty boy whose mother had (God forbid!) never stepped inside a Walmart and thought that everyone went to a champagne brunch on Sunday.

But Benson adored his mother, and she adored him. That's what they always said to each other in parting. Not I love you. I *adore* you. It was a little sickening, really, but Kat tried to act politely around Carmella—well, she tried not to roll her eyes at the things that came out of Carmella's mouth—if she was forced to sit through one of Carmella's three-hour champagne brunches. (Actually, the brunches were not that bad.) And there was a rather essential fact: Carmella owned the condo, and she only charged her son and Kat a nominal rent. And there was another monumental fact: Carmella controlled her son's allowance.

Kat Flowers lived with a thirty-two-year-old part-time model, part-time golf pro who got an allowance from his mother.

What in the hell was wrong with her?

Kat rationalized it this way. Number one, she lived in a great upscale community that she could never in a million years afford on her own. Number two, she'd been having a little trouble keeping a job in the last year. She was "between careers," she would tell people, not honestly telling them that her mouth was always getting her in trouble. So the price and security of the condo made sense. Number three, Benson was nice to her, nicer than any other boyfriend she had ever had. Granted, she hadn't had any nice boyfriends before Benson, so it wasn't too difficult to beat that standard. Benson, if he had the money, liked to buy her flowers or a new dress and take her out for lavish dinners in Old Town Scottsdale. Of course, more often than not, he had to ask his mother for his allowance.

What in the *hell* was *wrong* with her?

Their second-story terrace overlooked the pool—naturally, Carmella would only buy a condo that overlooked the pool—and it was not hard to spot Benson on a chaise lounge. Kat couldn't miss his long, lean, glistening-with-oil, Speedo-clad body. Benson prided himself on his year-round tan. Kat, who tended to sunburn, never went near the pool, but Benson was a regular. "Hey, Benny!" she called. "I'm home, so you better haul your ass up here!"

He didn't respond. His eyes were closed, and his foot twitched, keeping time to whatever song was coming out of the earbuds of his iPod.

"Don't make me come down there," she called uselessly. Benson had probably forgotten all about the time, lost in the music of his Adonis tanning. This was supposed to be her birthday celebration, damn it, and she was not going to go down there and drag his sorry butt out of the chaise lounge. Despite a couple of scotch shots and her time with Granny Nanny, Kat was suddenly in a very sour mood. She had failed to jump out of the airplane, and she didn't particularly want to be thirty years old.

She'd always thought she would be so much farther along in her life by this age. When she'd graduated from Northern Arizona University eight years earlier, she thought finding her perfect career would be easy, even though it had been difficult for her to pick a major. She had switched from political science to environmental sciences to theater to finally end up with a general, ambiguous degree in business because that was what everyone else seemed to be majoring in that year. "I can do anything I want with this degree," she had said at the time. "I can manage an interesting store that sells artsy collectibles, or run an upscale restaurant, or even, eventually, start my own company."

It had been so much easier said than done, especially when a newly-minted college graduate didn't really have the slightest clue what she wanted to do or who she wanted to be and had realized—too late—that she should not have majored in business. Plus, starting at the bottom was never her modus operandi, and even though she had been a good student, it turned out that, in the real world, she didn't take direction very well. At a small company in Scottsdale that sold air conditioning units, her first job had been in sales, and on the day that her car conked out and her boss wanted her to work overtime yet again, she'd quit. After that, she'd worked in various offices in various cubicles and stared at various boring spreadsheets. She never lasted more than a few weeks at any one place. Not surprisingly, that kind of thing did not look good on a girl's resume. Flitting around from job to job simply screamed to potential employers: unreliable, ditzy, beware of attention-deficit girl!

The truth of the matter was that she was bored stiff. She hated business, she hated cubicles, and she hated the weekly staff meetings—but not as much if they served muffins or donuts. "You'll find your way, dear," Granny Nanny kept assuring through a succession of retail, telemarketing, and restaurant jobs. "A college education is a tool for life." Sometimes, *rarely*, Kat wished that Granny Nanny would just smoke some pot and shut up.

Now, at the age of thirty, armed with her college education, her *tool for life*, Kat worked as a waitress at Tilted Kilt. She wore a tiny kilt and a bustier and served beer to paunchy, pawing, drunken men. The only thing that made Kat feel better was that, arguably, it was one step up from being a Hooters girl.

So now, with her mood growing increasingly sour, she was not going to watch her pretty boyfriend bask in the sun a minute longer. (What kind of man liked to tan anyway?) Kat knew she'd bought one for Halloween last year when she and Benson went to a party dressed as Bonnie and Clyde, and she found it in her underwear drawer. She filled the squirt gun with water at the white kitchen sink and went back out onto the terrace. Thanks to target shooting with Granny Nanny at Scottsdale Gun Club, Kat had become a pretty good aim. She aimed it right at his head.

"Hey!" Benson popped out of the chaise, looking around to see if any kids were splashing in the pool.

It was so satisfying. Kat squirted him again, right in the middle of his forehead. He looked up, and Kat sprayed him again. "We're supposed to be getting ready to go out and celebrate my birthday, Benny."

"Hey, Kat, stop being such a B. I must have fallen asleep. I'll be right up." He gathered up his towel.

He truly was a good-looking man, with his jet-black hair, blue eyes, and sculpted body. Of course, Benson worked out regularly. He had a personal trainer at Gold's Gym. And his tan. He had a nice, even tan. Kat couldn't help but notice how women stared at him when they went out, and she knew she should feel at least a twinge of jealousy or possessiveness. She knew she should probably have said on more than one occasion, "Hands off, bitch, he's mine." But she never had.

She went inside the whiteness and into the kitchen to empty the squirt gun at the white sink. And that's when she spied the stack of mail on the counter. The mail was where they always put it, nothing unusual about that. What was unusual was the envelope on top of the pile.

It was from her father.

"You should have just opened it, Kat," Benson said. "It's probably a birthday card, a simple birthday card from your father." He carefully buttered his dinner roll.

Some birthday celebration so far. Kat usually loved coming to El Chorro, with its fantastic view of Camelback Mountain, and she loved sitting on the patio and the cowboy memorabilia that decorated the walls inside. However, seeing that communication, that message from her father, had pushed her bad mood over the edge. "We're going to need another bottle of wine," she said to Benson.

She had not opened it. No, she had not. After all this time, why did he have to go and send a card or whatever it was? In the silent years, she could almost forget that he existed. She could almost forget that she had a stepmother and two half-brothers, who were four and six. Wait a minute. They would be how old now? Shit. They would now be eighteen and twenty, young men she didn't know and wouldn't recognize on the street. She took a big gulp of her wine. That was why she hadn't opened the card. It would be like opening a can of worms, and Kat had long ago buried those squirming worms.

She had thrown the card in the trash. Benson, unfortunately, coming up from the pool, walked into the kitchen at that moment, his towel draped over his shoulder. "What are you doing?" he asked, retrieving the card and reading the return address. "It might be important."

During the year of their relationship, she had, on a few scattered occasions, told Benson the basic facts of her upbringing before Granny Nanny—no elaboration, only the facts, and being Benson, he didn't try to dig deeper. But now, after ordering a second bottle of wine, he repeated what he had said in the kitchen, "It might be important."

"It isn't." Kat picked at her trout almandine, which she ordinarily devoured on the special occasions they came here, usually with Carmella, who would always pick up the check.

"How long has it been since you've heard from him?"

It just figured that Benson would pick *now* to start asking questions. "A while," she said.

"Like how long?"

"I don't think that cell phones had been invented yet." Kat took another gulp of wine.

"How did people live without cell phones?" Benson asked.

That was more like the easily distracted Benson that she sort of, kind of loved (maybe). "I don't know. How did people live without the internet?"

"Dark Times," Benson said.

"Prehistoric," Kat replied.

"How's your filet, sir?" Their handsome young waiter, who had said his name was Myron, seemed to have developed an infatuation with Benson. Currently serving time waitressing at Tilted Kilt, Kat noticed that he'd been to their table twice as many times as he'd been to the other tables in his station.

"Great." Benson gave Myron the same dazzling smile he gave to everyone.

"It's one of the house specialties," Myron said. "Did you see that commercial for Walmart prime steaks, you know, the one where they go to an upscale restaurant and replace the chef's steaks with the ones from Walmart?"

"I don't watch much TV," Benson said politely.

Kat rolled her eyes, not that either of the men noticed. Myron positively hovered, and Benson lied for no particular reason. Benson watched TV constantly.

"Well, they filmed one of the commercials here, and guess what? No one could tell the difference!"

"Wow," Benson said.

"I know, right? Chef Louie was not particularly happy about the whole thing, and naturally, we had to comp all the meals." Myron seemed genuinely happy to be sharing this information with Benson.

"Wow," Benson said again.

"Can I get you anything else, sir?"

"Some peace and quiet," Kat said.

After Myron hurried off, Benson said, "He was only making conversation, Kat."

"A good waiter is not supposed to hover while the guests are eating."

"You can be awfully mean for such a pretty girl."

Kat couldn't help but smile. That was the line that Benson always used when she was being especially peevish. Really, she should lighten up. They were having a fabulous meal at one of her favorite restaurants to celebrate her fucking thirtieth birthday. After all this time, the letter or card or whatever from her dad meant nothing, absolutely nothing. When they got home, she would not throw the damn thing away. She would take it out to the dumpster and burn it.

Kat gave Benson's line her usual reply, "We both know that you're the pretty one in this relationship." It was true. Her B.O. was jaw-droppingly gorgeous. Kat knew that she was attractive *enough* with her long reddish-blonde hair and blue eyes. People meeting her for the first time always guessed that she was Irish. Her father was primarily English, Kat thought, and as for her mother ... Well, she had no idea what ethnicity her mother had been.

"I hate it when you say that," Benson said. "It makes me sound so gay."

"Well, I think we've cleared it up that you're hetero." However, Kat would be lying to herself if she said she hadn't thought that Benson might be gay or bi on more than one occasion. He was just so damn pretty! But maybe that was the curse of all pretty men, to be mistaken for gay? However, if Kat were to continue with her self-confession, she would have to admit that their sex life was a tad bit *iffy*. Obviously, they did all the expected and standard things, but he just didn't turn her on like some of the bad boys in her slightly slutty twenties.

"Let's order dessert," Benson said nonchalantly, then added, "So, how long has it been since you heard from your dad?"

"A while! Can you give it a rest, Benson?" She did, of course, know precisely how long it had been since she heard from her father: ten years. After she ran away to Arizona and found Granny Nanny, her father had sent her a birthday card every year with a check for one hundred dollars. The card would always say something like, "I hope you're well" and "Use the money to buy something you need." And every year for those first four years, she would make a big show of writing a polite, terse note saying, "Thanks but no thanks," and send the unendorsed check back. Then, when she turned twenty-one, no more cards, no more checks. *Nada.* She tried to hide how much that had hurt her from Granny Nanny, but Granny

Nanny knew, and it still haunted Kat how much that ending of their scanty communication stung.

"Look, Kat, if my dad was still alive, I'd want to have some communication with him. That's all I'm saying."

Kat felt a flush of shame. Benson's dad had died racing a speed boat when Benson was ten, and he still sometimes cried about it. Really, it was no wonder that Benson became such a Mama's boy. "I'm sorry I snapped at you, Benny."

"After all this time—whatever amount of time it has been—he might be trying to tell you something. It might be important. That's all I'm saying." For Benson, his words were forceful.

"Maybe so," Kat placated. She needed to distract him again.

"I mean, maybe there's been a death in the family, or maybe your dad has cancer or some other terminal disease?"

"Jesus." In her anger and distrust, Kat hadn't really thought along those lines. Sometimes, the unbidden thought would come to her: What would she do if Granny Nanny became ill or got into some terrible accident? But her father? No. She had left him, locked him in a place in her heart where he didn't age, didn't change. He was practically nonexistent.

"Let's change the subject and enjoy the rest of our evening. I've said all I'm going to say." Benson reached across the table and patted her hand.

"Okay, good." Kat blinked. Where had those tears come from?

"Let's dance. They're playing our song."

Kat hadn't noticed that a band had started playing on the other end of the patio. Until now, she had not heard any music. She looked at the pretty man sitting across from her and felt a wash of tender sadness. "We don't have a song, Benson."

2

JUNE 1980

If one more person told her that rain on her wedding day meant good luck, Melody was going to have to slap them. She really would. She would smack the next person who said, "Rain on your wedding day means good luck, honey. That's all it means. Good luck."

Melody Callahan was not feeling lucky. The more appropriate word would be *trapped*, and when her mother knocked on her bedroom door for the third time, Melody said, "Five more minutes, Ma, five more."

"You don't want to be late for your own wedding, do you, sweetheart? Let me come in and help you put on your dress. The bridesmaids have started to arrive, and we need to get to the church soon, honey."

Melody turned up her transistor radio. Lipps Inc.'s "Funkytown" was playing. Currently number one on the Billboard Top 100, the song suited Melody's mood just fine.

"Don't you fret about the weather, Mellie. Rain on your wedding day means—"

"I know!" Melody shouted over the music. She knew it would not be appropriate to open the door and slap her own dear, sweet, well-meaning, clueless mother. "Five more minutes. Is Sylvia here?"

"She just arrived."

"Send her up, okay?"

"You're not going to let her help you get dressed, are you?" Claudia Callahan's worry was palpable through the closed door. "I'm the mother of the bride, and you're my only daughter. You wouldn't deprive me of this once-in-a-lifetime pleasure, would you? It would break my heart if my one and only daughter excluded me from the ritual of being the mother of the bride."

There was only one way to shut her up. Melody got up from the vanity stool and went to the door, opening it to her mother's worried face. Melody felt a rush of affection for the short, plump woman, who was already dressed in her mother-of-the-bride mauve suit. "Of course not, Ma." How could she? Her mother had worked night and day, cooking and cleaning for her domineering husband, three rowdy sons, and one and only daughter. It had not been an easy life for her, but Melody had never heard her complain, not even once. "I just need five more minutes. Sylvia can help with my hair and make-up, and then I'll call for you."

"Are you sure?" Claudia did not seem convinced.

"Yes, Ma, I won't forget. I promise."

Claudia was reluctantly satisfied. "I'll be waiting at the bottom of the stairs."

Melody watched her mother toddle down the narrow staircase of their South Side Chicago rowhouse. A product of immigrant Irish parents, Claudia had been the first generation born in America. The same was true for Melody's father, Frank. Both came from loud, boisterous, hard-drinking clans. Melody had often thought that her family—father, brothers, cousins, uncles—could serve as prototypes for every stereotype that had been labeled upon the Irish. It was too bad for her mother that so many patriarchal ideas still ruled the roost in Irish homes. It was 1980, for god's sake. It was time to modernize such old-fashioned notions.

Melody, for her part, was trying to do so. Her family had been appalled when she'd announced her senior year of high school that she would study nursing. Go to college? No one in their family went to college. If your collar wasn't blue, there was something *wrong* with you. Her three brothers, Francis Jr., Michael, and William had unquestioningly followed their dad into the bricklayer's trade and union. While Melody wasn't expected to do that, it had been assumed that she would become a secretary (because she was smart) until the time came when she would get married and quit to raise a passel of progeny.

Melody wasn't having any part of *that*. She had gone to school and graduated the week before. She and her best friend from nursing school, Sylvia Hammond, had just gotten jobs at Mercy Hospital. They were so excited! Everything had been going according to plan: finish school, get good jobs, and move out of their parents' homes.

And now this. Melody wanted to cry or throw up or throw *something*. She sat back down at her vanity and looked in the mirror. Her skin was blotchy, which added to her abundance of freckles, did not create a bride-worthy appearance. Not even close. She had, at least, started on her dark red hair—her best feature, she thought—using the curling iron and enough hair spray to get close to her usual poof and volume. Her ma had been asking for years: "Why do you make your hair so big, Mellie? You have such pretty naturally curly hair." Melody would answer: "It's the *style*, Ma." Claudia would shake her head mournfully.

"Knock, knock," Sylvia said as she walked in and closed the door quickly behind her. Seeing Melody's face in the reflection of the vanity mirror, she said, "You look like shit."

"Thanks," Melody said, her eyes filling, "I needed that."

"Sorry." Sylvia picked up a compact filled with different eye shadow shades and began applying dark blue on the lids of Melody's blue eyes. "You know that my big mouth just seems to open on its own accord sometimes. Ignore me."

"I need you to make me feel better," Melody said.

"And I came prepared to do that." Sylvia set down the compact and rummaged in her purse. She pulled out a joint. "As promised, I brought Mary Jane."

"Thank God." Melody waited while Sylvia did some more rooting in her voluminous bag for a lighter, and she felt close to tears again. Even striking, regal Sylvia, with her movie star platinum blonde hair and perfect figure, could not make the pink-flowered bridesmaid dress look good. With its high collar and poufy sleeves, it looked like something a matron in the 1890s would wear to a church ice cream social. Why had she let Claudia talk her into that hideous dress? Oh, right. She'd told her mother, "I don't care, Ma. Use your best judgment." It was a crying shame that Claudia's "best judgment" was *hideous*.

"I'm sorry about the dress." Melody took the lit joint from Sylvia.

"Yes. Well. I always wanted to know what it would be like to wear wallpaper. Now I know." Sylvia opened the window that looked out onto the neighbor's brick wall.

"I know you're a good friend if you're willing to shell out forty bucks for that thing. I'll pay you back."

"Don't worry about it. So I look like a 1940s parlor room for one day? What's the big deal?"

One day. This was just one day for Sylvia, but for Melody, this one day would change her life for *eternity*. She was twenty-two years old and about to marry a man she didn't even know very well. At this very moment, she should have been moving into an apartment with Sylvia in the newly renovated South Loop. They'd put a deposit down on a two-bedroom in the Transportation Building. Her *real life* would have finally, finally begun.

And now this.

"Who are all those fat girls downstairs? I thought I looked like the abominable flowered snowman in this dress. But you wallpaper a fat girl and *sheesh*." Sylvia's nostrils flared with smoke.

"My cousins. Ma thought I should have at least six bridesmaids, and since you're my only friend, that left the cousins to fill in. I haven't seen two or three of them in years."

"This is going to be a barrel of laughs, huh?"

"Oh, Sylvia!" Melody wailed.

Claudia must have had some kind of maternal radar. She was at the door in an instant. "Mellie, is something wrong?"

"Shit," Sylvia said. She cranked up the radio: "Please Don't Go" by KC & The Sunshine Band.

"Everything's fine, Ma," Melody shouted.

"Can I come in now? It's been five minutes."

"Five more minutes, Ma," Melody yelled. She could hear her mother's sigh through the door and above the loud music.

Sylvia turned down the music to a reasonable level. "You don't have to go through with this, Mel."

"Yes, I do."

"It's the 80s, Mel, and we're nurses. We know it's not a major procedure." Sylvia sucked down the last of the joint and threw it out the window.

Melody knew it wasn't a major procedure. She knew because she'd done it before. And Sylvia knew this, too, because she'd gone to the clinic with her.

"A simple D & C, that's it." Sylvia finished up Melody's hair.

"I can't do it again. I just can't."

"*Roe v. Wade*, Mel. Abortion is legal. Abortion is the answer to *unwanted pregnancies.*"

Melody believed this. She was a nurse—or would be soon. But she just didn't think she could go through with it again. Last year, it had been different. She and Sylvia had gotten chummy with a couple of roadies at a Michael Jackson concert. The guys had promised them backstage passes, but of course, that never happened. They'd all gotten really stoned, and she had ended up with the shorter of the two in one of the equipment buses. (Sylvia, who was almost six feet tall, always got the taller one, while she, at a mere 5'3", always ended up with the shorter one.) The next day, he—Melody could never remember his name—was gone, and she was pregnant.

This time wasn't much better. Melody had only gone out on three dates with the guy. She didn't know anything about his family, or really, much about him. He was older and seemed steady, unlike the guys she usually dated—which, admittedly, there hadn't been that many, and also, hooking up with a guy for a night couldn't really be called *dating*. Plus, she had been busy with school. She had plans. She would graduate, get a good job, move in with Sylvia, and begin her *real life*.

But she'd gotten pregnant. Again. It was embarrassing. She should know better. And she should quit smoking weed.

But there was another thing, too, something that she hadn't even told Sylvia about. She had this gnawing feeling that she would never get pregnant again if she didn't go through with this pregnancy. It was ridiculous. She knew this intellectually, but the gnawing feeling would not go away. The gnawing feeling said, "This is your last chance. Don't blow it, Melody." Try as she might, Melody could not escape this unfounded, unreasonable, non-scientific, gnawing feeling.

"It's not too late," Sylvia said.

"The church is probably already full of everyone in Daddy's union."

"No, it's not. They're probably all in the bar across the street."

It was quite possible. There was a bar across the street from St. Mary's. "Ma and Daddy would be mortified." She had not, of course, told them she was pregnant. They thought she'd had a whirlwind courtship, fallen madly in love, and was anxious to be a wife and mother. In their world, these things were the norm.

"They'd get over it. You're their darling little girl."

This was quite possible, too. Maybe Melody could feign some sudden, terrible stomach virus. Would they fall for that?

"You barely know the man," Sylvia pointed out for probably the hundredth time.

So very true. But what about the gnawing feeling that would not go away? What if it turned out to be the truest thing of all?

"Can you actually imagine yourself walking down the aisle at St. Mary's? Can you actually imagine the man standing at the altar, hands folded in front of him, waiting for you?" Sylvia asked.

Claudia knocked at the door. "I don't think we can wait any longer, Mellie. Honey, we should have been at the church thirty minutes ago." Her voice rose on every syllable. "The priest called and asked where we were, honey, so this is serious. Can I *please* come in now and help you put on your dress?"

Melody looked at Sylvia. Her thoughts whirred, and her queasy stomach cartwheeled. "It is a long aisle," she said. "A very long aisle."

Melody met Sylvia Hammond on their very first day at Resurrection University in September 1976. The orientation had been nerve-wracking for Melody. Looking around at the other bell-bottomed girls—and it was all girls—with their long, straight hair, she regretted her decision to wear a denim skirt, and she absolutely hated her curly hair. She kept asking herself: *What am I doing here?* She was, after all, from a middle-to-low income Irish Catholic family who lived in a Near Southwestern suburb. These girls, she imagined, probably came from the western and northern suburbs and lived in houses with white picket fences. Feeling dressed inappropriately and out of place, Melody could not help but wonder: What had possessed her to think she could become a nurse?

At lunch, Melody sat alone on the top front step and unwrapped the salami and red onion sandwich her mother had packed. It was adding insult to injury. Not only did she look out of place at this school, but if she ate the sandwich, she would smell out of place. She wanted to go home and pretend that she'd never wanted to be a nurse, that she had not been thrilled to be accepted at Resurrection University, and that the full scholarship had not seemed like a blessing from God. But she couldn't. Her brothers would never let her forget that she just *couldn't hack it.*

"I wish they would cut the crap," a smoky voice said behind Melody. "I can't wait to get my hands on a body, preferably one with multiple abrasions and contusions."

Melody turned around and looked up—and up and up. The blonde girl was strikingly tall. "Oh." It was the only response that came to mind, and Melody blushed at the inadequacy of it.

"I know this is awful to say, but I rather like the sight of blood. Most people are so squeamish about it, but the sight of a bloody nose or a gaping flesh wound never bothered me. I guess I grew up with it. My older brother was always getting in fights and coming home with this or that broken or scratched or scarred, and when I was eight, he got his hand stuck in the lawnmower. Now that was a *mess*."

"Dear God," Melody said. It wasn't that she was squeamish about blood—she might still want to be a nurse—but telling a story like that was a very odd way to introduce yourself to someone.

"It turned out okay. We found his pinkie in the grass and packed it in ice. They reattached it in the emergency room. I watched the whole thing, and it was fascinating. My brother screamed like a baby from start to finish, but it was still fascinating."

Melody's neck began to ache from looking up (and up and up). "Would you like to sit down?"

"Sure." The tall girl folded herself on the step next to Melody.

Melody was grateful to see that she, too, had worn a skirt. Maybe this was a sign? "So, I guess your brother is okay now?"

"Well, I don't know if he still had the pinkie when we buried him."

Melody, out of nervousness, had mistakenly taken a bite of the sandwich. She choked. "Oh," she said once more.

"Vietnam," Sylvia explained. "They advised us not to open the body bag. Can I have half of that sandwich? I forgot to bring a lunch."

Melody had lost her appetite, and as far as she was concerned, the girl could have the whole thing. However, she didn't want to appear to be *squeamish*. She broke the sandwich in half and handed one half to the girl. "Be my guest. I've got to warn you, though. The onions speak their own language."

The girl laughed. "Yeah, I could smell them from inside the building." She took a large bite. "Delicious." She took another large bite, swallowed. "I'm Sylvia."

"Melody." She tried not to stare too blatantly at this girl who ate with such appetite. (As it turned out, this was definitely a sign. Sylvia would prove to be a girl with many appetites.)

The third large bite, and Sylvia finished her sandwich. "So now you know my story," she said, wiping her hands on her skirt. "What's yours?"

"What's my—what?" This girl, Sylvia, didn't seem to be very good at transitions. She'd gone from blood to severed pinkie to body bag at an alarming rate of speed.

"Your story. I told you why I wanted to become an emergency medicine nurse. Now you tell me why you want to become a nurse."

"You didn't say you wanted to become an emergency medicine nurse." Melody didn't think so, but the conversation had covered a lot of ground in about a minute.

"It was implied. I was *eight*, and I sat in the emergency room and watched my brother's pinkie getting reattached. What eight-year-old girl would do that?" Sylvia lit a long brown More cigarette.

"Well, I'm pretty sure I don't know any eight-year-old who would do that."

"Exactly." Smoke flared from Sylvia's nostrils. "So, what's your story? Why do you want to be an RN?"

It was a good question, and it was one that Melody hadn't closely considered. She'd just wanted to become a nurse for as long as she could remember. She didn't think there was any one inciting moment that had sparked the idea—certainly no severed pinkie and blood-gushing, mangled brother's hand. Sylvia looked at her with such undivided attention that Melody fought hard not to squirm. "I guess … I want to help people?" she finally squeaked.

Sylvia looked so disappointed. "That's it?"

"Isn't that enough to want to help people?"

From the look on Sylvia's face, it was not enough. "That's a given. Nurses are altruistic, empathetic, caring, blah, blah, blah people."

Melody wondered if she should be offended. Surely, wanting to help people was a good enough reason to want to be a nurse. Wasn't it? But was it her real reason? "Look, Sylvia, I live on the South Side, and it's just assumed that I'll get married and have children. But I didn't have a high school boyfriend. I didn't want a high school boyfriend, and I don't want to think about children for a long time. I want to have a career, I want to make my own money, and I want to move out of my parents' house! Are those good enough reasons for you, *Sylvia*?" By the time Melody finished, she was panting.

Sylvia smiled, and her hazel eyes seemed to glint in the sun. "Now that's more like it, Mel. Those are *very* good reasons for wanting to be a nurse. Bravo!"

"Thank you," Melody said tightly.

"Hey, Mel, don't get your knickers in a knot. I didn't mean to upset you. Once you get to know me, you'll find out that I have a big mouth. I usually, but not all the time, mean well, but my big mouth seems to open on its own accord sometimes."

"I'm not upset." Really, Melody wasn't. It was actually a relief to admit to the reasons why she wanted to become a nurse. She didn't pine to become a saintly, loving healer. Hell, no. She just wanted to make enough money to live on her own. It probably wasn't a particularly lofty ambition, but it was *her* ambition.

"I live with my mom, too," Sylvia finished her cigarette and lit another. "She's had a hard time ever since my old man decided he wanted to go to Alaska and catch salmon. Well, that was his excuse at the time, and naturally, he never came back. This week, she thinks she has MS. Last week it was pneumonia. Next week, who knows? Kidney failure? Stroke?"

"I'm sorry." Melody wondered if Sylvia had any *good* parts of her story.

"Don't be. She's got a stash of pain meds that would embarrass Walgreens pharmacy."

The bell rang, and Melody started to gather up her belongings. "I guess we should go in now. Do you want to sit together?" she asked shyly. If she had this Sylvia for a friend, she might make it through nursing school.

"Let's play hooky." Sylvia smiled wickedly. "It's only orientation, and they already took roll call. They'll never miss us."

"Oh, I can't!" Melody said, shocked.

But she did; Sylvia convinced her. And Melody never regretted it. From that day forward, Sylvia Hammond would be her lifelong confidant, best friend, and partner in crime.

Because of Sylvia, Melody's years at Resurrection University passed quickly. And also because of Sylvia—at her urging—Melody decided to specialize in emergency medicine. She had always been a good student, and she sailed through the coursework (Concepts and Processes of Professional Nursing, Pathophysiology and Applied Pharmacology I & II). Initially, she had dreaded the clinicals where she had to work with actual patients. (Sylvia, outside the hospital, still referred to the patients as *bodies*). But Melody learned that she became a different person once she put on her uniform and hat. All her shyness evaporated, and she sounded, even to herself, like a person with authority. "You're a natural," more than one of her instructors told her. "You were born for this job."

Melody thought that it was too bad she had to take off the blue and white uniform with its action pleats. She wished she could wear it on the streets, to the corner market, to church, on the train, even to bed. She wished she could shower in the uniform that transformed her into a capable, confident person. But of course, she couldn't. Inevitably, when she took it off, she became plain old Melody Callahan from Bridgeview, who was expected to be home at a reasonable hour every night, to help her ma with the cooking and cleaning, to go to Mass and Confession every Sunday. Melody Callahan was expected to be, above all, a *good girl*.

Her parents and rowdy brothers did not treat her any differently. Melody wanted to shout at them, "I am trying to make something out of myself! Don't you think I deserve a little respect?" But as usual, she didn't say a word. It was as if they thought she was the secretary they'd expected her to become, going off day after day into the city to work in some nondescript office building, typing endless memos and taking dictation.

This all changed at one mandatory Sunday dinner toward the end of Melody's second year at Resurrection. They had all been to church, naturally, and Claudia had prepared her usual Sunday roast with potatoes and carrots and celery. (The repetition of the Callahan meals and the Callahan life inside 1113 S. Roosevelt weighed heavier on Melody's mind and heart daily. She longed to escape the tedium.)

As Melody remembered it, her father started the chain of events when he said to Frankie, "When are you going to marry that Wagner girl, son? A pretty girl like that won't wait forever."

Was he blind? Melody wondered. The Wagner girl, Ethel, had the face of a horse, with buck teeth and a slight mustache above her lip. Frankie had dated her for a couple of years. However, Melody thought that perhaps

Ethel, as homely as she was, didn't particularly want to marry Frankie. He was no prize.

None of her brothers were. They all had various shades of red hair, freckles, and washed-out blue eyes. They weren't exactly bad-looking, but they certainly didn't stand out in a crowd. Melody did realize she might be a little prejudiced against them because they were her brothers, but she didn't ultimately think that was the case. However, Melody thought that their real offense was that they were *uncouth*. Despite poor Claudia's best efforts, their table manners were more than dubious—elbows on the table accompanied with slurping sounds. And each of them would take his Friday paycheck and blow it at the corner tavern in a single night, leaving only a buck or two to put in the collection plate on Sunday. Melody would bet money that none of the neighborhood girls—and her brothers did not often venture outside the neighborhood, except for the occasional White Sox game—wanted to marry a Callahan man-child.

But then, why would her brothers want to leave home? They had Ma, their very own domestic servant, who uncomplainingly washed their cement-splattered work clothes and cooked their meals and made their beds. The list went on and on. They didn't pay the gas or water bills or contribute to the food budget. They had it made in the shade, so why in the world would they want to leave?

"I gotta save some money first," Frankie said.

"That means never, Pa," Mikey said. "The man goes through money like a pig goes through slop."

"I hear she won't put out," Willie contributed. "Is that right, Frankie?"

"Oh, dear," Claudia said, uselessly. She rarely spoke at meals.

"Mind your own business." Frankie helped himself to more roast beef.

"There comes a time when a man needs to move into his own home, start his own family," Daddy continued. For him, he was being persistent. He rarely criticized his sons, and never his one and only daughter. He was a good man, their father, although Melody thought his view of the world was totally antiquated.

"Why would I want to do that?" Frankie said.

"Aha!" Melody couldn't help but say. It was just what she suspected.

Claudia got up to fill the depleted meat platter. She had to do this often during their family dinners; her husband and sons were big eaters.

"Look who's talking," Frankie directed at Melody. "You're not going to move out any time soon. You've got no boyfriend."

Melody glared at him. He was the least attractive of the three with his stringy, orangish hair. "I have better things to do. As you well know, I'm studying to be a nurse."

Mikey, her second-least favorite brother, the one with the most freckles, said, "Nursie, Nursie, can I have a Band-Aid? I think I have a hangnail." He got the desired reaction from his older brother. Frankie snorted.

"Leave the girl alone," Daddy said.

"It's okay, Daddy. They're just morons." As Melody expected, they started grunting and scratching like apes. "I said *morons*, not gorillas." It was so typical of them.

"I need to ask you something later," Willie said to Melody.

Out of her three brothers, Willie was the one she loved the most. He was the best-looking of the three, comparatively speaking, and he was also the kindest. He was only eighteen months older than Melody, and they had been inseparable as children until Willie realized that Mellie, horror of horrors, was a *girl*. "Sure," Melody said. "You know where I'll be. In the kitchen, washing dishes with the *womenfolk*."

"Ask her now," Frankie goaded. "Ask her now, Willie boy."

"Yeah, Willie boy," Mikey chimed in, "ask her now."

"Shut the fuck up," Willie muttered.

Daddy heard. "We don't use that kind of language at the dinner table, son, especially at the Sunday dinner table."

Willie didn't usually use that kind of language, which made Melody wonder what he wanted to talk to her about. Maybe it was something medically-related? The thought of that gave Melody a small thrill of excitement. Finally, someone in her family would possibly take her career seriously and ask her a medical question. Hopefully, one she could answer. "You can ask me now, Willie, if you want." She didn't have her uniform on, but she tried to adopt an appropriate, nurse-like serenity.

"Later," Willie muttered, not taking his eyes off his plate.

"Let's just say that Willie does know the girls who put out," Frank said, smirking.

"Shut the fuck up!" This time, Willie could be heard by everyone at the table.

"Language," Daddy said.

"Oh, dear." Claudia fanned her hand in front of her flushed face.

Melody, wanting to appear nurse-like in front of her family, didn't stop to ponder the full significance of what Frankie had said. "What are your symptoms, Willie?"

Willie threw his napkin on the table and pushed back his chair. "I'm out of here."

"It's awfully warm in here." Claudia dabbed at her perspiring forehead with her napkin. "Could someone open a window?"

"The symptoms?" Frankie started to hold up fingers. "Well, there's Rebecca, Ann Marie, Clarissa, Donna, and Donna's mother."

"It burns when he pees," Mikey added.

"Balls the size of—"

Melody, later, would so regret being absorbed in her nurse role, trying vainly to get her family's respect. "You're saying that Willie has a venereal disease?"

"Bingo!" Frank said.

From Mike: "Willie boy has the clap!"

"It's Sunday dinner!" Daddy shouted.

"Oh, dear," Claudia said and toppled from her chair.

Clearly, Melody had been paying attention to the wrong patient. This fact gnawed at her in the days that followed, but she knew she would never make that mistake again. After Ma toppled from her chair, gasping for breath, her husband, her rowdy—and it would seem, promiscuous—sons, and her one and only daughter were stunned into silence. They stared, disbelieving, at the plump woman on the floor.

And then all hell broke loose.

Simultaneously, they jumped from their chairs. "Call an ambulance!" Melody screamed.

"You're the nurse! Do something!" Frankie screamed back.

This was not the kind of acknowledgment Melody had hoped for. She had desperately wanted them to respect her career, but this was carrying it way too far. Now she would be put to the test. "Call an ambulance!" she screamed again at her gaping, moronic brothers. "Stat!"

"What in the hell does that mean?" Frankie asked. He stood stock-still, unable to move.

"Now!"

That seemed to unfreeze her three brothers. They all rushed toward the kitchen phone, banging into each other as they went. "I'll do it," one of them said. "No, I'll do it," another said.

Melody knelt beside her mother, who gasped for air and clutched her chest. "Ma, can you hear me?" Melody looked into her terrified eyes and reached for her pulse. She, too, was terrified, but she was fighting to at least look like she was calm. What if Ma had a heart attack? She hadn't yet had a patient who had suffered a heart attack. She racked her brains. What were you supposed to do? She remembered something. "Daddy, run upstairs and get an aspirin." She was almost positive that aspirin would help in this situation.

"Ma, can you hear me?"

Claudia could only stare at Melody with those terrified eyes in her beet-red face.

Melody leaned closer. "Ma?" This was something they didn't teach you in nursing school. Sure, you were trained to act in an emergency, but when the patient was family, was your *ma*? How in the world were you supposed to remain calm, detached, *professional*?

Daddy came back down with the aspirin. He must have sprinted up the stairs. He had only been gone for seconds, and he wasn't a spry man. "Fix her, Mellie," he said tearfully. The lone aspirin bounced in his trembling hand.

It just figured. After all the years he had taken his wife for granted, Daddy now seemed to care very much. Maybe he was afraid of losing his cook and cleaning lady, Melody thought. No, that was unkind. Her parents loved each other very, very much, she told herself. Of course, they did. They just didn't show it.

Ma let out a strangling gasp, and Melody suddenly knew what was wrong. Her mother was *choking to death*. Melody was one hundred percent positive she knew what to do in this situation.

Her brothers ran back into the dining room. "The ambulance is on the way," one of them reported.

Melody let instinct take over. "I've got you, Ma." She lifted Claudia, grasped her around the ribs from behind, and gave three quick upward thrusts. On the third thrust, the piece of fatty roast beef that had lodged in Claudia's windpipe flew out of her mouth and splat-landed on Frankie's forehead.

"What the hell?" Frankie looked stunned as he reached for the half-chewed meat.

"Nice shot," Willie said.

"What is that thing?" Mikey asked.

"Roast beef." Melody helped Claudia to her chair. "Are you all right?" she asked her.

"I was eating, and then I couldn't breathe. I swallowed down the wrong pipe." Claudia struggled to get her breathing back to normal.

"What did you just do?" Daddy asked Melody. He was still as white as a sheet, and his outstretched hand still bounced around the aspirin.

"The Heimlich maneuver," Melody answered.

"Did you learn that in nursing school?" Mikey asked.

Frankie snorted. "No, doofus. Anyone can do the hymen maneuver."

"That was really cool, Mellie," Willie said.

"My daughter, your sister, just saved my life," Claudia said in wonderment. "I could have been a goner, I could have died right on my own dining room floor, but no, it didn't happen. It didn't happen because my daughter, your sister, saved my life!"

"My little girl," Daddy said.

Melody glowed with pleasure. She wanted to say to her brothers, "See? I can be handy to have around, can't I? I can be fast on my feet. I can save lives, you morons!" But she did not. She would be professional.

"Wow," Willie said.

"Anyone can do the hymen maneuver," Frank muttered, but no one was paying attention to him.

"Let's finish the meal," Melody said, sitting down at the dinner table. "Ma went to a lot of trouble to make this roast beef. Thanks, Ma."

Her brothers and Daddy followed her lead and sat back down and immediately returned their attention to their food. However, Melody noticed, they all chewed more carefully.

"What do the men at this table have to say?"

All four of them stared at her blankly.

"Don't you want to say thanks to Ma?" Melody knew she was pushing her luck, but she felt empowered. She'd just earned some acknowledgment and appreciation for her chosen career path and the grudging respect of her brothers, however short-lived it would probably be. "It's about time," she added.

"Thanks." The appreciation was muttered to their four plates.

"Oh, dear," Claudia said, embarrassed.

"That's more like it." Melody picked up her fork, and then—she couldn't help herself—she really pushed her luck. "Shall we get back to the topic of venereal disease?"

It didn't go over well, and she ended up volunteering to do the dishes.

Melody would always consider that Sunday dinner as a dramatic turning point in her life for two reasons. First, on that day, she knew with utmost certainty that she would be a good nurse. Her ma had been on death's threshold, and she, Melody, had saved her. And furthermore, she had remained professional throughout the ordeal. True, the incident had only lasted mere seconds, but that was beside the point. Grace under pressure, Melody vowed, would be her new motto. Grace under pressure.

Sylvia was not especially impressed with Melody's heroics. "Oh, that," Sylvia said when Melody told her about the event in elaborate detail. "I used to work in a restaurant, and I bet I did the Heimlich on thirty or forty customers. Someone was always choking on their stroganoff. It's a major health hazard. Most people do not know how to properly chew their food."

"I saved my ma," Melody insisted. It had been a big deal.

"Sure you did, Mel. Sure you did."

Melody dropped the subject. She loved Sylvia like a sister, but the problem with Sylvia was that she could sometimes act so superior to other people. Melody considered this a minor flaw, however. Sylvia's sense of fun and her generosity greatly outweighed her occasional spark of pseudo-superiority, and running around with Sylvia was always an adventure waiting to happen.

But for the first two years of nursing school, Melody felt as if she had not participated fully in Sylvia's grand plans. For example, Sylvia would suggest that they go to a jazz club on Illinois Street, where she knew the bouncer who would let them in, even though they were underage. Once they were in the club, Sylvia explained, no one would ask to see their IDs. Melody's response would be that she needed to be home by eleven. "Ma would be worried sick," she'd said. If Sylvia suggested that they go to an outdoor concert in Grant Park on a Sunday afternoon, Melody would say that Sunday dinners with her family were mandatory.

All that changed after she saved her ma's life. After that, Melody *grew up*. She was an adult, and she didn't need a curfew. She was an adult, and she didn't need to tell her ma and daddy where she was at every second of every day. She was an adult, and she didn't need to eat dinner with her family every damn night. She was an *adult*.

But she didn't have the money to move out of her parents' house.

Sylvia was in the same boat, with an AWOL father and wacko mother on top of the lack of money. "As soon as we graduate and start to make money, we'll get an apartment together. Think of the freedom," Sylvia said.

"We'll be career women." Melody loved the sound of those words.

"We can come and go as we please."

"We can eat on paper plates and never have to wash another dish," Melody said.

"We can have men stay overnight."

That part made Melody uneasy. At twenty years old, she was still a virgin. "We have to meet them first."

"Bars are good places for that," Sylvia said with authority.

"I can't wait," Melody said dreamily. She could perfectly picture a cozy apartment with high ceilings and an afghan-strewn couch.

"In the meantime, though, we'll have to make do."

And so they did. Since Sylvia's mom zonked out most of the time, they could pretty much come and go as they pleased at her apartment on Compton Street. In fact, Sylvia's mother, Thelma, didn't seem to care what they did. This fact became apparent the first time Melody set eyes on the tall, scarecrow-thin woman.

It was a Saturday morning in June, a week after Melody saved her ma's life. Amazingly, in the two years that she had known Sylvia, Melody had never been to her home, and during the walk up to the fourth-floor apartment, she could pretty much figure out why. The hallways stank of urine, garlic, and something else that she couldn't quite identify and hoped wasn't a dead rat. The place was almost, but not quite, a tenement, and it made Melody's parents' modest row house in Bridgeview look almost, but not quite, respectable.

"Luxurious, huh?" Sylvia said as they walked up the final flight of stairs.

"It's not so bad," Melody lied. She fought the urge to pinch her nose between her fingers.

"It's a dump, Mel," Sylvia cheerfully said. "We moved here from the burbs after Stanley came home in a body bag and dear old Dad left for Alaska, or wherever he decided to go. I tried to find him once, but you can't exactly phone a fishing boat."

"I don't suppose you can." Melody hoped the apartment smelled better than the hallways, but she would never place a bet on it.

"Anyway, it's easier for Thelma to score in the city."

Sylvia had told Melody numerous times that Thelma was a hypochondriac, but why would she say it was easier for her mom to *score*? That, to Melody, seemed to suggest something illicit.

They reached 4B, and Sylvia fumbled in her purse for the key. "Are you ready to meet my old lady?"

Thelma Hammond was probably not old, perhaps in her late forties, but Melody got her first close-up look at what years of pain and despair could do to a person's face. Thelma's green eyes seemed to be sunk into her face, which bore an abundance of crisscrossed fine lines. She was as tall as Sylvia, but her frighteningly thin shoulders were hunched. When they walked in, she sat in a green recliner smoking a More cigarette and watching *As the World Turns*. Even though it was in the upper 70s outside, the windows were closed, and she wore a grandmotherly cardigan. The apartment did smell better than the hallways—but only slightly.

"Thelma, Thelma, Thelma," Sylvia said with surprising tenderness. "It's like an oven in here." She walked to the front of the apartment and opened a window.

"I believe I've caught a chill." Thelma nervously twisted a wisp of her thin peroxide blonde hair in her fingers.

Sylvia walked to her mother and competently placed a hand on the woman's forehead. Sylvia, Melody had learned, was always competent. "You don't have a fever, Thelma," Sylvia said patiently.

"Nonsense. I have a chill, Sylvie. My whole body aches." Thelma lit another cigarette from the butt of her first.

Melody still stood awkwardly by the front door. The small, messy apartment, with its stacks of magazines on the floor and dirty dishes on the coffee table, did not seem to match up to Sylvia at all. The entire depressing environment did not match up to Sylvia. How could someone as vibrant and lively as Sylvia come from a place like this? Being Ma's daughter, Melody longed to find a bottle of Lysol and a rag and get to work.

"This is my friend, Melody, Thelma. You know, from nursing school."

Thelma noticed Melody for the first time. "Oh, yes, Sylvie talks about you all the time." She gave Melody a shy smile.

"How do you do, Mrs. Hammond?" Melody walked over to the green chair and shook the woman's hand. The bones felt as fragile as a bird's.

"Well, I have a chill. My daughter doesn't believe me, but it's true. I have a chill."

Sylvia sighed. "I believe you, Thelma."

"Would you like an aspirin?" Since Ma's near-death experience, Melody had been carrying aspirin (and band-aids and first aid cream and cough syrup) in her purse, just to be prepared, just so she would always have grace under pressure.

"Thank you, but no. I'm afraid that won't do. I need something a little stronger." She gave her daughter a beseeching smile.

Sylvia sighed again. "All right, Thelma. You win." She left the room and came back with a joint. "Here you go."

Thelma did not look happy. "Sylvie. I don't think this is the appropriate medicine for what ails me. I have a *chill*."

"It's the appropriate medicine, Thelma. We have company."

Thelma looked like it was news to her. She glanced at Melody, reminding her of the fact. "Oh, yes, it's nice to have company."

"Uh, thank you." Melody still tried to take it all in. As disconcerted as she was with the fact that Sylvia called her mother by her first name, it was nothing compared to the sight of the joint in Sylvia's hand. It wasn't that Melody had never seen one before; she had. Even though she'd gone to an all-girls Catholic high school, plenty of the girls smoked pot. But she'd never even been tempted. She was going to be a nurse, and nurses were above that sort of thing. A good nurse would not do drugs.

Thelma nodded toward the marijuana. "It's medicinal," she said as if she needed to explain its presence to Melody.

"Yeah, right," said Sylvia.

"It is medicinal." Thelma tried to light another cigarette—even though one was still burning in the overflowing ashtray—but her hands were shaking violently. "Damn it!" Thelma broke the cigarette in half. "Sylvia, you little shit, go get me my fucking medicine!"

"Fine," Sylvia said, her voice as calm as ever. She returned with a white pill and handed it to her mother. "Enjoy." To Melody, she said, "Let's go to my room."

Sylvia's room, unlike the rest of the house, was perfectly neat. A red and white quilt covered the twin bed, books were aligned on the bookcase, and a stereo sat on a table under the window. Sylvia flipped through her album collection, chose Paul Simon's "Slip, Slidin' Away," and put it on the turntable. She flopped onto the bed and motioned for Melody to take the vanity chair. "She's in a bad way today."

"What did you give her?" Melody was still trying to process what was happening in this apartment. Thelma might have started out as a hypochondriac, but that seemed to have now escalated into addiction. But was she addicted to pain meds or street drugs? Sylvia had said it was easier to *score* in the city.

"Today, it was hydrocodone's turn."

Hydrocodone was an opioid usually used to treat chronic pain. "Is it her back?" Melody asked. "Does she have chronic back pain?"

"Who the hell knows if she has *actual* pain. The point is that she *thinks* she does."

Melody wanted to ask many more questions, but the look on Sylvia's face told her that she better keep her questions and her opinions to herself.

"No use in letting this weed go to waste." Sylvia reached over and pulled a lighter out of her nightstand.

Melody was appalled. "I don't think we should." It would be just her luck to inhale once and then have the cops busting down the door. She'd go to jail, although she wasn't sure about the laws on marijuana, and Ma and Daddy would be mortified. Even her useless brothers had never landed in prison, which had to be a small miracle. And if she got caught, it would go on her record, and the ethics committee at any hospital would probably refuse to hire her. There was too much at stake.

Sylvia, of course, lit the joint anyway. "Have you ever smoked before, Mel?" She inhaled deeply.

"No, I haven't, and I don't plan to start now. We're going to be nurses, Sylvia, and nurses do not do drugs."

"In your view, Mel, nurses are so venerable they don't even shit." Sylvia took another hit and smiled. "Oh, come on, Mel. It's only pot. It's not bad for your liver like alcohol, and I'll bet you a hundred dollars that it will be legalized in the next few years. Really, it's harmless, and it wouldn't hurt you to lighten up a bit."

Sylvia's words stung, and Melody was tempted to march right out of Sylvia's room and this foul-smelling apartment. Essentially, Sylvia was calling her a prude. She should march out of the room and never speak to Sylvia again.

But she would miss Sylvia, who was the best friend she'd ever had. She would be doomed to eat dinner with her parents and brothers for the rest of her life. She'd never had a boyfriend, and she was twenty years old and still a virgin. The terrible fact was its truth. She was and had always been a prude. She would change that now.

Melody got up from the vanity chair and plopped on the bed next to Sylvia. She took the joint and inhaled. She coughed.

"You'll get used to it," Sylvia encouraged.

"I do not think that nurses don't shit." The second time, she managed to hold the sweet smoke in her lungs without coughing, and she was already feeling more relaxed. It was an amazing feeling, really. She was becoming somewhat detached from the moment, yet at the same time, she felt so *in tune.*

"You're a natural." Sylvia's voice sounded fuzzy.

"Grace under pressure," Melody said.

"Why not?" Sylvia nodded.

After they finished the joint and the album ended, Sylvia said, "I want to show you something."

Stealthily, Sylvia opened the door, and they tiptoed down the short hallway to the bathroom, even though there was no need because Thelma was passed out on the green recliner, her mouth hanging open and the TV still blaring. Sylvia took a key from her pocket and unlocked the padlock on the medicine cabinet. Motioning to the heavy lock, she said, "It's the only way I can keep Thelma under control."

"Good idea." In her heightened state, the padlocked medicine cabinet made perfect sense to Melody.

Sylvia swung open the door. "Take a look at this."

"Wow," Melody breathed. Sylvia had not been exaggerating when she said her mother had a pharmacy to rival Walgreens. Rows and rows of opioids crammed the shelves: fentanyl, hydrocodone, hydromorphone, morphine, oxycodone, pethidine, diamorphine, and more. "Where does she get all this?"

"Doctors, the streets. She has connections," Sylvia said vaguely.

"Wow," Melody said again. She was suddenly starving.

"We're going to be nurses," Sylvia said.

No cops had busted down the door, so Melody believed this to be true. "Yes."

"It might be a good idea if we tried these out, you know, to know first-hand what the effects of each one are."

If the effects of any of those drugs were half as good as the pot made her feel, Melody would be delighted. But she did have some reservations. The transformation from prude to party girl wasn't going to happen overnight. "Maybe one of each, over time."

"Right. One of each, over time." Sylvia closed and locked the mirrored medicine cabinet door. "It's purely research."

3

MARCH 2012

March Madness really sucked, Kat thought, as she brought a fourth pitcher of beer to the table where three men sat riveted to the TV watching Duke play against Wake Forest.

"The great thing about March Madness," the one with the beard said as Kat walked up, "is that there's always a chance that a Cinderella team will win. I've got huge money bet on Wheaton College."

"Not going to happen," the tallest, skinniest one said. "They always clutch at the free throws. You can't win this basketball tournament if you clutch at the free throws."

"You're full of shit, Andy."

"There is no way in hell that Wheaton will get past the next round. No way in hell, Pete, you asshole."

"Language, you dicks. *Our* pretty little Cinderella is bringing another pitcher of the nectar of the gods," the bald one said. "You're our Cinderella, aren't you, sweetheart?"

Kat knew that she should try to play along to squeeze another few bucks in tips out of these tightwads, but she just couldn't. She just couldn't. "I'm not your Cinderella," she said. "Obviously, I am your server, bringing you another pitcher of beer that you totally don't need."

"Our server, huh?" Pete leered. "What are you going to serve for dessert, Princess?"

A few possible scenarios flashed through Kat's mind. She could dump the pitcher of beer on the bearded guy's head, or better yet, she could divide it equally among their laps. She could flash them her boobs—which would be rather difficult since the push-up bra was very tight—but that would only egg them on. The scenario she leaned toward would be to tell them all to fuck off, but that would probably not sit well with management and would likely get her fired. And on this crowded, chaotic, awful night, Kat could think of nothing more humiliating than to get fired from Tilted Kilt. What would she tell Granny Nanny, who thought the sexy, faux-Scottish get-ups were *darling*?

"Who's buying this round?" Kat asked.

The men squabbled about whose turn it was to buy before the Andy guy said, "What are you going to do if we're out of money?"

Kat picked up the full pitcher of beer. "There's an ATM machine by the front door. I'll wait." Naturally, they coughed up the money, and again, on this fourth round, they didn't tip her, not even a lousy buck.

Kat went back to the bar and waited while Jessica, the bartender, filled the order for another table. Jessica had written her name on the blackboard above the bar, as all the female bartenders did, and dotted the i, not with the expected heart but with a butterfly. Very cute. Jessica was a whopping twenty-two, wore a D-cup, and had dimples as deep as the Grand Canyon. However, Jessica was the only person in the entire fleet of nubile, sexy, faux-Scottish lasses who had become somewhat of a friend during the four torturous weeks of Kat's servitude at Tilted Kilt. Jessica had worked at the bar for six months; she was a veteran of the place.

"How do you do this night after night?" Kat had wanted to ask the excruciatingly happy Jessica the question for weeks.

Jessica smiled and shrugged as she poured Jameson shots. "I don't know. I guess it's in my nature to be cheerful. And really, it's not so bad. I've had worse jobs."

That was a depressing thought. What kind of work had Jessica done before this? "Did you dig ditches or work in a sewage treatment plant or what?"

"Nope. I was a dancer at the Crystal Palace. Not your normal gentlemen's club. It was so low-class that the dancers had to put their own quarters in the jukebox before they got up on stage. Kind of dampened my performance, as you can imagine."

"Wow," Kat said. "I didn't mean to be nosy." That job did sound lower than this gig.

"No prob. Say, a few of us are going out after work. Do you want to come along? There's a nightclub in Old Town that stays open late."

It wasn't the first time Jessica had asked her to join a group of servers after work. Kat knew she should probably go at least one time, so she didn't appear completely anti-social, but she just couldn't. She just couldn't. She knew she looked okay because Benson had told her she looked *hot* in her sexy, faux-Scottish red plaid kilt, white knee socks, push-up red plaid bra, and white cover-up. But these little girls, with their nubile young bodies and without the beginning of crow's feet around their eyes, made her feel positively ancient.

"Next time," Kat said. "For sure."

"Are you sure? OMG, it's going to be such a blast." Jessica took a quick, furtive look around and then took a drink directly from the Jameson bottle.

OMG, Kat thought, *I really need to change my life.*

OMG, I really need to find some friends.

Since high school, she had meant to make some new friends ever since her best friend, Paula, had bailed on her three years before. She and Paula had done everything together. Paula was big on Groupon, so they had taken glass blowing lessons, cooking lessons (which in Kat's case, did not take *at all*), gone rock climbing, attended concerts, visited the Heard Museum, and had makeovers. And obviously, they had hit every bar in Scottsdale during their slightly slutty twenties. The list went on and on. Kat missed Paula intensely, although she was still mad at her. She couldn't help it. Even though she and Paula talked on the phone—but those conversations were becoming increasingly rare because Paula was now a mother—Kat would invariably work into the conversation, "You bailed on me."

"I did not bail on you," Paula would counter calmly as two babies screamed in the background. "I got married."

"Same thing."

"No, it's not," the newly serene Paula would say.

"And you moved all the way across the country," Kat would say.

"Raleigh is not ... Well, I guess Raleigh is all the way across the country."

"And then you plopped out two kids in two years," Kat would add.

"I did not plop. I gave birth."

"Same thing."

"No, it's not," the newly serene Paula would say. "When are you going to come to North Carolina and visit?"

"Soon. I need to scrape some money together, but I'll get there eventually. Soon." Kat doubted that she would ever make it to Raleigh, NC, and it wasn't because she didn't have the money. (Okay, one time she did have the money, but she went to Nordstrom's Last Chance and bought a used Prada bag. She was never going to tell Paula that story.) It was because Paula had two babies.

Kat was not particularly fond of babies. Okay, she didn't like them at all. All new mothers thought their babies were beautiful and precious and wonderful, and the best thing that had ever happened to them. It didn't matter that many babies looked a little toady or a little bit like that old vaudeville crooner, Jimmy Durante. All new mothers, who may or may not have been lying, thought their babies were *it*. Kat planned on never having a baby.

Kat was terrified of ever having a baby. For as long as she could remember—perhaps as soon as she could talk—she had wondered about her own mother and asked her father a multitude of questions: What was my mother like? Did she like ice cream as much as I do? Did she have a job? What color was her hair? Was she pretty? Did she have nice teeth? Why don't we have any pictures of her? *What was my mother's name?*

Eventually, her father got tired of any and all questions, not that he'd ever answered even one of them. Finally, with the familiar pained expression he always got when she asked questions about her mother, he said, "This is the last time I'm going to tell you, Katrina. Your mother died in childbirth. Period. End of story."

After two more days, Kat knew part of the reason she'd still not opened the card/letter from her father was that she didn't want a refresher course on her father's emotional barrenness. All through her childhood, he had been distant and cold. To tell your young daughter, "This is the last time I'm going to tell you, Katrina. Your mother died in childbirth. Period. End of story" was *mean*. He made it seem as if this unnamed, non-verbalized woman had never existed. Kat quit asking questions because she wanted any crumb of love she could wrench out of the man, but she had a gut instinct that the source of her father's coldness had to do with the woman who had died in childbirth.

She would have died in March, obviously, on Kat's birthday: March 22, 1982.

"Earth to Kat," Jim, the manager, said. It was clear it wasn't the first time he'd called her name.

She'd just gone through the motions while her mind was elsewhere, but miraculously, her shift was at an end, and she was trying to hightail it out of Tilted Kilt as quickly as possible.

"I've asked you three times," he said. "Do you want to or not?"

"Um, do I want to or not—what?"

"Do you want to pose for next year's Tilted Kilt calendar? It's an honor. Obviously, you have to try out for it, but as your manager, I'm nominating you." He seemed to think she was considering this magnificent offer. "You wear most of your clothes, you know. You've seen this year's calendar, right? It's on sale right at the front cash register."

She couldn't help it, even if it meant that she might lose her job. She started to laugh. "You've got to be kidding," she said when she could finally catch her breath.

"It's quite an honor," he repeated stubbornly.

"I'm sure it is," she gasped. "Ask me again when hell freezes over."

Her manager, Kat decided, must be delusional with March Madness.

Kat had not planned on running away on July 6, 1998. No, it had started out like any other sticky summer southern Illinois day. She overslept, which she often did at that time of year. Her upstairs bedroom did not have air conditioning. Only the modest house's downstairs was semi-cooled with a window unit in the family room and another in the kitchen. So Kat had difficulty falling asleep at night, tossing and turning in the sticky sheets until almost dawn. She awoke, feeling more tired and listless than she had when she went to bed, and she was getting pretty fed up from feeling so damn hot all the time. With temperatures in the upper 90s and the humidity matching, the heatwave had been uninterrupted for ten long days.

When she dragged herself downstairs that morning a little past ten o'clock, hoping that there were still some Cheerios left, Missy was not happy to see her. No surprise there. Missy was never happy to see Kat.

"You're finally up," Missy said flatly, her hands on her ever-increasing hips. When Kat's dad had married Missy eight years before, she had been model-slim and liked to brag about it, too: "I can't clear one hundred and five," she was fond of saying. "It doesn't matter what I eat. I could stuff my face with cake and cookies all day long, and it wouldn't change a thing. The pounds don't creep up on me." Well, the pounds were certainly creeping now. After giving birth to her two sons, the pounds had decided to *take residence,* primarily in her butt and hips. It was a source of great consternation to twenty-eight-year-old Missy, so she was continually dieting, which also meant that she was always crabby.

"I'm nominally up," Kat said. "Are there any Cheerios left, or did the boys hog them all?"

"Shane and Cody do not hog cereal, but it would serve you right if there wasn't any left. What do you expect when you drag your sorry ass down the stairs at noon?" Missy looked as if she could use a good night's sleep, too. There were dark ridges under her eyes, and it looked as if she had not washed her stringy blonde hair in a few days.

"Point of fact, Missy: It is ten o'clock, not noon." Kat picked up the cereal box still on the table and peered inside. Just as she expected, only crumbs. Her four- and six-year-old brothers were indeed cereal hogs.

"Why do you have to have such a smart mouth?" Missy turned away from Kat and started to swipe viciously at the kitchen counters. It was a good show. Missy was a terrible housekeeper, so the counters would probably only get a few slaps before she lost interest.

Kat was tempted to retort, "Why do you have to have such a dumb one?" But she resisted. What was the use? Ever since Kat had turned thirteen, right around the time she had her first period, her relationship with Missy had deteriorated into a series of pointless, petty squabbles.

They had been okay in the beginning, although it had been a total surprise to eight-year-old Kat when her dad brought home his pretty young bride one Saturday afternoon. He sent the babysitter home and told Kat that he and Missy had gone to the courthouse and *gotten hitched.* (Kat, at the time, had no idea what that meant, but she did know that you could hitch a horse. When Kat was eight, she loved horses.) She didn't even know that her dad had a girlfriend, but then again, why would he tell her? She had no idea where he went on the few nights he hired babysitters to watch her, and when he was home, they had a routine that never varied. She arrived home from school, took the key from the string around her neck, and let herself in. She would do homework, watch TV, and never let a stranger into the house until he got home from work. He would heat up some TV dinners or Campbell's soup, and they would eat in front of the evening news and then watch a sitcom or western until her father kissed her on the top of her head, telling her she was a *good girl* and sent her to bed. They were very quiet evenings for father and daughter, but Kat, having nothing to compare them to, thought they were perfectly normal.

And then came Missy. Because Missy was only twelve years older than Kat, she wasn't sure if she should treat Kat as a kid sister or a daughter. Missy finally settled on a sort of doll. She seemed to find great delight in outfitting Kat in frilly dresses and Mary Janes and would garnish her with ribbons and bows. At first, Kat, who was unknowingly starved for affection, loved all the attention. She wasn't nuts about the dresses, which hampered tree climbing and playing on the monkey bars at recess, but she let it pass when Missy said she could wear lipstick to school—why not? However, it slowly dawned on Kat that Missy didn't have a clue as to how to treat an eight- and then a nine-year-old girl. Then, one day, a grimy, boogery boy at school, a boy everyone made fun of, pointed to Kat and said, "You're a freak!" The dawning broke into a full realization. If the freakiest boy in her grade called her a freak, that was truly humiliating. It must mean that she, Kat Flowers, was a super freak in her throwback-to-the-fifties girly dresses.

Luckily, she didn't have to say something to Missy or throw a tantrum (not that she would have—she was a *good girl*) because it was at about that same time that Missy discovered she was pregnant. And her interest in Kat waned dramatically. The dresses and bows and hair braiding and lipstick were gone. When Shane was born, Missy's attention was laser-beamed on her new son, and basically, Kat could have been a fly on the wall as far as Missy was concerned. Oh, except for one thing. Kat was good for *fetching*. And Missy needed a lot of things *fetched* for the baby: diapers, bottles, booties, pacifiers, bibs, and comb, even though the baby had absolutely no hair. Just when Shane started to toddle, and Kat thought her fetching days were over, along came Cody, and the cycle started all over again.

Kat thought the fetching thing, although tedious, was not so terrible. At least it gave her something to do, some purpose in the household. No, the truly awful thing was her father's reaction to the baby boys. Quite simply, he seemed to adore them, picking one up in each arm and calling them his "little buckeroos." He even seemed to enjoy changing diapers and feeding bottles. If Kat didn't know better, she would swear that someone had kidnapped her solemn, serious father and replaced him with this smiling stranger. It was a crying shame, though, that his reaction toward his only daughter remained as distant as before.

It was probably inevitable that Kat, once she turned thirteen and the boys were one and three, started to spend as much time as possible away from home. She wasn't really doing anything wrong, and she definitely wasn't *acting out*, as Missy accused her of doing. No, Kat was hanging out with her friends, smoking the occasional cigarette or drinking the occasional beer, going to the mall, and developing the occasional crush on way too many boys. And then she met Bobby Baker.

It was her father's fault that she met Bobby Baker, although he didn't see it that way at all. It was the end of March, and Kat had just gotten her driver's license, which meant that she now had freedom—except that her father and Missy placed enormous restrictions on her use of the family station wagon. So it was surprising when, on a Saturday morning, her father asked her to take the station wagon to the local auto shop and get the tires rotated. "Are you kidding me?" she had said to her father. "You're going to entrust me with the sacred station wagon?" "See?" Missy had said. "There goes her smart mouth again." Her father let out his usual world-weary sigh and handed Kat the keys.

Most people would think that Bobby Baker was a little on the scrawny side, but not Kat. To her, he was a dashing figure: tall, lean, with longish brown hair and brown eyes and a perpetual cigarette dangling out of his mouth. Kat couldn't take her eyes off him when Bobby rotated the tires on the station wagon, and he finished way too quickly.

"That's it?" she said to him when he said he was done. She wished she had worn her favorite blue sweater, the one that matched the color of her eyes.

"Yep."

"There's got to be more to it than that," she said. Surely, rotating tires was a big deal.

"Nope."

"Do you have a girlfriend?" she blurted out, surprising herself. She could feel her face turn red.

Bobby looked at her thoughtfully, up and down. He took a cigarette out of the pocket of his t-shirt. "Nope," he finally said.

Okay, so maybe Bobby Baker wasn't the world's greatest conversationalist, but he was twenty-two, he had a Camaro, and he had a scorpion tattoo on his right bicep.

These qualities of Bobby Baker's were only a few that her father objected to when he found out that Kat was dating the neighborhood mechanic. Kat would never find out how her father heard she was dating Bobby. Where was his *distance* when a girl really needed it? "He's too old for you, Katrina," her father said over one spectacularly lousy dinner. Missy had outdone herself with something called Hawaiian meatballs.

"He is not," Kat said. "Pineapple does not belong in meatballs."

"See, Marcus?" Missy said. "There goes her smart mouth again. And for your information, young lady, this recipe came from *Redbook*."

"Well, then," Kat said. "Who am I to argue with the gospel of women's magazines?"

"Marcus!" Missy implored.

Kat's father went on, ignoring the squabble. He had become quite adept at it. "Bobby Baker is twenty-two, Katrina, and that is too old for you. Plus, he drives his car too fast, he has an ugly tattoo, and he's dumber than a brick."

"A dumb brick!" Shane shouted. His six-year-old sense of humor found this hilarious. Cody, following his big brother's lead, started to scream with laughter, too.

Kat had to yell to be heard over her bratty brothers' cackling. "He's actually quite intelligent, once you get to know him." Kat might have been stretching the truth a tad.

"He's a high school dropout, Katrina. How intelligent does that sound to you?"

Kat had not known this. "He has a GED," she blustered. She would have to ask Bobby about that later.

"He's dumber than a brick," her father repeated, "and he has a bad reputation."

"Most of the things people say about Bobby aren't true."

Her father put down his fork and folded his hands under his chin. "Which ones?"

Kat's brain ticked rapidly. Had Bobby been ticketed twice for going over a hundred in his Camaro? Yes. Had Bobby spent time in a juvenile detention center for stealing hubcaps? Yes. Had Bobby knocked up Lucinda Wilson when she was fifteen? Probably, although he said it could have been one of two other guys, too. "He didn't—" she stuttered.

Her father picked up his fork and speared a Hawaiian meatball. "Just as I thought. I don't want you seeing him, Katrina. Bobby Baker is a juvenile delinquent, a rebel without a cause. No, I take that back. Bobby Baker is too stupid even to know what a *cause* is."

"But—" What was she going to say? She couldn't say, "Don't worry about him getting me knocked up, Dad. We haven't even gone all the way yet." No, she couldn't say that.

"I don't want you seeing him, Katrina. Period. End of discussion." He chased the Hawaiian meatball with a big gulp of water.

"You heard your father," Missy added lamely.

"A dumb brick!" Shane shouted, sending him and his brother off again.

Kat did not listen to her father. If anything, his forbidding her to see Bobby only made her want him that much more. She would just have to be careful; that was all. She would sneak to his place in the dead of night if she had to. Even though he lived with his mother, she was usually dead drunk by nine o'clock, or so Bobby had told her.

"Your father forgot his lunch," Missy said to her now, her counter slapping completed.

Kat stood at the refrigerator, looking for anything edible. "So?" Kat said. "Can't he go to McDonald's or something?"

"You know he likes the same lunch every day. A bologna and cheese sandwich and an apple. Every day." Missy sounded weary. "Grab the bag out of the refrigerator and take it to him, would you?"

"Fine." Kat grabbed the bag, seemingly the only thing edible in the refrigerator. "Where are the keys to the station wagon?"

"I need the car. I have errands to run."

"Then why don't you drop off his lunch?" It seemed to Kat that the woman had no sense at all. If she was going to be out and about, why couldn't she take Marcus his boring bologna and cheese sandwich?

"Katrina, I am a busy woman, and you don't even have a summer job. Hop on your bike and take your father his damn lunch!"

It wasn't like she hadn't tried to get a summer job, Katrina thought, as she rode through town on her old Schwinn. What in the hell did Missy expect her to do? Commute to St. Louis, 96 miles north, without a car? Kat flatly refused to babysit, and she had applied at something like twenty businesses in Carbondale. But Carbondale was a college town, and most businesses slowed considerably during the summer months. She was too young to work in a bar or a restaurant, and she couldn't be a lifeguard because she wasn't a very good swimmer. Most of her friends had applied earlier than she had and landed jobs at the mall on the outskirts of town. So Kat did have to admit that waiting until June to look for a job was a bit late. And since she flatly refused to babysit, that left Kat Flowers jobless for the long, hot summer.

Plus, Kat needed her evenings free to spend with Bobby Baker, even if she didn't find him as attractive as she had when she first met him. She still loved him, sure. Hadn't she finally consented to *go all the way*? If that didn't prove how much she loved him, what did? The only problem was this: Now that they had gone all the way, it was all Bobby Baker wanted to do. Kat liked the sex part just fine, but every once in a while, she'd like to see a movie or grab a hamburger. "We're on the sly," Bobby kept reminding her, and being on the sly seemed to suit Bobby just fine.

She hopped off her bike in front of Barone's Trucking, where her father had worked as a dispatcher for as long as Kat could remember. Kat could think of nothing more boring than sitting at a desk all day long, fielding calls for produce pick-ups and deliveries, but her father had made a living doing just that. Kat had often wondered if her father had ever done anything exciting in his life or had anything exciting happen to him. It seemed unlikely. She knew nothing about his past. He always said there was nothing to tell, other than he had no siblings, and his parents had died before she was born. Obviously, her father had not been born for excitement. It was a shame, really, to live your life so monotonously.

"I brought your lunch," Kat said when she walked in.

Her father, as usual, was on the phone. He held up one finger, signaling for her to wait.

Kat took a seat in front of his desk and waited for the boring conversation about some misplaced tomatoes to end. Her father looked older under the unflattering overhead lighting, and Kat noticed that he was developing a bald patch on the back of his head. He looked every bit of his fifty-two years.

He finally hung up the phone. He sat back in his chair, made a temple with his hands, and stared at her.

Kat was immediately, uncomfortably on the alert. "What's up?" she asked.

"The jig," he said.

Kat's mouth went dry. "I don't know what you mean."

"I'll give you two words: Bobby Baker."

Kat decided that her best defense was to remain silent until she found out what he knew.

"I stopped by the garage this morning on the way to work." He continued to stare at her as if seeing her for the first time. "I needed a quart of oil for my truck," he added as if it was important.

Kat remained silent, but her hands were starting to shake, rattling the brown bag she still held in her hands. She leaned over and placed it on his desk.

"Bobby Baker didn't see me, or if he did, he's more of a moron than I gave him credit for." Her father leaned forward, still staring. "He was entertaining the other men with a story about the girl he's been screwing."

Kat's throat was too dry to swallow, and she sat miserably, waiting for the inevitable.

"Let me see," her father continued in an eerily calm voice, "how did he put it? The Flowers girl no longer has her flower, something along those lines."

"I can explain," Kat squeaked.

"You cannot!" Her father slammed his hands down on his desk and was out of his chair and around his desk so quickly that Kat didn't even have time to blink. "You have been whoring around with that lowlife, and I will not tolerate it! Do you understand me? I will not tolerate it!"

His slap was so quick and hard that it almost knocked Katrina off her chair. She knew that she had his hand mark on her cheek. Never in her life had he hit her; in fact, in her life, he had barely touched her. And now this. Her father had slapped her as hard as he could.

"I will not tolerate having a whore for a daughter!" he screamed at her.

Kat was sure that he was going to hit her again. Somehow she got to her feet and started to back away from him. "I am not a whore." She wasn't. She had gone all the way with Bobby Baker, but that did not make her a whore.

"You're a tramp!" her father shouted.

"No," she said, backing farther away from the pure hatred she saw in his eyes. She could not live with a man who looked at her with such loathing. She would run away. She'd go to Bobby's garage and convince him to run away with her. It was the only option.

Her father's breathing was hard and shallow, and he clenched his hands at his side. "Get out," he said. It was clear he wanted to hit her again.

Kat didn't need another invitation or warning. She turned and ran out the door, not stopping when he called something after her. She wasn't sure what he said—and didn't care—but later, much later, she would wonder if she had heard correctly.

Had he said, *Just like your mother?*

"Mother thinks we should get married," Benson said as casually as if he had just mentioned that they were out of milk or that there was a ten percent chance of rain next Tuesday.

Kat, munching on popcorn, wasn't sure if she'd heard him correctly. "Excuse me?" she said, her mouth still full.

"Mother thinks we should get married," Benson repeated without taking his eyes from the flat-screen TV. They were watching *The Hangover, Part II*, and one of the characters had just gotten a Mike Tyson-looking tattoo on his face. Benson absolutely loved the movie.

Kat did not. She'd wanted to watch *Beaches*, but they'd flipped a coin. She'd lost. Sunday afternoon movie-watching in the white, white condo was a routine they had fallen into somewhere along the way, and Kat didn't particularly enjoy it. She would much rather have taken a drive somewhere, anywhere in Benson's hand-me-down BMW, listening to Outlaw Country on Sirius radio. The BMW, of course, had been handed down from said Mother.

Kat choked down the mouthful of popcorn. "How many martinis had she had when she made this suggestion?" Carmella often came up with outlandish ideas after a couple of Appletinis.

"I don't know. Mother mentioned it when she called last night. She wasn't slurring or anything if that's what you're asking." Benson, his eyes still on the movie, laughed at a particularly offensive penis joke.

That was not what Kat was asking. No, not even close. Who in the world did Carmella think she was to suggest something like this to her son? (Well, Carmella would probably answer, "I'm his *mother*.") And another question: If Benson wanted to marry her, why didn't he ask Kat himself, instead of dropping this quiet bombshell? They never had, in their year together, discussed marriage. Really, in the few seconds Kat had to think about this semi-proposal concocted by her boyfriend's controlling mother, she could come to only one conclusion. She should be outrageously offended.

But curiosity got the upper hand. "Why does your mother think we should get married?"

"I don't know," Benson rotely answered while laughing at another stupid joke in the movie.

"Benson," Kat wrenched the remote control from his hand and pressed the off button, "you need to look at me. You don't just drop shit on my head like that and then pretend you're engrossed in a stupid buddy movie."

"I wasn't pretending," Benson said. "I love this movie."

Dear God, her boyfriend was a part-time model for a reason. Was he stupid? Was he spineless? Was he totally brainwashed by his mother? At that moment, Kat would answer *yes* to all three questions. Did she tend to be drawn to stupid, unsuitable men, beginning with the dumb-as-a-brick Bobby Baker? However, with patience, she asked Benson, "Why does Carmella think we should get married?"

Her handsome boyfriend of dubious intelligence squirmed in his seat. His smooth, pretty forehead furrowed in concentration. "She gave a couple of reasons."

"Which were?" Kat prompted.

"Well, she's been talking to a priest, and there's all that living in sin stuff." Benson still refused to look at Kat. Instead, he stared longingly at the blank TV.

"Staring at the television is not going to make it magically turn on, Benson," Kat said impatiently. "And when did Carmella start going to church?" Kat had always thought that champagne brunches were Carmella's main goals on Sundays, not mass.

Benson shrugged. "She's always gone off and on. She'll stop for a while, but then the guilt always drives her back."

Living in sin. What a total crock. If Carmella knew how infrequently they had sex, she might have second thoughts on that one. Shit. Had Benson told her that their sex life was pretty much a G-rated movie? Very likely. Shit. Kat didn't even want to think about it. She pushed on. "What was the other reason?"

"She said she wanted to have grandchildren before she got too old." Benson slowly inched his hand toward the remote.

Kat stuffed it under the sofa cushion. "Your mother is only in her mid-fifties, I think." Carmella went for Botox injections as frequently as most people went to the bathroom. Her face was flawlessly smooth—hell, it didn't even move—so it was impossible to tell how old she was. "Plus, Benson, I've told you countless times that I don't want to have children." At least she thought she didn't want them. She'd told Benson that all she knew about her mother was that she had died giving birth to her. If all a person knew about her mother was that single awful fact, it pretty much dampened her desire to follow in those footsteps. And Kat didn't want to hedge her bet; she wanted to live, damn it.

"Benson, why didn't you tell your mother that babies are not on my agenda?" Kat started to simmer. Wouldn't most boyfriends stand up for their girlfriends? Wouldn't most boyfriends tell their mothers to keep her nose out of their business? Oh, right, how could she forget? Most boyfriends did not get allowances from their mothers.

"You know how she is." It was the only explanation Benson could give.

"Yes," Kat said, "yes, I do. She's a conniving, controlling—"

"Let's put the movie back on. I don't want to talk about my mother anymore. You know I adore her."

Kat seethed. She did not particularly want to talk about Carmella anymore either, but it was clear from Benson's face, as guileless as a little boy's, that he had not told her everything. He had dropped this mother-thinks-we-should-get-married bombshell on her, and she wasn't going to back down until she had the whole story. "What else did she say, Benson?"

"Give me the remote, Kat."

"What else!"

"She thinks we should have a pre-nup." Benson spoke as if the words pained him.

Kat almost laughed. "I would expect nothing less of her. Go on."

Benson was back to staring at the blank television.

"Tell me, B.O., has she set the date? Has she hired a caterer? Has she picked out my hypothetical wedding dress?" Kat knew that the wise thing to do would be to shut up and pretend that this whole zany conversation never happened. But she wasn't going to be wise.

"You can be awfully mean for such a pretty girl," Benson tried.

Kat wasn't buying it. "Has she rented a ballroom, booked a band?"

In profile, Benson's perfect square jaw tightened.

It was then that the realization hit Kat. She wasn't really all that angry at Carmella, as pushy and nosy and controlling as she was. No, that wasn't it. Benson had said that his mother thought they should get married, but did he want to marry her? "Do you want to marry me, Benson?"

Benson's perfect square jaw tightened even more.

When was the last time he told her he loved her? For that matter, when was the last time she told him? Had they ever said it, or had they just assumed that they loved/liked/were fond of each other? Benson adored his mother, but how did he really feel about his girlfriend? Maybe he thought Kat added a splash of color to the bland KKK décor?

Kat tapped Benson's shoulder. "Benny, do you want to marry me?"

His voice was a whisper. "Not really."

This time, Kat did laugh. "That's okay, Benny. I don't want to marry you either!" She had never wanted to marry him, she realized, and she never would. Benson was sweet to hang out with, and this was the nicest place she had ever lived, but what in the hell was she doing here? She'd lived here for a year and didn't even know her neighbor's name. Kat didn't even have a key to the mailbox. She hadn't bought one single thing for the condo, nary a serape or a wooden spoon. It was all so ridiculous that Kat couldn't stop laughing.

"It's not funny," Benson said, finally turning to her.

"Yes, it is, Benny boy, it's ridiculously funny." Kat laughed so hard that tears streamed down her cheeks.

"Stop it! You don't look pretty when you laugh like that, and you sound like a hyena." Benson's pretty face turned a deeper shade of red.

That only made Kat laugh harder.

"Are you mocking me?"

It was too much. Kat would have bet money that Benson didn't know what the word *mocking* meant. "No," she gasped, "no."

Benson's face now looked like a mottled checkerboard. "Do you want to know the real reason Mother wanted me to marry you, the *real reason*?"

Kat struggled to get herself under control. "Sure, Benny, why not?" She would pack up her box of junk and leave. Granny Nanny would be happy to see her, but she'd probably be a little disappointed that her pot supply would be cut off.

"She thought that, if I married you, I might be faithful."

Kat was no longer laughing, but her sides ached with its aftermath. "What are you talking about?"

"I'm not a very good golfer," Benson said. "In fact, I'm terrible at the game."

"Of course," Kat rose to leave. It made perfect sense. Perfect. All those middle-aged, society-type ladies. Her boyfriend had been a gigolo. Wait a minute. Most of those women had been friends with Carmella, which would make her Benson's pimp. Had the women paid him for sex? It didn't really matter now. *Woe is the life of a pretty, pretty man,* Kat thought. But she didn't pity Benson.

When she carried her box back into the living room—it took her a whopping five minutes to pack—Benson had already returned to the movie. "I'll be seeing you, Benson," she said.

"I don't think so," he said absentmindedly.

"You're probably right." At the last second, before Kat left that white, white space for good, she went into the kitchen and grabbed the card/letter from her father off the counter where it had been waiting, unread, for a little over a week.

It was time to open it.

4

MARCH-JUNE 1980

Melody and Sylvia *researched* for the last two years of nursing school. And of course, in addition to the occasional fentanyl or hydromorphone, the effects of alcohol had to be wholly and thoroughly examined. Melody had not known or even imagined how *intoxicatingly* fun that research would turn out to be. They frequented folk clubs, Gate of Horn, the Quiet Knight, the Earl of Old Town; they frequented blues clubs, jazz clubs, and discos. They frequented the bars on Rush and Division Streets. Their tastes were eclectic. They would go anywhere and try anything—within reason, of course, and in semi-moderation. They were, after all, going to be nurses, who not only shit but who also vomited and passed out, in semi-moderation.

However, in the beginning, they always reassured each other that they were responsible in their research. Melody and Sylvia only gathered their data on weekends. Weekday nights, Melody still went home to Bridgeview, and Sylvia went home to Compton Street, but on Friday, after their last class, they hit the streets running. Hair was sprayed to hold the feathered Farrah Fawcett look in place, and they put on their jersey wrap dresses and platform shoes to look like the lead character in *Saturday Night Fever,* which they had seen three times. They didn't stop the party until noon on Sunday. That was their deadline. "We need to sober up," Melody said, "for classes."

"Back to the grindstone," Sylvia said.

This system was fine until their rotations began. If one of them had a clinical on a weekend night, a weekday had to be substituted. There was no other way around it. "We need to keep researching," Sylvia said.

Melody agreed. "We're college girls. We need to have fun before we graduate, and our real lives begin."

Thankfully, money wasn't a problem. Sylvia knew most of the bouncers in town, so they rarely paid a cover charge. ("Don't ask me how I know them," Sylvia said, and Melody never did.) They would usually only have to buy one drink before finding a guy who would pay for the rest. They were sexy, young, and became excellent dancers. It was always enough to get someone to notice them and pick up the tab. Always. It made them feel invincible.

Naturally, some of those guys would expect more than a dance after paying the bar bill. At first, this worried Melody. For the first month or so, she would drag Sylvia into the restroom at closing time. "I can't go through with it," she said. The guy who was "hers," always the shorter one, would be too fat or too thin or have hair that was too long or too short. Or his clothes would be wrong. Or he would have halitosis. There was always a reason.

"What's wrong with this one?" Sylvia said.

Melody would give her reason.

Sylvia would sigh. This would mean that she, too, wouldn't have a date for the night. However, they had both seen *Looking for Mr. Goodbar*, and by this point of the night were drunkenly wary. They would both leave with a man, or they would both leave without one. The plan was this: When they finally both decided to pick up a man, they would insist on going with their dates to the same apartment, or ideally, back to Thelma's place. Sad but true, Sylvia would give Thelma, to her great joy, two tablets of pentazocine. There was no doubt that she would be zonked out in her ratty green recliner.

After a couple of months of Melody's refusal to choose a date at closing time, Sylvia was fed up. "Damn it, Mel, just *pick* one. He doesn't have to be your soul mate or anything like that. He only has to be decent looking and seem like a nice enough guy. It's not like you're going to marry him." They were at Sylvia's apartment, dressing for another Saturday night on the town.

Melody applied kohl eyeliner around her eyes, a newly acquired make-up trick. "I am trying, Syl, but it just isn't that easy for me. Most of the guys we meet seem kind of *smarmy*." They really did. So many of them had three-piece polyester suits that didn't quite fit or wore too many thick gold chains that dangled against their hairy chests. One of "her" guys one evening—and this was the truth—had actually gotten a gold chain entangled in his chest hair. It had caused Melody to laugh so hard that she had to go into the bathroom and throw up. Sylvia had not been pleased. She claimed to have totally liked "her" guy, the taller one, that evening.

"Smarmy, farmy," Sylvia said. "I need to get laid. You need to get laid. We *both* need to get laid." She tightened the ties of the wrap dress and adjusted her bra, accentuating her impressive cleavage.

Melody did the same, although her result was not nearly as impressive as Sylvia's when she studied both of their reflections in the mirror. Her breasts were only B-cups, not D-cups. But that was not the reason that Melody had been so reluctant to choose a closing-time-date. "I'm scared," she said truthfully.

Sylvia took pity. "I know, Mel, I know." She patted her arm. "The first time is scary, but after a while, it's like riding a bike. You just get on and pedal."

Melody didn't know what she meant. Everything she had ever read (part of the *Joy of Sex* before she became too embarrassed and put it back on the shelf in the bookstore), and everything she had ever overheard about sex (all of it from Catholic schoolgirls), mentioned nothing about bicycles. "I'll try harder tonight."

"That's my girl." Sylvia sprayed her Farrah Fawcett curls a final time. "I have protection. We don't want to be nurses with gonorrhea, do we?" She gave her throaty laugh.

That was pretty much the last thing Melody wanted to be. "Definitely not."

"Just think of it as *research*, Mel, and you'll be okay."

That night, to bolster her courage and to *get it over with*, Melody drank an impressive amount of 7&7s. They were at a disco that Saturday, the Hunt Club on Rush Street, and with the strobe light cutting the room into whirling pieces and the Bee Gees' falsettos telling the crowd that they were "Stayin' Alive," Melody, for the first time, totally relaxed. The guy who'd been yelling in her ear and buying her drinks all night wasn't that bad. She tried to think. What was his name? Charley or Marley or something like that. Of course, he was short, but he had nice wavy blonde hair that just touched the collar of his cornflower blue suit. And he didn't have an overabundance of gold chains around his neck. He looked like he would do.

She told this to Sylvia in the restroom during Last Call. "I think I can do it with him ... Charley ... Marley." Was there a strobe light in the bathroom? She saw whirling diamonds of light, but it was a good feeling. It was.

"This is great news!" Sylvia had not been shy in the consumption department on this night either. "I really, really like my guy. His name is ..." She barked a laugh. Sylvia, with her deep voice, was incapable of giggling. "Whoops! I forgot his name. Oh, well. Hell's bells." She opened her tiny evening bag and took out two diazepams. "I think we need these."

"Okay," Melody said. She trusted her best—her *beloved*—friend without reservation. She swayed a little. Was there a breeze in the bathroom?

Arrangements were made, and Melody, Sylvia, and the two unnamed men went back to Thelma's apartment, where true to form, she was passed out on the ratty green recliner. The sight filled Melody with such compassion for the woman, such love for the darling, drug-addled hypochondriac, that she took an afghan off the couch and gently covered the doped-up mother of her best and beloved friend Sylvia. "God bless her heart," she said.

That was the last thing she remembered.

The next morning, she woke up in Thelma's bed with a pounding headache, a parched throat, and blood-stained sheets. It took her a moment to realize where she was and then—bam! She remembered what was supposed to have happened the previous night. Clearly, it had. It was only a little after seven, so Melody stripped the bed and tiptoed to the bathroom. Sylvia found her an hour or so later, still scrubbing at the sheets in a bathtub filled with water and Clorox. The stain was gone, but Melody still scrubbed.

"So, the deed is done." Sylvia yawned.

"Apparently." Melody was so hungover that she wanted to cry.

"Don't remember?"

"Not a thing."

"Not to worry. The first time isn't usually so great."

Melody had heard that story many times, but it seemed that the point was this: You should at least remember your first time. She was so hungover that she wanted to cry.

Sylvia sat down on the stool and peed. "I'll make some coffee. We'll talk."

In their first detailed discussion about sex, Melody learned a lot, but it would not be their last. And soon, Melody did have some experience to contribute to the conversations. Every Friday and Saturday night after that, she and Sylvia had closing-time-dates. Some names Melody remembered; some she didn't. Some nights she remembered; some she didn't. But it was all good fun. They were researching, and they were using condoms.

"No harm, no foul," Sylvia said.

"We're having the time of our lives."

"We need to go on the pill," Sylvia said.

Melody agreed. Condoms were not one hundred percent effective, but since they had become sexually active—much more so than either of them had planned—it was definitely time.

Their doctor appointments were for two days after the Michael Jackson concert when they got unbelievably stoned and tried morphine for the first time, and Melody ended up in the equipment bus with a roadie. The night was as big of a blank in her mind as her first sexual encounter, but the result was indelible. She was pregnant, and she could not have that baby and ruin her life. Abortion went against everything she'd been taught, but she didn't care. She wanted her life, not a baby.

After the abortion, as she left the clinic in Naperville, which was far away from her neighborhood on the South Side, feeling weepy and depressed and vowing that she would never go through that again, she said to Sylvia, "I think our research is over."

Three weeks after the abortion, Melody met Marcus. It was in a bar in the South Loop. She and Sylvia's newfound sobriety lasted one boring weekend when they played nine games of Scrabble and watched Thelma go in and out of consciousness. When she was conscious, she begged Sylvia for more drugs. It was her back this time. Thelma had strained her back when she leaned over to pick up a dropped cigarette, which ended up burning a sizable hole in the bright orange shag carpeting.

"I can't stand this," Sylvia said.

Melody, too, was bored out of her mind. She was not addicted to drugs and alcohol. Neither she nor Sylvia had any of the symptoms. It was the excitement she missed, the dancing, the people, the music, the sense of infinite possibilities that a Saturday night could bring. She supposed, reluctantly, that she did miss, just a little, feeling uninhibited after the first couple of gin and tonics.

"Maybe we could go to more low-key places, you know, neighborhood bars or something like that. We don't need to cut loose every time we go out," Melody suggested.

"Right. We don't need to get bombed," Sylvia agreed.

"We could be more selective about the men we sleep with."

"I suppose," Sylvia said.

So they found themselves on this late March night in Blackies. There was a nice-sized crowd, a jukebox played in the corner, and the drinks were cheap. But not cheap enough. For Melody and Sylvia, *free* was much better than cheap. They were getting dangerously close to finishing the one drink that they could afford to pay for when the bartender brought them another. Sighing with relief, they could relax for a little while longer; they didn't have to go home right away.

"The guy at the end bought these for you." The bartender nodded his head toward the end of the bar.

Both girls leaned over to look. It was Melody's first glimpse of the man who would ask her to marry him six weeks later. He was older than her—she would guess mid-thirties—with unstylishly short, nondescript brown hair and John Lennon round glasses. With his pressed blue jeans and red-checked flannel shirt, he looked decidedly *not cool.*

"Tell him we said 'thanks,'" Sylvia said to the bartender, who nodded and walked away.

"We're scraping the bottom of the barrel here." Sylvia took a sip and lit a More cigarette. "There is absolutely nothing going on in this place. No one's dancing and the joint is filled with old men, who seem to be cheap, by the way. We could still catch the El to the Warehouse." The Warehouse had been one of their frequent haunts before they decided to (kind of) go straight.

"I don't know." Melody snuck another furtive glance at the man sitting alone at the end of the bar. "The guy who bought us the drinks doesn't seem so bad."

"Are you kidding?" Sylvia's voice was loud, too loud, even for a bar.

"Shh," Melody hissed. "I don't want him to think we're talking about him."

Sylvia's glance toward the man at the end of the bar was not at all furtive. "He looks like an enginerd. Put a white button-down on him and a pocket protector, and you've got a classic enginerd. Plus, he's so *white*."

It was true. Even though most people in Chicago had the usual winter pallor, this man was very pale. He looked, Melody thought, almost luminous. "You can be so harsh, Sylvia, and," she pointed out, "he's the only guy in the place who has bought us a drink."

"True, but he still could use a mega-dose of vitamin D."

The man looked up from his drink just then and caught Melody's eye. He smiled, and it was a friendly smile, a warm smile. Melody smiled back. "I'm going to go thank him for the drinks. Do you want to come with?"

"I think I'll take a pass," Sylvia said in her superior, bitchy voice. "But you go. Knock yourself out, and see if you can finagle another drink out of the old man, would you?"

Melody picked up her drink and walked to the end of the bar. Even though all the other barstools were occupied, an empty stool stood on either side of him. Did he have body odor? Melody wondered. She would thank him quickly and get back to her seat.

When she got near enough to determine that he did not have B.O., did, in fact, smell like Aramis cologne, she thanked him for the drinks. "It was nice of you to buy them for us," she said.

"My pleasure," he said, again smiling his warm smile. The smile made his brown eyes crinkle, which made him seem a little younger. "Would you like to have a seat?"

Melody did not particularly want to sit down and make small talk to such an old guy, but it would be rude not to sit for a second or two. Plus— and Melody did not know why she felt this way—he seemed a little lonely. Why wasn't anyone sitting next to him? She sat primly on the stool. What did you say to someone of his generation? He probably didn't like the same music she did or want to go to concerts and dances. "Do you come here often?" she finally asked when it became apparent that he wasn't going to initiate the conversation.

"No. Do you?" He took a dainty sip of his Old Style beer.

"No." Okay, then, now what? Was she allowed to go? She felt a little like a schoolgirl waiting for permission to be dismissed. "Well, thanks again for the drink." She was anxious to get back to Sylvia, and the idea to take the El to the Warehouse was becoming more appealing all the time.

"You're very pretty," the man said.

Naturally, she blushed. (Damn her fair, freckled coloring and red hair!) The guys she and Sylvia had been hanging around with and screwing for the last two years were not the complimenting sort. Oh, they'd tell her she was cool or had a great ass or that her hair was *neat*, but that was about as far as it went. This compliment seemed genuine. "Thank you," she said, her face still aflame.

"Are you Irish?"

"Guilty as charged."

The man seemed to have decided something. He held out his hand. "I'm Marcus."

And then, miraculously, the conversation became easy. He asked her what she did, where she lived, how many brothers and sisters she had, what her plans for the future were, and on and on. He bought her another drink, and when he caught her glancing at Sylvia, who did not look happy, he bought her another one as well.

Melody, too, asked questions and found out that he was thirty-four (too old for her), had no siblings, his father had died years before, and his mother with whom he still lived (another big strike) suffered from dementia. When she asked him what he did, it was hardly surprising when he answered, "I'm a mechanical engineer."

Eventually, when it became apparent to Sylvia that Melody wasn't returning to her original barstool, she gathered up her things, moving to the other seat beside Marcus. "If you can't beat 'em, join 'em," she announced, seeming happy enough that Marcus was keeping a steady supply of drinks coming, even though he nursed the same Old Style all night. After another couple of drinks, Sylvia proclaimed to Marcus, "You're okay, Markie, you really are. For an old guy, you're all right."

Melody cringed. Why did Sylvia always do things like that? But Marcus smiled his very nice smile and said, "Why thank you, Sylvia, I appreciate that."

By the end of the night—and once again, she and Sylvia had made it to closing time—Melody decided she liked Marcus' company. As Sylvia later said, he might be a little bit fuddy-duddy, and Melody reluctantly agreed, but he certainly acted like a gentleman. For Melody, this was a new experience. Her daddy, as wonderful as he was to his one and only daughter, didn't do things like open doors or put his hand on the small of

Ma's back to gently guide her through crowds, nor did he take Ma's hand when they crossed a street. And her brothers? Forget about it. They were the opposite of gentlemen. They were *rough* men. And needless to say, the men she had been with had seen her as being useful for one thing: a ready fuck.

So after Marcus dropped them off that night at Sylvia's apartment because he refused to allow two women to take the El at that hour *unescorted* and he and Melody were standing outside on the stoop, he asked her for a date. He said, very primly in the chilly spring air, "Would you allow me to escort you on a date in the very near future, Melody?"

She was both flabbergasted and flattered. Marcus was too old for her, he lived with his mother, he was an enginerd, yet he was a gentleman. And if the truth were to be told—and she never told Marcus this truth—it would actually be her first date. So she answered, "Okay." He kissed her lightly on the cheek, another first for Melody, and called her two days later.

On their first date, they went to see *Coal Miner's Daughter*, and then he took her to Pizza Hut. He paid for everything, opened doors, bought her her own box of popcorn at the movie, and kissed her on the cheek. On their second date, he took her to the White Sox's opening game and then took her home to meet his mother, a sweet, white-haired, delusional lady who took an instant liking to Nurse Melody. They had a proper kiss on that date. Some time passed between their second and third dates. Sylvia felt left out and put upon, so Melody took up with her again on weekends. They were not quite as loose as they'd been, but Melody slipped and ended up sleeping/passing out with two guys she couldn't remember the next day.

So on their third date, at the end of April, Melody was feeling very guilty when Marcus picked her up in his slightly used but immaculately clean Buick. Marcus must have been missing her or was trying to win her over because he pulled out all the stops. He took her to Carmine's Italian Restaurant on Rush Street, and Melody was duly impressed by the white tablecloths and single rose in a vase on each table. Marcus asked for a wine list, which also duly impressed Melody, and ordered a bottle of Chianti.

The tart, red wine was delicious, and Melody told him so.

"Do you like this restaurant?" Marcus asked. He wore a suit, not a John Travolta *Saturday Night Fever* polyester suit, but a double-breasted suit made of real wool. A real suit. A grown-up man.

"It's ..." Melody looked around at the well-dressed crowd. Many had playbills with them and had come to the restaurant from the theatre. "Wonderful," she finished. She ordered the seafood pasta. It was so expensive, but Marcus said that money was no object, and it was also delicious. Melody had never been to such a nice place, and she was intoxicated with it.

And she was intoxicated with the wine. Marcus had one glass, and she had the rest of the bottle. She giggled frequently; she couldn't help it. Melody felt so happy! And because of her happiness, and because of the wine, and because she still felt guilty, when Marcus parked his Buick in front of Sylvia's apartment and kissed her good night, she wanted more. She needed more.

"Good night," he said.

"Not yet." She climbed on top of him. She unzipped his pants, hoisted her skirt, and pulled her panties to one side.

"Oh, Melody." Marcus didn't resist.

She thought she would never see him again. Thoroughly embarrassed, she didn't take his calls, and he called every day. He'd behaved like such a gentleman, and she'd behaved like a raging whore. He was twelve years older than she was, he was a little fussy, a little too particular, and she did not deserve him.

Then Melody, Ms. Fertile Myrtle, was pregnant again. "How could I have been so stupid?" she wailed to Sylvia. "I didn't even have a condom with me. I had no intention of assaulting him." Sadly, she and Sylvia had never gotten around to making another doctor's appointment to get the pill. They were too busy during the week with all their studies and the weekends ... Well, the weekends were for partying.

Practical, competent Sylvia didn't judge. "*Roe v. Wade*, Mel. Abortion is legal. Abortion is the way to get rid of *unwanted pregnancies*."

But almost-Nurse Melody could not go through with it again. The *gnawing feeling* would not let her do it one more time to atone for her own stupidity. She would have to break down and tell Daddy and Ma, and they would be devastated. They hadn't even met Marcus! She would end up working part-time and living in the row house on Roosevelt Street forever, dependent upon them for childcare and money. She would have to resign herself to the consequences of her actions. However, for some reason, even though she didn't know him well, she felt that Marcus had a right to know. After all, he wasn't getting any younger.

He was stunned, naturally. Melody had gone to his house in Evergreen Park and told him on his front porch on the first warm day that spring. She didn't pussy-foot around. She rang the bell, and when he came out of the house, looking so glad to see her, she blurted it out. "Marcus, I'm pregnant."

He was stunned for perhaps a second or two, and then he did what Melody had not expected. He did the gentlemanly thing. He dropped to one knee. "Melody Callahan, will you marry me?"

What was a girl to do?

The aisle at St. Mary's Catholic Cathedral was indeed long, very long. Melody stood in the vestibule, her arm linked with Daddy's, and stared at the miles and miles of the long white runner. It was endless.

"Are you ready to take the plunge?" Daddy asked. He looked uncomfortable in the rented black tuxedo. He was a small, bald man and rather stout, so of course, his rowdy sons had made the predictable penguin jokes.

No, she was not ready to take the plunge. What was she doing here, in this stained-glass church, the pews filled with family and friends and all of Daddy's union? Somewhere, in the distance, stood her betrothed, a man she barely knew, a man she had unprotected sex with once, a man she had kissed only four times.

Marcus, amid the flurry of the past few weeks, had been impeccably polite. After Melody had responded to his proposal with a very noncommittal "okay," he had done the right thing. They drove to her parents' house, and he asked her father for permission. Daddy had almost gotten down on *his* knees and said, "Thank the Lord! We had all but given up hope of anyone taking this girl off our hands."

It distressed Melody how merrily her parents took the news. "Mellie's getting married! Mellie's getting married!" These words were the background music for everything that went on inside 1113 S. Roosevelt. Even her brothers seemed to join in the excitement.

"You didn't even have to kiss a lot of toads, Mellie, before you found your prince," Frankie said. (How little he knew!)

"Mellie got a catch," Mikey crowed to his friends. "She's marrying an *engineer*." Melody highly doubted that he even knew what an engineer did. She certainly didn't, and it hadn't come up in her few conversations with her *fiancé*.

"Wow," Willie said. "This is so cool, Mellie." He blushed, then said playfully, "Do you need any advice about the wedding night?" Melody had taken him to the clinic to get penicillin for his very nasty case of the clap, and he'd been very grateful.

No one even remotely suspected that she was pregnant. Not their Mellie, their Mellie, who had never even had a boyfriend. They all assumed she was still a virgin. At this moment, in this church, she wished to God that she was still a virgin. Virgins, other than Saint Mary, did not get pregnant.

The sixth and last bridesmaid, Sylvia, her maid of honor, made it to the end of the aisle. The final words Sylvia whispered before she began that long and arduous trek had been, "You look terrified."

"I am terrified." Looking like a deer caught in the headlights was not an appropriate bridal look, but Melody couldn't help it. She was utterly, thoroughly terrified.

"My little girl," Daddy said fondly. "Shall we get this show on the road?"

The wedding march began, the pipe organ music filling the church. It was too loud. Melody wanted to put her hands over her ears. She wanted to run, but she couldn't move. Her right foot seemed incapable of crossing over onto that white runner.

"It's showtime." Daddy gave her arm a gentle tug.

She needed more time. "How do you know?" she asked. "How do you know you're marrying the right person?"

"Oh, little girl," Daddy smiled. "It's a leap of faith. You meet a gal, you get along fine, and you figure it's time to get married and get on with things. It's as simple as that. That's what me and your ma did."

A leap of faith, Melody thought. Maybe she could work with that. In the distance, she could see the six bridesmaids in their truly awful pink-flowered dresses and the groomsmen in their ivory tuxedos fanned out in front of the church. Marcus waited in front, a little apart from the rest, his hands clasped in front of him. From this distance, she couldn't make out his face at all.

She owed it to the bridesmaids to get married. She had made them wear wallpaper.

She could not remember what Marcus looked like.

The organist started the song again, and the entire congregation stared at her, the bride, who stood rooted in the doorway.

Daddy was getting a tad impatient. "The sooner we get this over with, Mellie, the sooner I can have a beer."

That was a pretty good incentive. The sooner Melody got this over with, the sooner she could get drunk. "Let's go," she said.

Step by slow step, Melody made it down that endless aisle, and an hour later, it was over. She would never remember the ceremony or the mass; she barely registered that Marcus stood beside her. She just followed the steps. She was very good at following procedure. Nursing school had taught her that.

At the end of that vague hour that would permanently stamp her life, the priest had the newly married couple turn to face the congregation and said, "I now present you with Mr. and Mrs. Marcus Arnold."

Melody was now officially Mrs. Marcus Arnold.

5

APRIL 2012

Kat arrived on Granny Nanny's doorstep with her two suitcases and her cardboard box of junk. Granny Nanny welcomed her with open arms, as Kat knew she would, and what's more, she didn't seem to be the least bit surprised to see her.

"Benson and I broke up," Kat said as she pushed through the screen door. "Well, I don't know if you could call it *breaking* up. It's more like we mutually dissolved our living arrangement."

"Pretty men are not what they're cracked up to be," Granny Nanny said. On this day, for some reason known only to her, she had decided to paint the old maple coffee table purple. She had the Sunday newspaper scattered on the floor and was on her knees beside the table. "This color is called Passion Flower. Don't you think that's lovely, dear?"

"Gran," Kat said, striving for patience since she didn't give a flying fuck about a hideous color with a ridiculous name. "I said that Benson and I are *kaput*. Shouldn't I be sad or something? Shouldn't I be bawling my eyes out?"

Granny Nanny looked up at her with her bright blue eyes. "Do you want to cry? Go ahead, if it'll make you feel better."

"That's the thing, Gran. I don't remotely feel like crying." Kat had tried to make herself feel sad on the drive over. She'd tried to remember the good times, and all she could come up with were a couple of Sunday champagne brunches. And Carmella had always been there with them. What she really felt, she realized, was relief.

"Then, don't cry."

"I'm going to miss the condo," Kat said.

"No, you're not."

It was true. Kat wasn't going to miss the KKK apartment, and she wasn't going to miss Benson either. What she regretted was wasting an entire year of her life dating and then living with Mr. Wrong. What if, while she was dating Mr. Wrong, Mr. Right had shown up, and she hadn't even recognized him? Oh, the hell with it. Kat didn't want to get married anyway.

"Hey," Granny Nanny said with a wicked gleam in her eye. "When I'm through painting this table, maybe we should take it over to the condo. It could be your parting gift, and God knows that place could use a splash of color. I've never seen anything like it. It was like walking into a freezer that had nothing in it but ice."

Kat laughed. The old maple coffee table painted Passion Flower would be hysterical in the presence of Carmella's designer furniture. "Carmella wanted us to keep it cold in case she dropped in, which as you know, she often did. I suppose she thought she'd keep better, or maybe I should say she thought the cold air would help to *preserve* her."

"That's the spirit!" Granny Nanny reached for Kat's hand to help her up. "I think it's time for a little bit of scotch."

"I think that's indeed what this situation calls for." They walked into the tiny kitchen at the back of the bungalow. "I'm sorry about the pot, Gran."

"Don't you worry about a thing, dear. I always have a back-up plan." Granny Nanny got out the Glen Livet and two shot glasses.

"But—"

"It's always a good idea to have a back-up plan, Katrina. It's always a good idea."

How in the hell could this sweet little old lady know someone who sold pot? Kat wondered. However, she knew better than to ask. Granny Nanny would never divulge her sources.

They sat at their usual places at the Formica-topped kitchen table. They each took a shot, and then Granny Nanny poured them each another. "This is a two-shot occasion," she said.

"At least a two-shot occasion," Kat said, remembering the card/letter from her father that she had put in her purse.

"Oh?" Granny Nanny cocked her head to one side and waited.

Kat knew that Granny Nanny could wait for a long time for Kat to finally spill her guts. Kat suspected that her gran would have the patience to wait forever if she had to, just to find out what troubled her dear Katrina. Kat had never told Gran how much she appreciated this but didn't really need to. Granny Nanny knew.

"There's this." She pulled the card from her purse and placed it in the center of the table between them. They both stared at it.

Granny Nanny, naturally, didn't say anything. She patiently bided time, waiting for Kat to spill her guts.

Finally, Kat said, "I wanted to throw it away, but Benson didn't want me to."

"I guess I have to give the pretty man some credit for that one," Granny Nanny said.

"I wanted to burn it."

"But you didn't."

"No." Obviously. The thing was still here, laying in the middle of the table, a little smudged and crumpled now, the ink on the address a little blurred.

"It's been a long time since you've heard from him."

Granny Nanny knew how long it had been since Kat had heard from Marcus Flowers: ten years. This card, or whatever it was after such a long silence, was what worried Kat the most. Pretty, dumb Benson had brought up an excellent point. After all these years with no communication, this thing had to carry bad news. Someone didn't, after such a long stretch of time, drop you a line and say, "Hope you're well. Let's get together for lunch sometime soon." People didn't do that.

So Kat was scared to open the envelope. And she was angry. And she was hurt. And she was humiliated. After communication ceased from her father, Kat had tried to call. (She didn't tell Granny Nanny this, but she suspected that the crafty little woman of indeterminate age did know.) The first few times, the phone rang and rang and rang. No person on the other end picked up, and there wasn't an answering machine that clicked on to take a message. The last time she called, a disembodied voice told her that the number had been disconnected. Her father and his new family had moved, or they had fallen on hard times and couldn't afford a phone line, or they had all gone to cell phones and no longer used a landline. It didn't matter what the reason was. What mattered was that her father made no attempt to let Kat know how to reach him by phone, or later, by email, Facebook, or text. She knew that she could have sent him a letter, but her pride wouldn't let her do that. What she dwelt on was that her father had wholly and finally cut her off.

"I'm not getting any younger," Gran prompted, her voice mild. She poured them each another shot.

Kat took the shot. "I could still throw it away. After all this time, he means nothing to me."

"Uh-huh." Granny Nanny's voice was noncommittal.

"Oh, what the hell! This thing is driving me crazy!" She would just get it over with once and for all. Whatever the old man had to say could not affect her now. *Oh, my God!* Kat realized he would be sixty-six. She tore it open.

It was a birthday card, and the front of it—a field of wildflowers—looked as impersonal as a birthday card you would receive from your bank or office co-workers. The script read, "On your birthday …"

Kat took a deep breath. "Here goes."

"Good luck, dear."

Kat opened the card. The script continued, "It's time to wish you well." Under that was her father's uneven scrawl: Marcus Flowers.

"You've got to be kidding me," Kat said. "After all this time, this is it? A crummy card with his *full name*. He couldn't even sign it 'your father,' or 'Dad.'"

"Well, I suppose I should say that it's the thought that counts." Granny Nanny looked as disappointed as Kat felt.

"Bullshit." Kat certainly hadn't cried when she broke up with Benson hours before, but she felt like crying now. After fourteen fucking years, how was it possible that her cold-hearted father could still reduce her to a sobbing mess?

"I agree." Granny Nanny poured them another shot.

"He didn't even put a check in it this time, not that I would have cashed it." Her nasty father had even denied her the satisfaction of returning his check.

"Cheap bastard," Granny Nanny concurred.

Kat got up and paced, furious with Marcus Flowers. The nerve of the cold-hearted, nasty, thoughtless man. "I feel like throwing something."

Gran reached across the table to the salt and pepper shakers. The black and white spotted cows had been on the table since before Kat came to live there. "I've always hated these things. Throw them."

"These little cows have been on the table for *centuries*, Gran. I can't throw them."

"They have not been on the table for *centuries*, Katrina. How old do you think I am?"

"I don't know! You won't tell me!"

A smile twitched at the corners of Granny Nanny's mouth. As usual, she would change the subject. "Sit back down at the table, Katrina. I'm getting a crick in my neck watching you pace back and forth. You're going to wear a hole in the linoleum, and I'm saving up for a new Glock. I don't want to waste my money on new linoleum."

Katrina sat down, suddenly depleted. She didn't have the energy that a full-blown pissy fit demanded. She put the spotted cows back where they belonged. "I'm just disappointed. I dreaded opening the card, but I guess I hoped that there would be something, some note or … something."

"I know, dear." Granny Nanny patted her hand. "But you need to turn the card over, Katrina. It looks like there's writing on the back." Gran poured them each another shot.

How long had the crafty, indeterminately aged woman known that? "Why didn't you tell me that sooner, Gran?"

"I don't know, dear. Maybe it's the scotch, but I'm rather enjoying the show. It sure beats painting the coffee table." Gran took her shot neat.

Kat took hers. She was never, ever going to win with Granny Nanny. Never. But she could live with it. She turned the card over; the handwriting was different from her father's. She read it aloud, "Your father had some tests done last Wednesday. We're waiting for the results. I thought you should know. Missy Flowers."

There it was: The bad news.

"She certainly isn't very specific, is she?" Granny Nanny got up and took some cheese out of the refrigerator and some crackers out of the cabinet. She didn't wobble at all. The crafty, indeterminately aged woman could hold her liquor.

Kat, on the other hand, felt the effects of the scotch. Her head whirled. "She isn't specific at all. What do you think this means, Gran?"

Gran sat back down with the cheese and crackers. "Don't you think, Katrina, that it's time you found some answers?"

The whirling in Kat's head was dense and loud, but the question cut through: *What was my mother's name?* She'd just broken up with her pretty boyfriend, who was a gigolo with an allowance, and she wore a mini kilt and padded, push-up bra to work. "Do you mean—"

"Road trip," Granny Nanny said, pushing the plate of cheese and crackers toward her.

Kat begged Granny Nanny to go with her on the road trip. "I'll do all the driving," she told her. "All you have to do is sit on the passenger side and watch the beautiful USA roll by. Come on, Gran, it'll be an adventure."

Gran was resolute. "This is your adventure, Katrina, not mine."

"I need your moral support." Granny Nanny had been the strong pillar that Kat leaned on since she was sixteen. And now, with plans to drive across the country and see her father after so many years, to ask him, once and for all, the questions he should have answered when she was a child, Kat needed Granny Nanny's support more than ever before. "Please, Gran. Please come with me."

"This is something you need to do on your own." She took pity on Kat then and patted her hand. "Everything will be fine. You really don't need me. You are much stronger than you think you are, Katrina dear."

Kat wasn't so sure about that. If a person looked at her life's resume, that person would not be impressed: crappy jobs, slightly slutty twenties, a pretty gigolo of a boyfriend. The list went on and on. Honestly, it was depressing to contemplate. "I hope you're right, Gran." Kat's voice didn't hold much conviction.

"I'm always right. Keep your chin up, get your ducks in a row, and hightail it to Illinois."

"You're just full of pithy sayings, aren't you?"

Gran just smiled.

However, that is what Kat decided to do—keep her chin up and get her ducks in a row. If Granny Nanny refused to go with her, implying nicely, in her crafty way, that Kat needed to grow up and start making adult decisions, Kat would do just that. Keep her chin up and get her ducks in a row.

Kat realized that being a thirty-year-old loser meant that you didn't have that many ducks. She didn't have a significant other, she didn't have children, and she didn't own a home. Hell, Kat thought that her ducks were more like Pepperidge Farm goldfish crackers. Basically, it boiled down to asking Jim for time off from work, getting an oil change for her Mazda, and getting someone to drive with her to share expenses. Pathetically, that was it.

She approached Jim the next night after work. The night had been busy, and Kat had made the most in tips that she ever had before. Knowing that she would be taking time off from the Tilted Kilt made her a lot nicer to the customers, and they responded by tipping her well. ("See?" Buxom Jessica said to her. "Guys like it better when you smile at them and don't tell them to go fuck themselves." Kat said, rolling her eyes, "I'll make a note of that.")

"Jim, I need to ask a favor." Kat had rehearsed what she was going to say to him. She wasn't going to tell him the truth. She wasn't going to tell him that she would be driving across the country to ask her estranged, possibly ailing father about the mysterious mother who had died while giving birth.

"Have you decided about the calendar?" Jim was emptying the register, counting out the one-dollar bills.

"What calendar?" For a brief second, Kat had no idea what he was talking about. She'd completely forgotten about his ludicrous suggestion that she—audition?—for the Tilted Kilt calendar.

"If you don't commit soon, like right now, I'm going to ask Jessica." Jim was a tiny man, barely clearing five feet. To make up for it, he talked in a strained, booming voice.

"Fine. Let Jessica do it. Now what I was going to ask—"

"I'm not happy with this, Kat, not at all. You were my first choice."

She could not afford to piss him off right now. Number one, she needed the time off, and number two, she needed a job to come back to. Kat would take every cent she had on this trip, and when she returned, she would be flat broke. "I'm very flattered, Jim," she said sweetly, "but it's not my type of thing."

Jim slapped the bills on the bar. "Maybe you're right, Kat. You don't have the right attitude for such an honor. You think you're too good for this place, don't you?"

She wanted to say, "You're damn right that I think I'm too good to be a waitress in this place. I have a BS, with honors, in business, you scrawny little runt of a man."

Instead, with as much feigned sweetness as she could muster, she said, "Truly, Jim, I'm very flattered, but I think Jessica will be thrilled with the *honor* of posing *half-naked* in the Tilted Kilt calendar."

Her feigned sweetness did not work on Jim. His face grew very red. "I could fire you, you know."

"For what?" This conversation was certainly not going as Kat had planned. She'd thought that Jim liked her, suspected that he had a little bit of a crush on her, and wouldn't object to her taking a week off. And here they were, arguing over a stupid calendar. Kat shuddered involuntarily. How many men masturbated to that calendar? It was gross, and it was grossly unfair that Jim was making such a big deal about it.

"For …" Jim searched for the word, "*insubordination*."

Kat laughed; she was done trying to be sweet. "Don't be ridiculous, Jim. Ask Jessica. She's got much bigger boobs anyway. Now, what I was going to ask you before you got all revved up about this calendar thing was—"

"You're fired," Jim sputtered.

His face was so red, and his body was so scrawny. To Kat, he looked something like a cherry lollipop. "You can't fire me for not wanting to do the calendar." She still hoped to salvage this conversation.

"I'm not firing you for not doing the calendar. I'm firing you because … because you're a lousy waitress!"

"I am not!" It's not that Kat aspired to be a great waitress, but she certainly didn't think she was lousy at it. It was a thoroughly offensive insult.

"You're rude to the customers," Jim yelled.

He had a point there.

"And you're just fired because I say so! I'm the manager here, and I can fire you if I want to."

Kat couldn't help herself. "Short men should not be put in positions of authority."

"You, you, you—" Jim said in a strangled voice.

"You can't fire me because I quit!" There was no way she was ever going to put this job on her resume.

"You're fired!"

"I quit!" Kat turned on her heel and walked out with as much dignity as she could muster in her mini plaid kilt and padded, push-up bra. Which wasn't much.

Naturally, she told Granny Nanny when she got to the bungalow, but Kat added the conclusion she had come to on the drive home. "Gran, I've decided to put a positive spin on this thing. It's time to move upwards and onwards. It was a nowhere job, and I need to move on to better things. I'll find a new job when I get back, a job that can actually be considered a career."

"I think that's an excellent plan," Gran said.

"But promise me that you'll never tell a living soul that I got fired from Tilted Kilt."

"My lips are sealed, dear."

Kat moved on to her next goldfish. There was absolutely no way she could afford the trip alone. She only had $700, but she refused to take the money that Gran kept trying to foist upon her. Kat kept reminding Gran that she was saving up for a Glock, a gun she had wanted for a long time, and for the first time ever, Gran miraculously gave in. Kat decided that the best thing to do would be to post an ad on Craigslist for a driving partner to Carbondale, IL, leaving immediately, all expenses shared 50/50. She was tempted to add, "Felons need not apply," but Granny Nanny talked her out of it.

"Make them come over for an interview. I can tell just by looking at a person whether or not he's a felon."

"It's not a good idea, Gran, to have people you're doing business with on Craigslist know where you live."

"Then why don't you put an ad in the *Arizona Republic*?"

"People my age don't read newspapers anymore, Gran."

"I am well aware of that awful fact, Katrina."

"We could meet them in the Target parking lot. How about that?"

"No, I want to meet them on my own turf. And don't forget, dear. I have a gun, and I know how to use it."

Kat finally, reluctantly conceded the point to her, and the first three people who showed up did not ring any warning bells for Granny Nanny. Not even close. The first was a woman in her early forties who was going through a divorce. Not only did she stop to cry after every sentence, but she also wanted to bring her sixteen-year-old son along for the ride. He'd just gotten his driver's license and wanted to help drive. The second applicant was a twenty-year-old gum-popping, giggling Valley girl, and the third was a man in his late twenties who explained that, because of his allergy medication, he might not be as alert of a driver as he should be. Kat vetoed them all. There was no way that she could spend 20-plus hours trapped in a car with any of them. The crying, a teenager's babble, the gum-popping and giggling, the sneezing and nose-blowing—all of it would be too much to bear.

"You're too picky," Granny Nanny said.

"If I had to ride in a car with any of them for such a long time, I would have to take your gun with me," Kat said, not sure if she would be tempted to use it on the passenger or herself. The situation looked grim. If she didn't get someone to share expenses, she couldn't go. And ever since the idea for this trip had been born, courtesy of Granny Nanny, her desire to go had grown stronger. Her need to go had grown stronger.

"Don't give up hope, dear. One more person is coming, and he sounded very nice on the phone."

"And not like a felon?" Kat teased.

"I'll know when I see him, dear."

He arrived on his bicycle promptly at two o'clock. Gran, peeking through the curtains at the front window, pronounced, "Definitely not a felon."

"Good to know," Kat said. She took the clipboard with her list of questions as she went out the door. "You're Lorenzo Delaney?"

"In the flesh," he said.

Kat rolled her eyes. She hated it when people said that.

"My friends call me Zen." He smiled.

Kat noticed his good orthodontia and consulted her clipboard. "Well, Lorenzo, why are you going to Illinois? Do you have any speeding or parking tickets? Are you willing to pay half the expenses? Do you have any contagious diseases? Since we will be in close quarters for many hours, do you have any irritating habits that I should know about?"

Zen took off his sunglasses and cocked his head at her. "Are you for real?"

Kat rolled her eyes. She hated it when people said that. "Yes, Lorenzo, I am *for real*." However, she did notice that his eyes were a striking shade—hazel, she supposed, a greenish, golden color.

"Okay," he said. "Law school. Speeding in 2004. Yes. No. Define *irritating*."

Kat had to smile. "Do you snore?"

"I've been told that I do not."

Kat wanted to ask: Who told you that you didn't snore? A former girlfriend? A former wife? A current girlfriend? A current wife? Instead, she asked, "What's with the bike?"

"I'm on a local team, and I thought I'd get a few miles of practice in." He went to her Mazda. "May I?"

She followed him. "May you what?" He had on an authentic biker's kit, complete with logos of sponsors. His legs were amazing, the thighs and calves ropey with muscle.

"Pop the hood."

"I already had the oil changed and all that other ... stuff." He stood by the hood of the car, waiting. "Be my guest," she said.

He studied the mysterious innards of her car for far longer than Kat thought necessary, his brow furrowed in concentration. His hair was sweaty from his helmet, but Kat thought it would probably be a light brown when the sweat dried. She wasn't used to being around sweaty men. Benson had preferred not to sweat. Even after a workout at Gold's Gym, the most he would allow himself to perspire had been a light film on his forehead. His hair, of course, didn't get matted with sweat like this guy. It was refreshing to be around a sweaty man. Kat took a tentative sniff.

"I stopped a block away and put on deodorant. I hope I'm not too offensive," Zen said from under the hood.

Kat was glad he couldn't see her blush. "Allergies," she said. "The olive trees." Kat didn't have any allergies.

"It's a little early for allergy season." Zen slammed down the hood. "How's your spare?"

"My spare what?"

"Tire," he said patiently.

"I think it's fine." Kat had no idea where her spare tire was located. She'd bought the car only two years ago when interest rates were rock-bottom, and she hadn't put that many miles on it, so the issue of a spare tire had never come up.

He found it in the trunk of the car. "It could use a little more air."

"Okay." He just kept staring at her, and Kat got another smile with its perfectly white, even teeth. She briefly wondered if he used Crest White Strips every day, but maybe it was his tan face that made his teeth look so white.

"Do you know how to do that, fill up a tire?"

"Sure, I know how to fill up a tire." She had no idea, but it suddenly seemed very important that he didn't know how incompetent she was about cars—or about anything else, for that matter. For instance, she doubted that she would ever tell him about getting fired from Tilted Kilt.

"You just take it to the gas station—"

"I know how to fill up a tire!"

"Okay," he said, "I'll take your word for it."

If he would stop looking at her like that, Kat could let it go. But he didn't, and she didn't. "You better not take my word for it."

"How about if we fill it up on our way out of town tomorrow?"

"That sounds like a good idea," Kat said.

And just like that, it was decided. Lorenzo would go with her, and they would leave first thing in the morning.

Zen was prompt again the next morning, arriving by taxi at 7:00 a.m. sharp. "Punctuality is an important quality in a man," Granny Nanny observed.

"Whatever," Kat said. Now that her departure time was here, she dreaded leaving Granny Nanny behind. "You could still come," she said, hugging the tiny woman once again.

"Nonsense. This is your time, Katrina."

Tears welled up in Kat's eyes. "I'm going to worry about you. There are a lot of creeps in this world who wouldn't think twice about taking advantage of a sweet little old lady."

"There is no need to worry. I have a gun, dear, and I know how to use it," Gran reminded her for the hundredth time. "Now, skedaddle. I have a million things to do today, and that handsome young man is waiting for you by the car." And with that, as Kat watched her, she went to the hall closet and got the vacuum cleaner. "Bon voyage, dear. Have a safe trip." She plugged in the vacuum, and it roared to life.

There was nothing left for Kat to do but pick up her suitcase and go to her car. She knew that Granny Nanny didn't want a big scene, and she knew that the dear woman, in her own way, was giving her permission to go.

"Do you want me to drive first?" Zen asked. He had a backpack flung over his shoulder.

"Is that all you're bringing?" He looked even better in a non-sweaty state. His hair was indeed light brown, with a slight wave to it. He wasn't tall—she would guess 5'10"—but he had an attractive muscular leanness.

"I sent some boxes ahead by UPS. Is that all you're bringing?" He pointed to her battered suitcase.

"I travel light." He didn't need to know that she hadn't traveled outside the state except for running away at sixteen. "I'll drive first."

"Suit yourself," he said.

"I don't have GPS, so I did a MapQuest," she said as she started the car. "We'll take I-40E to I-44E. 1541.39 miles. 23 hours and 41 minutes." She looked at the clock on the dashboard. "We should be in Carbondale around 7:00 a.m. tomorrow."

"What about gas and food stops? What about bathroom breaks?" Zen seemed amused.

"Oh, right. If we count those, we should be there about 7:30 then." She backed out of the driveway.

"What's your hurry?" Zen asked. "Is it some guy?"

"No, it isn't some guy." Her father certainly didn't count as a guy. However, Kat did have to wonder. What *was* her hurry? Her father didn't even know she was coming, and she hadn't allowed herself to consider a highly probable fact: Her father might not be happy to see her. The last time he saw her, he had slapped her face, hard, and called her a whore. It was not a favorable final impression, to say the least.

"Family reunion? Wedding? Funeral?" Zen turned in his seat to look at her with curiosity.

"Put on your seatbelt," Kat said. The only thing she could really rule out was the wedding. She was definitely not going to a wedding. A family reunion, sort of, and a funeral? She hoped not. If, after all these years, she traveled to see her father and he died before she got there and could ask him some questions ...Well, he just better not go and die on her.

"The spare tire," Zen reminded her, and they pulled into the first Shell station they saw. Zen came out of the convenience mart with snacks: Doritos, Pringles, Ding Dongs, Nutter Butters, and Diet Cokes. "I didn't know if you liked sweet or salty," he said when they were on the road again.

"Salty. Thanks." Suddenly, she was starving. She'd been too nervous that morning to have anything but coffee.

He handed her the canister of Pringles. "So why are you going to Carbondale, and how long are you planning to stay?"

"Are you going to jabber the entire trip?" she asked irritably. Kat didn't know why she was going to Carbondale, only that she had to. And she didn't have a clue as to how long she would stay.

"Fine. I'm only trying to make conversation. I'm really not that interested." Zen reclined his seat, put in his earbuds, crossed his arms, and closed his eyes.

Kat turned the radio to Outlaw Country and drove. And drove. And drove. Once they were past the Phoenix city limits, it seemed like the highway stretched out endlessly before her, flat and dry. Initially, she had wanted to go the northern route through Flagstaff and the mountains, but it added a considerable number of miles to her trip. Now, she wondered, why hadn't she done that anyway? What was her hurry to get to Carbondale? It wasn't out of the realm of possibility that her father, or Missy, would slam the door in her face. What would she do then? Turn around and come home with her tail between her legs, as Granny Nanny would say?

The lonelier and more monotonous the drive turned out to be, the more worried Kat became. She had gone thirty years without knowing anything about her mother, not even her name. Why rock the boat now? Why open a can of worms? Why not let sleeping dogs lie? She turned up the radio louder to try to drown out the Granny Nanny maxims that crowded her brain. She was almost to Albuquerque, had gone only 400 miles, and it wasn't too late to turn back. She could consider this a long day trip, nothing more than that. She would choose not to view it as an aborted adventure, or what it actually was: pure cowardice on her part.

"Are you getting hungry yet?"

Oh, yeah. Kat had a passenger. He would probably not be thrilled at the prospect of turning around. "No," she said, although the grumbling in her stomach denied that. She simply wanted to get off at the next exit and turn around. Besides, she still had the bag of Doritos.

Zen put the seat back up and stretched. "We need gas." He pointed to the gas gauge and its red light signaling low fuel.

Damn. Kat hadn't even thought about gas since leaving Phoenix, and she hadn't looked at any of the other gauges either. She really had no choice. "Okay, we'll stop for gas, and then I need to tell you something."

"Can't wait," he said, smiling.

"Are you always this cheerful when you wake up?"

Still smiling, he said, "I would be more cheerful if I had something to eat."

The next exit advertised an Exxon station and a McDonald's. Kat pulled off there. "I'll pump the gas while you run over to McDonald's. I'll take the Big Mac meal."

Zen seemed to be stretching every muscle in his body. He put one muscular leg on the trunk of the car and then the other. He put his arms over his head and swayed from side to side. He did a couple of squats and then a few lunges. "Are we still in a hurry?" he asked.

"Yes," Kat snapped and was immediately sorry. This Zen guy had been nothing but cordial, and she was acting pretty much like a bitch. If she was going to tell him that she was about to bail on him, the least she could do was sit down in a fast food place and tell him over a Big Mac and fries. "We'll go in and eat," she said.

"Such a small victory to savor," he said, still in annoyingly good humor.

Kat finished pumping the gas, and they walked next door. Kat immediately realized that it was a mistake. A four-year-old's birthday party was in full, riotous bloom, and little kids were everywhere—in the plastic ball pen, the tunnel slide, climbing over booths, cluttering the soda dispensers. To make matters worse, Ronald McDonald, in person, seemed to be an inciting incident of four-year-old hysteria.

"This is creepy," Kat said as a sticky little girl ran into her.

Zen helped the little girl up. "They seem to be having fun."

"Let's get this over with." She would eat quickly, very quickly.

"That's the spirit," he said.

They found an empty booth in the back, next to the bathrooms. As opposed to Kat's Big Mac, fries, and Diet Coke, Zen had ordered a chicken wrap, salad, yogurt with granola, and milk. Kat motioned toward his healthy selection of food. "What's the point?"

He just smiled his charming, annoying smile. "To each his own."

"You and Granny Nanny would get along fabulously." Kat took a huge bite out of her sandwich.

"She seemed like a nice lady." Zen took an excruciatingly small bite of his chicken wrap. "So, you live with your grandmother. Maternal or paternal?" He chewed slowly, too.

In contrast, Kat took another very large bite out of her burger. Lettuce strips and McD's famous, secret sauce dripped down her fingers. It was not very lady-like. "Neither."

He cocked an eyebrow at her. "Aunt?"

"You ask a lot of questions." Kat was beginning to think he would make a good lawyer, or a bad one, depending upon your perspective and if you were his client or the opposing counsel's.

"Just passing the time." Zen took a sip of milk directly out of the carton. "Nothing personal."

"Ha!" Kat said. "Obviously, asking questions is always personal." She froze mid-chew as the realization hit her. She'd come prepared to ask her father a list of personal questions and had even typed them out. It was a long list, twenty-two questions, and as she typed them out, she had become angrier and more convinced of her right to know the answer to these questions. She was *entitled* to know the answers, she told herself. For the first sixteen years of her life, his life had intersected and entwined with hers. Until they got to Albuquerque, she had been intent on prying out the information.

Or should Kat give Marcus a smidgeon of sympathy? He'd lost a wife in childbirth, true, and she'd been young and maybe beautiful, true, and it had been a great loss for him, true. However, people moved on, and Marcus had a daughter who should have been some consolation for him. So why had he closed down on her, withheld affection, acted like he wished she'd never been born? He'd never once gone to a Back-to-School night, or a band concert during her brief stint of trumpet playing, or a game during her even shorter career playing soccer. Not once.

Perhaps, Kat thought now, her father had never wanted her to know the answers because they were too awful, too tragic, or too painful for her to know. Perhaps his reasons were too achingly personal. This Zen guy asked her perfectly innocuous questions, and Kat felt somehow intruded upon for her own perfectly banal reasons. Kat started to choke.

Zen was around the table and doing the Heimlich maneuver in nothing flat. A piece of hamburger dislodged from her throat, and she gasped for air. "Are you all right?" he asked.

Kat, embarrassed more than anything, said: "You didn't need to do that."

"Better safe than sorry." Zen sat back down.

"Knock it off, will you?" She knew her face was still bright red, but her breathing started to return to normal. "It's like I'm traveling with Granny Nanny." That thought filled her with a sharp pang of longing and homesickness. She'd been gone a mere seven hours, and she wanted more than anything to turn around and go home to the sad little bungalow that desperately needed a coat of paint. If she did that, she would be continuing her thirty-year losing streak. But she was so damn scared!

Zen returned to his careful eating, calmly acting as if nothing had happened.

Kat, on the other hand, had lost her appetite, and this seemingly nice guy with the odd green/gold eyes chewed each bite thirty times. They would be here for hours at this rate, and Kat was anxious to get on the road, in one direction or the other. She caught herself drumming her fingers on the table and stopped. He had kind of saved her life, after all, and she should at least acknowledge it. "Thank you for kind of, sort of saving my life."

"No problem." He finally finished the first half of his chicken wrap.

Okay, then, that was done. Zen's questions had stopped, and the silence hung between them, louder than the screaming, sticky children. Sitting there made her anxious, and she almost wished she smoked so she would have the excuse of going outside. Should she head forward or turn back? Finally, when she couldn't stand watching him chew anymore, she asked, "How intent are you on going to Carbondale?"

"I'm not going to Carbondale."

Surprised and a little uneasy, Kat asked, "Then why are you riding with me, and where are you going?" Maybe he was a felon after all. Maybe she should have done a background check, but Gran's instincts were practically Pope-like in their infallibility.

"I'm going to Chicago. I thought I'd have you drop me off at the Amtrak Station." Zen started in on his yogurt.

"Wouldn't it have been easier to fly?"

"Money's a little tight right now—law school ... and other things. Plus, I've never seen this part of the country, and I like the occasional adventure, don't you?"

"I'm not quite sure," Kat admitted, not bothering to point out that he'd slept almost the entire way to Albuquerque (and certainly not telling him about her failed attempt at skydiving).

"Are you changing your mind?" Zen was almost done with his yogurt.

"What would you do if I did?" Time was running out, and now she wished he had to chew his yogurt.

"No problem. I'd hitchhike."

What would she do, continue her losing streak? And then Kat heard Gran's voice in her head (she was such a sly one, Granny Nanny): "This is *your* adventure, Katrina, not mine. This is your adventure."

Kat stood up. "Let's go, Lorenzo."

When Zen offered to drive the next shift, Kat didn't argue. What was the point? This guy was so exasperatingly pleasant that Kat doubted he had ever had a good knock-down-drag-out fight in his life. Besides, she needed time to think. What if Marcus did refuse to see her? Would she have to trail him like some inept investigator? Would she have to stake out at Barone's Trucking? Did he still work there? He had turned sixty-six in January, so there was a good possibility that he was retired. Did he take daily walks in the park? Did he play golf? Did he still eat the same bologna and cheese sandwich for lunch every day? She knew nothing about the man.

She never had.

"Do you want to stop in Amarillo?" Zen asked.

"No."

"Come on, I've always wanted to see it. If someone writes a song about a town, there must be something to see."

"What are you talking about?" Kat had pretty much ruled out the possibility that the guy was a felon, but she hadn't ruled out the possibility that he was nuttier than a fruitcake.

"You know that song, 'Amarillo by Morning,' right? It makes me want to know what the downtown area looks like. I really did drive up to Winslow one Saturday just to stand on a corner. You know that Eagles' song, right? The line that goes, 'I was standing on a corner in Winslow, Arizona, such a fine sight to see …"

"I know the song," she snapped. She loved that song, and Zen had a decent tenor voice, but she wasn't in the mood. She would rather sit quietly and fret. "Let's just keep going."

Zen stopped anyway, and Kat sat fuming in the car for thirty minutes while he went to check out Amarillo's downtown area. After that, he didn't bother to ask Kat whether she wanted to stop or if she wanted to drive. He stopped, and he stopped often—every hour or so—to get a cup of coffee, to use the restroom, to stretch his legs. Kat willed herself to say nothing. If she did, she knew he would ask, "What's your hurry?" And she had no answer to that question.

Somewhere, on a lonely, darkening stretch of highway between Oklahoma City and Tulsa, he said, "I've got it!"

She'd been partly asleep, lulled by the monotony of the landscape, and his outburst startled her. "Shit," she said. "You scared me."

"Sorry, but I've been trying to figure out where I've seen you before, and now I know. You work at Tilted Kilt, right? I went there a couple of weeks ago to watch a game, and you were waitressing. You weren't the waitress at my table, but I remember you because you chased down some freeloader who tried to skip out on his bill." He smiled happily.

Kat blushed; she remembered that night. It had not been her finest in her brief tenure at Tilted Kilt. She hoped that he hadn't overheard what she said to the guy. It had not been pretty. (Benson's voice rang in her head, "You can be awfully mean for such a pretty girl.") "I don't work there anymore," she said.

"Too bad. You looked good as a Scottish lass."

Kat desperately wanted to change the subject before he asked why she didn't work there anymore, and she knew he would. "What do you do for a living?"

He didn't answer right away, and Kat thought maybe she was off the hook and could go back to sleep. But no. Of course not.

"Right now, I'm on hiatus. I worked for Child Protective Services, but I got burned out. What do people do when they want to change careers?" He answered his own question. "They go to law school."

"Hmm," Kat said. Perhaps from now on, she could tell people that she was *on hiatus*. It sounded a hell of a lot better than telling people she had been fired from Tilted Kilt. For the first time, she wondered why she'd never contemplated going back to school. She'd never considered going to law school, but maybe going back for another degree wouldn't be such a bad idea. She always saw ads for culinary arts school on TV. The thought made her giggle. She could barely boil an egg.

Zen briefly took his eyes off the road to glance at her. "That's the first time I've heard you laugh. I was beginning to think you didn't know how."

Kat was too tired to be insulted. Plus, she hadn't exactly been Ms. Rosy during this trip. "I know, but I'm not in a very funny situation right now."

"I know what you mean," Zen said.

Kat highly doubted that he knew what she meant.

Then he surprised her. "I'm going to Chicago to see my dad. Pops had a heart attack last week." He stared straight ahead, eyes on the road.

Without thinking, Kat blurted, "I'm going to see my father, too. I haven't seen him in fourteen years."

"Why not?"

"It's a long story." Kat already regretted that she'd said anything to him about her reason for going on this trip.

"We've got time," he pointed out.

"Yes, but I don't have the patience to go into it."

"I've noticed that about you." Zen then let the subject drop.

The next thing Kat knew, Zen was gently shaking her. "How long was I asleep?" she mumbled. She hoped she hadn't snored or drooled.

"We're in Joplin, Missouri. We're spending the night, or at least what's left of it. It's 4:00 a.m."

"Wait a minute." She struggled awake. They were parked at a Motel 8. "The plan was that we were going to drive straight through."

"The wind is blowing like crazy," Zen said. "I could barely keep the car on the road. It's tornado season, and I think it's a good idea to stop for the night. I already got a room."

One room? In her slightly slutty twenties, this wouldn't have bothered her. But she'd just driven hours with this guy, who was a lot better looking than some of the guys she'd been with, and the thought of sleeping with him hadn't occurred to her. Go figure.

"A motel room is not in my budget."

"Don't worry about it," he said.

"I'll sleep in the car."

"No, you won't. We need to get inside."

Now that she was fully awake, Kat could hear the wind howling; the trees bordering the parking lot were bowed in half. She'd seen plenty of Arizona monsoons when the wind would suddenly kick up, blowing thick waves of sand, but she'd never seen anything like this. She remembered watching *Twister* years before, and even though it was only a movie, she still remembered the image of the semi and the spotted cow sucked into the eye of the storm. If this was a tornado, her car, with her in it, could be easily absorbed into the whirling air as if it were nothing more than a pick-up stick.

As soon as they were in the room, Zen turned on the TV to the local news station. They were definitely in the area of the impending tornado, and Kat could not take her eyes off the screen. The gray writhing mass spun like an out-of-control top. Then they heard the siren. "What do we do now?" Kat asked, panicked. Her first instinct was to run, but that was ridiculous. Where would she run to?

"Go get in the bathtub." Zen ripped the sheets and bedspread off the bed and lifted the mattress from one of the double beds.

Kat, terrified, did as she was told, for once. How did you escape from the inevitable? The town was directly in the path of the storm, and Kat suddenly remembered that it had been hit by a massive tornado the year before. Houses splintered like tinker toys, and the high school had been demolished.

Zen jammed the unwieldy mattress through the narrow bathroom door. He climbed in the tub with her, and she didn't argue when he positioned his back against one end of the tub, spread his legs, and pulled her against him. The back of her head rested on his chest, and they lifted the mattress over them.

Zen held onto the mattress with his right hand, his left arm clasped firmly across Kat's chest. She could hardly breathe, but that didn't matter. She could feel the steady beat of his heart, and she willed herself to concentrate on that, rather than the howling, wailing wind. She did not want to die like this, in the bathroom of a Motel 8 in Joplin, MO, in a stranger's arms. (She tried to console herself that Zen wasn't really a stranger. She knew his last name.)

"I'm not going to let you go," Zen shouted into her ear.

Kat took solace in that, too, because she believed him.

The room shuddered violently, and Kat thought: *This is it!* She should say something to this man, this not-quite-a-stranger. Her last words should be profound and noble, but the words that came out of her mouth were, "I'm scared shitless!"

Zen closed his arm around her even more tightly. "I've got you!"

The room gave one more lingering shudder. Some plaster fell onto the mattress, and the bathroom mirror crashed to the ground. Then, it was eerily quiet.

They huddled under the mattress for another minute or so, listening. "What's going on?" Kat didn't know why she whispered.

"I think it's over. It didn't touch down here." Zen's voice held a trace of wonder. "Unbelievable," he said. "That was a close call."

Cautiously, they removed the mattress, climbed out of the tub, carefully walked around the glass and plaster on the floor, and went into the bedroom. There, too, some ceiling plaster had fallen, and a lamp had jostled from the nightstand. It was unbelievable to Kat that the damage from that screeching wind, the *actual tornado*, had been so slight.

Zen opened the front door and gave a low whistle. "Come and take a look at this, Kat."

She went to the door, although she was still afraid of being sucked into that terrible, gyrating wind. Could a tornado come back? She looked out the door and gasped. They stood in an intact building, but right across the street where a strip mall had stood, barely thirty yards away, a pile of rubber remained. It looked like a giant had stomped on the buildings, leaving smashed timber, mortar, and brick. It was early morning, and Kat hoped that no people had been in those buildings. Surely, no one had been hurt.

"You see pictures on the news about this sort of thing," Zen said. "A tornado can go through a neighborhood and destroy one house but leave the one next to it standing."

Kat continued to stare at the rubble in the morning's dawning hour. She couldn't speak.

"It's just mind-boggling luck that this Motel 8 wasn't hit." Zen saw Kat's stricken face and put an arm around her shoulders.

Other guests came out of their motel rooms and surveyed the damage with hushed voices. Everyone could see how close they had come.

"We lived through a tornado," Kat finally said.

"We did."

And then Kat could cry. She'd been so terrified during the storm, and then it was over, abruptly. Now the whole thing just seemed unreal. And that is what she said to Zen, "This doesn't seem real."

"I know," Zen said softly, pulling her closer. "It's incredible."

Kat nodded against his chest.

"It's a miracle, really. It's a miracle."

"Yes," Kat agreed. She trembled all over as she surveyed the damage. "It's a miracle we're alive."

6

AUGUST-SEPTEMBER 1980

There was no honeymoon, not that Melody had been expecting one. She and Marcus hadn't discussed this topic, along with many, many others before their whirlwind courtship—if she could call it that—and marriage. But still, she had not expected to be so firmly *plopped* into the middle of Marcus' life, which revolved around his job at Motorola and his mother, Evelyn. Especially Evelyn. Melody moved into his mother's house in Evergreen Park on their wedding night, and it was not a promising start to their married life.

After somehow making it through the wedding ceremony, Melody drank a glass of champagne to help her get through the reception at the American Legion hall. Already, she was thinking: *What have I done?* Already, it was too late.

"Pregnant women are not supposed to drink, Melody," Marcus whispered to her at the dinner. They sat at the head table on a dais, flanked on either side by their attendants. Compared to her volume of six attendants, Marcus had only been able to scrounge up three co-workers that he barely knew. Three fat cousins had to walk down the aisle alone, and they were not happy about it.

"No one knows I'm pregnant, Marcus, so it's okay," she whispered back. She knew it didn't make sense because she was pregnant and should not be drinking, but the champagne had gone straight to her head, helped along by the pot that Sylvia had provided.

"I suppose one won't hurt," he said indulgently and patted her newly minted, married hand.

Melody resisted the urge to pull it away. "Right," she said. So when he left the table to dance with his mother (mostly leading her in a stroll around the floor), Melody drank another.

"This isn't such a bad party," Sylvia said, smiling happily. "The booze is tremendous."

Naturally, with Daddy and her brothers, it made sense to have an open bar. The drinks were not flowing; they were *rampaging*. "Yeah, the people running the bar are going to be fit to be tied when this is over. Daddy and my brothers will drink at least twice what they paid for, out of principle."

Daddy and her brothers were getting drunk with gusto, but Melody couldn't be mad at them. They looked like they were having a wonderful time. Daddy, as the father of the bride, his only daughter, went around to each table, slapping people on the back and accepting congratulations for a job well done. And Ma. Well, she acted like Queen for a Day, smiling broadly, then crying, then smiling, then crying, as relatives and people from the neighborhood came up to hug her or compliment her on the beautiful wedding. Melody, overhearing these compliments, wondered: *Are they blind? Can they not see the hideous bridesmaids' dresses?* She drank another glass of champagne.

About halfway through the endless night, Sylvia asked, "Shall we go powder our noses?"

It was their code, and it meant that Sylvia had brought some special treat with her. Melody wasn't having a good time, and Sylvia knew it. She'd danced the required first dance with her new husband and then danced with Daddy and Willie, but that was it. Loyally, Sylvia—who loved to dance as much as Melody—stayed by her side the entire night. Unfortunately, on Melody's other side was her new husband, who stuck to her like glue. Melody didn't know if it was because he was a terrible dancer or just antisocial. Marcus didn't know many people at his own wedding, but Melody suspected that her new husband was already staking his territory. She knew so very little about her *new husband*.

She shook her head at Sylvia and felt like crying. She didn't want their nights out, their nights of research, to be over. Did they have to be? Even though she was married, she could still go out with a girlfriend, couldn't she? Being married was not the end of the world, but at that moment, it certainly felt like it to Melody. She motioned to the waiter to refill her champagne glass.

"Uh, honey," Marcus said tentatively.

The hesitation in his voice and the fact that he had called her *honey* drove Melody over the edge. "On second thought, Sylvia, I think I do need to powder my nose."

After that, the night was a blur, and when Melody woke up the next morning in a strange bed, she at first thought that she and Sylvia had gone out the night before. And now she was lying in a strange bed because she'd once again gone home with a stranger. Her first instinct was to call out for Sylvia, but Marcus walked in the bedroom door with a breakfast tray.

"You're up," he said with his warm smile.

"Nominally." She struggled to sit up. Her head pounded, and she was dangerously close to vomiting. She hadn't had any morning sickness, so this was purely a hangover.

"I made you some toast and tea." He placed the tray gently on the bed. In addition to the toast and tea, he'd added a glass of orange juice, a single red rose in a glass vase, and a bottle of aspirin.

Melody quickly shook out two tablets and gulped them down with the orange juice. It was sweet of him to do this for her—she knew that—but she would have rather had some time alone to wake up more fully, gather her thoughts, possibly puke, and brush her teeth. The smell of chamomile tea made her feel even worse. "I'm a coffee drinker," she said.

"Oh, sorry." Marcus had on a crisp white button-down shirt, and yes indeed, a pocket protector. "I'll go make some coffee. I didn't know."

"Why would you know?"

"What do you mean?" He looked genuinely confused.

"Marcus, we went out on a whopping three dates, and now we're married. We don't know each other at all." Melody had a sinking feeling that this dance—this act of getting to know each other—would be utterly exhausting.

"I know enough," Marcus said, smiling.

What did he mean? He didn't even know that she preferred coffee to tea. Melody's mouth went even drier. Had they had sex the night before, and she didn't remember? Had she told him things last night that she planned never to tell him? She took a furtive peek under the sheet. She still had on the underwear she'd worn to her wedding. "Did we?" She blushed.

"The marriage has not been consummated." It was his turn to blush. "I didn't want to take advantage of you in your ... condition."

Perhaps the only thing Melody did know about her new husband was that, so far, he had behaved like a perfect gentleman. Perhaps he thought it would be harmful to the baby if they had sex? Even though it was the 1980s, some men still believed that. In her nurse's tone of voice, she would patiently explain this to him—not that she wanted to have sex with him in her present hungover condition. In fact, she wouldn't mind waiting a bit. Even though they were now husband and wife, and even though she'd slept with men that she knew less well (by a long shot) than Marcus, she was not eager to consummate the marriage. He was decent looking, maybe even handsome in a fastidious way, but so far, at least on her end, no sparks ignited between them. Not even a flicker.

"You passed out, and I had to carry you to bed. I slept on the couch." Marcus' voice didn't hold any accusation, not yet.

Melody blushed again. "I'm sorry." She was pretty sure that she wasn't the first bride in the USA to pass out on her wedding night, but still. She'd thought she was better than that. She was pregnant, and she shouldn't have been drinking in the first place—or done the Oxy.

"I'm sure you don't make a habit of doing that."

Oh, if he only knew! "Of course not," Melody said.

"It was the stress of the day," he offered.

"Sure," Melody agreed. Why not?

However, the stress of the wedding day could not explain why it took them six weeks to consummate the marriage. (By that time, they had already told Melody's family about the pregnancy. The prospective grandparents and uncles were giddy. "A grandbaby of my very own," Ma said. "That's my girl," Pa said, "right out of the barn!") Melody couldn't explain it. Marcus was sweet and attentive and often brought her breakfast in bed; it hadn't been a one-time thing. He didn't mind helping with the dishes or housework, either, which was an eye-opener for Melody. Melody wondered if her new husband, being a gentleman, would wait for *her* to say something. But as the days ticked by, she found it harder and harder to bring up the subject, and evidently, he did, too.

He was not shy about bringing up other subjects, though, the most frequent being this: "Melody, you don't need to work."

The first time he said it, they were washing dishes, and Melody almost dropped the plate she was drying. "Excuse me?"

"I've been thinking," Marcus continued in his mild, reasonable voice. "I make a good living, and you come home exhausted, Mellie. I hate to see you like that."

It was the first time he had called her *Mellie*, and it set her teeth on edge. Her *family* called her by that name. "I love my job," she said. True, it was grueling, hectic, and heartbreaking work, but Melody loved it because it made her feel so alive. She especially loved the shifts she worked with Sylvia; they were the only times Melody saw her in the six weeks she'd been married. Marcus hinted that he wasn't overly fond of Sylvia, but that wasn't the reason. (Melody was determined to never let her new husband tell her what to do.) Between working in the ER with its long, grueling, twelve-hour shifts, taking care of the house, and taking care of Evelyn, Melody didn't have much time. Besides, Sylvia had a new boyfriend that she was crazy about.

"It's really not necessary for you to work," Marcus said quietly, stubbornly.

It was very necessary for Melody to work. The job saved her sanity. She wanted to stomp her foot or break the dish in her hand in protest, but instead, she matched his quiet, stubborn tone in her reply. Already, she'd become quite adept at this. "I love my job, Marcus. I save people's lives."

"Yes, of course, you do," he placated, "but we don't want the stress of the job affecting the baby."

Marcus had quite a thing about stress Melody had started to notice. He avoided it at all costs, preferring to live quietly, monotonously, never varying from his daily routine. Five weeks into their marriage, and this bothered the hell out of Melody. "I'm pregnant, Marcus. I'm not incapacitated."

"I want people to know that I can take care of what's mine." Marcus drained the water from the sink and began to scrub it with the canister of Comet that he always kept nearby.

Melody wanted to yell at him that she was *not his*, but people did not yell in this house. Unlike the loud, rowdy house she grew up in, this house contained quiet voices and restrained sounds. Melody could often hear the grandfather clock in the front hallway ticking away the minutes of her life, a thing that wouldn't have been possible at 1113 S. Roosevelt Street. Melody felt swift tears rising. Even though Evergreen Park was next to Bridgeview, she felt like she rarely saw her family since her marriage. She sorely missed her Ma and Daddy. She even missed her brothers and their lousy table manners.

"I am going to keep working," Melody said quietly, stubbornly.

Marcus went on as if he hadn't heard her. "I want people to know that I provide for my family."

What people? Melody wondered. Marcus didn't seem to have any close friends, nor did he go to church or belong to the Eagles Club or a union.

"And if you stayed home, you could be Mother's primary caregiver."

So this is what he was getting at, and Melody should have seen it coming. "I'm not a geriatric nurse, Marcus. I'm not trained in that area. Besides, we have Belinda." Belinda, an at-home care person, came in to care for Evelyn every day. She was a large, black woman who did her job efficiently.

"Belinda does not show Mother enough compassion." Marcus poured more Comet and scrubbed the sink again.

"Your mother probably doesn't know the difference," Melody pointed out. Evelyn, a sweet, white-haired woman, seemed much older than her age of sixty-six. She was in an advanced stage of Alzheimer's and had good days and bad days. Even though Melody had only been living in the house for five weeks, she could see that the bad days were starting to outnumber the good days. The day before, Evelyn had looked at Melody suspiciously and asked who she was six times.

"I know the difference," Marcus said.

"Then hire someone else." Melody liked Evelyn; she did. But in her professional opinion, Evelyn should probably be placed in an assisted living facility staffed with doctors and nurses who knew what they were doing. It did no good to offer this opinion to her new husband, however. She could hear his voice in her head: "I can take care of what's mine."

Marcus, finally satisfied with his spotless sink, looked at her and smiled. "Well, perhaps we can compromise."

Melody was learning this, too. Marcus was very big on *compromise*. However, the compromises usually favored his opinions. She waited.

"On your days off, you can care for Mother."

Melody did not want to do this. She knew what that care would involve: bathing Evelyn, dressing her, feeding her, taking her to her assorted doctors' appointments and the hairdresser. (For no apparent reason, Marcus insisted that Evelyn's hair be styled each week.) However, Melody had married this man—and apparently, his mother. She had married him before God, in the Catholic Church, and she was having his baby because she had impulsively straddled him in his Buick after drinking way too much wine. What was she supposed to do? Run home crying to Ma? Announce to the world that she had made a huge mistake? Quit after six weeks of marriage? Her pride wouldn't let her do any of those things.

"I suppose we could try that and see how it goes," she said reluctantly.

"That's my girl." Marcus took her gently in his arms. "I'm going to buy you something so nice, Mellie."

Melody tried not to stiffen in his embrace.

He bought her a string of pearls, and of course, Ma noticed when Melody went to visit a few days later. Melody, her frustration growing, had gone to see Ma with the hope of soliciting some advice. Melody couldn't just blurt out that she'd married a man she didn't love. No, she would have to be careful. However, the pearls didn't give her a chance.

"Marcus bought you pearls!" Ma, who probably had not received a single piece of jewelry from Daddy since her plain gold wedding band, was giddy with excitement. "Are they real?" She fingered the single strand.

"Of course they're real, Ma."

"You are such a lucky girl, Mellie. Marcus Arnold is an upstanding man and a good provider." Ma called for Daddy to come and look at Mellie's pearls.

Daddy, also duly impressed, said, "Our Mellie landed her a fine one, didn't she?"

"That she did," Ma said.

When Ma finally quit going on and on about the pearls and about Marcus being such a fine man—who even took care of his invalid mother, God bless him—she remembered. "Didn't you say you wanted to ask me something, dear?"

It was out of the question that Mellie could try to seek some marital advice from Ma now. Ma was thoroughly convinced that her only daughter had married a saint. "Can I have that cinnamon Bundt cake recipe?"

After Ma carefully copied down the recipe, she whispered her parting words in Melody's ear. "It's a wonderful thing to marry a man who loves you a little more than you love him."

What *was* a girl to do?

So after six weeks of living together as husband and wife, Melody and Marcus consummated their marriage that night. Marcus treated her with care and kept telling her how special she was, how beautiful, and finally, he said the words, "I love you."

Melody burst into tears. She'd felt nothing during their lovemaking, nothing at all. Was it possible that she would ever come to love this man? Marcus took her into his arms and patted her back. He thought she was overcome with emotion.

And she was. But the emotion was not love.

The first time she felt the baby kick, Melody fell in love. She was sixteen weeks pregnant and brushing Evelyn's hair. "Oh," Melody said, dropping the brush and putting a hand on her slightly rounded abdomen. She knew this was coming. All the books she'd read said she would start to feel the baby move anywhere between sixteen and twenty-one weeks. Her baby had kicked at exactly sixteen weeks. Her baby was a genius.

Before, with all the rush to get married and settle into Marcus' precise house and life, the baby hadn't seemed entirely real to her. Her baby had seemed more like a condition to get through. She'd gotten herself knocked up (for the second time), and consequently, had to get married. She felt the second fluttering kick and now knew for a certainty that her baby was alive, living inside her. It was a fact; it was real. She was *with child*.

"Evelyn," she said excitedly. "The baby just kicked. Your grandchild just kicked for the very first time!"

Evelyn just stared at her with her brown, watery eyes and wan, vacant smile. "What baby?"

Melody sighed. On this, her first full day of caring for her mother-in-law, things were not going very well. Evelyn was having an especially bad morning and had already asked her three times who Melody was. Furthermore, Evelyn seemed to be missing Belinda. Melody pointed to her stomach. "The baby in here, Evelyn, your grandchild."

"Oh," Evelyn said. "Who are you again, dear?"

It was useless, but Melody was determined to be cheerful. She'd vowed to make the best of this situation. Really, what other choice did she have? "Let's go get some breakfast, Evelyn. How about oatmeal?"

Evelyn didn't want to eat breakfast, and Melody ended up feeding her. The woman needed to have something in her stomach before taking her medication, but with each spoonful that Melody brought to her mouth, the woman shook her head violently and clamped her lips shut. Melody's determined cheerfulness started to crumble. In another few months, she would be feeding her baby. Would she still be hand-feeding this old woman, too? It was disheartening.

Then Evelyn had one of her fleeting lucid moments that came randomly out of nowhere. "Marcus' baby crib is in the attic," she said. "I bought it at Sears and Roebuck in 1946. It was a very cold spring in 1946."

"That's terrific!" Melody's spirits lifted again. She could bring down the crib from the attic and see what kind of shape it was in. It might bring back some memories for Evelyn, and it would give Melody some purpose for this morning.

She settled Evelyn in the living room in front of the TV. She turned the dial through the channels, watching Evelyn's face. When she got to *The Price is Right*, Evelyn sat up straighter and smiled. *We have a winner*, Melody thought. To Evelyn, she said, "You sit right here, and I'll go up to the attic and get Marcus' crib, okay? You stay right here."

"Marcus." Evelyn nodded.

"Yes, Marcus." Even at this stage in her disease, Evelyn always recognized her son. Just the mention of his name seemed to calm her, so Melody repeated, "Marcus."

Melody had never been in the attic of this house and expected it to be like the attic of her parents' house, filled with clutter. Her parents' attic held all the remnants of Ma and Daddy's twenty-nine years of marriage: broken lamps, old mattresses, coats and shoes that looked like they came from the Depression era, an old Singer sewing machine, scrapbooks detailing their children's childhoods, old light bulbs. The junk was eclectic and useless.

One time years before, Melody had asked Ma, "Why do you keep all this junk? Who in their right mind is ever going to use one of these broken lamps or sleep on one of these lumpy mattresses?"

Ma had answered, "You just never know when something is going to come in handy."

"A starving, freezing person in Siberia would not have any use for this crap," Melody said, surveying the sea of clutter.

"You just never know," Ma said.

"A used light bulb is not going to do anyone any good," Melody pointed out.

"My future grandchildren might need them for science projects."

Melody let it drop. It was hard to argue with Ma's illogical logic.

Marcus' attic was nothing like her Ma and Daddy's. Not even close. It was as neat and bland as everything else in the house. A few neatly stacked and labeled boxes huddled in the corners. Melody counted. Nine boxes. All the stuff these people had accumulated in the last thirty-plus years in this house could be accommodated and compartmentalized into nine measly boxes. "Who are you people?" Melody asked the empty space. "Where are your keepsakes? Where are your *memories*?" Even though Ma and Daddy's attic contained, for the most part, utter crap, it also held a lifetime of stories. This attic did not.

The crib, of course, was easy to spot by the dormer window. It looked like it was in decent condition—no termite trails or rotted slats—and the next order of business for Melody was to figure out how to get it through the narrow door. She'd have to disassemble it and take it out a piece at a time. She went back downstairs to get a screwdriver and checked on Evelyn on her way. Evelyn napped in her chair, snoring softly. Good. Melody had some time.

Well, it was a thirty-four-year-old crib. It took longer than Melody thought to dislodge the screws from the dry wood. She didn't mind, though. The baby (her real, live *baby*) kicked again as she removed the headboard, and Melody allowed herself to daydream. Did she want a boy or a girl? Marcus, she supposed, would want a son, but Melody, in her heart of hearts, realized she wanted a daughter. Ma and Daddy would go absolutely nuts over a little granddaughter and probably spoil her rotten. Melody knew, too, that her brothers would be doting uncles.

Melody worked as quickly as she could until she finally had all the crib pieces down the stairs and propped against the walls of the upstairs hallway. Dusty and sweaty, she paused to wipe her forehead on her t-shirt. That was when Melody heard the TV and suddenly remembered Evelyn napping downstairs. How long had she been working on the crib? Was Evelyn still napping?

Melody took the stairs two at a time and turned the corner into the living room. Yes, the TV still blared, but no, Evelyn wasn't there. "Evelyn," she called. "Where are you?" There was nothing to panic about. Melody, an ER nurse, faced crises all the time. The old woman had probably gone into the kitchen to get a glass of water. "Evelyn," she called again. "Are you in the kitchen?"

Evelyn was not in the kitchen. It wasn't like the old lady thought she was in prison and needed to escape. She had to be around the house someplace. Then Melody glanced at the kitchen clock. It was noon. She'd left Evelyn alone for almost three hours! She ran to the bathroom, but no Evelyn. She ran to her bedroom. No Evelyn. She'd left the old woman alone for three hours!

Now it was time to panic. Melody ran from room to room with growing dread, checking under the beds, behind bureaus, behind doors, behind the shower curtain, and then ran down into the dank basement. It felt to Melody like a bizarre game of hide-and-seek and that she should shout, "Ollie, Ollie, all in free!" In her desperation—and making no sense at all—she checked the kitchen cabinets and drawers. Next, Melody ran into the yard and looked under the hedges and behind trees. She checked the garage and the unlocked car in the driveway. Nothing. Evelyn had vanished.

It was all Melody's fault. She'd been entrusted to care for the helpless, demented woman, and she had *lost* her. Evelyn had been her patient for the day, and Melody had really, really dropped the ball. She'd left Evelyn alone for far too long, and now there was an old lady who barely knew her own name wandering around the town somewhere. Evelyn was a lost soul on the loose.

Melody ran back into the house, and with shaking hands, dialed Sylvia. Sylvia, who was competent and calm in every crisis, would know what to do. Sylvia finally answered on the fifth ring, and Melody blurted out the predicament.

"How could you lose an old woman?" Sylvia did not sound overly sympathetic.

"I don't know, Syl. It's like she vanished into thin air."

"Well, she can't have gotten very far. How long has she been gone?"

Melody hesitated, reluctant to let even Sylvia know the full extent of her negligence. "I'm not sure. I was up in the attic, and she was watching TV—"

"Have you called Marcus?" Sylvia interrupted.

Dear Lord, she hadn't even thought about Marcus. He would be devastated if he found out about this. He adored his mother, and if he found out that Melody had let her out of her sight for even one second, he would … Well, Melody wasn't sure what he would do—hit her, strangle her, tell her to leave? She didn't know her husband very well at all.

"Maybe you should call the police?" Sylvia suggested.

"I don't want to get the police involved!" Melody's heart palpitated. Having the police know that she was monstrously careless with the old woman seemed even worse than having Marcus know. She already had a reputation at Mercy as a caring, attentive nurse, and here she had gone and lost—no, abused—her very own mother-in-law. It was unforgivable.

"Look, Mel, she could get hit by a car, or mugged, or abducted, or something. She might have fallen and gotten a concussion. You need to get in your car and go look for her."

The thought of Evelyn lying bloody in the street horrified Melody. She would be held responsible for losing and then killing an innocent senior citizen. She should be held responsible for losing and then killing an innocent senior citizen, who also happened to be her brand-new mother-in-law. "I'm a horrible person," Melody cried to Sylvia.

"You're not horrible," Sylvia said calmly. "Just get in the car and go look for her."

At that moment, the doorbell rang, and through the lace curtain that covered the window on the front door, Melody could make out what looked like a police officer. "Oh, dear God," she said as she hung up the phone. Was he here to tell her that Evelyn was dead?

She opened the front door, prepared for the worst, but standing next to the officer, looking small in an oversized man's coat, was Evelyn. "Evelyn!" Melody flung her arms around the woman. A profound feeling of relief washed over her, and Melody thought she might faint.

"I'm Officer Reynolds," the young man said. "Is this the Arnold residence?"

Melody nodded.

"I believe she belongs to you?"

Melody struggled to find her voice. "She belongs to me." She stepped back and took a good look at Evelyn. She had a small gash above her right eye. And why was she wearing a man's trench coat? "What happened? Where are her clothes?"

"I'm not sure. I got a call that," he cleared his throat, glanced at Evelyn, "an older lady was walking naked down Main Street. I picked her up and gave her my coat, but when I asked her where she lived, she seemed confused."

"She suffers from dementia." Melody inspected the gash on Evelyn's head. How was she going to hide that from Marcus?

"I figured that," the young officer said. "I took her down to the station, and another officer recognized her, said he went to school with a Marcus Arnold, so I looked up the address and brought her here."

"How did she hurt herself?" Melody asked.

"I don't know, ma'am." The young officer looked uncomfortable. "But I have a question for you. How did it come to be that an older woman with dementia was walking naked down the street? Are you her caregiver?"

Melody felt the heat rising in her face. "I was ... I'm not really... I just turned my back for a second ..."

"See that it doesn't happen again." He turned to go. "And you might want to have a doctor look at that cut."

"It's okay," Melody said. "I'm a nurse."

He glanced back, and the look on his face made Melody cringe with shame. "Are you now?"

She would never forget that look of withering contempt. She deserved it. Yet when Sylvia screeched up in a taxi seconds later, Melody enlisted her help to cover up the wound on Evelyn's head. Hopefully, Marcus would never know that his new wife had put his mother in jeopardy.

The wound was the first secret in their married life, and Marcus didn't even notice that his beloved mother had started to wear bangs.

7

APRIL 2012

They didn't arrive in Carbondale until well after noon. They hadn't been able to sleep, of course. They still rode the rush of adrenaline that comes with surviving a close call with all-powerful Mother Nature. They kept repeating to each other, "We survived a tornado. We survived a *tornado*." They weren't the only ones. The other motel guests seemed to be equally shell-shocked and giddy, as were the townspeople in the diner where Kat and Zen stopped for breakfast. Even to those seasoned veterans of tornado alley, a sense of awe at the sheer capriciousness of weather prevailed, a sense of relief from surviving another April storm, and the Midwestern practicality that assessed the damage and started to clean up. "That was an F-3," one old-timer said. "I've seen worse. I lived through the F-5 of 1964. Now, that was a tornado."

During the six-hour drive to Carbondale, Kat and Zen talked comfortably, mostly about the tornado, but also about some general family matters. Zen had one brother and one sister, and evidently, he adored his father. "He used to be an EMT," he told Kat. "You wouldn't believe the stories he can tell, and my mom, well, she's just a wonderful woman. My brother and sister live in the same neighborhood as Mom and Pops, and they've been taking care of things since Pops had his heart attack. I figure it's my turn to pitch in. Kent Law School doesn't start until the fall, and since I quit my CPS job, it seemed like the right thing to do. Go home."

"It sounds like you have a nice family," Kat said, surprised at the pang of jealousy. Granny Nanny was her family now, and Kat had convinced herself it was enough. But the way Zen talked about his family, making them sound almost *holy*, made her lonesome for something she hadn't thought she missed. Kat briefly told him about the birthday card and note from Missy. "I have no idea what my brothers are like, my *half*-brothers," she emphasized.

"Now's your chance to find out," Zen said.

"Maybe." However, Kat wasn't even remotely sure if they would let her stick around once she presented herself on their doorstep.

All too soon, Kat pulled into the Amtrak Station, which was adjacent to the Greyhound Station she'd fled from fourteen years before. Her hands grew clammy on the wheel. What was she doing here? The place looked the same, but different, too. Everything looked shabbier, or maybe everything looked so much smaller than she remembered. In 1998, the place had seemed huge to her, but then again, she'd been a cocky, scared teenager, thinking she was running off with the love of her life. So, in addition to being cocky and scared, apparently, she'd also been naïve, misguided, and just plain dumb.

"What time's your train?" she asked.

"Not until this evening."

Suddenly, Kat didn't want the journey to end. She didn't mind his company—not at all—and he had kind of, sort of saved her life on two occasions in about thirty-two hours. He was about to leave her just when she started to feel safe with him. "Why don't we go grab a cup of coffee, or maybe a beer?" A beer was a good idea; a shot of scotch was an even better one. Glen Livet, Granny Nanny's cure-all for everything. Actually, now that Kat had started to panic, what she needed was a shot of Granny Nanny.

"Sorry, Kat, but I'm beat." Zen yawned to prove it. "We haven't slept in hours, and I'm beat." He got out of the car and went to the trunk.

Kat followed. True, Zen had driven most of the way, but he'd slept all the way to Albuquerque. "You slept the first part of the trip," she pointed out. She couldn't let him get away. She needed more time to figure out what she would say when she knocked on the door of 126 North Hickory Street.

"I wasn't sleeping," Zen said. "I listened to you talking to yourself." He smiled his warm smile. "Quite entertaining."

Kat blushed. "I wasn't talking to myself." However, she knew that she sometimes tended to *think out loud*, as Gran had pointed out to her on more than one occasion.

"Thanks for the ride." Zen hoisted his backpack on his shoulder. "It did turn out to be quite the adventure, didn't it?"

"Yes." She tilted her chin up to look directly into his green/gold eyes. "Thanks for teaching me that mattress trick. It's good to know." She would show him that she didn't need him anymore. The trip might over, but what she most wanted to say was *don't go*. She extended her hand to shake his.

"Oh," he said. "I think we know each other better than that." He embraced her in a gentle yet firm hug. "After all, we survived a tornado together."

"It was a miracle," she said into his soft t-shirt. The tears would come whether she liked it or not. It wasn't like she wanted to date this guy or anything like that. After all, he would be living in Chicago, and she would be driving back to Arizona. However, she had become fond of him during their drive. He might have become a friend, and right now, she could really use a friend.

"You can do this, Kat," he said, breaking the embrace. "You can go and set things right with your father."

He did have an uncanny knack for channeling Granny Nanny. She'd have to give him that. "It was nice to meet you," Kat said formally.

"Much obliged." Zen tipped an imaginary hat and grinned. He turned and walked into the train station.

Well, that's that, Kat thought. She had nothing else to do but get in her damn car and work up some courage. The day was unseasonably cool for early April, so she turned on the car for heat. "Okay, Kat," she said aloud—shit, what all had she muttered when she thought Zen was sleeping?—"you have started the car." Step one, done. Then, she sat. Maybe she should go to a bar and get a drink? "No," she said out loud. "You need a shot of Granny Nanny." She dug her phone out of her purse just as it was pinging a text message from Zen: "If you can survive a tornado, you can survive this." Kat grinned. The guy really did have a knack for channeling Granny Nanny.

Kat didn't exactly remember the way to 126 North Hickory, which surprised her. A family-owned bakery had disappeared from the corner of Oak Street. The old Methodist Church on Waverly had been torn down and replaced with a KFC. When she drove by the campus, Kat noticed that a new engineering building had replaced the old one. And when she finally, after several wrong turns, made it into her old neighborhood, she saw that Bobby Baker's old auto repair shop had been boarded up. From the looks of it, it had been closed for a long time. Graffiti had been spray-painted onto every inch of plyboard.

However, Hickory Street looked pretty much the same, only so much smaller than Kat remembered. The houses looked like little square boxes carefully placed equidistance apart. Some had picket fences; most were chain-link. A rusted car up on cinder blocks rested in front of one house, and some needed a new coat of paint or a new roof. But for the most part, the structures and the yards were neatly maintained. It was a respectable neighborhood, a good place to raise children, with the grade school within walking distance. But it looked so small to Kat, so ordinary. It had absolutely no *pizzazz*. It probably never had, but Kat hadn't noticed it then. For her, it had been home.

She parked across the street from 126 North Hickory, turned off the ignition, and stared. Two white wicker rockers sat on the front porch. These were new, but maybe not. Kat didn't know if they'd been there for two weeks, eight months, or ten years. This house, her old house, could use a new coat of paint. Missy had insisted on painting the window trims blue fifteen years ago, and they were now flaked and chipped. The shrub by the front steps looked half-dead, and even though Easter had been a week earlier, a giant, rather gruesome, cardboard Easter Bunny adorned the front window.

A dull, green, nondescript sedan pulled into the driveway, and Kat slid down in her seat, silly as she knew it was. In this neighborhood, people would notice a strange car, especially a very dusty red Mazda that looked as if it had been in a tornado—and had been. Kat sat up straight. Damn it if she was going to act like some guilty fugitive who didn't belong here. But she had never belonged here, not really. Even if she had lived in the shabby house across the street, she had never really belonged here. Her father and Missy made sure of that.

Two young men got out of the car, and Kat immediately knew who they were—her half-brothers, Shane and Cody. From birth, Shane resembled Marcus, and he'd grown into the spitting image of him. It made Kat gasp. It was like she was looking at her father when he was twenty, and she'd never imagined him as a young man. To her, he'd always seemed and acted old. Shane was not as tall as Marcus, but he had his colorless brown hair and glasses. From her vantage point in the car, Kat could tell that his hairline was already starting to recede at the ripe old age of twenty. Cody, on the other hand, resembled Missy, with his blonde hair and blue eyes. He was about six inches shorter than his brother, and he was …

"Well, call it like you see it, Kat," she said aloud. Cody was fat, a doughboy of a young man. Each brother carried a backpack, and they walked into the house with nary a glance at the car.

"I'm invisible to them," Kat said to no one. She wondered if they remembered her at all. Surely, they must remember something about her. They'd been six and four when she left, hardly babies. However, if Marcus stayed true to form, he would have banished any picture of her from the house, just as he had with Kat's mother. He would have refused to talk about her, just as he had with Kat's mother. When Marcus said good-bye to a person, she was dead. Gone. Vanished. Even if she wasn't.

Kat felt an unreasonable and overwhelming urge to cry. She'd missed so much. Maybe she and her half-brothers, once they had grown out of their bratty stage, would have liked each other. Maybe they could have been friends and gone to movies and baseball games together. Maybe they would have all taken family vacations together, going camping and telling ghost stories around a campfire. Maybe. The *maybes* were endless.

Kat shook her head, hard. It was useless to think that way. She'd made a conscious choice to run away, and it was all Marcus' fault. He'd said horrible things to her and slapped her. Very possibly, he'd never loved her, and it wasn't fair. Parents should love their children. Period. Even if parents didn't particularly like their children, they should love them. Period. It was better to hold onto her anger at her father. He had denied Kat the basic rule of parenthood: *Love your children.*

Maybe it was even worse that he had denied his only daughter the slightest glimmer of what her mother had been like. She didn't know what her mother looked like, if her mother had a job, or if her mother liked to read novels or watched soap operas. He'd withheld his affection and deprived Kat of any concrete image of her mother. He had given her *nada*.

With her anger stoked just enough to make her knees stop shaking, Kat grabbed her purse and marched up to the front door. The giant Easter Bunny looked even more gruesome up close, with his large white teeth and an evil twinkling in his eyes. Kat took a deep breath and rang the doorbell. When the door opened, she took a startled step back. "Oh!" she said.

"You're here." Missy, who would only be forty-two, looked at least ten years older than that. Her blonde hair had large streaks of white, and the pounds that had started creeping up on her after the birth of her babies decided to settle permanently and multiply. Her shapeless blue housedress looked as if it were covering an extra-large bowling pin.

"I'm here," Kat said, trying not to stare. *What has Marcus done to you?* she wanted to ask. But she did not. It was none of her business what went on inside this house, and it hadn't been for a long time. An awkward silence followed.

"I thought it was the right thing to do, to write you that letter," Missy finally offered.

What letter? The woman had written her three short, ambiguous lines: Your father had some tests done last Wednesday. We're waiting for the results. I thought you should know.

"Yes." It was all that Kat could come up with. Missy wasn't waiting for Kat to thank her, was she? Kat wasn't about to do that. She'd come here for some specific answers, and she would be calm, concise, and professional about it.

Missy looked her up and down. "You grew up pretty good, Katrina."

Kat forced herself not to squirm under Missy's scrutiny, wishing that she had at least redone her ponytail. "I go by Kat now."

Missy continued her scrutiny and then concluded, "It suits you."

Was Missy complimenting her? "Thanks," Kat said uncertainly. "Is my father home?" It was near 5:30, the time Marcus had always come home from work, every single day, without fail. However, Kat speculated, he could be retired now.

"He's napping." Missy made no move to invite Kat inside.

An alarm went off in Kat's head. During her childhood, her father had never taken naps, not even on weekends. "I need to speak to him. I'll wait." The weather had turned even colder, and naturally, Kat-who-lived-in-Arizona did not bring a proper coat. However, she would camp out on one of the white wicker rockers if she had to.

"I think you should see him, Katrina, I really do—"

"Kat," she interjected.

Missy ignored her. "But I don't want you upsetting him."

"I'm not here to upset him." Kat knew that wasn't true. She probably would upset him, but tough luck. She had waited thirty years for some answers.

"Marcus has colon cancer. Stage four." Missy's faded blue eyes filled with tears.

"Oh!" Kat's hand flew instinctively to her heart. She'd imagined different scenarios about those unspecified tests in Missy's terse note on the drive here. Stage four colon cancer had not been one of them.

"I suppose you should come in." Missy opened the door a crack.

Kat squeezed in, numb from the cold and numb from Missy's news. What was her father's prognosis? Was he dying? Kat felt some of her resolve fade. She didn't think she could be calm, concise, and professional toward a dying man. It certainly wasn't polite. And he was her father.

"All these years, I kept telling him he needed to get a colonoscopy. You know, like that Katie Couric did on TV some years back. He pooped blood, but would he listen to me? No, he did not. Your father is a very stubborn man."

Kat knew that all too well. She followed Missy to the kitchen in the back. Like the neighborhood, the interior of the house looked much the same, but smaller. The same old couch, but the flat-screen TV was new. Pictures lined the mantle, but Kat didn't take the time to study them as she followed Missy's waddle to the kitchen.

Shane and Cody sat eating spaghetti in the same seats they'd always occupied at the old scarred oak table. "Look what the cat dragged in," Missy said. Oddly, her voice sounded pleasantly benign.

Kat thought she could have put it a little better than that. For Pete's sake, she'd just told Kat that her father might be dying, and then she went and said a thing like that. Missy Flowers, her stepmother, had not changed at all in all the years Kat had been gone. Kat swallowed hard and said, "I'm ... Katrina."

"I remember your red hair," Cody said, stopping his heaping forkful of spaghetti halfway to his mouth. Up close, he was quite cute—in a very cherubic way.

"I remember Mom was always telling you that you had a smart mouth," Shane said softly, grinning.

"I guess some things never change," Kat said, grinning back. Even his smile resembled Marcus' on the rare occasions when Marcus had smiled at her.

Missy shifted her feet and seemed unsure of what to do next. "Would you like some spaghetti?" she finally asked.

Kat hadn't forgotten Missy's lack of cooking acumen. Or those truly terrible Hawaiian meatballs. "No, thank you."

"It's okay," Shane said. "The sauce is Ragu."

"Impossible for even Mom to mess up," Cody added.

"Boys, boys, boys," Missy wearily said as if she had repeated those three words so many times that they had become a mundane mantra.

"I'll get you some," Cody said.

"Good, you kids eat, and I'll go check on your father." For a hefty short woman, Missy exited the room with surprising speed.

Kat didn't know what else to do, so she sat and accepted the heaping plate from Cody. Without thinking, she'd sat in the same chair she used to sit in and realized, simultaneously, that there were still five chairs around the table. It had been the four of them for the past fourteen years, but they'd kept her chair. It had to mean something, didn't it? Had her father secretly wished that she would come back home? If so, he had a funny way of showing it.

With Missy gone, the coast was clear for her half-brothers to pepper her with questions.

"Where do you live?"

"What do you do?"

"Do you have a boyfriend?"

Those were the easy ones for Kat to answer. "Arizona, I'm currently between jobs, and no, I don't, thank God."

Then came the hard ones. "Why have you stayed away so long?" and "Why are you here?"

Kat stuffed a huge bite (that rivaled Cody's) of spaghetti in her mouth and shrugged, trying to deflect the important questions. But they had patience, her brothers. Damn it, they had patience. They waited. Kat ate some more. They waited.

They won. Kat had emptied her plate, and she felt queasy from eating so much so fast. She supposed she owed them some answers. "I came back because I wanted to find out more—anything, really—about my biological mother. Also, I stayed away so long because …"

How could she explain it to them? For all she knew, Marcus was a loving father to them if the past held true. "You know, school, and then work, and things like that," she finished lamely. She looked at Shane and then Cody, and it was clear they weren't buying it.

Kat was not going to go into any more detail than that. She cleared her throat. "What about you guys?" They were polite, if not exactly forthcoming. Shane studied mechanical engineering at SIU and dated a girl who had a baby (hence, the gruesome Easter Bunny on the front door). Cody, a senior on the debate team, planned to attend Eastern in the fall to study restaurant management.

The whole conversation seemed surreal to Kat. She couldn't believe she was sitting in this forgotten yet familiar kitchen, talking with her half-brothers. They were related by blood but total strangers. They were charming enough, but Kat could feel their suspicion. And she couldn't blame them for that.

Their conversation started to stall, and Kat looked at the clock on the wall. Missy had been gone for an hour. Where in the hell was she? Was she hiding out somewhere in the house, or was she trying to persuade Marcus to see his daughter?

Without warning, Shane said, "Dad's dying." His voice trembled.

"Maybe two months to live." Cody looked ready to bawl.

Kat tried to swallow the lump that suddenly formed in her throat. "I didn't know," she said. Cody got up and blew his nose on a paper towel. Kat added, "I'm so sorry." She did feel sorry for them, but the man they knew as their loving father was not the distant man she'd known. She didn't understand what else to say.

"You can talk to your father now." Missy stood in the doorway. "But only for a minute or two. He needs his rest."

Wordlessly, Kat followed her down the cramped, narrow hallway to the downstairs bedroom, the one Missy and Marcus had shared for almost twenty-two years. As uncomfortable as the scene in the kitchen had become, she wanted to be back there. Now that Kat was about to see her father after all these years, she was more nervous and frightened than she had ever been. Too late, she realized she'd left her list of twenty-two questions in her purse in the kitchen.

It didn't matter. Kat knew that as soon as Missy opened the door to the darkened bedroom. It was the one room in the house that didn't look anything like it used to. The curtains were drawn, and Marcus and Missy's old double bed had been replaced by a hospital bed with cold metal railings. The shriveled gray man in the bed was a stranger.

"Who is it?" his voice croaked.

"Marcus, I already told you," Missy said with tender patience. "Katrina has come to see you. She can't stay long, though." She gave Kat a meaningful look.

She didn't have to worry about that. All Kat wanted to do at that moment was turn and run all the way back to Arizona and Granny Nanny.

"Go a little closer," Missy urged. "He doesn't hear very well anymore."

Reluctantly, Kat moved closer. The man vaguely resembled her father, but his remaining hair was white, his skin folded and wrinkled. But then he opened his eyes, and they were surprisingly clear. They were Marcus' eyes. "Katrina," he said.

"Yes," she whispered. She had no idea what to do. She should probably take his hand, but she couldn't bring herself to do it. She should probably feel fury, but that had evaporated as soon as she saw him. She was here to ask him questions, she knew that, but she had difficulty breathing in this room that smelled as antiseptic and sickly as a hospital.

"It's been a long time," he said.

"Yes," she whispered again. Here was her one chance to question him or berate him for being such a bad father to her and denying her information about her mother. Or to beg him for his love. Instead, she stood as mute and as still as a statue.

"This is a hell of a way to die," he said. "Nothing courageous or heroic about it."

The lump in her throat grew larger, and she had nothing more to offer him than what she had meagerly offered to his sons in the kitchen, "I'm so sorry."

"Now, your mother," he said, "she made a choice."

Kat leaned closer. He must mean that her mother made a conscious choice to have a baby—her, Kat—and this tidbit, this crumb of information, was more than he'd ever presented to her before. She took her father's hand.

He didn't seem to notice. "Many choices, I suppose, all leading to that one agonizing, heartbreaking decision. All this time, and I still can't forgive her for what she did."

Kat's tears started to fall. It was just what she had expected all along. Her father had never wanted her in the first place, and it was probably its own kind of hell to be responsible for and to try to love someone you'd *never wanted* in the first place. "You mean me, don't you? You never wanted to have a baby." Behind her, she could hear Missy gasp.

Her father looked directly into Kat's eyes. "No, Katrina, not you. *Her*. It was her, your mother. Melody." Just uttering her name seemed to exhaust him. He closed his eyes. "I'm tired now, exhausted."

Even though she hadn't asked all her questions, and even though there were so many things she still didn't understand, she felt like he had given her a rare gift: her mother's name. "Melody Flowers," she said.

"No, no," he said, his scratchy voice weakening. "Her name was Melody Arnold."

8

SEPTEMBER 1980

"I hope we get something good tonight," Sylvia said. "I'm going to scream with boredom if another mother brings in a kid with a sprained ankle or a measly 102-degree temperature. I'm in the mood for some blood and guts."

"Sylvia! We're not supposed to root for other people's tragedies." However, Melody said this with a smile on her face. She hadn't seen her best friend for weeks, ever since they'd cut Evelyn's hair to hide the gash, and she'd missed Sylvia terribly. They'd planned on getting together on two separate occasions, but something had always come up. Namely, Marcus.

On the first occasion, as she headed out the door to meet Sylvia for dinner, Marcus suddenly remembered that he had forgotten to pick up a prescription for Evelyn. "You don't mind staying here with Mother while I go get it, do you, Mellie? I'll only be gone for ten minutes."

Melody, with Evelyn's naked stroll down Main Street still fresh in her mind, knew full well that Evelyn could no longer be left alone for a second. But Marcus wasn't gone ten minutes. An hour and a half later, after she had already called the restaurant and tearfully told Sylvia she couldn't come, he returned with the prescription and an excuse. He'd had to go all the way downtown to get it filled because the local pharmacy was out of Evelyn's arthritis medication. "You understand, don't you, honey?" he'd said without a trace of remorse. Melody had nodded and gone to bed. When he came to bed later, he didn't seem to notice that her pillow was soaked.

On the second occasion, as Melody headed out the door, Marcus suddenly remembered that he had an "emergency meeting" at work. Melody highly doubted this was true because it had never happened before. (But then again, what did she know about Marcus' job?) "You understand, don't you, baby?" her husband asked. Melody nodded and called Sylvia at the restaurant.

Melody did not understand her new husband *at all.*

"What's the big deal?" Sylvia had asked on the phone. "It's perfectly normal to go out with a friend for dinner. *Perfectly normal.*"

Melody, embarrassed, had answered, "He says he can't stand to be apart from me for one second."

Sylvia had snorted. "That's fucking creepy, Mel."

"Newlywed bliss, you know?" Melody tried for a carefree laugh, but it came out sounding like a strangling cat.

"Bullshit," Sylvia had said.

Melody thought that pretty much summed it up.

However, she was still trying to make a go of this situation, still trying to view the scenario through rose-colored glasses. Ma and Daddy couldn't stop talking about the pearls, and when she and Marcus went on their rare visits—and Ma and Daddy had never been to Marcus' house—Ma and Daddy practically genuflected at his feet, her brothers not far behind. Ma and Daddy were perhaps not the best judges of character, but Melody had never known them to be utterly wrong about a person. So, it must mean that it was her. She missed something that everyone else could see.

Except for Sylvia, of course. On this night that they were finally together, working the same shift, standing at the nurses' station, waiting to see what this night would bring, Sylvia said, "If you quit this job because he wants you to, you're playing right into his hands."

Melody wished she hadn't told Sylvia about that. Sylvia harped on it constantly. "I'm not going to quit, Syl. Relax. I'll take maternity leave when the baby is born, but I'll be back to work as soon as possible."

Sylvia arched her eyebrow.

"I promise," Melody said, and she meant it.

Sylvia seemed satisfied. "Okay, then. I believe you. Now, about the little rugrat. Is she still playing soccer in your belly?"

Melody didn't have time to answer because "CODE TRAUMA NOW" resounded throughout the department on the overhead pager. Instinct and training took over. She and Sylvia glanced at each other, then raced toward the trauma room of the ER. They, along with the MD Attending,

MD Resident, OR Residents, and Respiratory Specialists, quickly donned gowns, gloves, and glasses. They entered the trauma room, and all eyes focused on the patient as she was lifted from the paramedic's stretcher to the hospital stretcher. The paramedic began his report: female, approximately seventeen years old, high-speed motor vehicle accident, unconscious at the scene ...

Melody surveyed the patient and wanted to weep. The girl was so young, covered in blood under a white blanket. One of her arms—or perhaps both—appeared to be broken, shattered glass clung to her hair, and deep cuts lined her face around her eyes and nose. Her head was swollen, bloody, and bruised. This poor girl was someone's daughter. Did her parents know where she was? Were they waiting for her at their dinner table, beginning to worry that she hadn't appeared? Were they ever going to see her again? Always, when a trauma patient came in, Melody had these overemotional moments when she pitied these unknown victims and their families. Why did such terrible things have to happen? Why did people have to get hurt, maimed, or die? To make matters even worse, these accidents often resulted from carelessness, stupidity, or just plain bad luck.

Melody took a deep breath and got to work. It took sheer will to put those feelings aside and concentrate on what she needed to do. She had to remain professional; she had to have grace under pressure. She was still new at this job, and hopefully, over time, her heart wouldn't feel like it was breaking every time a patient like this young girl came in. Melody fervently prayed that this would be the case.

The attending doctor began his verbal assessment of the girl as Sylvia, Melody, and the others worked quickly to get the young patient's clothing off. Then they brought the necessary equipment to the bedside to perform emergent imaging to make sure there wasn't any damage to her internal organs. Sylvia began to document the trauma findings on the trauma flow sheet as the doctor dictated, while Melody's role was to locate intravenous access to immediately begin administering fluids, medications, and blood products. Her first attempt to place a needle in a vein in the girl's left forearm failed. The girl's bones were broken, and the veins there were weak. Melody looked for another vein and could easily place a large IV in her right wrist, followed by a second large IV in her right antecubital area, the area inside her elbow. The doctor ordered blood products, and

Melody grabbed a bag of blood from the trauma room coolers and started giving it through the IVs.

The poor young girl was losing a lot of blood, so the doctor could not fully assess her injuries. With her blood pressure low and her heart rate fast, she was breathing at a rapid pace. They would have to place a ventilator down her throat to allow it to breathe for her. The resident yelled out the doses and medications he wanted to use for the intubation, and Melody quickly drew them up in a syringe. When he asked Melody to administer the medications to paralyze, sedate, and take away all feelings of pain the patient might be experiencing, Melody felt utterly relieved. *She can't feel any pain now*, Melody thought. *She can't feel any pain.*

A couple of minutes later, the patient was moved to radiology for X-rays and CT scans. The entire trauma process had lasted mere minutes, but to Melody, it felt like hours. She was sweating, and her heart pounded as they took the patient away.

"Now that was something," Sylvia said when they were back at the nurses' station. "I bet we have the best trauma team in the entire city."

Melody agreed. She was proud of her role as part of Mercy's remarkable trauma team. However, she wished she didn't find the misfortune of others so gut-wrenching. It must be her hormones. After the baby was born, she wouldn't be so emotional. She would be totally and utterly Professional with a capital P. "I hope we've had our excitement for the night," she said.

But they had not.

The next patient limped/staggered in. He was a black man in his mid-thirties, Melody guessed. "Help, Help!" he shouted. "I've broken my leg."

"You wouldn't be walking on it if it was broken," Melody pointed out.

"I want one of you bitches to take a look at it now! Damn it, I pay my taxes!" he shouted.

"I highly doubt that," Sylvia said under her breath.

The man reeked of alcohol, and his dilated pupils told Melody that he was probably high on some other drug, too. "I just need you to fill out this form." Melody pushed the clipboard toward him.

"Paperwork, paperwork! Do you bitches have some government conspiracy going on here? I said I broke my leg! I need a shot of morphine."

Melody and Sylvia looked at each other. The man was obviously after something to keep his drug high going. "Sylvia, why don't you call Dr. Doolittle and tell him we have a patient who needs morphine." Dr. Doolittle was their code for calling security. They hadn't had to use it yet, and this man was probably harmless, but Melody thought it was better to be safe than sorry, especially since the man had staggered in during the one and only time they had no one in the waiting room.

Sylvia nodded, reaching for the phone. "Will do. Dr. Doolittle is the best. Why, he can even speak to the animals."

"What you talkin' about?" the belligerent man said.

"Let me take a look at that leg," Melody said to distract him. She walked around the counter. "Lift your pants leg."

"No, sirree. Not until I get my morphine shot."

"Come on," Melody coaxed. "I promise I won't hurt you." She squatted down in front of the man and reached for his pants leg.

The next instant, his hands were around her throat. "You bitch, I need a morphine shot!"

Melody couldn't breathe. She slapped futilely at the hands around her throat, but his grip got even tighter.

"Holy shit!" Sylvia flew around the counter with a clipboard in hand and started swatting at the man's face. "Let her go, you piece of shit. Let her go!"

Melody saw black dots swimming before her eyes and knew she was about to pass out. This horrible man was depriving her of oxygen. This horrible drunk man was depriving her baby of oxygen. She did not want to die this way.

Sylvia kept swatting and cursing, and suddenly, the man loosened his grip. Melody toppled over, gasping for breath. Where in the hell was security?

Sylvia was gasping, too. She stopped swatting and pointed toward the door. "Get out of here! *Now!*"

"Bitches," he said and spat. The blob of spit landed on Melody's gasping, red face.

"Get out!" Sylvia screamed.

The drunk, high man with the professed broken leg bolted out of the room just as security arrived. "What seems to be the problem here?" the shorter guard said.

"Would you chase after that fucker, you moron!" Sylvia said. "He tried to strangle a nurse." She helped Melody up. "Are you okay, Mel?"

"The asshole tried to strangle me, and then he spat on me," Melody croaked. "No, Sylvia, I am not all right." What she felt was humiliation. How had she let herself get in that position? She should never have walked around the counter, and she should never have knelt in front of a drunk and aggressive man. She should have known better, yet she'd acted like an idiot.

"Our shift is almost over," Sylvia said. "I think we need a drink."

"It's eight o'clock in the morning, Syl, and I'm pregnant." Melody massaged her neck. She was sure that creep's fingers still marked her skin.

"Minor details, minor details. We can go to my place and have a real gab fest, like in the good old days."

The last thing that Melody wanted to do was go home, and she really needed a friend right now who would listen to everything that was on her mind. However, she said, "Marcus will not be happy."

"That makes it even better. But first, I need to swing by and check on Thelma. I haven't seen her in a couple of days, and I'm suffering from a daughter's guilt."

Melody knew a daughter's guilt all too well. "Okay."

Melody had not been to Thelma's apartment since before her marriage and was struck anew by the odor as they walked up to the fourth floor. During their two years of *research*, she'd become immune to the sour smells of urine and garlic and that indescribable stench that she'd once attributed to rats (and which she now realized was actually despair). It was an unexpected Indian Summer, and even though it was only a little past eight o'clock in the morning, the place was stifling.

Sylvia was thinking along the same lines. "This place smells like a vermin sauna. I swear, one of these days, I'm going to call the health department."

"Then Thelma can come and live with you in your shiny, refurbished apartment in the South Loop," Melody panted. The steep steps sucked the air right out of her lungs, and either she was horribly out of shape or just pregnant. Or maybe she was simply beat because of the stress of the last twelve hours. Boy, could she teach Marcus a thing or two about *stress*.

"On second thought, let the vermin rejoice." They reached the fourth floor, and Sylvia took out her key. "Ready or not, Thelma, here I come," she sang out.

As usual, Thelma was asleep in the ratty green recliner, the TV blaring. Sylvia walked over and turned it down. "Thelma, I came to pay you a visit, and I brought Melody. You remember Melody, don't you?"

Melody tried not to gasp. Thelma had been scarecrow thin before, but now she was skeletal. She'd lost a lot of hair, and what remained stuck out from her scalp in wispy, greying clumps. The clutter in the room—dirty dishes, overflowing ashtrays, crumpled papers, and take-out containers—had grown even worse, and from the smell of things in here, Melody would guess that Thelma hadn't bathed in quite some time. "Syl," she whispered, even though Thelma was still passed out, "this is …"

"I know." Sylvia, who never cried, looked close to tears. "It's awful. She absolutely refuses to get any treatment, and I've hired four different caregivers to come in and watch out for her, but they all quit because she's so nasty to them. The last one didn't even last a full day."

"She's so thin, probably only about eighty pounds. You could pick her up and carry her someplace, whether she wants you to or not." Melody did not understand the situation. Uber-competent Sylvia was dropping the ball here.

"Don't you think I've thought of that? Don't you think I've said that to her? She said if I did that, she would know that I don't have respect for her. She said that I would *break her heart*. I'm her daughter, the only person she has in the entire world—a nurse to boot—and I can't even take care of my own mother!" Sylvia cried in earnest now.

If Melody thought she'd understood a daughter's guilt, she now knew that she didn't hold a candle to Sylvia. She went to Sylvia and put her arms around her. "I know you try," she consoled. "I know you try."

"I cleaned out the medicine cabinet before I left. I started to refuse to refill Thelma's prescriptions, so then she had them delivered. I've called her doctors and explained the situation, and then she switches doctors. She's got contacts on the street, too."

"Where does she get the money?"

"Disability, social security, welfare, who knows? Addicts are very crafty people."

It was the first time Sylvia had ever called her mother an *addict*, and Melody knew how painful it was for her to say it aloud.

"When I even try to clean up around here, she gets offended. I don't know what to do."

"We'll think of something," Melody said. "I'll help you."

Sylvia nodded. "Thanks, Mel." She gently shook Thelma's shoulder. "Thelma, it's me, Sylvia, and I brought Melody."

Thelma awoke with a congested snort. "Who's there?"

Sylvia put on a fake cheerful face. "Your daughter."

"Oh, yes," Thelma said as her eyes began to focus. "My lovely Sylvie, and you brought your pretty red-headed friend."

"Melody," Sylvia prompted.

"Of course," Thelma said, smiling weakly.

Melody gave her a quick hug. Thelma's bones felt like brittle twigs under her thin skin. "It's good to see you again, Mrs. Hammond."

"How've you been, Thelma?" Sylvia was a good actress. Her voice sounded conversational, almost nonchalant.

"Oh, you know, honey, this and that, good days and bad days. I think I have thyroid cancer, though. I saw a program on television the other day—maybe it was Tuesday?—and I have all of the symptoms. All of them."

"You don't have thyroid cancer, Thelma," Sylvia said calmly, as she always did.

"Oh, but I do. You don't know what pain I've been in."

Melody felt for the poor woman. Thelma had been in emotional pain for years, and look what it had turned into: a miserable life as an addict.

"You don't have thyroid cancer, Thelma," Sylvia repeated.

"What do you know?" Thelma said sharply.

"Well, I am a nurse," Sylvia began.

"You don't *listen* to me, Sylvia! I'm your mother, and you don't even *listen* to me! I have thyroid cancer!" She reached for her trusty pack of Mores and saw that it was empty. "Son of a bitch!" she cried.

"I have a pack in my purse." Sylvia bent down to get it.

"I don't want your lousy cigarettes! If you loved me, you'd go down to the corner drugstore and buy me a carton of cigarettes." Thelma's entire body shook uncontrollably.

"You know that I love you, Thelma." Sylvia's voice was still calm. She was a pro. After all, she had been taking care of Thelma for years.

"A carton of cigarettes!"

"Okay, Thelma, Melody and I will go get you a carton of cigarettes."

Melody followed Sylvia out the door. "How long has this been going on?" she asked when they were on the street. When she and Sylvia were doing their research and spending countless weekends in the apartment, Thelma, when not asleep, was docile as a lamb—until she wanted her "medication." This antagonism was completely different.

"A couple of months, I guess. I have no idea what Thelma's on." Now that she was out of the apartment, Sylvia dropped the fake cheerfulness. "For all I know, she could have graduated from opioids to heroin."

Melody shuddered involuntarily. How could addicts do what they did? Why didn't they just stop? She had studied the psychology of addicts in nursing school, but she just didn't get it. Why didn't they simply *stop*?

Once at the corner drugstore, neither Melody nor Sylvia was particularly eager to get back to the apartment, so they thumbed through some magazines on the newsstand and sampled some colognes at the make-up counter. They flirted with the idea of getting makeovers from the overly made-up, overly friendly saleswoman but then decided it would take too much time. They bought the carton of cigarettes and trudged slowly back up the four flights of stairs at the apartment building.

"It's showtime," Sylvia said when they got to the door. She adjusted her face into a bright smile.

Melody did the same, thinking how much she admired Sylvia's bravery, her fearlessness, her loyalty.

"Ready or not, Thelma, here I come!" Sylvia sang out once more as she flung open the door and walked in.

Thelma wasn't in her ratty green recliner, and Melody felt the alarm singe through her veins. Thelma rarely left that chair, and the sight of its emptiness set off warning bells.

"Oh, my God! Thelma!" Sylvia turned to Melody with a look of pure terror on her face. "Melody, where is my mother?"

They found her on the bathroom floor, curled into a fetal position, blood coming from her nose, mouth, and eyes. Even though Sylvia valiantly tried CPR, and even though the ambulance arrived in record time, they both knew it was too late.

"I took too long buying those damn cigarettes," Sylvia cried to Melody after they took Thelma away. "I should not have left her alone in that agitated state. What have I done?"

Melody stayed with Sylvia for hours, comforting her. It was not the time for Melody to tell her best friend—whose mother had just died of an overdose—that she was worried to death about her pregnancy. She had not felt her baby move for five days.

9

APRIL 2012

"Do you have everything you need?" Missy asked as she ushered Kat out of the dying man's bedroom.

What in the hell kind of question was that? Kat had not been home (could she still call this chipped-painted house her home?) in fourteen years, and when she arrived, she found out that her father was dying of cancer and still withholding information. He had given Kat her mother's name, yes, but that was it. Still no explanations, still no declarations of love or apology. Still *nada*.

Even the information about her mother's name confused Kat: Melody Arnold. Their surname was Flowers, so what did it mean? She asked Missy.

"I have no idea, Katrina. Your father never talked about your mother." She slowly inched Kat toward the front door.

"Not once?"

"Not once." Missy cleared her throat. "Unfortunately, Katrina, we don't have a spare bedroom. I suppose I could make up the couch—"

"That's all right, Missy," Kat interrupted. "I have a place to stay." Well, she did if you counted her car. "I'll grab my purse and be out of here. Thanks for letting me know … about Marcus."

"I thought you should know."

In the kitchen, her half-brothers were still sitting at the table, which surprised Kat. It seemed like she had been in her father's room for hours, but when she glanced at the clock, she saw that she'd only been in her father's presence for a mere five minutes. Fourteen years out of his life and five minutes in his presence. If she let herself dwell on that dismal fact, the entire can of worms that she had buried in her heart would start squirming out. She would not, could not let that happen.

"Well, guys," she said as she picked up her purse, "I'll be seeing you." Would she ever see them again? The odds, she supposed, were stacked against it.

"Are you leaving?" Cody asked. "You just got here." He was eating another plate of spaghetti, just shoveling it in without seeming to taste it.

"He eats when he's upset," Shane explained when he saw Kat's widened eyes. "Things are rather bleak around here."

"Yes," Kat said slowly, "I can see that."

"Why don't you spend the night?" Cody asked.

"Because I ... well, I ... have someone waiting for me." She had no one waiting for her (another dismal fact), and with both her half-brothers looking at her with their earnest eyes, they suddenly seemed as young as they had when she'd left years before. She realized she felt sorry for them. Because they loved their father, they were suffering as they watched him die. She, on the other hand, was not in this family's equation. And she was leaving again. She had the luxury of leaving again—or was it merely cowardice? Probably cowardice, but she hadn't been included in the love here, so why should she participate in the grief?

"She's got better things to do, Cody," Shane said.

"It's not that I've got better things to do—" Kat began.

"It's okay," Shane interrupted. "We understand."

What did they understand? she wondered. What had they been told about her? Had they cried when she left? Had they asked about her over the years? Kat shifted her feet uncomfortably. Perhaps a better question would be: Why did she feel so guilty leaving them here as she walked out the door yet again? It made no sense. They lived here; she did not.

"We understand." Cody, apparently, still echoed his older brother.

"Well, I'll be seeing you," Kat said again, desperately wanting to escape but seemingly not able to drag her butt out the door.

"That would be good." Cody nodded glumly.

"Oh, you almost forgot this." Shane held out Kat's cell phone. "You left it on the table."

"I'm always doing that." Kat took the phone. "I've left the damn—darn—thing in so many bars—restaurants—bathrooms, cars, stores... You wouldn't believe where this cell phone has been. Why, if it could talk, it would have quite a story to tell …" She stopped when she realized she was babbling and blushed. "Well."

"I took the liberty of adding both of us to your contact list." At that moment, Shane looked and sounded so much like their father that Kat shuddered. "I hope you don't mind."

"Mind? No! It's good, great! Thanks! Adios, amigos!" Then Kat fled the kitchen and the house, giving a quick wave to Missy, and sprinted across the street to her dusty red Mazda. She jumped in and locked the doors—(against what?)—and gave a huge sigh. She hadn't let herself feel just how tense she'd been in that house. How long had she been holding her breath?

As she started her car, Kat realized she hadn't given her half-brothers her phone number. Should she have done that? It would have been the polite thing to do, an exchange of telephone numbers, a you-give-me-yours-I'll-give-you-mine type of thing. "Oh, well," Kat said aloud, "I'll probably never see them again. They seem like decent guys—surprise, surprise, given their mother and father—but Marcus will die soon, and Missy will probably remarry—that is, if anyone will have her—and they will go on about their lives …"

She was babbling again, aloud, and to *herself*. "Get a grip. You are so done *thinking out loud*. Enough!"

She drove around the corner, away from the house, and parked the car. She had no idea what she was going to do next. True to her damnable track record, she hadn't thought ahead. It wasn't that she'd thought her reunion with Marcus would be a cozy, heartfelt homecoming. He would explain everything she wanted to know, tell her that he had made mistakes and was sorry and that from now on, things would be wonderful and terrific. It was not that. Well, perhaps, she had harbored a slight hope that would be the case. However, she had not predicted that the reunion would be so short, so abrupt. She would google her mother's name. Now that she had it at long last, she would do that. But then what?

What was she supposed to do? She hadn't planned on heading immediately back to Arizona, but what were the other alternatives? Should she sleep in her car, take sponge baths in dirty gas station restrooms, buy her food from Dollar Tree—a loaf of white bread and a jar of peanut butter—and poke around town for a while? She could ask the local businesses, the neighborhood market and drugstore and auto shop and diner, if they remembered a Melody Arnold. Yet already that presented a problem. These businesses no longer existed, having long since been replaced by conglomerate chains: Kroger, Walmart, Shell, Denny's. Kat had no idea if her mother had held a job, belonged to a church, or had friends in the Junior League. Hell, for all she knew, her mother could have been a long-haul truck driver or a staff sergeant in the Army or a piano teacher. She still knew nothing at all.

What had her father meant when he said that Melody Arnold had *made a choice*?

Melody restarted the car. There was only one thing to do at this point. She would go to a bar, get a shot of scotch, and call Granny Nanny. Screw the budget. The situation called for Granny Nanny's cure-all, Glen Livet.

The bar she chose—actually, it was the first bar she saw as she came into the downtown area—did not have Glen Livet. With a name like Zeke's Tavern, Kat should have surmised this, but with her usual impetuousness, she saw that it was a bar and had a red neon OPEN sign blinking, so she parked and went in. Although it was late afternoon, the tavern had the same twilight feel that casinos had, the blurring of night and day, the timelessness of good timing non-productivity. Kat's eyes adjusted immediately. She was very familiar with this kind of atmosphere, as both an employee and a patron.

Kat took a seat at the bar. She wasn't happy with the selection of cheap scotch the bartender—presumably Zeke—offered, but she smiled sweetly and ordered the least offensive one. Then she dialed Granny Nanny's cell. Granny answered on the second ring. "Get the Glen Livet," Kat said.

"Certainly, dear," Granny Nanny said. "I was thinking along those lines myself."

Kat smiled as she heard the clanking of bottle and glass on Gran's kitchen table. It was two hours earlier in Arizona, only 2:00 p.m., but if Granny Nanny was thinking along those lines—well, it was time for a shot. "Ready, dear," Gran said.

Kat took her shot at the same time she knew Gran was taking hers at her kitchen table in Scottsdale. She quickly filled her in on the events that had taken place at her father's house: seeing Missy and her half-brothers,

Marcus' cancer and prognosis, the scant information about her mother's actual name.

"Why do you think she had a different last name, Gran?" Kat motioned to Zeke to refill her shot glass. This was definitely a two-shot situation. Screw that damn budget.

"Perhaps she wanted to keep her maiden name? Liberated women do that, you know."

"In the early eighties?"

"Some women have been liberated since the dawn of time, dear. It is not a new concept. Why, back in my day, I knew lots of women who kept their maiden name when they married."

"And what day would that be, Gran?" Maybe the crafty old woman would slip and finally give away her age.

No such luck. "Never mind, dear. What is your next step, Katrina?"

"I have no idea, Gran. I was hoping you could give me a hint." She took her second shot. If not Gran, then maybe the liquor would enlighten her.

"Now, why would I do that, dear?"

"Because you love me, because I'm a stranger in a foreign land with next to no resources, because I'm a big, fat loser who's always fucking things up. Take your pick."

Granny Nanny chuckled. "Katrina, Katrina, Katrina."

"What, what, what?" Kat knew she was too old to be calling her zillion-year-old gran and begging for advice, but still. She was at a loss, and it was probably—no, certainly—her own damn fault. What a mess she was.

"You're going to be fine, dear," Gran said in her infinitely patient voice. "I have the utmost faith in you."

"Gee, thanks." She motioned for another shot. What the hell. She would be spending the night in her car anyway, no need to drive because she had no place to go. This shot was probably going to cost her a pint of blood. She vaguely remembered driving by a blood bank somewhere in this no-longer-familiar town. How much would they pay if she donated her blood? Or could she find a fertility clinic that needed some fresh eggs? She was wealthy in unused, unharvested eggs. Which place would pay more? Which place was more desperate? Which place was more hopeless than she was? Perhaps she was getting a little drunk.

"I could wire you some money. I would be glad to do that, Katrina," Gran said.

Kat felt a wave of love for this sweet old lady wash over her, and tears sprang. "I'll be fine, Gran, and you're saving that money for a new Glock. I'm just feeling sorry for myself. I don't want you to worry." She downed the unwise third shot. The crappy scotch tasted like turpentine.

"I'm not worried, dear. I know you can take care of yourself."

Kat thought Gran must have been blinded by love for the last fourteen years. On Gran's end of the phone, Kat thought she heard a man's voice. "Do you have company, Gran? I thought I just heard a man's voice."

"Well, Mr. Williams is a man."

"Mr. Williams is there?" Mr. Williams was a dapper-looking man with a pencil-thin white mustache, who lived two houses down from Gran. He must have been in his late 70s or early 80s, and he was always impeccably dressed in a black pin-striped suit that looked like it came from a 1940s gangster movie. All that Kat knew about him was that he was a widower and kept to himself.

"That appears to be the case," Gran said nonchalantly.

"Wait a minute. I've been gone for some thirty-odd hours, and you have a boyfriend?" In the fourteen years that Kat had lived with Granny Nanny, she'd never known her gran to have a boyfriend. But then again, knowing Granny Nanny, she could have kept a few men on the side without Kat's knowledge. It was distinctly possible. Kat would have to have another shot to absorb this news. That crafty old woman! She could sure move fast when she wanted to.

"Mr. Williams is a dear friend," Gran said loudly, evidently for Mr. Williams' benefit. Then, whispering, she said to Kat, "He has the goods, you know, the *weed*."

"Mr. Williams is your *supplier*?" Kat started to laugh.

"I told you I had my sources, dear."

Kat struggled to get her laughter under control when she realized that the other patrons in the bar, all men, were staring at her. "Jesus, Gran."

"What about your young man?" Gran nimbly changed the subject, as usual.

"What young man?" Kat had stifled her laughter. Now she had the hiccups.

"Your driving partner, the prompt, polite, and handsome fellow who was definitely not a felon."

Funny, she hadn't thought about Zen at all since she'd gone to her father's house. "I dropped him off at the train station. It turns out that he was going to Chicago." It occurred to Kat that he was probably still there. Hadn't he said that his train left tonight? Maybe she should go see him and say good-bye. No, she wouldn't do that. There was absolutely no reason to do that. It was the crappy scotch talking.

"I see," said Gran.

What in the hell did she see? "He kind of, sort of saved my life two times during the trip out here." Kat hiccupped.

"That's nice, dear." Gran seemed suddenly distracted. "But I'm afraid I must go. Mr. Williams and I have some business to discuss."

"Sure, Gran." Even though Kat lacked a prescribed purpose at this exact moment, Granny Nanny did not. She needed to buy her pot. "I love you," Kat said.

"I love you, too, dear. Call anytime."

After Kat hung up, there was nothing to do but pay her bill, which was much cheaper than she had expected. Carbondale was not Scottsdale, and she would not have to donate blood or eggs just yet. She was suddenly and completely exhausted. So much had happened in less than two days, and all she wanted to do was curl up in a nice warm bed and sleep for a week. But she didn't have a bed. Her car would have to do.

She drew her not-warm-enough jacket around her as she went out the door into the chill air. It was only around five o'clock, but the cloud cover made it seem much later than that, or maybe it felt later than that because she was so very, very tired. She started walking across the gravel parking lot toward where she'd parked her car. She hadn't noticed what a dubious neighborhood this was in her preoccupation to get to a bar and call Granny Nanny. Yet another boarded-up business sat across the street, and next door was a tattoo parlor with a skull and crossbones neon sign. A gust of wind rolled empty beer cans across her path, and all Kat wanted to do was get to her car, lock the door, and get the hell out of Dodge. How had she not noticed that this neighborhood, as Granny Nanny would say, was probably chock-full of felons, and likely, juvenile delinquents? She hurried toward the safety of her Mazda, which she had parked at the far end of the lot.

The parking lot, mostly empty when she arrived, was now full of pickups and jeeps, large automobiles, tall ones. That was why she couldn't see her short compact car. All the man-vehicles dwarfed her girl-car. That's why she couldn't see it. She practically ran when she got to the end of the row. Just past the mega Ford 250, her car would be waiting for her, her sweet red car, her home away from home. Literally.

She rounded the bed of the mega Ford 250 and stopped. Her car wasn't there. She blinked. Her eyes must be playing tricks on her, or she was disoriented. Yes, she was disoriented, confused. Her sense of direction sucked. She'd probably parked her car at what she thought was the end of the lot, when in fact, it wasn't. She must have passed it. Her car must be huddled somewhere in the middle. She retraced her steps, at a full run now, back to the beginning of the row. No red Mazda. She ran back to where she was now sure she had parked her car. No red Mazda. An empty space. Gone in sixty minutes. Gone in sixty minutes, an excessive amount of time for a felon in this felon-riddled neighborhood to steal her car.

It was a cosmic bitch slap: Some fucker had stolen her car!

Lucky for her—haha haha—that when she ran back into the bar, near hysterics, babbling incoherently about stolen … bed … home… cancer … car, Zeke took pity on her, told her to sit down, gave her another shot of crappy scotch, and mentioned that the guy at the end of the bar was an off-duty cop. "Dick'll take care of you, honey. Neighborhood's gone to hell in a handbasket lately. Not the first automobile stolen from this lot, rest assured of that. Used to keep a shotgun under the bar, but damn Illinois gun laws took care of that. Pricks in Springfield—no, the pricks in Chicago—think they can overrun the goddamn Second Amendment of the Constitution. Politics in this state are as corrupt as a wolf in a hen house. Bunch of pricks! Sheesh!"

Dick took care of her, writing down a car description, license plate number (which she did not know), and the car's contents (clothing, make-up, computer, money!). At that point, after another shot, courtesy of the magnanimous Zeke, Kat was too numb to cry or think coherently. Could she hitchhike back to Arizona? How many days or weeks would it take her to walk 1541.39 miles?

"Is there any place I can drop you off?" Dick kindly asked after he had written everything down. "You got folks nearby?"

Kat shook her head. "Cosmic bitch slap."

"Beg pardon?"

"Nothing." They were sitting in his squad car, and the kindly Dick looked at Kat expectantly. "Take me to the Amtrak station," she said. "Please."

Kat felt a swaying, rhythmic rocking that slowly brought her to consciousness. *This is nice,* she thought. *Am I in a hammock or on a boat?* The rocking was soothing, comforting. She could stay like this forever, floating in an ill-defined dream that had something to do with water—or was it scotch?

Then brakes screeched, and Kat woke up, banging her head hard against a window. "Where am I?"

"Well, you are not in a hammock or on a boat. You're on the Amtrak, the Illini," a pleasant voice next to her answered.

Kat turned her head sharply and was immediately sorry. "Shit." Her head throbbed, and her mouth tasted like it was full of sour cotton balls. "How did I get here?" She narrowed her eyes at the man sitting next to her. He looked something like Zen. It was Zen. What in the hell was going on?

"Not on your own accord, I can tell you that. You're heavier than you look." Zen's smile crinkled the corners of his green/gold eyes.

"You carried me onto this train?" Kat tried to search for the memory between the throbs in her brain. "Are you *kidnapping* me?"

"Are you *kidding* me?"

"I'm confused." Kat shook her head. Big mistake. "Ouch!"

"You're probably still drunk." Zen uncapped a water bottle he had on the tray next to his computer. "Here." He handed it to her.

Kat gulped down the bottle, still searching for the memory of him carrying her onto the train, searching for *any* memory to explain how she came to be in this seat, next to him. The last thing she remembered was that she had dropped him off at the Amtrak station. No, wait. She had gone to her father's house, and he was in a hospital bed, and then she had gone to a bar and called Granny Nanny …

"Cosmic bitch slap," Zen prompted, taking the empty bottle from her hand. "Stolen car, or as you put it, 'your home away from home had been stolen by some felonious motherfuckers.' Your language gets quite colorful when you drink, Kat Flowers. You could make a sailor blush."

Kat blushed now. "I'm sorry if I said anything to offend you." Things were starting to come back to her now.

"You said quite a few things that offended me. I made a list." He started to reach for his backpack.

"Oh, God!" Kat said, genuinely mortified. He'd seen her shit-faced drunk, she had probably sworn at him, and yet here he was, sitting next to her—after carrying her onto this train.

"Now, I'm kidding."

It didn't make Kat feel any better. What in the world had she said and done when she found him in the station? She knew it would all come back to her sooner or later, and she was not looking forward to the resurfacing. "I'm offering a blanket apology for everything."

"Accepted," he said.

"I was in a state."

"You were in quite a state," he agreed, "before you passed out."

"This story just keeps getting better and better." (At least she was wearing jeans. If she had been wearing a skirt and had passed out, legs sprawled ... Dear God, she was such an idiot.) "You didn't leave me," she said. He certainly could have left her passed out on a bench or on the floor. After all, he didn't know her from Adam. If the tables had been turned, would she have lugged an almost-complete-stranger onto a train?

"Of course I didn't leave you. You were in a state, a state of unconsciousness." He reached into his backpack and pulled out a Subway foot-long. He unwrapped it, and without asking her, gave her half.

So now he was feeding her, too. And she was grateful. She took a huge bite. "Did you buy my ticket?"

He nodded. He could even eat a cold cut combo sandwich loaded with onions, lettuce, tomatoes, green peppers, and black olives neatly. He didn't drop a thing.

Unlike her. She already had enough garnish in her lap to qualify as a salad. "I'll pay you back."

"Yes, you will."

So, he wasn't a perfect Good Samaritan. And where was she going to get the money to pay him back? She'd worry about that later. "Really, I am grateful."

"You would have done the same thing." He wiped his mouth neatly with a napkin.

"I'm not so sure. I don't know you very well—even though you kind of, sort of saved my life a couple of times on the way to Illinois, you know, the choking and the tornado—but I think you're probably a nicer person than I am."

He chewed thoughtfully, nodded. "Probably."

Well, that was settled. Zen was a nice guy, and she was a drunken, foul-mouthed bitch. Complete opposites, no yin and yang, yet here they were together again. "Where are we going?"

"I told you where I was going, Chicago. Now you're going, too. We're stopped at Champagne right now. The next stop is Homewood, then Chicago. We'll take another train to Oak Lawn Park, where my sister will pick us up."

"I don't particularly want to go to Chicago." Did he think she wanted to stay with his parents or something? She was grateful to him for not leaving her passed out in an Amtrak station, sure. As it unfolded in her non-illustrious life so far, being in public transportation stations did not bring out her finest moments. But Chicago? How was she going to get home from there? What if they found her car, and she would have to go all the way back to Carbondale to get it? He was taking her *way* out of her way.

"Did you have a better plan?" he asked.

She hadn't had any plans at all. "No," she admitted. She was already done with her sandwich, and he was barely a third of the way through his. Add that to her list of inadequacies that he was discovering about her: sloppy, piggy eater.

Passengers had disembarked and embarked. The train blew its whistle and started to chug forward. Zen finally finished his sandwich, crumpled the paper, and put it into the plastic bag. Then he said, "I gather it didn't go very well with your dad."

"Father. Marcus. I never called him Dad." She looked out the window into the darkness and felt a sense of loss more profound than she ever had before. She had never had a *Dad*. When she could finally speak, she said, "No, it did not go well at all. He's dying."

"I'm sorry," he said softly.

"Me, too." She was sorry, sorry that she would never really know the man. She should have gone back to his house after the theft of her car. She knew that. She should have told Missy that she would be sleeping on her couch indefinitely. No, she should have demanded that she be allowed to stay. But she had been unable, or unwilling, to make herself do that. Why hadn't Granny Nanny told her that was the right thing to do? Because

Granny Nanny had assumed Kat would know that was the right thing to do. As usual, Kat's ragged epiphanies came too little, too late. As usual, her pride put up roadblocks. Her damn pride.

"What's your next step?" Zen asked after a while.

"I wish I knew." Kat turned her face from the window to look at him. He'd been so nice to her, and why? He barely knew her, yet he was taking her to his home. It had to be one of the nicest things anyone had ever done for her—aside from all that Granny Nanny had done. His generosity, his niceness, made her want to cry. Embarrassingly, she sniffled. "Well, there is something. He gave me my mother's name. Funny, though, she had a different surname—Arnold, instead of Flowers. Maybe she kept her maiden name?"

"Maybe, or maybe your dad—your father—changed his."

Kat sat up straighter. "Why would he do that?"

"You'd be surprised. Working at CPS, we saw it all the time. Sometimes, men changed their names to get out of paying spousal or child support. Sometimes, women changed theirs to escape a domestic violence situation. Sometimes, people just want to get lost, to forget the past, to start over. There is any number of reasons for a person to change his or her name." Zen opened up his laptop.

Could that be the case? Kat wondered. Had her father changed his name? It seemed far-fetched. Her father had led the most boring life of anyone she'd ever known. However, as Zen just said, people could have many reasons for changing their names. "Can we google Melody Arnold?" she asked.

"I'm already on it."

What was one more disappointment in a very long day of disappointments? Still, Kat had let herself believe that when they googled her mother's name—Melody *Arnold*—information would pop up, perhaps the hospital she'd been born in, or her mother's age or occupation. But once again, she stared *nada* in the face. "I don't get it," she said. "Everyone and everything is on the internet these days. Why, I could probably find out exactly when Brad Pitt took his last shit, or what Pamela Anderson's bra size is." Zen looked at her quizzically. "If I were so inclined, that is, which I'm not," she quickly amended. "I don't even read tabloid magazines." Actually, she did.

Kat would purposely get in the grocery store's longest line to give her a chance to flip through the latest edition of *Star* or *In Touch* or the *National Enquirer*. She was also no stranger to People.com. She felt herself blush yet again. Why did this guy always make her blush?

"We're talking decades ago, Kat. Plus, the internet is not infallible."

"Well, it should be," she snapped.

Zen sighed and closed his computer. They had tried every other search word they could come up with—Carbondale, childbirth, Kat's birthday, with no results. "You're cranky when you're hungover."

"Right. I'm foul-mouthed when I'm drunk and cranky when I'm hungover. That's me, Katrina Flowers, or Katrina *Arnold*, in a nutshell." She was so tired and disappointed and frustrated that she wanted to curl up into a ball and cry for a week. But the train was pulling into Union Station, and she had somehow, for some reason, ended this terrible road trip without a car, in a strange city, with very little money, and with an almost-complete-stranger. She didn't even have a toothbrush, and she was getting more than a little weary of cosmic bitch slaps.

"Home sweet home," Zen said, gathering his backpack and his duffel bag. "One more train, and we're there."

Kat had no choice but to pick up her purse and follow him, dazed, through Union Station, then out the door for a freezing ten-minute walk to Millennium Park Station, and onto the next train. Zen's sister, Lorraine, was waiting when they arrived.

She threw her arms around her brother. "I'm so glad you're home! You stayed away too long this time, you stinker. You didn't even make it home for Christmas!" She hugged him tighter, a shorter version of her brother, with his same sandy hair.

"Yeah, but I got the fruitcake." Zen returned her hug with equal enthusiasm.

"Well, okay, then. You were still participating in the Delaney tradition." She finally broke the hug. She turned to Kat. "Mom's fruitcake is horrible, but none of us have the heart to tell her. Every year, she bakes dozens of the damn things, and we act like they're delicious. I always take mine home and stick it in the freezer. I throw it away when I think that a decent enough amount of time has passed." She stuck out her hand. "I'm Lorraine."

Kat shook her hand. "Kat," she said, managing a tired smile. It was after two in the morning, and this woman brimmed with energy. Kat decided she was perky, and even though she was not a huge fan of perky people, something was appealing about Zen's sister. "Thanks for picking us up this late."

"Oh, no problem. I'm a night owl, and when you've got two little ones, you get used to getting by on little sleep." She looked Kat up and down. "So what brings you to Chicago, besides my brother, that is." She gave Zen's ribs an affectionate jab with her elbow. "Business or pleasure?" she asked slyly.

"More like a lack of options," Kat said, realizing that Lorraine assumed that she was Zen's girlfriend. Usually, she would have quickly set this woman straight, but she could barely keep her eyes open.

"I'll explain everything in the morning, Rainey, but right now, we need some sleep." Zen took her elbow, steering her to the lone car in the parking lot.

"Oh, yes. Of course! You two have got to be dead tired, and I'm just yapping away. It's so good to see you, Zen!" She practically skipped beside her brother.

Again, Kat had no choice but to follow. In her tired, hungover, disoriented state, she barely noticed her surroundings. The only thought that semi-crystallized was: *She has a car. I am so jealous. What felon is driving my car?*

"How's Pops?" Zen asked.

"He's better, Zen. He's much better. His doctor says he needs to change his diet—no red meat and cut down on his sodium intake—and exercise more, but he should make a complete recovery."

"That's good news," Zen said.

"It sure is." Lorraine started the car. "Both the folks wanted to wait up and see you, but I insisted that they go to bed. 'There'll be plenty of time to see Zen in the morning,' I said to them. I told them I'd get you settled."

Once at the two-story brick house, Lorraine led them upstairs, and Zen went to his childhood bedroom at the end of the hall with only a tired nod toward Kat's general vicinity. (*Right back at you, buddy,* she thought. *So even superheroes needed sleep.*) Kat's room was Lorraine's childhood room. Its single bed had a pink-ruffled bedspread, a white desk stood under the one window, and the walls were still adorned with Lorraine's old cheerleading and prom pictures. It just figured that Lorraine had been a cheerleader.

"Mom and Pops don't like to change much around here," Lorraine whispered.

"It's very nice," Kat politely whispered back. She could afford to be polite. She could be excruciatingly lovely because she'd just realized she was coming to the end of a very long bad dream. When she awoke, she would be back at Granny Nanny's, and she would have her job at Tilted Kilt. No, wait a minute. Maybe that had been a bad dream, too?

"The bathroom's next door," Lorraine whispered. "Please, make yourself at home."

"Muchas gracias," Kat whispered.

In the dim light from the ballerina night light plugged into the wall socket, Lorraine looked puzzled. "We're Irish," she whispered.

What in the hell was she talking about? "I'm very happy for you." Kat smiled, demonstrating her happiness. She was thrilled. There was a bed only a foot away.

"I'll see you tomorrow." Lorraine quietly shut the door.

Kat fell face first, fully clothed, onto the pink-ruffled bedspread, and slept.

10

SEPTEMBER-OCTOBER 2, 1980

The next week, Melody did not go to her scheduled doctor's appointment. In fact, on the morning of the appointment, she refused to get out of bed at all. Marcus was not happy with her. He had rearranged his schedule, he said, to go with her. (Marcus worked from nine to five every day, and Melody wondered what it was that he had to *rearrange*.) "I don't feel well," she said to him. She managed a barely convincing sniffle.

"All the more reason to go. I even hired Belinda to come and take care of Mother. She's already downstairs."

That, at least, gave Melody a small measure of satisfaction. Marcus wasn't exactly cheap—and he was capable of splurging on occasion, like with the pearls—but he was very conscious of every dime spent. He would probably say he was *careful* with money; Melody would say he was *controlling*. Shortly after they were married—long, long weeks before—Melody came home with her first paycheck, excited. Finally, she'd made some money of her own, and the first thing she would do was go to the bank and open her own personal checking account. The endless possibilities of what she could do with the money were thrilling. She could go to a proper stylist (not Mrs. Chesky, who lived next door to Ma on Roosevelt and ran a beauty parlor out of her basement) and get her hair done. She could go to Marshall Field's and buy something without first checking the price tag. She would, after all the years of scrimping, have some freedom.

Marcus didn't see it that way. When Melody came in, giddily waving the check on that Friday afternoon, he'd looked at the amount and said, "This is wonderful, Melody. It will help with household expenses. I'm very proud of you. I'll deposit it with my check the next time I go to the bank."

"But," she said, feeling as if he'd just pulled out the rug from under her happiness, "I thought I'd open up my own personal account."

"Why would you need to do that?" He had already taken the check from her hand, folded it, and put it in his pocket.

"Because ..." She was at a loss to explain: *Because I earned it, and it's mine?*

"Do you have any idea what it costs to run this household, honey?" Marcus filled the tea kettle with water from the tap. At this early stage in the marriage, his tea-drinking habit was already driving Melody up the wall. Why couldn't he drink coffee like a real man?

She didn't, of course, have any idea how much money it cost to run this household, *his* household. She had only lived in this damn house for a week. "I can help with the expenses, Marcus, if you just tell me—"

"Mother's medications each month alone are astronomical," he continued.

"But," she stammered. Surely, Marcus didn't think she needed to contribute to his mother's expenses?

"It's very complicated, kitten. I have an organized ledger, and you don't need to worry about a thing. I can take care of everything." He smiled at her affectionately.

"I could certainly learn if you'd teach me." She didn't particularly want to learn Marcus' anal accounting system, but she did want him to stop looking at her and talking at her like she was a somewhat backward child.

"No need for that. We're married, and I will take care of you. I'll give you plenty of money when you need to buy groceries or something for the house."

He was making her money mundane; he was blending it in with his. Still, he possibly had a point. Wanting to have access to her own money was probably being selfish on her part. Hadn't Daddy always handed over a small allowance to Ma every Friday? Yet Melody still felt uneasy with this arrangement. Finally, she said, "What about when I want to buy a new dress?"

He smiled again at her affectionately, indulgently. "Of course, honey. You can have money anytime you want. All you have to do is ask."

So far, she hadn't asked.

Now, as he stood at the foot of the bed, waiting to go to the doctor with her, he said, "Mellie, I've really looked forward to this. I want to hear our child's heartbeat."

So do I, she wanted to say. *So do I.* And Marcus looked so earnest standing there that she felt pity for him for the first time. "I'm sorry, Marcus, but I can't in good conscience go to a doctor's office when I might be contagious with a cold or the flu. I could infect so many people who might already be sick with something else. You understand, don't you?"

He looked unconvinced. "Mellie—"

"You're going to have to trust me on this one, Marcus, okay? I'm the health professional here, and I know what's best." He looked so forlorn that she wanted to cry. "Okay … honey?" She had never called him an endearment before, and it seemed to cheer him up.

"Okay, *honey.*" He came over to her side of the bed and kissed her on the top of her head. "You'll call and reschedule right away, though, right? I want to hear our child's heartbeat."

She nodded and held her breath until he left the room. Then she let the tears fall. She hadn't felt the baby move in twelve days, and she should go to the doctor. Melody knew that; she did. But she couldn't. She couldn't because she was terrified that he would tell her that something was wrong with her baby, her child, whom she'd fallen in love with when she felt him move the first time.

Something was wrong with her baby.

No! Something was not wrong with her baby.

She had been working too hard, she was overly tired, and she was adjusting to being married and moving into a new house with a new husband and his demented mother. One of those factors alone would make anyone anxious. Still, when you put them all together… Well, that could make a person's nervous system, constitution, and physical stamina entirely out of whack. The baby kicked all the time, and Melody was simply not paying enough attention.

Something was wrong with her baby.

No!

She needed to get out of this house and get her mind off the baby. Wallowing in bed would only make matters worse. Never mind that she'd told Marcus she was ill. He wouldn't be back for hours. She would take the train into the city and visit Sylvia, who she knew wasn't working today either. Quickly, she got dressed and went downstairs, telling Belinda that she'd changed her mind and decided to go to her doctor's appointment after all, even though she knew she shouldn't, even though she was ill.

She gave Belinda another one of her unconvincing sniffles and added a cough for good measure.

The doorman at Sylvia's building let her in, and Melody rode the elevator up to the eleventh floor, thinking, as she had on the few occasions she'd visited Sylvia in this beautiful, newly refurbished apartment building: *This could have been mine.* She didn't want to think that thought, but it came unbidden, and once again, it managed to bring tears to her eyes. As she stepped out of the elevator on Sylvia's floor, she shook her head and squared her shoulders. It wasn't right to be jealous of her best friend. She'd made her decision to marry Marcus and have this child, and that was that. Period. There was no backing down or second-guessing. She would make the best of the situation, and once the baby was born, everything would be different. She would have a family, and she would learn to love her husband, the father of her child. She would, damn it, she *would*.

Sylvia did not come to the door for quite a while, and just when Melody was about to turn away, feeling utterly disappointed and close to tears again, Sylvia opened the door. She wore a blue terrycloth robe, and her platinum hair was disheveled. The remnants of the previous night's mascara ringed her eyes.

"I should have called," Melody quickly apologized. She knew that Sylvia had been having a rough time since Thelma's death, yet Melody had been so wrapped up in her own problems that she hadn't stopped to consider that Sylvia might have chosen today to do some wallowing of her own. "I could come back another time, Syl," she said, although in her head she was begging, *Please let me come in.*

"No, no," Sylvia said, opening the door wider. "I'm glad you're here. Come in."

Sylvia's usually neat apartment looked like a disaster area. The couch was overturned, empty beer and vodka bottles littered the coffee table, and clothing—a man's—was strewn over another chair and the floor leading to the closed bedroom door. Just then, the door opened, and a man stepped out, wearing nothing but a hangover. He looked at them with bleary, bloodshot eyes. "Morning," he mumbled.

"Get your clothes and get out," Sylvia said brusquely. To Melody, she said, "Let's go into the kitchen and make some coffee."

Once they were in the small galley kitchen, Melody said again, "I should have called, Syl. I didn't know you had company."

"He isn't company," Sylvia said flatly, banging the kettle onto the stove. "Instant all right?"

In the kind of mood Sylvia was in, Melody didn't dare ask if it was decaf. "Sure." Maybe this was the mysterious boyfriend Sylvia had been so crazy about a few weeks ago? Maybe they had a huge argument the night before? Something was definitely out of kilter here, and Melody had a feeling that she was intruding, that there was something she wasn't supposed to know about. That was absurd, though. Didn't Sylvia tell her everything?

The front door slammed just as the kettle started to scream. "Thank God, he's gone." Sylvia poured the boiling water into two mugs and added instant coffee. "What a scumbag."

"Big penis." Melody instantly wished she hadn't verbalized that thought. However, the man had been standing before her stark naked, and she couldn't help but notice. At least compared to Marcus' penis, he had been huge, although she tried very hard not to look at Marcus' penis.

"Trust me. That's his only attribute."

Melody followed Sylvia back into the messy living room, and together they righted the toppled couch. So many questions swirled around in Melody's brain, and she settled on the one she thought was the least innocuous. "Is that your boyfriend?"

"God, no." Sylvia settled back into the couch and closed her eyes.

Melody waited. She didn't want to pry, but she was burning with curiosity. The man's hair had been shaggy and greasy, and he'd been scrawny, except for his one attribute. What had Sylvia been doing with that kind of man? Admittedly, they'd made some dubious choices during their research phase, but Melody was pretty sure they hadn't stooped that low.

"That was one of Thelma's dealers," Sylvia finally said, her eyes still closed.

"What? Why?" That would be the last person that Melody would expect Sylvia to be associating with.

"I don't know." Again, Sylvia's voice was flat. "I haven't been myself since Thelma passed."

"That's understandable," Melody soothed, even though she still didn't understand.

Sylvia opened her eyes and looked at Melody. "I tell myself that I'm trying to find some closure, trying to make sense out of what happened to poor, helpless Thelma. I thought I could track them down and tell them what they'd done to her. I thought I could make them see that they were ruining people's lives."

"Why don't you call the cops? I mean, if you know their names?"

"Call the cops? Are you kidding me?" Sylvia reached for her now cold instant coffee. "You didn't want to call the cops when you lost a demented old lady. You think I should call the cops and rat on drug dealers who, quite possibly, are connected to the mob? I value my life too much to be put on some mobster's hit list. I'd have to leave Chicago—and I *love* this town—and leave my job and move to some godforsaken place. I have an aunt who lives in Arizona. Do you think I should tell the cops and then hightail it out to the desert?"

Melody, taken aback by the ferocity in Sylvia's voice, also felt hurt. She was only trying to help her friend, who was obviously in pain, but now Sylvia was sleeping with drug dealers who had helped destroy her mother's life? It made no sense. It also made no sense that Sylvia was mad at *her* for making a simple suggestion. Melody got up to leave. "I was only trying to help," she said stiffly.

Sylvia grabbed her hand and pulled her back down to the couch. "I know, I know. I'm sorry, Mel. I have been a complete mess since Thelma died, and I have no idea why I'm doing the things I'm doing. I start out with the best of intentions, but then I end up getting high with them, and sleeping with them, and then hating myself in the morning. This was the third dealer. You need to stop me, Mel. You need to stop me before I'm hopelessly out of control." Sylvia put her face in her hands and sobbed.

Melody moved next to her and took large-boned Sylvia in her arms, knowing even as she did so that it was small solace for her dear friend. What would she do if she lost Ma? She couldn't even bear to think about it, and here her best friend was agonizing over the loss of her mother to a senseless drug overdose. Sylvia had been acting out her grief in a senseless, terrible way. But wasn't that the nature of grief, that it did, in fact, make people do senseless, terrible things?

"I'm here for you." Melody patted Sylvia's back. "I'm here for you."

"I know." Sylvia straightened up and wiped her eyes on the sleeve of her robe. "I love you, Mel."

"I love you, too, Syl."

"I'm going to pull myself together, and I'm going to get through this."

"We'll get through this together."

"We'll get through this," Sylvia repeated. She reached for a vodka bottle on the table and saw that it had a shot or two remaining on the bottom. She slugged it down and lifted another bottle. "Just not today."

Three days later, Marcus said, "I'm taking you to lunch."

That surprised Melody. She hadn't really thought about it before, but in the months of their marriage, they had not once gone out to a restaurant. In fact, the last time they'd gone to a restaurant had been the night they went to Carmine's, and she drank too much wine and then climbed on top of him in his immaculate Buick.

"What about work?" she asked. She was scheduled for the night shift, but Marcus was supposed to leave for work at that very moment.

"I'm taking a personal day."

This, too, was surprising. Marcus had already missed a precious hour out of his workday when they were supposed to go to her doctor's appointment. However, he seemed excited about something, and Marcus was not a man to get overly excited about anything. "What are we celebrating?" She tried, but she couldn't quite get the suspicious tone out of her voice.

"Do we need a reason? I'm taking my beautiful wife out for a nice lunch, and that's that."

That's that, she thought. Marcus said it was so, and it was so. She managed a smile. "That'll be nice." Maybe it would be. Maybe they would talk about something other than what needed to be done to the house, or Evelyn, or what she should make for his dinner. Maybe they would finally get to know each other a little bit better.

In the Buick an hour later, Marcus was still in his happy mood, which made Melody—irrationally, she knew—uneasy. "Where are you taking me?"

"It's a surprise." Marcus actually hummed.

"It doesn't have to be anything fancy," she said.

"My wife deserves the best." He reached over and patted her hand. "But we need to make a quick stop first."

She'd been right to be suspicious and uneasy of Marcus. They were driving north on Moreland Avenue, and Melody noticed how the leaves were starting to change color to gold and fiery orange. She almost remarked to Marcus about how she was glad that fall was here, but he made a sudden sharp right turn into her doctor's office parking lot. "What are you doing?" Melody cried, and immediately, panic washed over her, seizing her heart, making her break out in a cold sweat. She did not want to go in there. He could not make her go in there.

"Surprise!" he said. "I called and made an appointment with Dr. Crowley, and it's a good thing I did, too. You naughty girl, the receptionist said you hadn't called to reschedule, but luckily, she squeezed us in. We're going to hear our baby's heartbeat!"

"Marcus, no," she whispered.

"What's the matter, Mellie? This is a momentous occasion, and you look like you've seen a ghost."

"I'm feeling a little light-headed." That, at least, was true. "I think I need to eat something. That's it. I need to eat something." She would make him take her to a restaurant, and she would have time to think of some excuse as to why she couldn't see the doctor today.

"Come on, Mellie." Impatience crept into his voice like a snake. "We're already here, and the doctor is expecting us."

She could not go in there.

"Mellie." The impatience had notched up his voice. "I am thirty-four years old, I have married a beautiful woman, and I am about to become a father for the first time. I want to hear the baby's heartbeat, and perhaps, if we're lucky, they can do an ultrasound, and we can see our baby. Let's go in now."

She could not go in there. If she went in, she would know for a certainty that something was wrong with her baby. "Marcus," she began.

Marcus had had enough. He was out of the car and around to her side and opening the door. He took both of her hands and pulled her out of the car. Her knees buckled, but he caught her. "I've got you," he said. As he propelled her towards the office door, he added, "There is nothing to be nervous about, Mellie. Everything is going to be fine. This will be one of the most wonderful days of our life so far, with many more to come. I promise you."

They didn't have to wait; they were expected. Melody was whisked into an examining room and given a gown to put on, and then a nurse came in and checked her vital signs. "Everything looks good," she said. "How have you been feeling since your last appointment?"

Melody's voice choked. "Fine. I feel fine." How would she ever explain to this nurse, to the doctor, and to Marcus—especially Marcus—that she had ignored her suspicions. She had hoped she'd been mistaken, and even though she was a nurse, she had ignored the obvious. Could she say to them: *I hoped I was wrong? I hoped the baby was still alive? I hoped for a miracle?*

Dr. Crowley, a kindly man in his late sixties (who had delivered thousands of babies, he told Melody), came into the room then, followed closely by Marcus. "We are well on our way," he greeted Melody, "over halfway through the pregnancy, and we have a very excited father here who is going to hear his baby's heartbeat for the first time!" He washed his hands at the sink and then approached Melody on the hospital bed. "Any changes from the last time I saw you?"

Melody shook her head, mute. She had lost all ability to speak. She wished she'd bolted from the car as soon as Marcus had opened the door. But where would she have gone? Where did a person go when she was running away from the inevitable? She slowly leaned back until she reclined on the bed, prone and still.

"Are you ready?" Dr. Crowley disentangled the stethoscope from around his neck.

"Yes, sir!" Marcus hurried to the other side of the hospital bed and took Melody's hand.

The kindly doctor placed the earpieces in his ears and the cool, silver disk on Melody's belly. He listened. He moved the disk to a different position. He listened, moved the disk again. He listened, moved the disk again. "Hmm," he said.

"May I listen?" Marcus asked.

Melody lay still, listening to her own heartbeat. It was steady, regular, and if she concentrated hard enough, she might be able to block out everything that was going on around her, everything that was going on inside her womb.

"Hmm," the doctor said again. To the nurse, he said, "Let's get the patient into the sonogram room."

"Is everything all right?" Marcus asked, anxious.

"Nothing to get alarmed about." Dr. Crowley patted Marcus' arm. "Why don't you go to the waiting room and have a cup of coffee?"

"I don't drink coffee. What's going on? Melody," he pleaded, "what's going on?"

"I don't know," Melody lied, suddenly very, very tired. She was numb with fatigue. (Later, she would realize what a blessing that numbness had been. Yes, later, she would know it had been a gift, however temporary.)

When Marcus began to hyperventilate, the nurse quickly led him out of the room. Dr. Crowley turned to Melody. "Have you been feeling the baby move?"

"Not for the last day or two." Another lie. It had been fifteen days since she'd felt her baby move. Fifteen days—two weeks and one day.

She was wheeled to the imaging room down the hall, and the ultrasound told the story. The umbilical cord was wrapped around her baby's neck. Her baby had been strangled by the very cord that connected mother and child, the baby's lifeline for oxygen and nutrients. Her lifeline to the baby, her baby's lifeline to her. Symbiotic. Tit for tat. Mother Nature at her finest.

Melody had not been up to par.

"There is no way to predict when stillbirths will happen," Dr. Crowley consoled. "Unfortunately, it can happen to anyone. I'm sorry, Melody."

"Thank you," she said. Thank you? That wasn't the right thing to say, was it? Her mind was an anesthetized fog rolling, roiling in. A doctor told a mother he was sorry that her baby had died, and she responded with *thank you*. That could not possibly be right.

"There could have been possible birth defects," Dr. Crowley said from somewhere far, far away.

"Thank you." *Thank you for telling me that my baby was not perfect? What the hell do you know? My baby was a genius. My baby kicked at precisely sixteen weeks.*

It was Melody—*the mother*—who had failed the baby.

"We'll have to induce labor …"

Marcus was too distraught to drive, so they took an ambulance to the hospital, not to Mercy, but to St. Matthew. Melody couldn't have stood going to Mercy, where she was known, where they would pity her for her inability to keep a baby alive. She was a nurse, damn it, a *nurse*.

Marcus was in the expectant fathers' waiting room while she endured eight hours of labor, all the while knowing that it was a lost cause, that her baby would be *stillborn*. Still born. Still born. *Still born*. No, it was better to endure the labor alone, without the weeping Marcus by her side, without the constant chant he'd taken up since he found out: why, why, why?

She gave birth to their dead son at 8:08 that night. She did not look at him or hold him.

She had failed him.

She had not been up to par.

11

APRIL 2012

There was no clock in the room, and her cell phone was dead, so Kat had no idea what time it was when she awoke. However, that wasn't as alarming as the panic that gripped her when she sat up. Where was she, and who was that perky, smiling girl staring down at her from the collage of pictures on the wall? The memory of the previous day seeped slowly back.

"Oh, shit," Kat groaned. It had not been a bad dream.

She was never going to drink scotch again.

If she hadn't stopped at Zeke's Tavern, her car wouldn't have been stolen. If she hadn't taken this road trip, she would know exactly what she had known before. Nothing. But hadn't she been happy? Wasn't ignorance bliss?

Kat knew the answer to both of those questions: not really. She'd felt that something crucial was missing all her life, and she was right about that. She was almost positive that she was right. Not knowing anything about her family history was wrong on all levels. She had been an orphan, even though she had a father. Now her father was dying.

And she would indeed be an orphan, a thirty-year-old orphan who lived with her adopted gran. And who didn't have a job. How pathetic. So what was she doing here, in a strange house, in a strange city, surrounded by strangers? Her mission to find out about her past had been a complete bust. She would have to admit that, and then she would have to move forward. No looking back, and no regretting past mistakes. Her new mission would be one of self-improvement. She would reinvent herself. She would go back to Arizona and find a decent job; no, she would find a *career.* Maybe Zen had the right idea, and she, too, should go back to school. Surely, there was something in the land of employment that she would be good at, that she would enjoy and find worthwhile. Surely?

But first, she needed to get some money to get back home. (Forget about selling blood or her fertile eggs. Maybe she could sell a kidney? As far as she knew, a person only needed one.) She already owed Zen money for two train tickets and half of a Subway sandwich, which would deplete what little cash she had in her purse. Her money, like her options, dwindled before her eyes. She sincerely hated the idea, but she would have to call Granny Nanny and ask her to wire money for a plane ticket. No, too expensive. She would ask for just enough money for a bus ticket.

She would be right back where she started fourteen years before. How pathetic.

There was absolutely no point in lying in bed, fretting, trying to prolong the start of this day. She got out of bed and made her way to the bathroom. She gasped when she looked in the mirror. "You look like shit," she said to her reflection. She had dark circles under her eyes, and her right cheek had a big red blotch from sleeping so hard. Her long reddish blonde hair—her best feature—was stringy and tangled. She looked more closely. Yep, the icing on the cake. She had crumbs in her hair. Little pieces of bread had probably flown out of her mouth when she gobbled down the sandwich. It was something to add to the self-improvement list—better table manners. "Well, I don't have to worry about Zen finding me attractive," she said to her ghastly reflection. "Not that I want him to find me attractive," she added.

Someone knocked on the bathroom door. "Kat?" It was Zen.

She didn't want him to see her looking like this. Frantically, she clawed at her hair and splashed water on her face. "Just a minute."

"Mom thought you might need a few things to freshen up," he said through the closed door. "I've already filled them in on your situation, you know, the stolen car, your stuff and most of your money gone."

Who was *them*? "Oh, okay." She might as well open the door, just a crack, and see what he was offering. After all, she had nothing, no toothbrush, makeup, or toiletries.

He held a small pile of clothes, and on top—God bless his soul—was a new toothbrush wrapped in plastic and a tube of toothpaste. She had never been so excited to see a toothbrush. "Thank you!"

"No problem. This is some of Lorraine's stuff if you're interested." He smiled.

It just figured that he would look fresh as a daisy (as Granny Nanny would say). "I'm very interested," she said, taking the pile. "Thanks." Not only did this man continually make her blush, but he also made it so that she was always thanking him.

"See you downstairs," he said.

The hot, hot shower made Kat feel much better, and brushing her teeth ... Well, that was pure heaven. She put on one of Lorraine's t-shirts and a pair of white cotton underwear—definitely not her usual style, but beggars could not be choosers (as Granny Nanny would say). She combed her long hair up into a ponytail, and the reflection in the mirror no longer looked like a zombie from *Night of the Living Dead*. In fact, Kat felt quite human. She went downstairs.

Apparently, *them* was Zen's entire family: Mom, Pops, Lorraine and her two little girls, and his older brother, Phillip. They were gathered around the dining room table, drinking coffee and juice. Breakfast, it would seem, was long a thing of the past. They all looked at her with friendly, expectant faces, and Kat had the distinct impression that she'd been the topic of conversation. Well, why not? Zen had dragged home a soon-to-be-orphaned, thirty-year-old woman with whom he had traveled across the country, and then that woman had her car stolen while she was drinking shots of scotch in a dubious tavern. Kat had to admit that it made for a rather interesting story. She just wished that it wasn't *hers*.

"Hello," she said. "I'm Kat Flowers." (Or was she Kat Arnold?) Her stomach, at that precise moment, decided to rumble loudly. Of course. "Oh!" She blushed, embarrassed.

"I do believe the girl is hungry, Mother," Tanner Delaney said. It was clear that Zen had gotten his warm smile from his father. Although still in a bathrobe, he looked surprisingly robust for a sixty-something man who had recently suffered a heart attack.

"That sounded just like Tony the Tiger," Megan, Lorraine's three-year-old, said.

To Kat's further mortification, everyone laughed. However, they didn't seem to be laughing *at* her. She managed a smile. "Excuse me."

"Let me get you some blueberry pancakes," Zen's mom said. She was a short woman with streaks of grey in her auburn hair. Like her husband, she must have been in her mid-sixties, but her face was practically wrinkle-free.

"I don't want you to go to any trouble," Kat said, even though blueberry pancakes sounded heavenly. Her stomach growled again. Damn it.

"No trouble at all, sweetheart. There's still plenty of batter left. I can whip you up a stack in a jiffy. You just missed the rest of the clan," she said as she arose. "Benny, Lorraine's husband, had to go to work—he's on seconds at the plastics plant—and Janet, Phillip's wife, had to take their three boys to soccer practice. They all wanted to meet you, too."

Why? Kat wondered. "I'm sorry I slept so late," she said. She still had no idea what time it was, and being in this cozy house with these friendly strangers only added more to her sense of unreality.

"Have a seat." Zen pulled out a chair next to him. "Another family tradition, Saturday morning brunch."

"Like the fruitcake," Kat said as she sat down. She doubted very much that this brunch included champagne, and she could use a glass right about now.

"Jesus, that damn fruitcake," Pops said. "Someone should tell your mother that her fruitcake needs a lot more rum. A *lot* more rum."

They all nodded, smiling, and Kat knew, without being told, that no one in this family would ever tell her that. What's more, they would probably vehemently defend the rum-lacking fruitcake to anyone outside the family who dared to criticize their mother's infamous Christmas offering.

"Where are you from?" Phillip asked. He was taller than Zen, with the same sandy hair that ran in the family, but Phillip's hairline receded slightly.

"Arizona now, but Carbondale originally." Zen poured her a cup of coffee, and Kat gave him yet another grateful smile. When was he going to stop being so nice to her? His *niceness* was starting to get on her nerves. She wasn't used to it.

"It's funny," Lorraine said, hoisting Megan and the other daughter, Tammy, onto her lap. "I've lived in Illinois my whole life, but I've never driven farther south than Springfield."

"Well, I lived in Carbondale until I was fourteen, and I never visited Chicago." Kat hadn't thought the fact was particularly odd until just now. Then she remembered another long-forgotten detail. Her eighth-grade class had taken a year-end field trip to Chicago to visit the downtown museums, and she had desperately wanted to go. Everyone in the class was excited by the trip, not so much for the cultural enrichment, but because they would stay overnight in the Sheraton by the Chicago River. Water balloon fights and forbidden hook-ups danced in everyone's mind. Before Bobby Baker, Kat had a mad crush on Peter Wentzel, and she'd vowed to her girlfriends that she was going to make out with him on the trip. However, Marcus had refused to let her go. He'd said Chicago was too dangerous, that it was a filthy town. She cried and pleaded with him, but he wouldn't budge. She had tearfully—then angrily—pointed out that she would be the *only one* in the *entire class* who didn't get to go on that special trip. "So be it," he'd said. "You are not allowed to go to that city. Period."

"Here you go." Zen's mom set down a large stack of blueberry pancakes in front of Kat. "Enjoy."

Kat reminded herself to watch her table manners. Use some self-control. On her new mission of self-improvement, she would have a long way to go in that department. She picked up her fork and looked around the table. They all stared at her with their friendly, expectant faces. Were they going to watch her as she ate? "These look delicious." She cleared her throat uneasily.

"So, what's new in the neighborhood?" Zen asked.

Once again, she had to be fucking grateful to him. His family was immediately off and running with tales of who was getting divorced, who had lost their jobs, and who was currently hitting the bottle too hard. Lorraine's little girls went into the den to watch cartoons, and the conversation segued into the weather, then the family's shared history. As the stories turned to this topic, Kat's ears perked up. Evidently, the Good Samaritan, superhero Zen had not been an angel.

"Remember that time you broke Joey Bosco's nose with a baseball bat?" Phillip asked.

"It was an accident," Zen said. "I told him not to stand behind home plate when I was batting, but he did it anyway."

"What about the time you set off the fire alarm at school? Everyone ran out into the freezing rain and had to stand there for hours while the firemen searched the place. You were grounded for a month after that prank." Lorraine laughed.

"I had an English test that afternoon, and I hadn't read the book." After the fifth or sixth story of his pranks, Zen was blushing and getting a little defensive.

"Lordy, Lordy, you went through a wild spell," Zen's mom said.

"A spell?" Phillip said. "Zen went through a wild streak."

"Boys will be boys," Pops said fondly.

Kat had finished carefully eating and was thoroughly enjoying the conversation. It was an enormous relief to find out that Zen Delaney was not perfect. She wished they would graduate from the childhood pranks to juicier stuff.

"Jeanie Graciano said to tell you hi," Lorraine smirked. "I ran into her in Jewel. She was buying condoms naturally."

"Who's Jeanie Graciano?" Kat asked. Zen's face was bright red, and if she had her phone charged, Kat would take his picture. She knew the photo of Zen's embarrassment would cheer her up in her new regimen of self-improvement. It would be a constant reminder that even seemingly perfect people were not perfect.

"No one," Zen muttered.

"She was an old flame of Zen's," Lorraine said, still smirking.

"Jeanie Graciano was an old flame of every guy in this neighborhood," Phillip added with a snort.

"I want details," Kat said.

"I think it's time to change the subject." Zen pushed back his chair. "The kid brother has taken enough Saturday brunch abuse."

"I'm calling a truce," Pops said. "Okay, everyone?"

Lorraine and Phillip reluctantly agreed.

Kat was sorry to see the ribbing end, especially when it became immediately apparent that the next subject of brunch conversation would be her. (Since they weren't serving champagne, perhaps she could ask for a beer, or would that make her look like a lush?)

"So, you were in Carbondale visiting family?" Zen's mom asked.

"Um, yes." Kat shifted uncomfortably in her chair. All eyes at the table were again on her.

"That's nice, dear. Families are so important. Do you have any brothers or sisters?"

"No, I mean, sort of."

Zen's mom cocked her head. "Sort of?"

"Two half-brothers." She really didn't want to explain anything to this woman, but then again, Zen's mom had allowed her to spend the night in her home and then fed Kat blueberry pancakes. She owed her *something*.

"Oh," Zen's mom said knowingly. "Divorce."

"No, not a divorce." Kat automatically looked to Zen for help, but he wasn't offering any. He had his arms folded over his chest, and his chair tipped back. Obviously, it was her turn.

"Priscilla, you don't need to grill our guest," Pops said.

"I'm not grilling. I'm just interested. Families are very important." Priscilla was absolute on that point.

Quickly, Kat said, "It wasn't a divorce. My mother died in childbirth."

"Oh, that is so sad!" Lorraine said. "I had such a hard time getting pregnant—three miscarriages—before I had the girls. I can't imagine not being around to see them grow up."

Kat opened her mouth, but no words formed. What should she say to that? Something along the lines of, *You're damn right that it's sad. It sucked. It wasn't fair. I was screwed from birth.*

"I'm sorry, Kat. We are prying. Please forgive us," Priscilla said.

"Maybe we could call the Carbondale police and see if they've found your car," Phillip suggested, trying to change the subject.

But then Kat could not stop the words, the dreadful words, from pouring out. "I never even knew my mother's name. My father never told me anything about her. I ran away at sixteen, and for fourteen years, I had minimal communication with him until my birthday last month. I got a card. He only signed his name, but my stepmother wrote on the back that he had undergone some tests. So I decided to drive across the country to see him and finally have him answer all my questions. I wrote a list, twenty-two questions, but when I got there, I found out he was dying of colon cancer." She hadn't realized tears had fallen until her words dwindled, and she was sitting there with wet cheeks and her napkin bunched in her hand.

"Kat," Zen said softly, putting a hand on her arm. His family looked stricken.

"But he finally told me my mother's name. At least I now know that."

Priscilla's motherly instinct took over, and she came around the table and placed her hands upon Kat's shoulders. "I'm sorry, Kat. We're all so sorry."

"Her name was Melody Arnold," Kat sobbed. "At least I know that."

"Melody Arnold?" Pops said. The color drained from his face. "You're Melody Arnold's *daughter*? Jesus, Mary, and Joseph!"

"What's wrong, Pops?" Zen asked, alarmed.

"I'm going to call the ambulance." Lorraine knocked over her chair as she stood up. "Is he having another heart attack?" Her eyes darted around the table. "Is he?" she said to no one in particular.

"I'll drive him myself to the emergency room," Phillip said. "With everyone's help, we can carry him to the car. It'll be faster than an ambulance."

"Dear Lord." Priscilla rushed to her husband's side. She fiddled with his top pajama button, trying to loosen it. "Can you breathe?"

"Enough, woman!" he bellowed, clearly able to breathe. "Enough, all of you! I am not having a heart attack. I'm just knocked for a loop. That's all. Just knocked for a loop. I never thought I'd live to see this day. Melody Arnold's daughter. I'll be damned." He stared at Kat like he was seeing a ghost.

"Did you know my mother?" Kat's tears had stopped in all the commotion she'd caused by only mentioning her mother's name. It was unsettling and confusing. How could this man, a former EMT in Oak Lawn Park, know her mother? She had always thought—or just assumed, without any hints or disavowals from her father—that her mother lived in Carbondale, 332 miles south. Tanner Delaney must have her mother confused with someone else. He'd recently suffered a heart attack, and maybe his medication had jumbled his memory. That had to be it.

"No, I didn't know your mother." His family and Kat looked intently at him, relieved that he didn't have a heart attack but mystified at his reaction to the woman's name.

It was just as Kat had thought, yet she felt disappointed. She knew it was silly of her. There was no way this man could have known her mother.

"I need to have a private conversation with our guest," Tanner Delaney said slowly. "I know that privacy is a rare thing in this house, but that's how it's going to be. Priscilla, will you bring me my scrapbook, the red one?"

"The red one," his three adult children whispered. They looked at each other and filed out of the room silently, but Zen did look back briefly, his eyes full of sympathy.

Kat had no idea what was going on, but it did not bode well. She felt a chill and shivered. Suddenly, she wanted to leave the room. Suddenly, she wanted to run from this house and these people. The way she felt right then, she believed she could run the entire way back to Arizona and the comfort of Granny Nanny without stopping to eat or drink. Without breathing. Without thinking.

Priscilla brought in the red scrapbook and placed it on the table, leaving without a word.

Kat stared at the book. EMTs were called to help with accidents, medical emergencies, and even stupid things, like when a kid got stuck in a tree. And of course, they were called if a woman went into labor unexpectedly or had complications. She took a deep breath to calm her nerves. She already knew how this story ended. Her mother had died in childbirth. The red scrapbook probably contained newspaper clippings of his patients who hadn't made it. It was sad; it was awful. It was possibly gruesome.

But what had her mother been doing here, in this town that her father had thought of so disparagingly? Perhaps her mother had been in Chicago on business or to visit a friend or family? Perhaps her mother—*oh, no!*—had been on her way to the hospital when she was in a terrible car accident? Kat had always assumed—without any hints or disavowals from her father—that her mother had died on a clean, white hospital bed. That was as far as she'd gotten in her imagination. Her mother had passed away in a hospital. Something unforeseen had happened in the delivery, something the doctor hadn't predicted, like an adverse reaction to anesthesia. Another thought occurred to her for the first time. Had her mother had a heart attack?

Tanner Delaney watched her, not saying a word. "Are you sure you want to know, Kat?" he asked kindly. "I could just put this away."

She wasn't sure at all. After thirty years of believing that this was what she wanted— finally, the truth—she wasn't sure at all. She was terrified, and it was ridiculous. She already knew how the story ended. "The truth will set you free," she said. Her lame smile trembled, wobbled, slid off her face.

"I don't know about that. I saw a lot of things in my years as an EMT, too much. A lot of the cases ... Well, there didn't seem to be any rhyme or reason to them at all."

"Tell me about my mother's ... case." Kat tried to swallow the lump in her throat. It was time; this was it. Some act of fate or karma had chosen Zen to be her traveling companion across the country, chosen him to put her on a train, and chosen him to introduce her to his father, who'd been present at her mother's death. "I mean," she said softly, "can you tell me anything positive, or uplifting, or ..."

Tanner leaned toward her, his face earnest. "Well, my partner, Capino, said it was a godsend. And after all his 'Jesus, Mary, and Josephs,' I had to agree. I actually went back to the church after what we witnessed."

Godsend. Jesus, Mary, and Joseph. Back to the church. After what we witnessed. His words echoed in Kat's brain.

"Now, some people in the town thought it was the most bizarre—" He stopped and corrected himself. "Most people in town thought it was a miracle."

"A miracle," Kat repeated. As long as she could look into this kind man's eyes, she could forestall the foreboding, forestall the inevitable. In seconds, she would know what happened to her mother. She would know the truth. Whether it would set her free was still unknowable.

"That's right." Tanner nodded emphatically. "A miracle. It was a miracle that you survived." Without taking his eyes off her, he opened the red scrapbook, which fell naturally to the well-worn page. He pushed it in front of her.

Kat read the *Chicago Tribune* article title: "A 'Miracle' Born from Tragedy." She looked up at him, and he nodded.

"It's like I said. You, Katrina Arnold, were the miracle."

12

OCTOBER 1980

"It was not your fault, Mellie. Dr. Crowley says that this type of thing occurs more frequently than people think. It was not your fault." This had been Marcus' refrain for weeks now: not your fault, not your fault, not your fault. Even in the throes of his own grief, which had been overpowering, he'd offered up the refrain as a condolence to her. Melody had never seen a man cry like that.

But Melody knew that it wasn't true. It had been entirely her fault. She'd known that something was wrong with the baby for fifteen days, yet she'd done nothing about it. She was a nurse and the baby's mother, yet she'd done nothing about her suspicion and fear because she hadn't wanted to know the truth. Her body had provided a safe haven for her baby. She must have done something wrong. No, that might not be it. Perhaps she was not fit to be a mother to the baby. She had not been up to par. She was *guilty as sin*, and she was being punished. She deserved to be punished, but her precious baby boy did not. Did. Not. He had been stillborn. *Still born.*

She managed to hold it together when Marcus asked to name the baby Marcus Junior. Melody did not want that. She hadn't picked out a name, but one thing was certain. She didn't want to call him that; she did not want to name her son after anyone. Didn't he deserve his own one-of-a-kind name? Still, she agreed. She owed Marcus that, she supposed. After all, hadn't she failed him, too?

She also managed to hold it together during Marcus Junior's funeral and burial in Marcus Senior's family plot. She supposed she owed Marcus Senior this, as well. Even when they placed the tiny white coffin in the ground, she had not cried. Even with all the sobbing around her, and even when Ma cried in her arms, Melody had not shed a tear. The others mistakenly thought she was brave. "Our Mellie has such courage in the face of adversity," her family could be heard saying at the reception afterward at the house on Roosevelt Street. "Our Mellie is so brave."

She was not brave. She was holding onto, for as long as possible, the catatonic numbness that had overtaken her in the doctor's office. Without being asked, just instinctively knowing what Melody needed, Sylvia had brought her diazepam. Melody hadn't taken any drugs since the night of her wedding, and in those four months, she'd forgotten the loveliness of the drug. She'd forgotten how soothing it was to exist in a place where your senses dulled, and the whirling chaos of life around you slowed down. The diazepam was just what she needed; it was the key to her survival.

Vodka helped, too, when Melody took a leave of absence from her job. Since she didn't have to face the pitying stares of her coworkers, or worse, their looks of accusations, Melody saw no harm in pouring a little vodka into her morning orange juice. It was an official drink, after all, a screwdriver. It was a real cocktail, listed on bar menus throughout America. And Melody discovered that vodka could be added to any number of juices: cranberry, grape, grapefruit, tomato. "Good, Mellie," people around her said. "You're not eating much, but at least you're drinking juice. That's a good thing, isn't it? She's drinking juice." Melody drank a lot of juice.

She even managed to hold it together when Marcus disassembled the crib and put it, piece by piece, back up in the attic. Melody had sat on the bed, juice in hand, and watched him as he carefully pulled the crib apart, tears silently coursing down his unshaven cheeks. Idly, Melody thought: *I didn't even have time to buy a mattress or sheets or blankets for that crib.* Idly, she thought: *The baby would have needed a mobile.* Idly, she thought: *My poor baby was going to sleep in a musty old crib. How much would a new one cost?* Idly, she thought: *Why hasn't Marcus shaved?*

The days passed in a diazepam-vodka haze. Belinda came back fulltime to take care of Evelyn, and Marcus did the shopping, cooking, and cleaning. At first, people came and went from the house, paying their respects and bringing over casseroles and pies. Melody thanked them all but did not encourage small talk. She wanted them gone. However, when the condolences tapered off and then stopped altogether, she felt enraged. Had they forgotten her baby so soon? What was wrong with them? She poured more juice, concluding that there was no need for her to change out of her pajamas, or what's more, to even get out of bed. No need, no reason, nothing at all.

Time crawled and blurred day and night. Melody was unaware of the days of the week or the changing fall season outside her door. (Later, she would be told that it was a brilliant fall. She would remember nothing of leaves turning crimson and fiery orange or the last warm days of the season. All she would remember was that her baby boy was born on October 2.) She'd been in bed for some time now. Her hair was stringy and dirty, and she couldn't remember when she last showered. She couldn't remember much of anything at all, but she didn't give a damn. However, she was getting low on vodka, and about that, she did give a damn. She cared very much. Sylvia was due to drop off another bottle, secretly hidden in her voluminous purse, sometime soon.

Marcus knocked tentatively on the door. "May I come in?"

Melody sighed. Since the ... hospital procedure ... he'd been sleeping on the couch downstairs. Marcus said he was giving her time, that he understood. (What in the hell did he understand? She didn't understand anything.) He didn't even have to come into the room before the ringing in her head started: not your fault, not your fault, not your fault. He was probably trying to bring her more food. She sighed again. "I suppose."

He did, in fact, carry a tray with a grilled cheese sandwich and some tomato soup. The abundance of casseroles, ham, fried chicken, pies, cookies, and cakes had been thrown away. Because there wasn't enough room in the freezer, Marcus had been unable to freeze and neatly label and date them all. "How are you feeling this evening?"

Aha! she thought, *it's evening.* And then: *Can you put vodka in tomato soup? Tomato juice, tomato soup, what's the difference?* "You know." Melody shrugged. She felt the same as she had on all these countless days and nights, nothing at all.

He put the tray on the nightstand, knowing that she would not touch it. "I've been thinking, Mellie. This whole thing—the baby—is not your fault."

"Stop." Mellie held up her hand. The man was a scratched record.

"Well," Marcus said. Uncertainly, gingerly, he sat on the edge of the bed.

Melody moved over. Although he smelled like his usual Aramis cologne and had shaved, she did not want to touch him. He'd cleaned up and looked handsome in his usual fussy, fastidious way.

Marcus adjusted his wire-framed glasses and cleared his throat. "I've been reading a book by this woman named Elizabeth Kubler-Ross, a psychiatrist." He cleared his throat again. "It's about the five stages of grief."

Melody had read the book during nursing school and thought it profound at the time, but now she did not. What did this woman, this psychiatrist, really know about grief? Had she had a baby boy who was *still born*? If not, she didn't know anything. "I've read it," she said.

"Okay then, good." Marcus looked at the floor for a few moments, trying to decide something, then he took Melody's hand. "I don't know any other way to say this, Mellie, but I think you—we—need to move forward. This has been a terrible tragedy." He choked up. "We lost Marcus Junior to forces unknown to us, something beyond our control—"

"Are you talking about God?" Melody interrupted. She needed to hurry him along. He was clearly intent on saying something to her, but Sylvia was due any minute, and Melody's glass of grapefruit juice held the last drops of the Smirnoff bottle.

"I suppose I am." Marcus cleared his throat again.

It took sheer will for Melody not to roll her eyes. *Jesus,* she thought, *get on with it.*

Marcus took a deep breath and nervously caressed Melody's hand. "We can have another baby."

Melody snatched her hand out of his. "What?"

"Another baby. I'm not talking about right now, of course." His attempt at nervous laughter fell flat and hollow. "I mean, honey, we're young, and everything must happen for a reason ..." His voice faltered.

Melody stared at him, horrified. She felt a staggering, wretched shifting inside her rib cage.

"I'm thinking in two or three months, when you're fully rested, we could try again. Another baby would help us recover. And of course, I want a child." Marcus tried not to sound pleading, but he did.

Melody continued to stare at him. She had recently—how many weeks ago?—given birth to their *dead* baby, and he was talking to her about another baby? (Another *dead* baby?) Dear Lord. He was insane. She'd married him because she had to, because she'd been pregnant. Their marriage was a sham, born out of necessity. *Born* out of necessity. *Still born.*

"Marcus," her voice was a choked whisper, "you don't understand. I want that precious little boy! I want that baby back!"

And that's when she really lost it.

By the time Sylvia arrived, the bedroom looked like a disaster area, with broken lamps and picture frames, torn sheets, and the stuffing ripped out of pillows. At first, Marcus tried to stop her tirade, saying, "Mellie, Mellie, it's all right. It's all right." And: "Please don't break that lamp. It's one of Mother's family heirlooms." That further fueled her rage, and she lunged at him, knocking his glasses off his face when she scratched his right cheek. He left her alone then, leaving her to her crying, her throwing, her shredding, her insatiable grief.

Melody didn't know how much later Sylvia arrived. It could have been minutes or hours. To Melody, it felt that she had shed a lifetime of tears. They didn't help. The pain did not go away, nor did the image of the impossibly small white casket being lowered into a gaping black grave. She clawed at her face, hair, arms, legs, and chest. She needed more drugs. She needed more juice. But neither of those would be strong enough to help her now. The floodgates had opened to a grieving hell.

Sylvia found her huddled in the corner, howling, with a blanket over her head. She knelt beside her. "I'm here for you now, Mel, I'm here. I've got everything you need to make you feel better, okay? Let's start by taking the blanket off your head."

Underneath the blanket, Melody shook her head. She would stay in this position indefinitely. Why venture out into a cruel and heartless world that let innocent babies die? Her poor, poor baby. He hadn't even had a chance.

"Come on, Mel. I know this is horrible for you, but we can get through this together. Let me help you."

Melody shook her head again, but she did stop howling at the sound of Sylvia's confident, soothing voice, the voice of a competent nurse.

"Come on, honey." Sylvia tugged at the wool blanket.

Melody tugged back.

"I'm not playing tug-of-war with you." Sylvia picked up Melody's huddled, dwindled mass and put her on the bed.

Melody was so surprised that she didn't resist when Sylvia then ripped off the blanket, and the sight of her did give Melody the smallest glimmer of solace. Sylvia must have been out on a date or at a club. She wore a tight black dress and high heels that elevated her to a height well over six feet tall. Her platinum blonde hair fell to just below her shoulders, and the whiteness of it, the contrast to the black dress, made it seem that her face was surrounded with an elongated halo. "It hurts too much," she said to the apparition that was Sylvia.

"Yes." Sylvia reached into her purse and pulled out the bottle of Smirnoff. She twisted off the cap and handed it to Melody.

Melody took a long, burning gulp, then another. It did little to ease the pain. How would she ever be able to make this sharp aching go away? How many weeks had it been since her son had died? She took another long gulp. Her empty stomach, her empty womb, her empty heart churned in revolt.

Sylvia took the bottle from her. "Let me help you." And she did. She led Melody to the hall bathroom, held her head while she vomited juice, vodka, and bile, then ran hot water in the tub, and helped Melody undress and get in. Sylvia closed the lid of the stool and sat down while Melody bathed. They passed the bottle of vodka back and forth.

The warm water did feel nice. Melody hadn't realized that every muscle in her body ached until she felt the soothing water. They were in a different bathroom in another house, but the scene seemed so familiar. How many times had Sylvia done this for her during their research period? How many times had she done it for Sylvia? "Seems like old times," she said after they'd been silent for some minutes.

"Not quite." Sylvia reached for the bottle.

Not quite indeed. So few months had passed from that time of carefree partying, and now here they were, professional nurses, one who had recently lost her mother and one who had recently lost her child. "I feel so old." Melody leaned back against the porcelain. "So old and so tired."

"We're twenty-two, Mel. We're only twenty-two."

"Unbelievable." In the few months she'd been married to Marcus and living with his demented mother, she'd aged, at least mentally, ten years.

"We still have our whole lives ahead of us." They were three-fourths through the vodka, but Sylvia didn't sound drunk at all.

Melody, on the other hand, felt the effects of the liquor. Vodka worked so much faster when she ate little for days and when she did not join him with his sister, juice. "You sound like that's a good thing."

"Of course it's a good thing. We're twenty-two, Mel, for god's sake. *Twenty-two.*"

"You forget that I'm married to ..." Melody suddenly could not remember her husband's name. It was right on the tip of her tongue, but it wouldn't form through the vodka. "Mr. Fuddy Duddy," she finished.

"I didn't forget," Sylvia said.

"I did! I just forgot his name!" Melody giggled. How could she be laughing at a time like this? It was the vodka, without his sister.

"You don't have to stay married to him, Mel. I mean, you didn't have to marry him in the first place."

"I'm a good Catholic girl." Melody hiccupped. "Well, I used to be. I'm not so sure anymore. I don't think I'm anything." She reached for the bottle.

"You are a good nurse and a wonderful friend."

"I'm a wreck." Melody slid down into the cooling water. How nice it would be to stay there indefinitely. It was even better than being under the blanket. Until her lungs started to burn. She broke the surface of the water. Not yet. Not yet.

"You don't have to stay married to him, you know," Sylvia said this mildly, but she accompanied it with a penetrating gaze.

"Well, I kind of promised God," Melody slurred.

"People get divorced all the time, even Catholics." Sylvia took a towel from the rack and held it out to Melody.

"What would Ma and Daddy say? They think Mr. Fuddy Duddy walks on water." How odd. She still could not remember that man's name.

"Sorry, Mel, this is definitely not the time to be talking about such things. You know me and my big mouth. However, this time, I think it's the vodka talking."

"Vodka talks?" *Wow!* Melody was impressed. She knew it did amazing things, but talk? What a fantastic talent!

When it became clear that Melody was incapable of reaching the towel, Sylvia helped her out, dried her, and dressed her in clean pajamas. She led her back into the bedroom that was miraculously clean with a neatly made bed. But no lamps or pictures. Melody thought before she fell into a deep, drunken, blessed sleep, that it must have been Mr. Fuddy Duddy who'd worked such wonders. Maybe she would remember his name in the morning.

Two weeks after Melody hit rock bottom in her grief and tore up her bedroom, she went back to work. It was therapeutic to think of others rather than herself and her lost baby boy. (She had decided never to refer to him as Marcus Junior. It was not his name; it was not who he might have become.) She would work her twelve-hour shift and come home tired. But not tired enough. Although wonderful in his way, Vodka had been supplemented by rum, gin, tequila, and brandy. Her doctor, sympathetic to her story, had given her prescriptions for Xanax and Valium. So she was able to muddle through her workdays and sleepless nights with these aids. She would put one foot in front of the other and hope that time—like everyone said—would heal the hurting, that time—like some miracle drug—would miraculously cure her.

However, on the days she wasn't at work, getting through the hours was sheer hell. Evelyn got worse by the day, and the dreary house reeked of her ailment, old fried foods, and general disuse. The only time Melody had tried to open a window to air out the place, she discovered that it had been painted shut. The window would not open; it wouldn't budge. She tried other windows, and it was the same story. They were all painted shut. It reduced Melody to tears. She was stuck, stuck in this house, and she wanted out.

However, she couldn't. What would people, especially her parents and her brothers, say? Melody supposed that from the outside looking in, people thought they were a suitable match. Marcus was kind to her, Marcus helped cook and clean, Marcus had supported her when they lost the baby (and hadn't that been her fault?), and Marcus had bought her pearls. Marcus didn't drink or run around with other women or squander his paycheck. Marcus was a gem.

The problem was this: Melody did not love him, and she didn't think she ever could or would.

How could she explain to people that she didn't love him because he was too nice to her, because he loved her too much? It didn't make sense, but it was true. It made her skin crawl when he said things like, "I love to dote on you, Mellie." *Dote.* Like she was some beloved pet. Or when he would say, "You're my darling little flower, Mellie." *Flower.* What kind of a man said crap like that? A man like Marcus, a thirty-four-year-old who lived with his mother and craved routine and avoided stress and excitement, a man who had no friends or hobbies. Unless you counted her. Melody was his hobby.

Sylvia hadn't brought up the subject of divorce again since that terrible night, and neither had Melody. What was the point? Sylvia thought the solution to Melody's loveless (on her part) marriage was simple, but Melody knew it was not so. She hadn't tried hard enough to be a good wife to Marcus, and she hadn't given Marcus enough credit for being a good man. From now on, Melody would hand over her paychecks to him without glowering or making a snide remark. She would be more attentive to Evelyn and not complain when it was her turn to feed or dress her. Melody would buy curtains to cheer up the drab brown house with its brown shag carpeting and brown vinyl couch. She would try her best to be nice to her husband.

But it was so hard. On the nights when Melody wasn't working, they ate dinner, washed the dishes together, and then sat and watched television. Marcus would watch anything: *Dallas, The Dukes of Hazard, MASH, Three's Company, Diff'rent Strokes.* He would sympathize with the dramas' characters, saying "what a shame" when someone was mistreated or had a bodily injury. But it was the sitcoms that most got on Melody's nerves. Marcus would laugh outrageously at the stupidest jokes. The man never laughed in real life, but an unrealistic, predictable situation comedy would have him practically rolling on the floor.

It was on one of these boring, endless evenings that Melody suggested something new. "Why don't we go to a movie? It's still early enough." They could. Dinner in this house was served precisely at 5:45, and television watching, after the dishes were washed and the sink cleaned with Comet twice, began strictly at 6:30. It was now 6:45, and if they hurried, they could catch a 7:00 show.

"We can't leave Mother." Marcus didn't take his eyes off the TV. "Besides, movies are a waste of money, and most of the time, they're morally corrupt."

Melody snorted. "Morally corrupt?"

"Nudity, sex, violence," Marcus responded.

"Those things are why I like going to the movies," she said to him, just to rile him up.

It wasn't happening. "No, they're not, kitten. You like wholesome movies, just like me."

God, *kitten*. That was a new one. Melody let it drop. "What about taking a walk one of these evenings?"

"It's turning cold out, Mellie, and then there's Mother." A commercial was on, and Marcus flipped through the *TV Guide*.

Melody wanted to yell at him: "You treat that damn *TV Guide* like it's some kind of Bible." Instead, she took a deep breath and said, "We could go over and visit Ma and Daddy one of these evenings." She would never have predicted this strong wish to visit her parents. For all those years, she had been so eager to move away from them, and now she longed for the infrequent visits to Roosevelt Street. It's what marriage to Marcus could do to a woman: turn her inside out.

"When we took Mother over there the last time, she became extremely agitated."

That was true. The old lady had been terrified of all the loud noises and comings and goings of her brothers and their friends. "Marcus, why don't we hire someone, anyone to come and watch Evelyn once a week or so? It would be nice if we could vary our routine a little more, you know, do more social things—maybe even with other people?"

"We have a fine routine, kitten, a fine routine. Most people are not as fortunate as we are." The program came back on, and Marcus was once again immediately engrossed.

Case closed. Melody wanted to remind him that she was only twenty-two, that she was too young to be living like part of a middle-aged couple. And she wanted to tell him that sitting here, in this bleak house, night after night, made the sadness grow and grow and grow until it enveloped her completely. The alcohol and the Valium and Xanax only did a little to blur the gnawing edges that were always there. She was consumed by them, haunted by them, and taunted by them. "You killed your baby," they said, "you, you, *you*."

She stood up suddenly. "I'm going to the store. We're out of milk."

"No, we're not, kitten. I picked up a gallon on the way home from work." Marcus didn't take his eyes off the flickering screen, and he wouldn't until the next commercial.

"We're out of coffee, then." She had to escape this house *right now*.

"We're fully stocked, honey. Sit back down and enjoy the show."

"I hate this show." Melody's voice cracked. Everything was cracking: her heart, her will, her life. "I'm going out."

"Where are you going, and why?" A Nair commercial came on, so Melody now had Marcus' full attention. He looked genuinely puzzled.

"None of your business." She grabbed her coat from the front closet and her purse.

Marcus followed her to the front door. "This is not a good idea, Mellie. It's starting to rain, and the roads might be slick."

"I don't care." The Buick was parked in the driveway by the side of the house, and she ran to it. It had started to rain, and the drops were fast and fat. She slammed the car door shut and locked it. He couldn't get her here. She started the car and backed down the driveway. She was almost to the end, almost on the street, when she heard what sounded like an explosion. She slammed on the brakes, her heart pounding. Had someone shot at her? Had Marcus shot at her? She knew he had a gun in the nightstand next to his bed. He'd bought it some years before, he had told her, for protection.

The next thing she knew, Marcus knocked at the window. His face looked distorted through the rain-streaked glass. She had no other choice but to roll down the window. "What happened?"

"You had a blowout, baby, a flat tire. Come inside now. It's raining too hard to change it now. I'll change it in the morning."

She needed to escape. She needed to get out. Surely, a flat tire wasn't that big of a deal. "Tell me what to do, and I'll change it," she said. Marcus would probably think the tears sliding down her cheeks were just the rain.

"It's too complicated, honey. And it's raining. Come inside now. *The Love Boat* is about to start. We both love that show."

It was rainy and cold and too dark to walk anywhere. Again, no choice. Melody followed her husband inside.

13

APRIL 2012

There were no adequate words to describe what Kat felt after she read the article. It was incomprehensible to her. For thirty years, she'd wanted to find out about her mother, the woman who had died in childbirth while giving life to her daughter. In Kat's mind, she'd been heroic and tragic, a young woman who had given her life to bring her child into the world against impossible odds. Oh, Kat had fantasized about it many times, imagined that her mother might have begged the doctors in her dying breath: "Don't worry about me. Please, please save my child. She is the one who shall live!"

A consequence of this fantastical imagining of her mother's death was that Kat had spent her entire life feeling guilty. It had been beyond her control, of course. She'd been a baby, but that didn't stop the guilt. She was the one responsible for killing her mother, and Kat had always known, without being told, that her father held her responsible, too.

Bullshit. This Melody Arnold woman had tried to kill *Kat* when she climbed up the 100-foot light tower and jumped. So many questions ran through Kat's head. How could a nine-months pregnant woman in labor escape a hospital and then climb up a rickety ladder to the top of a light tower? How was that physically possible? Why had she thought her baby was dead even after the doctors let her hear the heartbeat through a stethoscope? Why had she decided to jump? What had possessed her?

Your mother made a choice, her father had said.

Well, that was the understatement of the century.

Her mother had jumped, probably convinced that the fall would kill them both. Ha! Kat supposed she got the last laugh on that one. She'd been cushioned and saved by the amniotic sac and delivered at the scene by two paramedics, one of whom sat next to her now. Dear God, it was no wonder she'd been such a screw-up her entire life. With a beginning like that one, her life was destined to be a bumpy ride.

And she'd thought getting her car stolen was a cosmic bitch slap. Ha!

"Mr. Delaney—" Kat tore her eyes away from the article. She should thank him, shouldn't she? If he and the other one, Capino, hadn't been so fast-thinking, she wouldn't even be here. She wouldn't be alive. It was unbelievable.

Tanner Delaney no longer sat next to her. Kat had been so engrossed—overwhelmed, stunned, speechless—when reading the article that she hadn't noticed him leaving. She had no idea how long she'd been sitting there. It could have been minutes; it could have been hours.

"Mr. Delaney," she called. Her voice sounded thick as if she had been crying, but she hadn't shed a tear. When she talked about her mother earlier, she had cried, but not now. She would never shed another tear over this Melody Arnold, a woman who tried to execute a double suicide.

Her father had been waiting in the expectant father's room. Had he thought that his wife—this Melody Arnold—had been giving birth down the hall? Had he been pacing the floor, talking nervously with the other expectant fathers, waiting for a nurse to come at any moment and tell him that he had a daughter or a son? Had a police officer shown up instead to make the grim announcement, or had someone in the hospital rushed in breathlessly and told him that his wife had vanished into thin air? Surely, Marcus Flowers hadn't suspected that his wife would do something like she did. Surely not.

But had Marcus Arnold suspected?

"Mr. Delaney," she called, louder. She knew he was trying to give her space to absorb all of this, but she suddenly didn't want to be alone any longer. There were too many questions, all shrouded with mixed emotions, running through her head.

Mr. Delaney came into the dining room, followed by another man. They sat down at the table. "This is Mario Capino, Kat, the other EMT at the scene. We thought you might have some questions."

Hell, yes, she had questions, but she doubted if they could answer the most important one: What had possessed Melody Arnold to jump?

"Jesus, Mary, and Joseph." Capino looked awestruck. He must have been in his early sixties, with a thick head of white hair and an etched brown face.

"My words exactly," Delaney said. "I was quoting you. They were the first words you said when you saw her little leg."

Kat knew what they were talking about. The article had said that when they turned this Melody Arnold woman over, a baby's leg—her leg—protruded from the abdomen, twitching. Her leg had been *twitching*. They both stared at her as if she were an apparition or a freak, or as Mr. Delaney had said, a miracle. "I'm pleased to meet you," she said awkwardly. "I hope I didn't put you to any trouble."

"No, no trouble at all. I just live a couple of blocks over on Palmer Street."

That wasn't what she meant. Absurdly, she was referring to the day thirty years before when they'd delivered her at the scene of a fatal accident. Not an accident at all. A suicide. "I mean ... Well, thank you."

Both men nodded. "All in a day's work," Delaney said, "although it wasn't a typical day."

"Never saw anything like it before or since." Capino was still staring.

"Do I have something in my teeth?" She smiled, hoping she didn't sound rude, but their staring made her uncomfortable. She wasn't that baby from thirty years before. Well, of course, she was that baby, but it was going to take some time, a lot of time, to get used to that idea, that she had been a baby born from a *tragic leap*.

Both men relaxed. "I never thought I'd live to see this day, Tan. What a blessing. You're a pretty girl, Kat Arnold. Is Kat short for something?" Capino asked.

"Katrina. Katrina Flowers," Kat corrected.

"Ah, married." Capino nodded knowingly.

"No, I'm not married."

"Zen brought her home," Delaney supplied by way of explanation.

"That boy sure knows how to pick them," Capino said, still nodding.

"I'm not with—" Kat stopped and shrugged. At this point, it didn't matter if they thought she was Zen's girlfriend.

"It's a small world," Delaney said.

"Gets smaller as you get older," Capino agreed.

Kat could imagine them with a checkerboard between them, two aging men philosophizing about life. They were sweet and had obviously been very good at their job, but she needed to get down to the nitty-gritty. The article stated the facts, but she needed to know what was between the lines. "Do you remember anything else about that day?"

"I remember it like it was yesterday," Capino said.

"Never forget it," Delaney agreed.

"You arrived at the scene ..." Kat prompted.

"We were second at the scene. A young police officer was there, white as a sheet." Delaney had a faraway look in his eyes, remembering.

"He'd tried to talk her down." Capino looked at Kat and cleared his throat. "Tried to get her to change her mind, but he didn't know if she could hear him."

"It was a windy day and cold," Delaney added.

Had she heard him? Kat wondered. Had she heard him and ignored him, intent on killing herself and her unborn baby? It was horrible to contemplate the *purposefulness* of what Melody Arnold knew she was going to do.

"After we delivered you—"

"We always worked real good together as a team," Capino interrupted.

"Damn right, we did." Delaney pumped Capino's fist across the table.

"After you delivered me ..." Kat prompted once again.

"I wrapped you in my coat, and we rushed you to the hospital," Delaney said.

"We had to leave the ... uh ... her. Crime scene, you know."

Crime scene. Suicide was a crime. What was more, Kat suddenly realized, it would not have been a double suicide. It would have been a suicide and a *murder*.

"What then?" Kat asked. "What about the father?" It was strange how easily she could shift into the third person, distancing herself from the scene: *that* Melody Arnold, *the* father. Was she in shock? She seemed to be behaving normally, but maybe she wasn't, and these nice men who had saved her life were too polite to tell her.

"Well, our job was done after that. We waited until the hospital checked you out and were relieved when your vital signs were good. You had a broken left leg, though," Delaney said.

Checked the baby out, not me, Kat wanted to say but didn't.

"And then we went and had a beer to celebrate," Capino said happily.

"As I recall, we had many beers to celebrate." Delaney reached over and pumped Capino's fist again.

"What about the father?" Kat asked again.

Capino looked thoughtful. "I don't recall hearing anything about the father. Do you, Tan?"

"Nope." Delaney shook his head. "I kept thinking there'd be some follow-up story, you know? Maybe something about when you went home from the hospital, or something about the grandparents. Hell, I checked the obituaries for a couple of weeks after that, and I didn't find a thing."

"Damnedest thing," Capino agreed. "It was a major news story. Everyone was talking about it and then not a peep. It was like you and your father just disappeared."

And that was exactly what had happened after the "miracle born from tragic leap." Marcus Flowers, aka Arnold, had taken his daughter and disappeared.

"I don't understand it. I don't think I'll ever understand it. How could a woman do such a thing? If Melody Arnold didn't want to have a baby, she could have had an abortion, right? But why carry a baby to full-term and then decide to jump off a 100-foot light tower? None of it makes sense." Kat peeled the label off a Heineken bottle. After Mario Capino left and Tanner Delaney went upstairs to nap, Zen had magically appeared and asked if Kat wanted to go for a walk. She had responded, "As long as that walk has a bar as its final destination." Zen had taken her hand and led her to his favorite local haunt, Melnick's, a dark, narrow place that still had an old-fashioned jukebox in the corner.

"I don't understand it either," Zen said for probably the tenth time. "It's a pretty amazing story." So far, he'd let Kat spout and said very little.

"I don't think *amazing* is the right word. The word that pops into my mind is *gruesome*; another word is *bitch*. That Melody Arnold was a bitch." Of all the emotions that Kat felt since learning what Melody Arnold had done, anger emerged as the front-runner. What her mother had done was supremely selfish. Her unknown mother had been an incredibly selfish *bitch*.

"Are you sure your dad never told you about the woman who jumped from the light tower?" Kat asked again.

"No, Pops never talked about the people in the red scrapbook."

"I guess it's rather obvious why he didn't," Kat said wryly. She finished her beer, and Zen automatically motioned to the bartender for two more.

"Why do you think she did it?" Kat had asked this question many times, too.

Zen shook his head. "You're probably never going to know the answer to that."

Probably not. And it was killing Kat. In a way, she almost wished she didn't know what had happened. Ignorance was bliss and all that sort of thing. If she didn't know the story, she wouldn't be questioning why Melody Arnold had jumped off that damn tower. But now she did know the story, and she wasn't going to be completely satisfied until she knew the *why*.

"Don't take this the wrong way, Kat," Zen said hesitantly, "but maybe your mother—"

"Melody Arnold," Kat interrupted. She refused to think of that incredibly selfish bitch as her mother.

"Melody Arnold," Zen amended. "Maybe she had a mental illness?"

Well, that would be just perfect. Her mother might have been a wacko. Melody Arnold might have had bipolar disorder or something. And didn't mental illness sometimes run in families? That would mean that she could have inherited something, which would actually explain many things about her past. Just perfect. "Do you have any better explanations than that up your sleeve?"

"Nope."

"Shit." Kat took a big gulp from the fresh beer.

"What are you going to do now?"

Even though the light in the bar was dim, Kat could see the compassion in his eyes. It was almost enough to push her over the edge and make her start to bawl. Not over her mother, but over that look in his eyes. "I wish I knew," she said. This whole trip had been a series of *what's next*, with nothing going according to plan, especially with this bit of incomprehensible knowledge. Earlier in the day, which seemed more like weeks ago, she'd decided to ask Granny Nanny to wire her the money to go home. However, she didn't think she could do that now. Knowing what she now knew was worse than not knowing for thirty years. To her, the story was half-finished, incomplete, and she somehow had to figure out the rest.

"Maybe you could hire a private investigator?" Zen suggested.

"With what?"

"Good point."

On the short walk to the bar, Kat's phone had started to ring. (Zen had naturally, thoughtfully charged up her phone with his charger.) She hadn't recognized the number and almost hadn't answered it. She should have listened to her instincts. Officer Dick from Carbondale said they had found her car completely stripped and with all her possessions gone. Of course. So even if she wanted to sell her car for cash—a remote, half-baked idea—she couldn't. Selling a couple of her eggs was starting not to sound like such an outlandish idea, after all.

She needed money to buy time. She could still ask Granny Nanny to wire money, but she felt it was wrong to do that. What kind of person took money from an old lady? Besides, if she somehow found a way to get back to Arizona and did this research from a distance, she felt she would be missing something. Where had this woman lived? Where had she worked? Kat would have to see these places for herself if there was the slightest possibility that she would ever understand Melody Arnold.

So if she were going to stay and try to figure out her mess of a mother, she would have to get a job and a place to stay. "I guess I'm going to have to figure this out on my own."

"I'll help as much as I can," Zen said.

She hoped he'd say that.

"In my free time," he added. "My job starts in a few days."

"What job?" He was going to law school in the fall, but he hadn't mentioned a job during the cross-country trip.

"Well, since Pops is on the mend, I didn't see any point in sticking around and freeloading off my parents. I called a college buddy of mine, and he hooked me up with this catering company. It's a part-time thing, and I'm going to live with him until school starts. He's got an apartment in the South Loop."

Kat knew her face fell, and she couldn't stop its falling. It was ridiculous, she knew, yet she felt like he was abandoning her. They'd been through a lot in the brief time they'd known each other: a cross-country trip, a tornado, and the spooky, impossible discovery that his dad had been present at Melody Arnold's fatal jump. In that short time, without her wanting it, she had come to depend on him. "Congrats, I guess."

He leaned forward and took her hand. "I'm sure Mom and Pops will let you stay as long as you need a place."

"I couldn't ask them to do that." She took her hand from his. "I mean, they're nice people, your folks, but I couldn't put them to that much trouble." She felt dangerously close to tears now, and it took all her self-control to keep them at bay. This handsome, excruciatingly nice man didn't owe her a thing. He'd already paid for her trip to Chicago and let her taste his mother's awesome blueberry pancakes. He also happened to be the son of the paramedic who had delivered her.

"We'll figure—"

At that moment, a pretty, petite blonde woman burst through the door. "I heard you were in town, Lorenzo Delaney. How long did you think you could hide from me? I called your house, and your mom told me you were here. It's so good to see you!" She rushed over to the table and plopped herself in Zen's lap. The kiss she gave him, in Kat's opinion, was not platonic.

"Wow." It was too dark in the bar to see if Zen blushed.

"I take it that you know each other," Kat said dryly.

"Kat, this is Carrie." Zen tried to undo her arms from around his neck. "We went to high school together."

"We were high school sweethearts," Carrie squealed. "We went to senior prom together. You remember that night, Zen. It was the first time we—"

"I remember," Zen said.

Carrie kissed him again. "We have so much to catch up on!"

Kat decided she was a gusher. She went way beyond Zen's sister's perkiness. Carrie was like a cute little puppy wriggling around on his lap while the words just *gushed* from her mouth. It was a sickening display, but it wasn't like she was jealous or anything like that. Why would she be? Zen was not her boyfriend.

"Do you mind if I join you?" Carrie had already hopped off Zen's lap and pulled out a chair.

"Do I have a choice?" Kat knew that she did not.

"Excuse me?" Carrie sat down anyway.

"Sure, you can join us." Zen gave her one of his charming smiles, the one that crinkled the corners of his green/gold eyes.

Damn it. Why was Zen giving one of those smiles to Carrie? But it didn't matter because Kat was *not* jealous. "I have a phone call to make."

Kat abruptly stood. "You two kids can just catch up all you want." She hated how surly she sounded, but it didn't matter. Her surliness was lost on them.

She would call Granny Nanny. That's what she needed. She should have done it hours ago, and only the thought of hearing Gran's voice almost cheered her up. Almost. When she opened the front door, she was just in time to see a crack of lightning, hear the sonic boom of thunder, and feel the first big, fat drops of rain. She looked up at the sky. "Are you kidding me? Do you really think I need this, too?"

She had no choice but to go back inside because it wasn't like she had a car to go to, after all. She sat at the far end of the long bar, as far away as possible from Zen and Carrie, who were deep in conversation, their faces close together and their arms touching. Not that it did any good. The mirror on the back of the bar reflected their every move. She made herself look busy by shuffling around in her purse for her phone. "I'll take a shot of scotch," she said when the bartender came over.

"A shot?" He raised a bushy eyebrow. "Most people like to sip their scotch."

"I'm not a sipper, okay?" The very last thing she needed right now was a bartender telling her how to drink her scotch.

"Okay," he said, staring at her and then pouring her shot.

She punched in Granny Nanny's number, praying that she wasn't at the gun club where she couldn't hear its ringing. She wasn't. Her gran answered on the third ring. "It's me again," Kat said, relief washing over her. She felt like she hadn't talked to her in ages, even though it had only been twenty-four hours since she made the last call while in Zeke's Tavern in Carbondale. Kat felt like she had lived another alternative, surreal life in that short time.

"I know it's you, dear," Gran said. "I have caller ID. Your name pops up every time you call. It's rather a shame. Back in the day, you didn't know who would be on the other end of the line when you picked up the phone. There was a kind of mystery about it. Now you know who's calling every single time."

"Yeah, it's a shame," Kat said. "Are you sitting down?"

"I'm going to need some scotch for this, aren't I?"

"I hope the bottle's full."

"You know me. I always have an extra one tucked away under the sink behind the Lysol and another on the laundry room shelf behind the Tide."

Kat hadn't known that, but it made sense. Gran never ran out of scotch.

"I'm ready, Katrina," Gran said a moment later.

The words spilled out of Kat's mouth. She told Gran about her car getting stolen, how she'd passed out in the train station, and how Zen had carried her onto the train and taken her home to Oak Lawn Park. Then she took a deep breath and told Granny Nanny about a woman named Melody Arnold who, at nine months pregnant, had climbed a 100-foot light tower—and jumped.

It was the first time Kat had ever known Granny Nanny to be stumped for words. Kat could hear a glug of scotch pouring into a glass. "Did you hear me, Gran? She jumped. I don't know if I would've ever found out about this. When Zen googled her name on the train, nothing came up. But then Zen's dad happened to be a paramedic on the scene when it happened. Can you believe this? The whole thing is just bizarre."

When Granny Nanny finally spoke, her voice was slow and thoughtful. "I've seen and heard many things in my life, Katrina, but this really takes the cake."

"You can say that again." When the bartender came over with the bottle in hand, Kat nodded. He poured.

"It puts a whole different spin on your father, too, don't you think?" Gran continued in her slow and thoughtful voice.

"I haven't gotten that far in my thinking yet." As far as Kat had gotten in her thinking was the glaring fact that her father had taken his baby daughter, changed their names, and disappeared. Then this thought came like a lightning bolt bright enough to match the one she'd seen outside. What if she had relatives on her mother's side—grandparents still living, or aunts, uncles, and cousins? Her father had always insisted that he had no one, but what about this Melody Arnold? What was her maiden name?

"It's a lot to take in, dear, a lot to take in."

"I think I need to stay in Chicago for a little while to figure things out." And when Kat said it aloud to her gran, she knew that it's what she had to do. She didn't know how she was going to do it, but she had to. If she could discover who her parents had been, she would finally begin to understand herself.

"Your adventure has taken a new turn," Gran said.

"I think it's more like it's veered off course." Kat had about forty dollars in her purse. The rest of the money for the trip home had been in her suitcase because she'd thought it would be safer there. Right. How was she going to make this work?

Gran, apparently even over the phone, could always read Kat's thoughts. "I'm going to wire you some money."

"I can't, Gran."

"Nonsense. This is how it's going to be. I don't want to stay awake at night worrying about you, Katrina, even though I know you can take care of yourself."

Kat felt sorely tempted, but she wasn't going to do it. "Nonsense right back at you. You live on a fixed income, and I don't want to stay awake at night worrying about *you*."

"Would it make you feel better if I told you that Mr. Williams and I are working on a business plan? He is a very knowledgeable man, and we've come up with a humdinger of an idea. So that's that."

"What kind of business plan?" What could two old people come up with? They certainly couldn't sell a well-worn kidney at their age, or any other decades-old organ, for that matter.

"None of your business," Gran said mildly.

"Look, if you don't tell me, I'm not going to take the money. I'll leave it at Western Union, or wherever it goes to." Kat wasn't exactly sure how the concept of wiring money worked.

"You are a dear, Katrina, but you can be so stubborn."

"Tell me something I don't know. The plan, Gran, what is it?"

Granny Nanny let out a sigh. "Well, we are going to expand Mr. Williams' business. That's all you need to know."

"I thought Mr. Williams was retired," Kat began, and then she remembered. "You're going to sell pot with Mr. Williams?" she asked incredulously. Even for Granny Nanny, this was far-fetched.

"It's perfectly legal to sell marijuana for medicinal purposes in Arizona now, you know. And there are plenty of people our age who could use a little something to relieve the pain and suffering of old age. We would be doing a great service—"

"Wait a minute, Gran," Kat interrupted. "Are you telling me that you and Mr. Williams are going to sell pot to senior citizens?" She had to wonder if Mr. Williams was senile and if, in a brief time, he'd drawn Gran into his loopy world. "What are you going to do? Go to senior citizen homes and sell it?" After the events of the past three days, Kat had seriously thought that she would never laugh again, never find anything funny, but really, this was hilarious. She started to snicker.

"We were thinking along the lines of *assisted* living homes, Katrina, and it's not funny."

"Yes, it is." Kat was laughing now. She'd even caught the attention of Zen and his beyond-perky-gushing Carrie.

The sweet old lady on the other end of the line started to giggle like a schoolgirl. "Okay, it might be a little funny. However, this is the point, Katrina. You will have the money tomorrow morning, and that's that."

"I'll pay you back, Gran," Kat said, still laughing. "I promise."

"I know, dear, whenever." Gran still giggled, too. "I told you it was a humdinger!"

"What's so funny?" Zen asked after Kat hung up the phone. He walked over to her with miniature bombshell Carrie still draped over his arm.

Kat was having a hard time getting a hold of herself. She was mentally and physically exhausted and a little tipsy on top of that, but she couldn't stop laughing. "Oh, it's nothing," she gasped. "No, it's everything."

She gasped one more time. "Well, shit, Zen, I guess it's just life."

14

NOVEMBER-DECEMBER 1980

"I miss Thelma's candy store, too," Sylvia said, taking a bite of her beef stroganoff. "You've got to give the woman credit for that, I guess. She sure knew how to accumulate the goods. I still don't know how she did it."

They were treating themselves to lunch at the Walnut Room on the seventh floor of Marshall Field's. It was a large room with a domed ceiling, and soon the store would erect the giant forty-five-foot Christmas tree in the center of the room, under the dome. It had been a Chicago tradition for years. Families came and saw Santa Claus and then had lunch in the Walnut Room. Melody made a mental note not to come this year. She wasn't yet ready to see all the excited little kids dressed in their Christmas outfits, their faces shining with expectation.

"I'm just thinking that I need a little something more to take the edge off, but only until I get through all this shit," Melody said.

Sylvia nodded emphatically. "I know what you mean. I think about Thelma all the time. Thelma, my mother, the hypochondriac, the addict."

Thelma died less than a month before Melody's labor had been induced, and Sylvia's pain was still raw, too. Plus, she was still in self-recrimination mode. "I should have done more to help her. I saw what was happening," Sylvia said often. Melody had finally, tearfully told Sylvia that she'd had suspicions that something was wrong with the baby but hadn't done anything about it. On the rare occasions that Marcus grudgingly consented to Melody's going somewhere without him, she and Sylvia confided in and consoled each other. After all, they were, more or less, in the same boat.

Plus, they were both on similar meds, alcohol and anti-depressants. The last time Sylvia had gotten really high, she said, was when she'd foolishly spent the night with her mother's third drug dealer, the one with only one attribute. However, even though today had started with great expectations, they were both a little glum. For Sylvia, it started when they walked past the Clinique make-up counter on the first floor, and she saw a woman about their age getting a makeover with her mother. For Melody, it began when she walked into the bathroom and saw a mother changing her baby's diaper.

"When I'm not feeling horrible about the baby, I feel, basically, nothing at all." Melody picked at her Cobb salad. She knew Sylvia would understand, and she did.

"It's a kind of numbness," Sylvia said, "but more than that. I call it the super blahs."

"And the world seems colorless."

"Drab and washed out."

"It's tiring to keep trying to pretend that you believe things will get better in time and that you're functioning normally."

"Exhausting," Sylvia agreed, taking a sip of her wine.

"We're quite the pair, aren't we?"

"Yeah." Sylvia gulped down the rest of her wine. "But we need to snap out of it. This is getting us nowhere. From now on, we should ban pity parties."

"I'm all for banning the pity parties, but how do we go about doing it? It's not like we can throw ourselves into our work. We already do that." Melody would do anything to feel something, to feel *better*. Anything.

"Well." Sylvia had devoured her lunch and started work on the basket of bread. "It's not like we can ask for time off to travel somewhere exotic, or even to Peoria, for that matter. I suppose we could volunteer for some noble cause, but I personally prefer to get paid if I'm going to be noble. That leaves two things: fucking and drugs."

Melody shuddered. "Forget the fucking. I try to avoid it at all costs."

"I don't blame you." The sympathy in Sylvia's voice was genuine. "So I guess we have a winner. Drugs it is."

That was what Melody had actually meant when she told Sylvia that she needed something to take the edge off. She'd been obsessing over their days of research and all the opioids they'd tried: the oxycodone, fentanyl, and hydrocodone. Melody had never felt happier in her life than those two years, and she wanted—no, she needed—to feel that way again. She needed painkillers to kill the pain. It was as simple as that. Still, she hadn't wanted to blatantly come out and say to Sylvia, "Where can we score some drugs?" So she'd casually mentioned Thelma's medicine cabinet. Though, of course, Sylvia knew what she was getting at all along.

"Drugs it is. How do we go about this?" Thelma's candy shop, with its infinite variety, was all the experience that Melody had in obtaining drugs. Looking back, she realized how amazing their access to the painkillers had been, and she didn't have the slightest idea of how to go about this business of buying drugs. Were deals done in alleys, or restaurants, or parks? She would probably have to pay cash, but that was a problem she would worry about later. "What about—"

"No." Sylvia's voice was firm, almost sharp. "We are not going to deal with Thelma's *associates*. They're all scumbags and street lowlifes. I never want to see any of them again."

Melody remained silent, but as usual, Sylvia could read her thoughts on her face.

"I know I slept with them. I'm pleading temporary insanity, okay? I want those three weeks expunged from the record." Sylvia, even though she was fair-skinned, was not prone to blushing. Yet now her face turned bright red.

"Consider your temporary insanity expunged." Melody didn't judge or hold Sylvia's reckless behavior against her. As bad as it had been to lose the baby, losing a mother would be horrible. Losing Ma was unthinkable.

They each ordered another glass of wine. Melody had come up with an idea during all her sleepless nights, but she knew it was far-fetched, wrong, dishonorable, and downright illegal. It started when she went to the hospital pharmacy to get vials of amoxicillin. It had been a particularly bad day for her, one of overwhelming sadness, or as Sylvia put it, a day when the super blahs plagued her. She signed out for the key, and when she unlocked the cabinet, the rows of bottles beckoned to her. How easy it would be to take an extra bottle, to simply write one bottle of morphine or codeine on the inventory sign-out sheet and pocket the other. So many people had access to the cabinet. Who would ever be able to pinpoint her? Melody had quickly dismissed the notion, of course. She could lose her career. She didn't need to be medicated that badly. It was a ludicrous idea. Yet it kept coming back to her as she tossed and turned in bed next to the sleeping, snoring man she'd married. Those rows and rows of bottles. Just there. All she had to do was slip one into her pocket.

Still, tentatively, against her better judgment, she said, "The hospital."

Sylvia didn't act surprised. "Yes."

"We couldn't."

"No." They had ordered apple pie for dessert, and Sylvia took a large bite. "Although I know for a fact that the new resident, skinny Dr. Adams, has dipped into the stash on occasion."

Melody gasped. Dr. Adams, an up-and-coming resident in neurosurgery, was obnoxious and bossy and treated the nurses with disdain, but he was highly regarded by the other doctors, who thought the young man was brilliant. "How do you know?"

"I saw him do it. I was shocked at first, but then I thought, well, he's under enormous pressure, and maybe his nabbing some Quaaludes was a one-time thing. Or maybe it was for a relative or something." Sylvia shrugged. "Who knows? I can tell you one thing, though. I bet it happens a lot more than we would think."

"Do you really think so?" Sylvia was probably right. But even though she had vaguely considered swiping some drugs herself, Melody couldn't help but feel somehow offended by a health professional physically doing such a thing. They were supposed to treat patients with the drugs, not take them themselves.

Sylvia nodded. "Are you going to eat that pie?"

Melody pushed her untouched pie toward Sylvia. "We would never do such a thing, take drugs from patients."

"Right. No matter how desperate we got."

"No matter how desperate," Melody echoed with much less conviction than Sylvia. It was an unfortunate fact. Each day, she became more and more intimately acquainted with that word, with that feeling. *Desperate.*

"Hey, Mr. O'Malley, how are you feeling today?" Melody knocked on the door of the old man's room and walked inside.

Ed O'Malley had been rushed to the ER by ambulance the week before. He'd collapsed mysteriously, and his daughter had called the ambulance. After the usual tests, the doctor on duty diagnosed the man with lung cancer, stage four.

"But he never complained, not once," his daughter said after the doctor told her the diagnosis.

At that point, the old man lying in the ER hospital bed looked at Melody and winked. "I'm tough as nails. This cancer business is for the birds."

Melody had been stopping in for a quick visit after her shifts ever since. He was a tough old man, but he was also a sweetheart. The only thing they could do for him was to keep him as comfortable as possible, but as his daughter had pointed out, he never complained, not once.

Melody had come to look forward to her visits with him. He told wonderful stories about his years as a railroad conductor for the Chicago transit system.

"I saw some things in my time, let me tell you, Miss Melody. I'm pretty sure that Al Capone was on the train one time. The man was a lot shorter than you would think, for a gangster," Mr. O'Malley said on one visit.

"Are gangsters supposed to be tall?" Melody teased.

"If you're going to carry a loaded gun, you better know how to use it," Mr. O'Malley said.

"I agree," Melody answered.

"My neighbor lady liked to plant petunias. Every year, she planted those damn cheap flowers. 'What about roses?' I would say to her, but no. Every year, she plants those damn cheap petunias."

"I prefer roses myself," Melody said.

"That a girl, Miss Melody, that a girl. Do you think you could get the kitchen to give me cherry Jell-O? I'm not a fan of the green stuff they serve here."

"I'll see what I can do."

"The Chicago Bears are going to win the Superbowl this year. That Mike Ditka is one hell of a coach." Mr. O'Malley winced in pain, but he did not utter a word. He reached for the bottle of morphine on his tray.

"If the Bears go to the Superbowl, I'll host a party, and you can come." Melody helped him get the cap off the bottle.

"Is Thanksgiving on a Thursday this year?"

"I believe so," Melody said.

It didn't matter at all to Melody that their conversations were not only one-sided but also disjointed and circuitous. She still enjoyed the old man's company, his still-bright blue eyes, and his wicked sense of humor. She looked forward to such a conversation today, but she saw Carlita, another nurse, replacing a bag of fluid on the IV when she entered the room. Mr. O'Malley appeared to be sleeping, and he looked small and skeletal under the white hospital blanket.

"What's going on?" she asked Carlita.

"Mr. O'Malley just had a bad night." Carlita's voice was overly cheerful. "He's taking a little rest now."

Melody knew what the IV meant. Mr. O'Malley had taken a turn for the worse. It could happen so fast with cancer or with any disease. Even though she hadn't been a nurse for very long, Melody was sure she would never get used to how quickly people could pass from this world. Even though she had seen too many deaths already, she would never get used to people dying. But it was a hazard of the job. It was also a hazard of life.

"Not much time left," Carlita whispered on her way out. "Poor old guy."

"Oh, no," Melody whispered back. She knew the man was in his eighties and had been a two-pack a day smoker since he'd been a teenager, but it was still sad. Just yesterday, he had been full of life, or as he would say, full of piss and vinegar. Now he was still, his eyes closed, his mouth and cheeks sunken. Someone had taken out Mr. O'Malley's dentures, and Melody knew that if he regained consciousness, he would not be happy about that. He was very proud of his "eight hundred-dollar choppers."

The only thing that gave her comfort was that he couldn't see her cry. She stood by his bed and patted his hand. Then she leaned over and gave him a soft kiss on his forehead. "It's Melody, Mr. O'Malley. I stopped by to say hello, but I guess tomorrow would be better for you. You have a nice rest, and I'll make sure the kitchen gives you two cherry Jell-Os for dinner. You take care now." She gave his hand a final pat.

She cried hard now. She reached for the box of tissues on the nightstand, and that's when she saw it. The bottle of morphine.

The sight of that bottle with all the relief it promised paralyzed her. Morphine could work on the limbic system and cause increased feelings of contentment. *Morphine could make her feel better.*

But she couldn't take a patient's medication, especially if that patient was dear Mr. O'Malley. What if he suddenly woke up and needed it? She wasn't that desperate, was she? She had her Xanax, her Valium, her vodka. They should be enough to tide her over until she felt better, or normal, or however she used to feel before everything went black. She couldn't remember what that feeling was.

The Xanax, the Valium, and the vodka were not enough.

She glanced at the old man. He was dying from terminal lung cancer. He wasn't going to wake up. The IV drip contained all the morphine and other drugs that he needed to ensure that he was as comfortable as possible. He no longer needed the oral doses of morphine.

And she did.

But what if Carlita came back and saw that the pills were missing? Why hadn't she taken them away when she hooked up the IV? Perhaps Carlita hadn't noticed the pills at all. Perhaps the hospital had an overabundance of morphine, plenty enough for everyone who needed it.

Melody glanced one more time at the dying man and made her decision.

Did Melody feel guilty after she stole a bottle of morphine from a dying man? Yes. Did she feel guilty enough to return the next day and discreetly place the precious pills back on Mr. O'Malley's nightstand? No. However, she did secret away the drugs for a few days in her underwear drawer to make sure that no one in the hospital mentioned the missing pills or started to question the nurses. She was nervous at work during those days, paranoid almost to the point of distraction, but no one said a word.

Finally, when she thought the coast was clear, she went to Sylvia's apartment and shared her stash. She dumped the contents on Sylvia's kitchen table. "I stole these tablets from a dying man," she said, not daring to look at her best friend. "I can't believe I did it."

Sylvia took a sharp intake of breath. "Amazing."

"Please don't think I'm a terrible person. I already think I'm a terrible person, but I don't want you to share that thought." She didn't know what she would do if Sylvia reprimanded her. She would probably become completely undone.

"I didn't think you had it in you," Sylvia said.

"Me either," Melody said glumly.

"I don't think you're a terrible person." Sylvia sat down at the table, still staring at the pills. "Whose were they?"

"Mr. O'Malley's."

"Oh, he died last night." When she saw Melody's stricken face, she quickly added, "He never regained consciousness again, Mel. He never knew, and I'm sure he wouldn't think any less of you if he did know."

Maybe the old man wouldn't have cared, but what she'd done was still wrong on every level. Perhaps she should go to his funeral—and do what? Atone in some way? She'd only met Mr. O'Malley's daughter once, and technically, he hadn't even been her patient. Sylvia, she knew, would tell her she was overly sensitive, that she was wearing her heart on her sleeve, that she was unprofessional. Death, Sylvia would say, was part of the job.

"Let's try these babies out." Sylvia divvied up the pills. "Pour us each a drink, and we'll give a toast to Mr. O'Malley. We'll get a jump-start on Thanksgiving."

The next day was Thanksgiving, and it was the one thing that Melody had been looking forward to. Marcus could not object to visiting her parents on a major holiday. It was Callahan family law, even more important than mandatory Sunday family dinners. They spent the holidays together. Period. She'd told that to Marcus point-blank, and for once, he hadn't tried to cajole her into changing her mind.

"You are truly the best, Syl," Melody said as she unscrewed the vodka bottle. "I'm glad you're coming tomorrow."

"Thanks for inviting me."

Neither one of them stated the obvious. Sylvia had no place else to go.

The next day, Melody and Marcus, with Evelyn in tow, arrived at 1113 S. Roosevelt Street a little after noon. Ma always served dinner at 2:00, but she wanted everyone in the family to *socialize* on holidays, not just eat and run. So it happened, every year, that her husband and three sons were pretty much sloshed by the time everyone sat down to dinner.

This year Melody planned to not be far behind them in the drinking department. She hadn't dared to take another morphine tablet because she had to be functional enough to help Ma in the kitchen. Ma always cooked too much food, waking at 4:00 in the morning to cook the turkey, stuffing, green beans, succotash, creamed corn, mashed potatoes, gravy, cranberry salad, and six pumpkin pies with homemade whipped cream. Everything was time-consuming, made from scratch. The family ate, the men went into the living room to watch football, and Ma cleaned and scoured, and carefully put away the good china. That was Ma's Thanksgiving and Melody's, too.

However, Melody wouldn't mind this year. She looked forward to spending time with Ma, even if it was in an overheated and cluttered kitchen, and she was going to drink just enough to elevate her mood a little bit. No, Melody wasn't going to take any morphine. She needed to hoard those precious tablets. The evening before, she and Sylvia were amazed at how relaxed they felt and how *contented* they were after ingesting the pills. Melody felt like she was floating, untethered by dismal reality. She hadn't felt that good in a long, long time.

Eventually, she had to call Marcus to come and get her. She and Sylvia had lost all track of time, and she missed the last train to Evergreen Park. She told Marcus that she thought she got food poisoning at the restaurant. (They hadn't gone to a restaurant.) She told him she was a little loopy because she was light-headed from all the vomiting.

Marcus, of course, wasn't pleased. He'd thrown his coat on over his pajamas, and his brown hair stood up in points. "I have been pacing the floor, worrying about you, kitten. I guessed you were at Sylvia's, and I must have called her apartment seven times." A light snow had begun to fall, and Marcus drove cautiously through the streets.

"Sylvia's phone is out of order." Marcus had called at least eleven times. Knowing it was him, she and Sylvia ignored the ringing and giggled as they played a game of make-up-a-word Scrabble. It had been hilarious, the words they had come up with (oonza, bbycok jintalo). Wonderfully hilarious.

"I would appreciate you telling me when you are going out, where you are going, when you will get back, and how I can contact you. That kind of communication is essential between a man and his wife."

A *man* and his wife, not a *husband* and his wife. It was so Marcus. "Aye, aye, sir!" She almost lost it in a fit of giggles, but she held on.

Marcus looked at her sharply. "What's wrong with you?"

"Nothing." Then she remembered. She subdued her voice to a whisper. "Food poisoning."

Marcus turned into their driveway. "It's stress, honey. I know it's stress. My little flower is working too hard." He could switch gears into sympathetic mode now that he'd solved the situation.

"Sure," Melody said. It was always a safe bet to agree with Marcus when he was obsessed with *stress*.

He turned off the ignition and turned to look at her. The streetlight reflected off his glasses. "I love you so much, Mellie, so much. Your welfare is of great concern to me."

As usual, Marcus ended up screwing up his heartfelt sentiments with some crap that sounded stiff and old man-ish. Her *welfare* was of great concern to him. Melody sighed and sat up straighter, now that he was looking directly at her. She tried to hold her head up properly, but it was suddenly very, very heavy. "I know, Marcus."

"And I think, kitten, that Sylvia Hammond is a bad influence on you."

This was not the first time he'd said this to Melody, and the flash of anger that it incited helped to sober her up for a moment. "No, she isn't, Marcus. She's my best friend and a wonderful person, a wonderful nurse. She is most definitely not a bad influence on me. Maybe if you had some friends, you would know what I was talking about." She wanted to offend him, to wound him, to make him mad.

It never, ever worked. "All I need is you, Mellie," he said softly.

"And Evelyn," she said snidely.

"Her, too."

"Well, I need Sylvia." Melody opened the car door. "And you better be nice to her tomorrow."

Marcus, damn him, was being nice to her. He was polite to everyone; he was in his perfect gentleman mode. Shortly after they arrived, and he'd deposited his mother in the wing back chair in the living room where she could look out the window, he came into the kitchen and offered to help. He should have known by now that the men in her family did not help in the kitchen, but then again, he was *Marcus*. Flustered Ma accepted his offer and put him to work mashing the potatoes. Melody was incensed. She had so wanted this time alone with Ma. She wanted to talk about the baby (not Marcus, Jr., *her* baby) and what she'd been going through. She wanted to subtly hint to Ma that all was not rosy in her world. She hadn't exactly planned how she would broach the subject, but now it no longer mattered. Marcus, knowingly or unknowingly, had seen to that. When Sylvia came into the kitchen, offering help, Marcus, smiling, said to her, "Thank you, Sylvia, but I think we have it under control." Sylvia rolled her eyes at Melody, and that was when Melody unwisely decided to sneak another drink.

By the time they all sat down to dinner, Melody was as sloshed as her daddy and brothers. Sylvia, perhaps, was even worse. Frankie, Mikey, and Willie didn't have dates, naturally, and since Sylvia had been alone with the men during the prep time before dinner (Evelyn did not count), she had manned-up to the occasion and matched them drink for drink.

"Our Sylvia is such a fine gal." Willie, her favorite brother, looked at Sylvia with unabashed lust.

"She is so very tall and fine." Frankie, too, looked like he was undressing Sylvia with his eyes.

"Va-va-voom" was Mikey's original contribution.

"I love you all so much!" Sylvia gushed. "Well, not so much Marcus and … what's her name." She nodded toward Evelyn. "But I can learn to love them, too, in time. I am a very loving person."

"Isn't this jolly?" Daddy beamed around the table. "I haven't been this jolly since Mellie's wedding."

Oh boy, Melody thought, *we are in such trouble here.* Everyone had been very drunk at her wedding, herself included. By the end of that evening, she'd been told, her daddy and brothers had to be forcibly removed from the American Legion bar. She looked at Ma, who didn't seem to be the least bit perturbed by the drunken state of her family. Poor, poor Ma. She was so used to the situation that she didn't even notice it. Melody wanted to weep for her poor, poor Ma. "I love you, Ma," she whispered, but no one heard her because they were laughing at an entirely inappropriate joke that Frankie had told about a traveling salesman who met a farmer who had a daughter who liked to …

It was Marcus who reminded them that they had forgotten to say grace.

"Well, I'll be damned." Daddy pounded his fist on the table, making the water glasses and beer cans tremble.

"Oh, dear." Ma nervously glanced at Marcus and Evelyn. She twisted her linen napkin in her chapped, hard-working hands. "What must you think of us? We always say grace. Truly, we always do."

Marcus, unlike the rest, had not yet touched his food. With a bib tied around her neck, Evelyn slept in her chair, entirely oblivious to the religious faux pas. "I'm sure it was just an oversight, Claudia. Everyone just got caught up in the festivities." He patted her hand. "Don't you worry about what I think."

He is such a hypocrite, Melody thought. They had not set foot inside a church since their wedding day, not once.

"I'm sure everybody here is very thankful and can say a silent prayer to themselves," Marcus said soothingly.

He was unbelievable, so smug in his checkered wool vest. Melody had never wanted to hit him more than right then. Her anger might be irrational—and drunkenly induced—but she couldn't help it. He'd butted in on her time with Ma, and now he was butting in on her family. Was she the only one who noticed this?

"Everyone should pray a silent prayer of thanksgiving," Daddy instructed. "I'm sure the Lord will think it's good enough."

There was a two-second silence.

"We need more gravy, Ma." Mikey held up the empty gravy boat.

"I'll get it, Ma," Melody said. Marcus sat across the table from her, and Melody made an uneven detour around the table on the way to the kitchen. Everyone at the table was so loud that she knew no one would hear her when she bent down and whispered in his ear. "Will you just stop it? Will you stop trying to run the show? My family was a family way before you came into the picture, mister." She knew it didn't quite make sense, what she was saying, but she just wanted him to shut up. In truth, she didn't want him there at all. If there had been any gravy left in the gravy boat, she would have poured it all over his head.

He smiled at her and shrugged. He hadn't heard her.

When she returned from the kitchen with the gravy boat, and after talking herself out of the impulse to pour it all over Marcus, her brothers were bickering. "Come on, Sylvia, which one of us would you go out with?" Frankie said. His face was flushed bright red with alcohol.

"She thinks she's too good for the likes of us," Mikey said.

"I treat women better than these two," Willie said.

"Huh!" Frankie said. "You screw—"

"Boys, boys, please," Sylvia placated. Even though her red lipstick smeared around her mouth, she didn't seem to have lost her allure. "I can't go out with any of you. You're Melody's brothers. You're like family to me."

Why had she ever thought she missed them? Melody wondered. They were whiny and immature and had the gall to hit on her best friend on a holiday. If she sat at this table long enough, she could work up rage toward everyone. They were all behaving stupidly on this sacred holiday, and it had been something she had looked forward to. (Wait a minute. Thanksgiving wasn't sacred, was it? Thanksgiving was always on a Thursday. She was pretty sure she'd told Mr. O'Malley that. Poor, poor man. He was dead. She had stolen his pills.)

No one in her family—the family she'd longed to come home to—had mentioned her baby. No one. They had mourned him at the funeral; she had seen them cry. Yet now, weeks after her baby was *still born*, they had forgotten about him. It was intolerable.

The boys' squabbling grew louder, and Daddy started pounding on the table again. "You need to settle down, all of you. You're upsetting your mother."

Melody glanced at Ma. She was deep in conversation with Marcus and not paying any attention to the commotion at the other end of the table. What was he saying to her? Lies. It was probably all lies. Marcus had a way of doing that to a person, making the person believe that what he said was true. It was the tone of voice he used—calm, rational, unruffled. He could tell a person that the world was flat, and just for a second, you believed him. After five months of marriage, she knew that about him now. But Ma didn't. She should warn Ma.

Her brothers, supposedly grown men, now kicked each other under the table. It was unbelievable.

"Take it outside, boys, before you knock over the table." Daddy didn't seem inclined to do more to stop what would be a sibling brawl. Granted, he had seen them fight many times, but holidays were usually off-limits. He opened another beer.

Sylvia sat stoically in the middle of them, smiling, smoking a cigarette. She was probably enjoying herself, and for the first time, for the merest of seconds, Melody felt rage toward her, too. Could this Thanksgiving get any worse?

Yes.

Marcus stood up. "I would like to say something. Frankie, Mikey, Willie, do you mind?"

Melody didn't know how they could hear him over their ruckus, but they did. They stopped bickering and kicking and looked at Marcus.

It was eerie, the sudden quiet. Melody, too, looked up at her husband, and without warning, a sense of dread began to build. What had he said to Ma? What was he going to say now? Why in the hell did her family listen to him? He wasn't a part of them; he wasn't related by blood. These people were her family, not his. *Hers.*

"I am honored to be in this home for the first Thanksgiving that Mellie and I have had as man and wife. Mother is, too." He glanced at Evelyn, who had not awakened during the meal, and her bib did not have a single stain.

"We all suffered a great loss this year," Marcus continued, his voice becoming graver, moving into a lower register. "A tragedy."

Sniffling began—immediate, drunken sniffling.

Melody had wanted them to talk about the baby, but not like this, and not initiated by *him*. Marcus acted like a minister, professor, or motivational speaker with his formal tone and regal demeanor. But she'd seen him grieve, too. She had witnessed his terrible grief. But now he did not act like a bereaved father, not at all.

"But with tragedy, we must move forward—"

Was that the secret—*moving forward*? Had everyone done that but her? How could they? Her baby had been a living being. She'd felt him move inside her and knew he was alive. He had been a genius, making his presence known to her at only sixteen weeks, his butterfly presence. She started to cry softly.

"And there will be more babies. Believe me, we will try." Marcus' voice was now offering hope and redemption. He winked.

Snicker, snicker. Grown men, her brothers, *snickering*. Marcus' audience was eating it up. He had them in the palm of his hand.

"On this Thanksgiving Day—Mellie's and my first—I just want all of you to know how grateful I am for my beautiful wife, who is the love of my life." He choked up a little on that and reached into his pants pocket.

The dread had now climbed up from the pit of Melody's stomach into her throat. She was afraid she would be sick. How dare he do this! How dare he make a mockery of their lost baby, and how dare he make a spectacle like this in front of her family. The love of his life? Lies. All lies.

"Since we had such a whirlwind courtship, I didn't get a chance to give Mellie this." He opened the black velvet box and presented it to the table: a ring with a large diamond surrounded by smaller emerald and ruby baguettes.

On cue, his captive audience again gave the appropriate response: oohs and aahs.

"Would you look at the size of that thing?" Willie said with awe in his voice.

"My goodness," Ma said breathlessly.

"It was Mother's. She wanted me to give this to Mellie with her blessing." Evelyn still slept in the chair. "Come around the table, Mellie. I want your family to see me put this ring on your finger, where it belongs."

Mellie couldn't move. She did not want the ring. She did not want any more rings—or pearls, for that matter—from this man. She knew what he was trying to do. He was trying to bind her even more closely to him and to Evelyn, too, trying to seal her fate with her family and best friend as witnesses. As witnesses and as his willing accomplices.

Except for Sylvia. When Melody shot her a frantic glance, Sylvia shook her head furiously. "No," she mouthed, "don't do it."

Sylvia was outnumbered. "Come and let Marcus put the ring on your finger," Ma said. "It's so beautiful." The others echoed Ma's words: "Go on, Mellie, go on."

Their eyes were upon her. They expected her to accept the diamond ring from her husband because it was the right thing to do, in their eyes. What young bride wouldn't be shedding tears of joy at such an elaborate and beautiful gift? There was again no choice. Marcus had set it up beautifully. She got up slowly, her limbs feeling wooden, and went to his side.

He slipped the ring on her finger. "A perfect fit."

"Our Mellie is a lucky girl." Daddy had to wipe the tears from his eyes.

Melody did not say a word, and she did not give Marcus the kiss everyone expected.

The stones felt heavy on her hand.

By mid-December, Melody's supply of morphine ran out. She had tried so hard to ration the pills, only taking them when she felt extremely low or agitated. She had only taken them when it was absolutely necessary, like on the two-month anniversary of the baby's birth. And when nights in front of the damn TV, with Marcus' horrible sitcoms blasting canned laughter, became so unbearable that she wanted to run screaming from the house. The pills had become a safety net, a special treat. When things got really bad, when she felt the angst and depression drilling into her skull, tearing her apart, she knew she had a way to cope.

Now they were gone. Sylvia's, unfortunately, were gone, too. It would be all right, Melody kept telling herself. The pills were only a temporary crutch. She really didn't need them. If she believed in what Marcus said, all she had to do was *move forward*, put one foot in front of the other, and she could get through each day. It was that simple.

She didn't believe Marcus. It wasn't that simple. She needed more time to heal and get over everything that had blindsided her in the past year: an unplanned pregnancy, marriage to a man she barely knew, the loss of the baby she had come to love. She needed more time. And more pills.

Christmas had been sheer hell to get through without the help that morphine gave. It was supposed to be the happiest time of the year—Melody had always believed that—but this year had been horrible. She didn't see merry people and the spirit of giving. She saw frantic people with too little time to get everything done. She saw the great divide between the haves and the have-nots. She saw way too many people wheeled into the ER injured and maimed because they tried to drive home drunk from yet another Christmas party. She saw complete and utter bullshit.

Now it was New Year's Eve, and there were only two halfway cheerful things about it. First, it signaled the end of the holiday season, and second, it marked the end of a truly dreadful year. Neither one was worthy of celebration, so Melody had volunteered to work the night shift. No paper hats and tooting horns and confetti for her. No champagne toasts and singing "Auld Lang Syne." She would work and hope that all the parties didn't wreak too much havoc on human lives. She would put on her starched uniform and her hat and be the professional that she was. She would be competent. She would have grace under pressure. She would try not to think about anything but the job.

So far, it wasn't working. The night had been slow—a good thing, of course, but it wasn't midnight yet—and she'd been stuck on the shift with Linda Carlson. Linda was a couple of years older than Melody and Sylvia, and neither could stand working with her. She constantly jabbered about her stream of boyfriends, the brand of makeup she currently used, and the clothes she intended to buy with her next paycheck—all of it stupid and shallow. "She acts so high and mighty," Sylvia once said about her, "and everyone knows that she's the hospital slut." Melody had been trying to look busy with paperwork during most of the evening, but it wasn't detouring Linda.

"My boyfriend, Gino, just bought a brand-new Mustang. Did I tell you that already?" She hovered over Melody's right shoulder.

"I believe you mentioned it," Melody said. *Only ten times*, she thought.

"He's going to be somebody someday. He's going to take over his dad's pizza shop soon, and he plans on opening pizzerias all over the city. He should be rolling in the dough soon. Haha, get it? Rolling in the *dough*."

"Good for him." Everyone knew that Linda had dated a string of losers and slept with some unmarried doctors. Some of the married ones, too.

"He's not too tall, but his physique, let me tell you about it. He's got muscles on top of muscles. He lifts weights."

Melody could feel Linda's breath on the back of her neck. "Uh-huh."

"And when we make love, let me tell you, he's got an enormous—"

"Jesus!" Melody interrupted. "I'm not interested in the size of your boyfriend's cock."

Linda just kept jabbering away. She didn't listen or reciprocate in conversation. No, she just rambled on endlessly, and obviously, it was impossible to hurt her feelings. "I hoped for an engagement ring for Christmas. We've only been dating for a few weeks, but when it's right, it's right, you know?"

Melody wanted to say, "No, I don't know anything about when it's right, it's right. I married a man I didn't love, the first almost-boyfriend I ever had." But she didn't say anything, hoping that her silence would get the message across to this blabbering idiot.

No such luck. "Say, didn't I see you with a big rock on your finger a few days ago? I knew you were married, but this ring is new, right? Why don't you have it on?"

"It gets in my way." Melody turned to face her.

"Gets in your way?" Linda said, incredulous. "Why, if I had a big rock like that on my left hand, I'd be showing it off to everyone."

A big rock. That's what it was, definitely. It felt heavy, unnatural on her hand. She hated it. Every time she looked at it, it was a glaring reminder of Marcus, just as he had intended it to be. As soon as she got to work, she stowed it in her locker. When she went grocery shopping or ran errands, she put it in her purse. Basically, every time Marcus was out of sight, she took off the ring. "It gets in my way," she repeated.

Before Linda could offer a blabbering reply, Dr. Reynolds rounded the corner. "Good. You're not too busy." He wrote on his prescription pad, tore off the slip, and put it on the counter. "I need two vials of diamorphine. Could you get it for me? I'll be in room 236." And he was off, his white coat flying out like wings.

"That man is always in a hurry," Linda said. "I hear he's—"

"I'll go," Melody cut her off. The woman's thick, nasal Chicago accent was shredding her nerves.

Melody walked down the hall toward the pharmacy, signed out for the key, and noted the medication she was taking. Even as she unlocked the appropriate cabinet, she was not thinking of taking anything. Even in her desperate, morphine-deprived state, she was not thinking of stealing any medication. It was only when she opened the door and saw the rows and rows of bottles—all those amazing drugs—that she stopped short. Her heart started to beat rapidly, and it became hard to breathe. "You are not going to take anything," Melody whispered. "You have opened this cabinet hundreds of times, and you have not taken anything. You are not going to take anything now."

But there were so many of them. It was like opening Thelma's candy shop, magnified hundreds of times. There were so many of them, so many painkillers that would kill the pain. "I need more time," she whispered to the bottles. "If I just had a little more time, I could get over this."

She felt like she was watching from a great distance as she took the two vials for Dr. Reynolds and the bottle of morphine for herself. She quickly closed and locked the cabinet and was turning, stuffing the bottle in her pocket.

"What are you doing?" Dr. Desoto stood in the doorway.

"I—" Melody's face drained of color.

"I've always had a fondness for redheads," Dr. Desoto said as he closed the door.

15

APRIL 2012

Kat had four days to solve the riddle of Melody and Marcus Arnold's lives. After that, Zen was moving into the city, and Kat could not, in good conscience, impose on his parents' hospitality any longer, even though they did seem happy about her staying. Granny Nanny's money arrived the next morning, and Kat felt terrible when she picked it up, but what could she do? On this part of the adventure, she would have to rely on the kindness of strangers—and Gran, once again. And pay everyone back as soon as she could.

Four days. It would certainly be enough time to find out everything Kat needed to know about the stranger who had jumped and inadvertently given birth to her. When she thought about it, her father was a stranger, too. He'd evidently led another life before her birth, not that he'd ever shared it with her. He hadn't shared anything about his past with his only daughter. She had been born to strangers, and they had remained strangers. But they had not been kind.

Kat borrowed Zen's computer and got to work. When she added "tragic leap" to Melody Arnold's name, the *Chicago Tribune* article showed up, but that was the extent of the information that the internet revealed about the woman. It was painful, but Kat forced herself to reread the article, searching for clues she might have missed during her first shocked reading. She'd missed a lot. Melody Arnold, from Evergreen Park, had been twenty-four when she jumped, six years younger than Kat now. Kat tried to remember what she'd been like at that age. She probably had a dead-end job and a loser boyfriend. She probably hadn't had a clue as to how a grown-up should behave, but that didn't mean she was going to cut this Melody Arnold any slack. Not yet.

Kat had also missed the perhaps most telling detail about Melody Arnold when she first read the article in Tanner Delaney's red scrapbook. She had been an ER nurse at Mercy Hospital. The woman had been a nurse! It made it even more stupefying that she would think her baby was dead, even after the doctors tried to reassure her that the baby was alive by letting her listen to the heartbeat through a stethoscope. Maybe Zen's hesitant suggestion that she might have had a mental illness wasn't so far off base. The woman had been in labor, checked into a hospital—different from the one she worked at—and then somehow escaped to an abandoned railroad yard some miles away. It was definitely crazy behavior.

Or maybe the woman had been depressed, and something or someone pushed her over the edge. Maybe it had been a family tragedy, or marriage to Marcus Arnold had not been what she'd hoped for. Now that was a definite possibility. Maybe Melody Arnold had gotten knocked up and had to marry Marcus, or they were in the process of getting divorced. Had he been as cold to his wife as he had been to his daughter? Kat sighed. Every question she had led directly to another question.

Next, she went to the Peoplefinders website. If she ordered profiles on Melody and Marcus Arnold, it would take a few days to get the reports emailed to her. And they were expensive, at least for her. Plus, she wasn't sure if the Melody Arnold that the website located in Pullman was *her* Melody Arnold. The newspaper article said she was from Evergreen Park. Would the site even carry a profile on a woman who had committed suicide three decades ago?

It seemed to Kat that she was getting nowhere when she had no time to lose. She closed the computer and tried to think of a plan. Even if she got more facts on Melody Arnold, she still might not find out the most important thing: Why did the woman jump? Kat still sat at the dining room table, staring into space, not getting anywhere, when Zen walked in. His bike and other belongings had arrived that morning, and he'd immediately hopped on the bike and gone for a ride. After he walked her home the night before, he'd gone out again, and she hadn't spoken to him since.

"How's it going?" he asked.

Like the first time they'd met at Granny Nanny's, his hair was matted with sweat, but he did not look unappealing. It was unfortunate, in Kat's opinion, that he didn't smell either. "It's going nowhere. I've got questions chasing questions."

"What did you find out?" He started to stretch, hands on hips, lunging forward.

Kat tried not to stare at his muscular calves. "Pretty much only what the *Tribune* article stated."

"That's enough to get you started, isn't it? You know where she was from and where she worked."

Zen must have read the article more thoroughly than she had the first time through. "I know those facts, but I still don't know anything about her. For example, what was her maiden name? If I knew that, I could track down her family."

"That's easy enough. Melody Arnold's maiden name would be on your birth certificate." Now Zen was doing squats.

Shit. Why hadn't that occurred to her? "I know that." He'd been in the room for about thirty seconds, and he'd already accomplished more than she had in the last hour. To change the subject, she asked, "How was your date last night?"

"It wasn't exactly a date."

"Not that I care," she added, too late.

He grinned at her. "Not that you care," he echoed.

"I really don't," she said, her face coloring.

"Carrie's an old friend. She's going through a rough patch and just needed a shoulder to cry on." He finished his squats.

"Right."

It was his turn to change the subject. "Didn't the article mention a police officer at the scene? He might be a good starting point."

Shit. Kat hadn't thought of that either. Zen had missed his calling. He should have been a private investigator. "I was thinking along those lines myself." She averted her eyes. Granny Nanny had always told her that her eyes spoke the truth, no matter what her mouth said.

"Why don't you see if you can find out where he lives? I'll jump in the shower and go with you since I know this area well from all my high school cruising days. If you don't mind, that is."

"I'd like that," she said and meant it.

Less than thirty minutes later, they were on Greg Simpson's street. She had still been struggling to find him on the internet when Zen appeared showered and dressed in jeans and a t-shirt. He produced a phone book and found the number instantly. Of course. But it was Kat who made the phone call to make sure he was the right Greg Simpson and would be home. Remembering the looks she had gotten from Tanner Delaney and Mario Capino when they knew who she was, she told Officer Simpson right off the bat: "I'm Kat Flowers. I'm the baby who survived the 100-foot leap from the light tower." He'd whistled. "I'll be damned," he said. "You'd be thirty years old now, right?"

Zen parked in front of Officer Simpson's house. "Do you want me to go in with you?"

"Yes, please." She'd just assumed that he would, but she could see his point in asking. Maybe some people would like to find out more details about their mother's death alone, but she was not one of them, and suddenly, she felt filled with dread. Did she genuinely want to know the sordid details? Tanner Delaney and Mario Capino had not gone into much detail about the state of Melody Arnold's ... body ... the condition of the body. Kat realized now that they must have avoided the subject to protect her. If Officer Simpson went into greater detail, it would make it much more real to her.

She still didn't quite believe that a pregnant woman had jumped from a light tower.

It was an article in a newspaper.

Kat didn't want it to be real.

Greg Simpson, in his early fifties, had aged well. He wore his salt and pepper gray hair in a short military cut, and he opened the door before they had a chance to ring the bell. "It's nice to meet you. I never thought this day would come."

"I still have nightmares about it," he said later after his wife had brought them iced tea. (Officer Simpson pointed out, for no apparent reason, that it was his second wife.) "Not as frequently as at the beginning, but I still have them. I was only twenty-two when it happened." He shook his head.

Now that she was face-to-face with the only witness of Melody Arnold's suicide, Kat found that it was hard for her to speak. The man had witnessed the woman's jump, and the dread that had started in the car grew. She'd waited her entire life to know her mother's story, only to find out that it was a nightmare. She felt pity for this man—and for herself, too—but not for Melody Arnold.

"It must have been traumatic for you," Zen said, breaking the silence that had fallen over the three of them.

"Yes. I've been on the force for almost thirty-one years now, and I've never seen anything like it. Thank God." He took a sip of his iced tea. "Damn it, Virginia, you made the tea too sweet again!" he called out.

"If you want unsweetened tea, you can make it yourself," Virginia's voice called from the kitchen.

"The woman is from the South," he explained to Kat and Zen. "They like sweet tea down there. We've been married for twenty-five years now, and I still can't get her to make unsweetened tea."

Another awkward silence fell, and Kat wondered where to begin. She cleared her throat to find her voice. "Thank you for seeing me."

He smiled for the first time. "My pleasure. I didn't find out until later that the baby—you—survived. That, at least, was a comfort. I was pretty shaken up when the EMTs arrived."

"My dad was one of the EMTs," Zen said. "Tanner Delaney."

Officer Simpson nodded, not looking the least bit surprised. "Good man."

Again, the awkward silence. Kat was beginning to think they shouldn't have come here. The man obviously didn't want to talk about it, and she didn't really want to hear it. Kat looked over at Zen, trying to signal that she wanted to leave. She reached for her purse.

"I got the call at 4:35 p.m. on that March Sunday," Officer Simpson said out of the blue. "She was already climbing the tower when I arrived. She was far enough up that I wasn't sure if it was a man or a woman, so I didn't know she was pregnant."

Kat put her purse back on the floor. Zen leaned forward, listening, his hands clasped.

"She climbed slowly—with determination, I guess—one rung at a time. When people asked me later how she did it, I said *sheer will*. That's the only explanation I had for it then, and it's still the only explanation I can come up with now. Sheer will." Officer Simpson stared at a place on the wall behind Kat and Zen as his memory formed into words.

"I yelled for her to come down, but it was a windy day, and my siren was still blaring, so I don't know if she heard me. For years, I felt so guilty that I couldn't do more, that I couldn't make her climb back down that tower, that I didn't have the time to climb up and get her. Years. But I've finally concluded that she wouldn't have climbed down. I think her mind was made up."

Kat felt a chill go through her body. The woman had been determined to jump. She could hear her father's words in her head: *Your mother made a choice.* "Her mind was made up," she whispered. "She was going to jump."

"The way I remember it, or maybe this is just the recurring image of my dreams, it was more like a swan dive." He shook his head vigorously as if to clear it. "I'm sorry." He looked directly at Kat. "I'm sorry I made you cry."

Kat hadn't realized she was crying, but when she touched her cheek, she felt the slippery wetness of a tear. "Oh, I'm not crying." She wiped her hand on her jeans. "I'm fine." However, she didn't feel fine. *Confused* was more like it. And hurt. Her mother had clearly not wanted her. "I mean, this is all new to me. I only found out about it yesterday."

Officer Simpson nodded. "Your father didn't tell you." It was a statement of fact.

"No, he always told me my mother—Melody Arnold—had died in childbirth."

"Don't think I can blame the man. He was torn up about it, as any man would be, I guess."

Her father, stoic Marcus Flowers, had been torn up about it? The man who so rarely showed any emotion? "You interviewed him?"

"I tried. I went to the hospital afterward. Marcus had been sedated by that time. They said he had been out of control and had pretty much busted up the waiting room, which he had. I saw it with my own eyes: broken chairs, shattered vases, a smashed window. But even though he was sedated, he was still crying and shouting: 'Why?' and 'Tell her to come back to me now! She's the love of my life!' I'd never seen a man cry like that before, or since. Thank God." Officer Simpson looked uncomfortable. He shifted in his chair. "I thought I'd go back the next day and interview him."

"What did he have to say?" Zen was still leaning forward in his chair, listening intently.

"He wasn't there. The hospital wanted to keep him overnight, but when a nurse checked on him at 2:00 a.m., he was gone. Can't say I blame him for that one either. The last place you'd want to be after something like that is chained to a hospital bed, alone with your thoughts. It could drive a man crazy, I would guess."

"Chained?" Kat whispered. Even though she had three decades of anger stored up against her father, she didn't want to imagine him chained to a bed.

"Not chained, exactly, tied. They had to restrain him." Officer Simpson shifted again in his chair. "Sorry."

Kat touched her cheek. More tears.

"Hey, Virginia, do we have any more of that cinnamon coffee cake left? Our guests could probably use a little refreshment," Officer Simpson yelled in the vicinity of the kitchen.

"No!" Virginia called back. "You ate the whole damn thing last night after supper."

"We're okay," Zen said politely. "The iced tea is enough." He took a sip to prove it and then went back to his intently listening position. "So did you go to Marcus Arnold's house to interview him."

"I tried that, too, of course, but he'd already gone. His whole place was cleaned out, and there wasn't any need to pursue him. It was a clear-cut suicide. I witnessed it with my own eyes. No one pushed Melody Arnold off that light tower." A veil of sadness seemed to drop over Officer Simpson's face. He repeated, "No one pushed her. I saw it with my own eyes."

A clear-cut suicide. The words roiled in Kat's brain. Clear. Cut. Suicide.

Zen gently asked, "What about the baby?"

Officer Simpson looked at Kat sympathetically. "As I recall, he didn't take the baby from the hospital. I think one of his wife's relatives took her home when she was discharged a few days later. I'm not sure of those details. I was onto about three or four other cases by then."

"But he obviously went and got the baby later," Kat said. She meant to defend her father, and she didn't know why. Had he been scouting for a new place to live? Had he wanted to get settled someplace new before he brought his baby home? More questions, more questions.

"That's correct," Officer Simpson said as if the case was closed.

"I think we've taken up enough of your time." Zen glanced over at Kat

Kat knew she probably looked as fragile as she felt when Zen gently helped her to her feet. She needed to get out of there fast before she fell to pieces in front of the only person who had witnessed Melody Arnold's suicide. "Thank you, Officer Simpson. You've helped me a lot."

"I hope I helped," he said, walking them to the front door. "It was the damndest thing I've ever seen." He shook his head as he opened the door for them.

Kat took a deep gulp of air on the porch, but it didn't help clear her brain or make her feel better. There were too many thoughts running through her head. The pregnant woman had climbed the light tower with sheer will, determined to jump. It had been a clear-cut suicide; no one had pushed her off the tower. Her father had left town without his daughter.

"One more thing," Officer Simpson said as they descended the steps. "I don't know if this will be important to you or not, but Melody Arnold had a gray overnight bag with her. She left it on the ground next to the tower. After I tried to interview Marcus at the hospital, I went back to the scene to get it. It was gone, and no one there had seen it. It was one more mystery of the case."

"Who would have taken a pregnant woman's overnight bag?" Kat asked as Zen drove to Mercy Hospital. "It would probably have all the usual things, something for the mother and baby to wear home, toiletries, reading material. Maybe a homeless person took it?" Kat felt slightly better than she had when she left Officer Simpson's house; she felt like she could breathe again.

It was a beautiful spring day, and they rolled down the car windows. When they passed an elementary school playground, and Kat saw the children playing on the swings and monkey bars, she was glad to be reminded that there were everyday things in the world, such as kids horsing around at recess. Not everyone in the world had just found out that their mother had been determined to jump from a 100-foot light tower on a cold and windy Sunday afternoon. It was true. Some people did lead normal, happy lives.

"Well," Zen carefully said as he turned into the parking lot, "I guess it could have had a note in it, a suicide note."

Damn it. Why was he always one step ahead of her? "No one has mentioned a suicide note, not the article, not your father and Mr. Capino, and not Officer Simpson."

"If it was in the bag, they didn't find it because someone took the overnight bag to prevent them from finding it." Zen turned off the ignition.

"If that was the case, then someone didn't want people reading what was in the note." They were only speculating, but for Kat, the idea started to take seed. "If someone didn't want people reading the note, then Melody Arnold had something to hide."

"That could be," Zen agreed, "or maybe she was running away from something. Maybe she got into some hot water and couldn't see any other way out."

"Hot water? It would have to be *scalding* to go to the length of escape that she chose. For crying out loud, she was a nurse. What kind of trouble could she get into?" As soon as she said that, it came to her. She looked at Zen.

"Drugs," they said simultaneously.

It was a preposterous idea, and Kat knew they must be jumping to conclusions from a fact-less plateau. "Oh, come on. We're being ridiculous. We still don't know anything about her."

"Probably." Zen drummed his fingers on the steering wheel. "But working for CPS, I saw a lot of messed-up, crazy things."

"Is that why you quit?" Kat was curious. Zen was such an easy-going guy that it would seem like nothing would get under his skin. However, he'd probably seen horrific cases involving neglected and abused children. On the road trip to Illinois, he hadn't talked about anything like that.

"Another time, Kat. Are you ready to go in?"

Something must have happened to him, but he was right. Now was not the time to talk about it. Kat only had four days to try to piece together the puzzle of Melody Arnold's life. "Do you think that someone who worked there thirty years ago will still be there? What are the odds?"

"Not good."

The odds weren't good at all. When they asked the young receptionist if she knew anyone in the ER who might have known a woman named Melody Arnold, who had worked at the hospital thirty years before, her eyes glazed over. She looked like she was in her early twenties, and to Kat, she was jarring to look at. She wore scrubs with pink and blue bunnies bounding over the surface of her sizeable girth, but the scrubs didn't disguise the blood-dripping dagger tattooed on the back of her neck or the boa constrictor snaking up her right arm.

"That was a long time ago," she said. "That would be like ..." Her name tag read DeDe, and DeDe was having a hard time doing the math in her head.

"Thirty years ago," Zen supplied.

"Wow," DeDe said. "We have some old RNs around here, but I don't know if they're that old."

"We're talking about someone in his or her early fifties. Surely, you have people of that age or older working here." Kat wondered why a hospital would hire such a nitwit. But then again, this nitwit had a job, and she did not. She forced herself to smile. "Could we just talk to someone a little older than you, please?"

"Nurses get pretty burned out around here." DeDe tried to explain herself. "They see all kinds of stuff. On some days, it's kind of like watching a horror movie like *Chainsaw Massacre* or *Friday the 13th*, the bloody, gory ones. I'm not kidding."

"Oh." Kat shuddered. She hadn't stopped to consider the *particulars* of an ER nurse's job, the accidents or gunshot victims or anything bloody at all. It wasn't that Kat was squeamish about things like that, but she'd always considered that it was in her best interest to avoid seeing or being in such situations. (And she didn't go to horror movies, and neither had Benson. In retrospect, it was the one good thing about him.) However, she now had to wonder: What kind of things had Melody Arnold seen? Had it been too much for her? Had something she'd seen in the ER pushed her to climb that tower? Again, more fucking, confusing questions, and Kat needed to find some answers. Soon.

"Maybe you could tell us where HR is located?" Zen suggested. "I doubt if they keep hospital personnel records for over thirty years, but—"

"Oh, wait," DeDe interrupted excitedly. "There is a new nurse. I mean, she's new here, but she's old. Maybe she could help you? Her name's Linda."

It was unbelievable. This young girl had the I.Q. of one of the bunnies frolicking on her scrubs. They needed a middle-aged nurse who had worked here thirty years before. "I don't think you understand," Kat began.

"I think I heard something about how she used to work here years before but had to come back to work because of a divorce or something." DeDe smiled, showing the Invisalign on her teeth. The smile was directed solely at Zen. "Are you seeing anybody?" she asked.

"Are you kidding?" Kat practically spat. She'd seen this kind of behavior before, of course, many times in her line of work—if you could call it that—the boldness of young girls with males. Flirting was a lost art, and while she should be glad about that fact because she had always sucked at flirting, she wasn't happy about it now. Zen was old enough to be DeDe's ... older brother. Shit.

Zen, unperturbed and probably used to such things, smiled back. "I'm flattered, DeDe." He then put his forearms on the counter and leaned slightly towards her, but not too much, just enough to give her a false glimmer of hope. "Now, where can we find Nurse Linda?"

DeDe dimpled. "She went to the cafeteria a few minutes ago. I'll take you there." She came around from behind her desk and linked her arm with Zen's. "Do you listen to rockabilly? I'm a big fan of the Reverend Horton Heat. He's coming to town at the end of this month."

Seething, Kat had no choice but to follow. She wasn't jealous—of course not—but how could Zen let this fat little girl with braces put the move on him? How dare her! They were on a fact-finding mission, and this little tatted up tart was yet another speed bump in the road. If she lay down in the middle of the road, this little girl could be a speed bump. "It's not my problem." Kat unwittingly said it aloud.

"What?" Zen turned his head to look at her over his shoulder.

"Nothing." She really must stop thinking out loud. Kat would put that on the self-improvement list, which seemed to grow longer every day.

They wound through the hospital's halls, which looked like they hadn't been remodeled since the 1980s when Melody Arnold worked there. The dominant color was green, the shade of a jar of Gerber strained peas, and the beige linoleum cracked in places. The interior halls that they passed through were dim, windowless. Kat shuddered. She didn't like hospitals in general, but this place was downright depressing. They healed people here, she reminded herself, but then came the accompanying thought. People also died here.

Yet this hospital was where Melody Arnold had worked and where Kat, the surviving baby, had been brought after the determined jump from the 100-foot light tower. How strange to think that she, as a newborn, had been here once before. She hadn't expected to feel any connection with the place, and she didn't. What it felt like to her, in addition to depressing, was *eerie*. It was like the place gave off bad vibes or something. She couldn't quite put her finger on it. She would talk to Nurse Linda and then get the hell out of Dodge.

"She's in that table in the corner." DeDe pointed her chubby finger at a woman with dyed blonde hair the color of dried hay. She sat alone at the table, eating a hamburger.

"Thanks, DeDe." Zen patted her hand and gently extracted his arm from her vise-like grasp.

"Don't forget," she said as she reluctantly backed away.

"I won't." Zen gave her a wink.

"Oh, for crying out loud," Kat said, taking Zen's arm and walking quickly toward the table.

When they asked Nurse Linda if she could spare a minute or two, she gave them a denture smile and motioned toward the other chairs. "I'm glad for the company. I haven't worked here in over twenty years, and these new nurses at this hospital are a cliquey lot."

She had deep smoker creases around her mouth, and even though she was only in her early or mid-fifties, she looked much older than that. Time, or life, had not been kind to her. Then Kat had a fleeting thought: Would Melody Arnold have looked this old?

"I'm Kat Flowers," she said, "and I know this is a long-shot and rather strange, but I was wondering if you remember a nurse who used to work here whose name was Melody Arnold? It would have been in the early eighties." At the suspicious look that Nurse Linda gave her, Kat added, "I'm doing some family research."

"Melody Arnold ..." Nurse Linda fumbled in the pocket of her scrubs and pulled out an E-cigarette. She looked around furtively and took a quick hit, then replaced it in her pocket. "I've known a lot of nurses and doctors, too, and then, of course, there's the story of my life. It's quite the saga. I've been married four times and had a kid with each one of the bastards. The first one, Gino, well, he promised me the moon. He was going to become rich—self-made, you know—by opening a string of pizzerias, but did that ever happen? Of course not. The bastard couldn't keep his pecker in his pants. And then the second one, well, he ran out on me, too. And then the third and then the fourth, and now here I am, a fifty-six-year-old woman back at work. Do you think they would pay spousal support? Ha!" She looked at Zen.

"That's too bad," he said sympathetically.

Kat wanted to wring his neck. It was glaringly apparent that this woman didn't need any encouragement to go on and that she was just getting wound up. Kat had no other choice but to cut to the chase. "I'm asking about Melody Arnold, the woman who jumped from the light tower on March 22, 1982."

Nurse Linda gasped and reached into her pocket again for the E-cigarette. "Oh, my God! I haven't thought about that in years!"

"Subtle," Zen said under his breath.

Kat ignored him. It had been bad before at Officer Simpson's house, asking about the woman who had tried to kill her. She'd felt the walls closing in and a tightening in her chest that made it hard to breathe. Here, it was even worse. "Did you know her?"

"I worked with her, but I wouldn't say I knew her. She wasn't talkative when she was on the job. She would always try to get me to stop talking, even when it was slow. She said that we should always be professional. Melody was very big on being *professional*."

Just Melody. Not Melody Arnold. The familiarity of only the first name made Kat's heart beat faster. *Melody* had been a real person, and someone had known her. It was a good thing that Nurse Linda was a blabbermouth because Kat felt her throat closing up again, making it difficult to speak.

"She was a pretty little thing, red-haired with freckles—Irish through and through, you know. I think she came from a pretty big family, but maybe that's just me guessing. Irish Catholic, South Side, and all that. But she sure never opened up about any of that to me. I know that she and that friend of hers—what was her name?—talked about me behind my back, but I was just being friendly, you know? Do you think they ever invited me to join them for a drink after work? Ha! They probably thought they were too good for me, and now, when I think back on it, they were kind of bitchy towards me."

Zen covered Nurse Linda's hand with his. A good tactic. It shut her up immediately. "Do you remember anything else?"

Nurse Linda needed another puff on her E-cigarette before she could continue. She used her left hand this time, not disturbing Zen's hand on her right one. "Let me see ... Oh, yes, she had this big diamond ring that her husband gave her. It was quite a rock, but she seemed kind of embarrassed about it. She took it off as soon as she got to work and put it in her locker. I told her once, 'Melody, if I had a rock that size on my finger, I'd flaunt it.' But she didn't do that. Maybe she thought it would get in the way of caring for the patients? Who knows? She was a good nurse, though. I'd certainly have to give her that. I didn't work that many shifts with her before she—you know—and I started a couple of months after she did."

Zen looked at Kat and saw that she couldn't speak. Once again, he stepped up to the plate. "You've been very helpful."

However, Nurse Linda was on a roll. "After her ... accident, you would not believe the shock at this place. No one could believe what had happened. We were all just flabbergasted. We were all asking each other if we should have seen it coming. Melody was kind of quiet and mostly kept to herself, except when that snotty friend of hers—why can't I think of her name?—was around. Her friend was tall, I remember, with this platinum hair piled under her hat—we wore real uniforms then—and boy, you could see her coming a mile away. Melody did seem kind of sad sometimes, and one of the nurses told me she thought Melody had a miscarriage or something, but I asked her point-blank one time, and she looked me directly in the eye and said, 'No, I did not miscarry.' The way she said it, I believed her, and of course, I didn't ask her again. All in all, Melody was a very quiet person."

The wealth of information overwhelmed Kat, mostly because Nurse Linda had been in the actual presence of Melody Arnold. She had spoken to her, worked next to her, possibly even *touched* her. Melody Arnold had been a young, red-headed nurse in this very hospital, and she had probably eaten in this same cafeteria. Kat needed air—the sooner, the better. She looked at Zen.

But Nurse Linda wasn't done, and the E-cigarette was out in the open now. "When the baby came here—I'm just starting to remember that part of the story—all the nurses couldn't believe that she had survived that fall. She was such a pretty little baby with a broken left leg, but otherwise in good shape. I think all of us wanted to take her home with us, and we were sad when they came and took her home. I wasn't here that day, and I've got to tell you, I cried when she was gone."

"Thank you so much." Kat stood up. She'd started to sweat.

Nurse Linda didn't seem to notice. "There's a lot of gossip in this hospital—you wouldn't believe how much—and I don't want to tell you anything that isn't true, but there was a rumor that—"

Kat fled, but she did hear over the buzzing in her head, Nurse Linda, still talking, say, "Family research, huh? Well, that girl does bear a family resemblance to Melody Arnold. I just now noticed it."

Zen knew better than to ask how she felt when they got back in the car. Kat wouldn't have been able to answer him anyway because the truth was that she didn't know how she was feeling. Or to be more precise, she didn't know how to explain what she was feeling. In her life to date, she had never been in a situation like this, nor had she ever imagined being in a position like this, so she hadn't exactly had enough time to warn and prepare her emotions. Her wildest dreams had never led her to the discovery that Melody Arnold, who happened to be her birth mother, had been a good ER nurse, a quiet person, nine months pregnant, and she had decided to take a nosedive off of a 100-foot light tower for no apparent reason. It was no wonder that when she'd badgered him with questions about her mother throughout her childhood, her father had answered, "Period. End of story."

That part of the story was beginning to make sense. Who would want to tell his child that kind of truth? Holy shit. It put an entirely different spin on things if Marcus Flowers, aka Arnold, had been trying to protect his daughter from that terrible information, if he thought he was doing the right thing by withholding the truth. That part, Kat could understand. However, while he was withholding the truth, why did he also withhold his love?

Because she reminded him of Melody? Kat possibly might have looked like her, sounded like her, thought like her, or acted like her. Officer Simpson had said that her father was a broken man after the suicide, and he'd called Melody Arnold the love of his life. Nurse Linda had said there was a family resemblance. And then more words from her father came back to her. She was in his office, and he'd just accused her of whoring around (even though she had only slept with Bobby Baker) and slapped her face, hard. She'd fled from that scene, too, and he had called something after her. In her hurry to get away from him and his accusations, Kat hadn't paid attention, but an echo came back now: *Just like your mother.* Was that what he had hurled after her on her way out the door?

With her mind doing somersaults, backflips, and cartwheels, Kat didn't notice where they were until the car stopped. They were in a Target parking lot. Zen looked at her with something like hope in his eyes. "Retail therapy?"

It was a thoughtful gesture, yes, but still. "I'm not really a shopping kind of gal," Kat said, although when she absolutely had to shop, she did go to Target, along with Ross and TJ Maxx. How did he know that?

"Maybe you could start? It might make you feel better, get your mind off everything that's been showered on you."

"Showered on me? It feels more like a giant bird took an enormous shit right on top of my head." Which would explain why she was having trouble breathing. It was nearly impossible to gulp in air through a pile of shit so enormous.

Zen let that pass. "A group of us are going bowling tonight, and I thought you could pick out something to wear. Not that you don't look fine already, but maybe you'd want to pick up some make-up, or whatever you do to make yourself look like you used to look?"

Used to look. Kat was almost positive that she hadn't even looked in a mirror this morning. She pulled down the visor and looked in the small mirror. Not good. She'd brushed her teeth, but she certainly hadn't washed her hair or showered. She looked down at her jeans, the pair she'd worn for days. "That's not a bad idea," she said, embarrassed. This guy, in mere days, kept seeing her at her absolute worst. "You don't have to keep being so nice to me, you know."

"I don't mind."

"You can stop at any time."

"No."

"Suit yourself, but I'm not going bowling tonight. I've got to figure out how to get my birth certificate. I doubt that I can go to the Office of Vital Records and get one when I have a different name on my driver's license, so I'll have to see how long it takes to get one online and how expensive it is."

"Or you could call your house and talk to one of your brothers or your stepmother and see if it's there, which it probably is. They could scan it and email it to you or just tell you your mother's maiden name. However, you really should get a copy. You'll need it if you ever get a passport." He followed her into the store and grabbed a shopping cart.

Damn it. Why *wasn't* Zen a PI? "That's a possibility, but I'm not going bowling."

He wore her down. During their navigation through Target, as he helped her pick out a new pair of skinny jeans, a couple of tops, and some ballerina flats, he wore her down. "What do you want to do, sit around and stew all night? Nothing is going to change the story if you don't do any more research this evening."

During dinner at Applebee's, he wore her down. "Would you really rather sit with my parents and watch the History Channel? Come on, Kat."

Finally, she agreed to go. "But I am not going to have a good time."

But she did, despite herself. In addition to Kat and Zen, there were two other married couples, one couple he had known since high school. ("Prom king and queen," Zen whispered to her, "high school sweethearts, still married.") The other couple he had known since college. ("No one thought they'd make it this long, used to fight like cats and dogs after too many beers at frat parties," Zen whispered, "but you never know.") And then there was John, the college buddy Zen would be rooming with in the South Loop. And then there was Carrie, naturally.

Yet it was such a relief to not be *stewing*, as Zen put it. It was a non-competitive game. Strikes and gutter balls were cheered equally, the beer flowed, and no one talked about anything more serious than the merits of the White Sox versus the Cubs. Zen, always polite, didn't fill in the others on Kat's story, and she was once again grateful. When the married couples announced that they had to get home at ten o'clock—their babysitters had a curfew—Kat was disappointed.

"Let's go into the bar and get a nightcap," Carrie suggested.

So far, she had not been overly clingy with Zen, so Kat readily agreed, along with Zen and John. But when they were seated at the bar according to Carrie's plan—Kat, John, Carrie, and Zen, all lined up like ducks in a row—Kat realized she was trying to get Zen as far away as possible from everyone else to engage him privately in conversation.

So be it. Kat still felt an adrenaline high from the bowling and pleasantly tipsy. After all, she'd won the last game. Even though the games were friendly and all in good fun, Kat had to admit that she might have been a bit competitive. "Tell me about yourself, John," she said conversationally. She really didn't care a whit what was going on between Carrie and Zen. (One of these days, though, she was going to get that bitch alone and say, "Will you grow up and quit acting like you're in high school, you drama queen?")

He was a good-looking guy, and not in a pretty boy way like Benson O'Shea. He was a little over six feet, with dark hair with just a touch of grey at the temples, although he was only Zen's age, thirty-four. John told her that he worked in finance and trained and ran in marathons in his spare time. "What about you?" he asked.

His gray eyes looked at her attentively, and Kat was glad that Zen had the foresight to make her go shopping. Even though she initially didn't want to come, she'd showered and tricked herself out a bit, nothing overdone, just trying to go back to how she *used to look*. Kat ordered a shot of scotch. "I'm just in town visiting," she said. There was no need to go into any detail with this guy. She was in a decent mood, and she wanted it to go on a little longer. Tomorrow, she knew, would be a different story.

"So," he asked, "are you and Zen an item?"

Kat's laugh came out more like an unattractive snort. "Oh, hell no. We just drove across the country together, that's all."

John whistled a sigh of relief. "Good. That's what Zen said, too."

For some reason, this did not make Kat happy, and she felt a little bit of her buzz ebb away. "Oh, really?"

John looked sheepish. "I hope you don't mind, but during the game, I took him aside and asked him. You're a knockout, and Zen's my best friend, and I didn't want to cross any boundaries. I know you're not in town for long, but I thought maybe we could go out before you left?"

Maybe she wasn't thinking clearly. It had been another long day capped by beer and scotch, but it almost sounded like Zen had given John permission to ask her out. "Believe me, there are no boundaries to cross," she said, avoiding his question.

"I'd like to show you the city," John said. "Chicago's a great town."

He had nice eyebrows, Kat thought, and a nice mouth and straight, white teeth. Really, he was quite attractive—but *not pretty*—and she had gone out with so much worse material during her slightly slutty twenties. He seemed nice enough, too, but he certainly didn't make her heart do any calisthenics.

But that wasn't being fair to John because no one had, not since Bobby Baker—and look at how *that* had turned out.

However, Kat tried very hard not to notice that when Zen Delaney came into a room, there was a change in the atmosphere, a static charge.

But she knew it was only because she was in a highly charged emotional situation. That was the explanation.

Politely, she said, "I'm only going to be in town for three more days, John, but thank you for asking. The next time I come back to Chicago, you can show me the sights." Kat didn't think there was much of a chance that she would ever come back.

"You have three days left, right? Can I have one? I have vacation time coming, and I could get tomorrow off, just like that." He snapped his fingers, smiling.

"I don't think—" Something made her look past John, toward the end of the bar where Zen was. Her heart didn't do calisthenics; it dropped. Zen was kissing Carrie, or Carrie was kissing Zen. It didn't matter; they were *kissing*. Kat quickly averted her eyes. She wished a magic Visine existed, so she could put drops in her eyes and make that image go away.

It would take away a precious day of research, but Kat had just seen Zen kissing another woman. It changed things. "How *about* tomorrow?" she said, not flirtatiously, but factually. She would never learn how to flirt.

16

MARCH 1981

"I won't tell," Dr. Desoto said on New Year's Eve in the hospital pharmacy. "I think we can come to some mutually satisfying arrangement." He was already taking off his white coat, and he ran his hands through his thick silver hair, smoothing it. "I've always had a fondness for redheads," he said again.

"I don't know what you mean," Melody stammered. She was trapped. The pharmacy had one door, and he stood directly in front of it. He wasn't a large man, but he was certainly taller than her five feet, three inches, and one hundred and ten pounds. She didn't stand much of a chance of pushing him out of the way.

"You know what I mean." Dr. Desoto locked the door and approached her, unzipping his fly.

Unfortunately, she did know what he meant. Should she scream for help? The hospital was practically deserted on this holiday night, but even if someone did come in answer to her screams, what would she say? Seventy-something-year-old Dr. Desoto, who everyone thought was half-senile, was trying to rape her? And what would he say in answer to that?

That he had caught Nurse Melody Arnold red-handed, trying to steal a bottle of morphine. There would be a disgrace, possible criminal charges, and her career would be over before it had even really begun. Even if she denied the supposed allegation, it would be her word against his, nurse versus doctor, and she knew who would win.

She couldn't see any way out of this situation, but she gave it one last try. "I'm married."

"So?" He dropped his pants, exposing his shriveled, varicose vein-laced legs.

"I'm Catholic," she said in a shaky voice.

"So am I," he answered.

"This is not professional behavior." Her voice grew even weaker. She didn't know where to look—certainly not at his old-man legs—but his cold blue eyes held more than a glint of malice.

"Neither is stealing medication from a hospital pharmacy." He stood directly in front of her now.

"This is the first time, I swear." Melody's legs shook violently. "I'll put it back, and we can forget the whole thing. I'll never do such a thing again. I promise. I don't know what came over me."

Dr. Desoto crossed his arms and didn't release his cold stare. He wasn't buying any of it.

"I did it for my mother-in-law ..." Melody's voice trailed off. She'd lost. She'd lost control of the situation when she took the bottle of morphine off its shelf. And now it was safely in her uniform pocket, and even in this situation that was about to turn very ugly, she didn't want to put it back. That was the horrible truth. She didn't want to put the precious painkillers back.

She averted her eyes from his face and dropped to her knees.

Naively, she'd thought that would be the end of it, but no. Three months later, Dr. Desoto still cornered her in the elevator or called her into his office. It was blackmail, of course, but there was this: He wrote her prescriptions for morphine, as well as Oxy and different types of hydrocodone. And as the prescriptions grew, so did the favors. Blow jobs were not enough. They'd met at a motel on Montrose on three separate occasions, and on each occasion, Dr. Desoto—he wanted her to call him Stanley, but she could not—was getting more perverse. During the last meeting, he'd tied her to the cheap bed with his expensive belt, and the bruises on her wrists did not go unnoticed by Marcus.

"What happened to your wrists, flower?" He was all concerned, taking her hands in his and gently turning them over. "These are some nasty bruises."

Marcus couldn't even begin to know how truly *nasty* those bruises were. Such things were simply not in his comprehension. Melody withdrew her hands from his prying, concerned gaze. "At work. I did it at work. I was on the ground, trying to adjust the wheels of a gurney, and the lock slipped. The wheels ran over my wrists." It was a totally unbelievable lie, which she then embellished. "The patient was obese, over three hundred pounds."

"Oh, baby, you need to be more careful. You could have broken them, but I suppose we should consider you lucky that you didn't." Marcus kissed her on the top of her head.

Lucky. That was something Melody certainly wasn't. If she'd been lucky, the sadistic Dr. Desoto wouldn't have caught her stealing, and she wouldn't be trapped in this messy situation. "Yes," Melody said to her husband, "I'm very lucky."

When she noticed the bruises from Melody's latest go-round with Dr. Desoto, Sylvia's reaction went beyond concern to outrage. "That sadistic creep!" she spat. "He has now gone too far, Mel. I'm afraid that one of these days he's going to seriously hurt you. We've got to put a stop to this. I can't let you keep taking all the pervert's abuse, not while I share in the profits."

They sat in the hospital cafeteria, eating lunch, but Melody had no appetite. She pushed the mushy pieces of roast beef around on her plate. Naturally, she'd told Sylvia what was going on from the very beginning, and she'd shared the drugs with her from Day One, knowing that Sylvia, if the tables were turned, would do the same. "I know," she said miserably, "but how am I going to stop it? I don't want to ruin my career."

"You're not Dr. Demented's slave!" Sylvia said with such force that a line of spit trickled down her chin.

"Shh!" Melody furtively looked around. It seemed like she did a lot of looking over her shoulder these days, on guard for the approach of Dr. Demented, wary that others would somehow find out about this affair, or whatever it was. Or find out about the drugs. On rare occasions, when the weight of her life (or *stress*, as Marcus would call it), when the dark hole started to close in, Melody had started sneaking into the bathroom, locking herself in a stall, and swallowing a pill. That was the one thing she hadn't told Sylvia. She was too ashamed.

"Sorry." Sylvia dabbed at her chin. "But he makes me mad enough to spit. Literally. The whole thing is so tawdry. That's the perfect word for it, Mel, *tawdry.*"

"But he is supplying us with drugs," Melody pointed out. She pushed her plate away. In addition to making her feel paranoid, this tawdry affair made her feel nauseated most of the time. She'd lost weight, and her face was growing gaunt, yet the steady supply of morphine and Oxy and hydrocodone was wonderful.

"Damn it," Sylvia said, "therein lays the conundrum."

They fell silent, both thinking. "I could tell Dr. Demented I have a venereal disease," Melody said.

"I could make an anonymous phone call to his wife," was Sylvia's suggestion, "or to the ethics committee. That might be better yet."

Both of those were possibilities, but Melody had a gut feeling that Dr. Demented would not go down quietly. "I'm pretty sure he'd implicate me, too. He wouldn't want to go down on a sinking ship alone."

"The next time you're supposed to meet him, I'll go instead." Sylvia threw her silverware onto her empty plate. "He probably wouldn't even notice. He probably thinks a piece of ass is a piece of ass."

Melody felt the hot rush of blood to her face. Even in front of Sylvia, she was embarrassed. She had been reduced to a piece of ass, and it was all so humiliating. Yet there were the drugs that made her life with Marcus at least tolerable. What was she going to do? "Maybe he'll have a heart attack?" she said without conviction.

"A massive coronary, dropping dead on the spot." Sylvia nodded. "I like the image of that. It's what the fucker deserves."

Melody stiffened. Over Sylvia's right shoulder, she saw the man approach. "He's behind you," she whispered. "Don't say anything, Syl, I'm begging you. At this point, we can't jeopardize anything."

"I won't say anything," Sylvia said grudgingly, "but can I kick him in the balls?"

Dr. Desoto passed by their table, and without pausing or looking at either one of them, dropped a folded note in front of Melody. She waited until the old doctor was out the door before she opened it.

"I take it you've been summoned," Sylvia said.

Melody's throat constricted, and she could only nod. He wanted her in his office *now,* and she knew what that meant. She would be on her knees. Again.

"Where are you going?" Marcus' voice was reed-thin, almost a whine. "I don't like you going out alone at night, Mellie. It's the fourth time this month." He followed her around their bedroom, from the closet to the vanity, and when she went down the hall to use the bathroom, he waited outside the door.

A double life. Melody felt like she was leading a double life, and it certainly wasn't as glamorous as a James Bond movie would have one believe. Whenever Dr. Demented snapped his fingers, Melody jumped. It was part of the arrangement, a fact of the arrangement, and Melody was having a harder and harder time making up excuses for Marcus. Lies and more lies, requirements for the leading of a double life.

The first time Melody left to meet the sadistic old doctor at the motel on Montrose, she'd told Marcus she was working a double shift, but when she turned her paycheck over to him, he commented that there had been no overtime payment. "Where's the extra money?" he'd asked her.

"There must have been some mistake," she told him. "I'll talk to the accounting department tomorrow." Of course there had been no overtime, so she ended up borrowing money from Willie to make up the difference. She had yet to pay him back.

The second excuse she tried was this: "I'm going to go visit Ma. She's recovering from a bad case of the flu." More lies.

"I'll drive you." Marcus was already walking to the tray on the front hall table to fetch his keys. "I'll get Evelyn, and we can have a nice visit with your folks. You'd like that, wouldn't you, kitten?"

Panicked, Melody blurted out, "She's probably still contagious, Marcus. Why would you want to expose yourself and Evelyn to that?"

"If she's still contagious, then you probably shouldn't go," Marcus said in his most reasonable tone of voice.

"She's my *mother*. My *mother* needs me." She held her breath, hoping that the mother card would shut him up. It did. However, for the next few days, Marcus insisted that Melody call her ma to see how she felt. He was never far away, and Melody was glad that Marcus didn't hear—even though Ma's voice on the other end of the line was loud and irritated—her reply to the repeated questions about her health: "Mellie, I'm fine! Why do you keep asking me that question? You sound like a broken record."

For the third excuse, she used this gem: "We're having a staff meeting at the hospital."

"At eight o'clock in the evening?" Marcus said in disbelief. "Don't they know that *Fantasy Island* is on?"

Jesus, Melody thought, *her husband lived on a fantasy island.* "I guess not," she'd said. "It's the only time everyone could make it." That was so blatantly untrue that he should have questioned it. People at the hospital worked around the clock, so there would be no time where everyone could make a staff meeting. But Marcus, with his nine-to-five mentality, didn't raise questions. The plane landed on his beloved, mythical island, and he was already engrossed.

Flimsy, transparent excuses, fibs upon fibs, mushrooming into lies. It was exhausting to keep straight what Melody had said and when. Utterly exhausting. Still, she couldn't sleep at night, and she tossed and turned next to her snoring husband. (This, after she had once again rebuffed his suggestion that they try for another baby. Another baby. It was unthinkable to Melody.) More and more frequently, she needed to swallow a pill to jump-start the day, to focus her groggy mind.

Now, outside the bathroom door, Marcus said, "I'm beginning to wonder if I should hire a private investigator, Mellie."

Melody flung open the bathroom door. Her face, she was sure, was chalk white. "What?"

Marcus took a step back at the vehemence with which she hurled open the door. "I was just making a joke, honey." He gave a feeble laugh.

Marcus never made jokes, and Melody wondered if there was a seed of truth to his "joke." Would Marcus actually do something like that? It would be just like Marcus to check her gas mileage. Had he already done that? It was something else to worry about. She took a deep breath to compose herself and said as sweetly as she could muster, "Don't you trust me ... honey?" She rubbed his arm for good measure.

"You don't give me a reason not to, do you, flower?" He covered her hand with his, grateful for the rare touch.

"Of course not." She turned away and closed the bathroom door, breathing hard.

On this night, the fourth after-work tryst with Dr. Demented, she told Marcus that she was going to Sylvia's house.

Marcus' mouth made a hard line. "You know what I think of her."

"You've made it abundantly clear, Marcus, but I'm going."

"Now, baby," he cajoled, "why don't we just have a quiet, relaxing time at home. *Charlie's Angels* is on tonight."

"No, Marcus, I'm going to see my *friend*," Melody said with unusual forcefulness and left the house without a backward glance, without waiting for Marcus' rebuttal.

She truly was going to Sylvia's house—to meet Dr. Demented.

After weeks of trying to get Melody out of an increasingly impossible situation, they had devised a plan. "We have to document the sadistic fucker in the act," Sylvia concluded. "Butt naked, old man penis throbbing, and you, preferably, in an extremely uncompromising situation."

At first, Melody had been horrified. "If you take a picture of him butt-naked, that also means that you will be taking a picture of me butt-naked. I don't want anyone to see me like that. I don't even want you to see me like that."

"I have seen hundreds of naked bodies, Mel," Sylvia reminded her. "Hundreds, and if memory serves me correctly, which it does, I've even given you baths before."

"That's not what I'm talking about. It's just that you would see … It's just that I would be … It's just that it would be so *pornographic*."

"Exactly! That's exactly the look we're going for, what we need to catch on film, the *pornographic* nature of this whole thing. If we would ever need to show the pictures, we would want people to know how *pornographic* and *tawdry* Dr. Demented is."

"I don't like it." There had to be a better way. Unfortunately, Melody couldn't think of one.

"I do." Sylvia was adamant. "He's blackmailing you; we'll blackmail him. Tit for tat. Poetic justice. An eye for an eye. It's perfect."

"I might think it was perfect if I was not the one who was going to be tied spread-eagled on a bed." Just the thought of it made Melody shudder with shame. She'd fallen so low, lower than she had ever thought possible, which is another reason she needed the drugs. When she took Oxy or hydrocodone, she could prevent herself from thinking about it. The drugs could erase everything—the guilt, the shame, the very facts of her life. Her very own *tawdry* life.

"It's unfortunate but true, Mel. The more sadistic he gets, the better in the long run for us. Better ammunition, I guess you could say. I'll use my new Polaroid. We'll have immediate evidence, proof that he can't argue with. Besides, I'll be right there, hiding in the closet. If he goes too far, I'll crack him over the head with a baseball bat."

"Just great, Syl, then we'd have a possible homicide on our hands."

"Good point," Sylvia acknowledged. "I might get carried away because I would like nothing better than to bash in the old creep's head." She considered the alternatives. "I'll use my mace instead, temporarily blind the old fart."

So that's where they were on this particular night of *reckoning*, as Sylvia had come to call it. When Melody arrived at Sylvia's apartment, a half-hour before they expected Dr. Demented, she was a nervous wreck. Suppose the old man's hearing suddenly became acute, and he heard Sylvia in the closet? What if, for some mysterious reason, the camera malfunctioned? What if the horrible old man—a supposed *healer,* for christ's sake—carried a gun and would shoot them both?

Then there was this utterly demoralizing thought. What if, even after she and Sylvia had the Polaroids stored in a safe place—say a safety deposit box in a bank—the wretched doctor decided to call Marcus and tell him everything? Her husband would know her for what she was, a disgraced, conniving, felonious, drug-using whore. He would divorce her, and she would have nothing. The car and house were registered in his name, and he owned the furniture as well. She would have no property. In Marcus' moral certitude, he would call the hospital and tell them about the stolen drugs, and she would have no source of income. She would have—and be—*nothing,* all at the age of twenty-three.

On the other hand, Marcus might not divorce her. He might forgive his baby, his honey, his kitten, his flower. He would stand by her and support her and make her see the errors of her ways. But he would make her pay. In his mysterious, upstanding way, he would make Melody *pay and pay for the rest of her life.* In a way, in most ways, that would be worse.

"You're letting your imagination get the best of you," Sylvia said when Melody blurted all this out. "None of that stuff is going to happen. This is a good plan." However, her hands shook as she poured them each a stiff drink. At the same time, automatically, they each swallowed an Oxy.

"How long does it take each Polaroid to develop?" Melody asked nervously. "How long between pictures?"

"You let me worry about that. Everything will be fine." The intercom buzzed, and Sylvia gave Melody a hard hug. "Go let him in, Mel. It's showtime."

Thank God for drugs, Melody thought, as she went to the intercom and told the doorman to let her guest up. The edges of her emotions were already softening, the tautness of her muscles relaxing. Sylvia had gone to her hiding place in the closet, located three feet from the foot of the bed, leaving the door slightly ajar, her large-boned frame hunched as far in the back as possible, waiting. Melody turned on some music loud enough to mute a camera's clicking, poured two stiff drinks, and waited.

Dr. Demented's first suspicious words were: "Whose apartment did you say this was?" He looked around, eyeing Sylvia's plaid couch and poster-covered walls: Michael Jackson, Jackson Browne, Kool & the Gang. "It looks like some college kid's." He threw his coat on the back of the bean bag chair and vainly smoothed his thick silver hair.

"She's not a college kid," Melody said, "and don't you think it's cozier than a motel room? There's a nice stereo, too. Isn't the music relaxing?" She'd been instructed by Sylvia to *play nice*, to throw the despicable old man off guard. It was hard to even get out those few words. Usually, she said nothing at all.

"Huh," Dr. Demented grunted. He grabbed one of the drinks on the coffee table and gulped it down. "The doorman, not a good idea. This is the last time we meet here."

"Okay," Melody said meekly. Her heart had started to beat rapidly, despite the drugs. She had just sighted a picture on Sylvia's bookcase, a picture of the two of them taken a year before at a party. She moved over slightly to block his view. "Another drink?" She quickly poured straight vodka.

He gulped it down. "Enough pussy-footing around." His smile turned into a sneer. "I'm here for one thing, and you're here for one thing."

"Yes, I know." She looked away. She absolutely despised this man.

"The floor," he said. "Get down on the floor."

No! That was not part of the plan. Melody's mind raced. "The bedroom is right through that door." Melody pointed with a shaking finger. Could Sylvia hear what they were saying? "I put on clean sheets."

"The floor." Already, he was opening his medical bag where he kept his supply of belts and nylon ropes. *In his medical bag.*

"The floor is filthy," Melody rushed out. Then she looked at it, and it was, thank God. Sylvia must not have had time to vacuum. The floor was littered with potato chip crumbs, and there was a bright maroon stain—red wine, ketchup, blood?—that Melody had never noticed before.

That statement caused Dr. Demented to pause in his preparations. Although he was a mediocre doctor at best, he did have an eye for when things were *not sterile*. "Your friend is a slob," he announced.

Melody would swear that she heard Sylvia snort in the next room and say, too loudly, "You're the slob!"

"In here." Melody led the way into the bedroom.

They stripped, not looking at each other, as they always did. It was so strange to Melody, this odd moment of delicacy, before he tied her to the bed and invaded every orifice of her body. So with the aid of another Oxy that she had taken with the straight vodka and knowing that Sylvia was nearby, Melody no longer cared what she looked like, splayed and helpless. She closed her eyes and turned off her brain, willing herself to ignore the pain and humiliation. It would be over soon. It would never happen again.

Sylvia did not interrupt. Jesus, where was Sylvia? Had she fallen asleep? Damn her to hell if she had fallen asleep in that closet and wasn't doing her job. Nurses did not fall down on the job. Nurses were good and kind and noble. Nurses were *professionals*. Melody was definitely going to let Sylvia have it. Yes, she would. She would let Sylvia have it when this was all over, although she wasn't really mad at Sylvia. Sylvia was her best friend, and Melody loved her so much …

"Get dressed," Dr. Demented said. He was already dressed, hair smoothed, nothing out of place, just a doctor making a house call.

Melody squinted her eyes, making him small and far, far away. She sat up and struggled into her skirt and blouse, not bothering with the underwear. Where in the hell was Sylvia?

"What did you take tonight? You were practically comatose."

"What does it matter?" Melody stumbled after him to the door. Something had happened to Sylvia. She was gone, or maybe she had never been here? Had the whole thing been a dream? No, no, the whole thing had been a nightmare.

"I'm not writing you any scripts tonight. You're taking too many opioids. Why, you can barely function." He had his medical bag in hand, his coat thrown over his arm. "I'm a little concerned, Nurse Arnold."

Was he a little concerned? Melody couldn't tell. When she squinted her eyes again, making him far, far away, he looked so small, just a regular man, a tiny man, and not that doctor of perversity.

"And I don't like fucking a comatose woman," he added.

"It's a good thing you do like fucking with your eyes closed." Sylvia came out of the bedroom, a handful of pictures in one hand, a tape recorder in the other, her eyes red and puffy.

Sylvia had been crying! Melody didn't understand. Why had Sylvia been crying?

"Nurse Hammond!" Dr. Desoto coughed. "Is this your apartment? What do you have in your hand?"

Melody propped herself against the couch. Was that fear in the little man's voice? No, that was *concern*.

"Evidence." Sylvia approached aggressively and waved the photos in his face. She towered over the little man. "Evidence of your sadistic, filthy nature. This is never going to happen again. Do you hear me? Never!"

"What do you think you're going to do with those?" Dr. Desoto cleared his throat. "I will say it was consensual."

Sylvia shook the tape recorder at him. "The sounds coming from Melody on this tape do not sound *consensual*."

"If you show anyone those pictures, I'll tell the hospital about the drug theft," Dr. Desoto said in as forceful of voice as he could muster.

He was such a *tiny* man. Melody swayed back and forth against the couch.

"That's right." Sylvia leaned over to get right in his face, mere inches separating them. "And then you and Melody can both have your reputations ruined. You'd be going down in a blaze of infamy after all your years as a respected—by some—doctor." She selected a picture from the pile. "This one, especially, shows you at your finest, wouldn't you say?"

Dr. Desoto flinched.

"Leave her alone, and no one will ever see these pictures. I mean it. Leave Melody alone."

"No more scripts." Dr. Desoto backed away and opened the door. "No more drugs, ever."

"We don't want them," and Sylvia sped his departure by pushing him out the door, slamming and locking it.

Later, Sylvia said to Melody, "It was all I could do to keep from killing him. I couldn't get the angle right at first, and I felt so helpless, watching what he was doing ... and you were so helpless ... and the anger ... and then I had to remind myself why we were doing this." All of Sylvia's bravado and anger had seeped away with her tears. "But it's over now. He'll never hurt you again."

"It's okay." They had switched roles, and Melody was now the one offering comfort. "I think I passed out. I don't really remember. Besides, Sylvia, I knew you'd be a professional."

They never talked about that night again.

17

APRIL 2012

Finally, Kat felt like she had a break in the case. She didn't exactly remember doing it, but she must have drunk texted Shane before she plowed face-first into perky Lorraine's bed, too tired and emotionally spent to even take off her clothes. (It did *not* matter that Zen had kissed Carrie; Kat was *not* jealous.) The text was an embarrassment, a garbled mush of misspellings: Do u kniw whre ur dad kept the famlly's brthh ceturkficates? Great. Now her kid half-brother probably thought his older sister was an idiot. But even if he did—God bless him—he had texted back: Yes.

Excited, Kat called him before she had even gotten out of bed, hoping that he was more prompt at answering his phone than she was. He was. "Shane, I got your text," she said breathlessly as soon as he said hello. "How do you know where Marcus keeps the birth certificates? Oh, and sorry about my garbled text. Late night."

He chuckled. "I guessed that, and it wasn't that hard to figure out. It's not exactly calculus. Although calculus is actually my best subject."

Okay, so he had the brains in the family. Kat was glad he couldn't see her roll her eyes. To Shane, who so eerily resembled her father but had taken the time to help her, she said, "Good for you. Now, where did you find them?"

"Where he's always kept them, in the second drawer on the left-hand side of his desk. It's where Dad keeps all his important papers."

Kat, of course, had not known that crucial fact. Had Marcus moved his important papers to the desk drawer after she left home, or had they always been there, right in front of her? What, exactly, did Marcus consider to be *important*?

"I was surprised that your birth certificate was still here. Why didn't you take it with you?" Shane asked.

"Well, I was sixteen and in a hurry, and I haven't needed it before."

"You don't have a passport?"

Zen had mentioned the same thing. Apparently, everyone in the world thought she needed a passport. "I promise I'll get one as soon as I get back to Arizona. You can send the birth certificate there. Let me give you the address."

"I have the address. It's right here in the folder."

Kat's heart tightened. So Marcus had kept her address, Granny Nanny's address, in with his important papers. What did it mean? Had he perhaps thought about her from time to time? Kat shook her head. She would have to contemplate all these facts later. She had gotten so much information in such a short time that she was having trouble processing it all. "Thanks, Shane. I do appreciate all the trouble you've gone to."

"It wasn't any trouble." His voice was hesitant. "This isn't about a passport, is it?"

She might as well tell him the truth—at least part of it. She owed him that. "No, I'm trying to find out about my mother, my birth mother. Marcus never told me anything about her, and I'm trying to figure out who she was. I'm in Chicago now, trying to piece together the story."

"Oh," Shane said, "you mentioned that while you were here. I guess it's something like checking out ancestry.com, right?"

"Right." Kat made a mental note to look at that site. She was surprised that PI Zen had not yet mentioned it. "So before I let you go, I need to know her maiden name."

"Sure," Shane said. "Let me see … Callahan. Her name was Melody Katherine Callahan."

Melody Katherine Callahan. The suicidal woman's birth name. Kat's heart tightened again. She did not and would not feel anything toward Melody Arnold, the determined, selfish bitch who had climbed the 100-foot light tower to swan dive to her death, taking her unborn baby with her. Yet this additional name, the original name of the woman … Well, it almost made her seem like a completely different person. Plus, there was this: Katherine/Katrina. Was there a connection? Probably not, Kat decided. Most definitely not. She was stretching.

Shane had been talking during Kat's reverie. "We moved Dad to the hospital yesterday," he said, his voice thick. "It seemed to me like he was getting better, but you know, it was getting to be too much for Mom, even with the home nurse coming in for five hours a day. I guess the doctors know what they're doing, right?"

Kat's heart had now tightened into a hard ball in her chest. "I'm sorry." She knew she should ask him if there was anything she could do. It was the polite, appropriate thing to say in a situation like this, but she couldn't make herself do it. In the last two days, she had caught a glimpse of who her father was, or had been, but there were still too many confusing questions. But Shane's pain hurt her, too. Damn it; it punctured the hard ball in her chest.

"Do you think you'll be coming around any time soon?" Shane's voice was almost inaudible.

Kat had not even considered the possibility until now. "I'll try, Shane. I can't guarantee anything, but I'll see if I can make it down before I go back to Arizona." She wasn't going to take the easy way out and tell him that her car had been stolen, she was strapped for cash, and she was indebted to too many people already. She wasn't going to tell him how difficult it would be for her to see her father one last time. For once in her life, she was not going to take the easy way out.

"That's good. It would mean a lot to Cody and me. You're the only sister we've got."

She hadn't been a very good one. "I'll try," she said one more time. She didn't know how she could swing it, but she really would try. She, too, had some amends to make.

Kat still held the cell phone in her hand, staring at it, when there was a knock on her door. Zen's voice: "Your date is here."

Holy shit! It was another thing she hadn't remembered from the night before. She had agreed to let—what was his name?—show her around the city. She really could not afford the missed day of research, and she should have said no, but then she had seen Zen kissing that gushing Carrie. But she was *not* jealous.

His name was John. That was it: John. He was a nice-looking man, and she could probably use a break from the emotional roller coaster that her life had become in the last few days. It would do her good to take her mind off things. And it would be her first date since pretty boy Benson. She must be improving. In her slightly slutty twenties, she would have had a lot of dates by now—if she used the term *date* loosely.

She was obviously late, although she didn't remember agreeing on a time. She gathered her new clothes to take to the bathroom and flung open the door. Zen still stood there, she discovered, when she ran into him. "Shit," she said, dropping the clothes.

"Good morning to you, too, gorgeous." Ever the gentleman, Zen bent down to pick them up.

Why did he always have to see her at her absolute worst? She was still in the rumpled clothes from the night before, her hair snarled around her face, which was streaked with the remnants of last night's makeup, and her teeth felt furry. Zen deposited the clothes back in her arms and stood there staring. Kat wanted to sink through the floor. "He's not exactly my date," she said, apropos of nothing, and blushed.

"He thinks he's your date." Zen stood in front of her, blocking her way to the bathroom.

"Well, he would be wrong." Under Zen's steady scrutiny, Kat grew even redder.

"Where are you going to go?"

"Where did you and Carrie go the other night?"

"I'm only asking you a simple, friendly question." Zen leaned against the doorjamb and folded his arms across his chest.

"I'm only asking you a simple, friendly question," she echoed. She was definitely losing this staring contest. Zen's green/gold eyes were mesmerizing, and she did not want to be mesmerized by Lorenzo Delaney, who, by some trick of chance, karma, or fate, always seemed to be coming to her rescue. Well, Kat Flowers did not need a knight in shining armor. However, she did wish that he wasn't so damn nice or so good looking—and not in a pretty boy Benson way.

"I took Carrie to visit her grandmother. She fell and broke her hip, and now she's in a nursing home. Carrie's very close to her grandmother."

"Oh." Now, of course, she felt like complete shit. However, was he playing the grandmother card because he knew how she felt about Granny Nanny? Maybe she was overly suspicious, but Zen's mouth twitched. Was he trying not to smile?

"Your turn," he said.

"He's going to show me the city." For the life of her, she again couldn't remember the name of the guy with whom she wasn't going on a date.

"For the entire day?"

"Oh, for crying out loud, Zen. I have no idea. I can't even really remember what we talked about last night," she blurted. "What's with the inquisition? What's next? Are you going to tell me I have a curfew?"

Now Zen was smiling. "Hold on, Kat. I was teasing you like I used to do with my sister. John's a good guy, and I don't care where you go. I hope you have a great time." He straightened up.

So he was teasing her like he used to do with his *sister*. He thought of her as his sister. It was a good thing that she didn't harbor any romantic feelings for him, none whatsoever. "Very funny. You're a riot, Zen, a real riot." She started to move past him, then stopped. "Tell Carrie that I'm sorry about her grandmother." That, she sincerely meant.

Zen's smile could not get any broader. "Carrie's grandmother is alive and well and living in Boca Raton. She plays golf every Tuesday and bridge every Thursday."

"That was low."

"You need to learn how to take a joke."

"You're a jackass." She tried to walk away from him with as much dignity as her rumpled clothes, bad breath, and snarled hair would allow.

"Thank you," he called after her.

Kat slammed the bathroom door and took a quick glance in the mirror to see what Zen had been staring at. She looked even more appalling than she had imagined. Kat hadn't remembered dripping ketchup down her chest when she'd eaten a hamburger while they bowled. She took the fastest shower of her life, put her wet hair in a ponytail, and swiped at her lashes with mascara. That was it. After all, she wasn't going on a date.

Or was she? When she finally made it downstairs and into the living room, Kat noticed with embarrassment that John was more nicely dressed than she in khaki pants, a dark blue polo shirt, and expensive-looking Italian loafers.

"You're even prettier than I remembered," John said, smiling.

Now, *that*, thought Kat, was a joke. "I'm sorry to keep you waiting. Let's get this show on the road." It was not a date, and she wasn't going to run back up the stairs and blow dry her hair and change, although she wanted to.

"Gladly." He took her elbow and steered her toward the door. "I have the whole day planned."

Kat couldn't help but glance over her shoulder. Was Zen watching? Was he lingering in the doorway, thinking, "I should be the one taking this girl to see the sights of Chicago?"

Nope. Kat, despite herself, felt a pang of disappointment.

For the rest of the day, she tried to put Zen and Melody Arnold out of her mind. She felt guilty that she wasn't doing more research and that she had hastily accepted this date to prove some stupid point to Zen when there wasn't any point to prove at all. However, John tried valiantly to keep her entertained.

"To really get to know the city," he said, "you need to walk it."

He hadn't been kidding. They walked from his apartment in the South Loop to the museum campus, past the Field Museum, Shedd Aquarium, and the Planetarium. He bought tickets to the Art Institute, and they strolled through the remarkable Impressionism gallery and up the stairs to the new Modern Wing. Then they walked through Grant Park and Millennium Park, where they bought hot dogs and sat at a bench looking at the infamous Bean, which Kat thought did look like a giant kidney bean.

"It's actually called Cloud Gate," John explained, "but everyone in Chicago calls it The Bean. On the west side, it reflects the Chicago skyline."

John had fed her tidbits of information like that for the duration of their non-date, playing tour guide with ease. Kat was grateful for that; it eliminated the need for chit-chat. And even though her feet ached, she'd enjoyed herself. The day was sunny and warm ("It's ten degrees above normal for this time of year," John had informed her), and it had been a pleasant experience. But she was ready to go home. Well, not home. Back to Zen's parents' house in Oak Lawn Park. John was a very nice guy, a little stiff, perhaps, but nice. However, Kat did not feel any *zing* in his presence. None whatsoever. Granny Nanny would probably say that this was a failed experiment, like her ghoulish goulash. Granny Nanny, as usual, would be right.

John had other plans. They were not done walking. They went back to the lakefront for the next leg of their journey and walked north, past the Columbia Yacht club, DuSable Harbor, and over the Lake Shore Bridge to

Navy Pier. They walked to the end and back, and by that time, Kat, who was tired and hungry, desperately wanted to go home. One lousy hot dog had not been enough for all the walking. As they left Navy Pier, Kat said, "This has been great, John, I've had a good time, but—"

He looked at his watch. "If we hurry, we can make it to Sears—I mean Willis—Tower before it closes. We'll have to walk fast, though."

"I thought we had been walking fast." John had mentioned again that he was a marathon runner, and there had been no need to reveal that tidbit of information. Their walking pace had surpassed many shuffle/run joggers on the lakefront. Her feet and lower back ached.

John looked at her and blushed. "I'm an idiot. I've been walking you too hard, haven't I? I get so excited about this city, and I didn't know when I'd get another chance to show you how great it is. Do you want to take a break? We could stop someplace and get a drink. I know a great place on Rush Street."

The desire for a cold beer waged battle with the desire to go to Oak Lawn Park. The beer won. "How far is it?"

"We'll take a cab," John said, his arm already in the air, flagging an approaching taxi.

This was more like it. Sitting in the dark bar with a Negroni in front of her (John had insisted that they made good ones here), Kat felt infinitely better. She still wanted to go back to Oak Lawn Park, but she'd decided not to be a bitch about it. After all, he was a good friend of Zen's, and oddly, she didn't want word to get back to Zen that Kat Flowers was a lousy date. She'd decided this once the throbbing in her aching feet subsided—and after she had drunk half of the Negroni. "What did you say the name of this place was?"

"Carmine's. It's my favorite Italian restaurant in the city. The fried calamari here is excellent."

She stifled a groan. *On your best behavior,* she reminded herself, *remember your self-improvement plan; John's a friend of Zen.* So instead of saying, "Would you quit acting like a fucking tour guide," she said, "That sounds great. Let's order some."

They ordered the appetizer and another drink, then moved to a table by the front window for dinner. Kat wouldn't say she was enjoying herself, but the alcohol definitely made her less edgy. After a couple of glasses of pinot noir (excellent, according to John), she was doing an impressive job of dodging the questions he asked her.

"What do you do for a living?" The red wine had slightly stained John's mouth. He looked like he had inexpertly applied lipstick.

"I'm between jobs."

"What kind of jobs? What company?" he persisted.

"I majored in business." That part was true.

"Excellent."

John's overuse of the word *excellent* was grating on her nerves, but she smiled her wine-stained smile. "Yes, it is *excellent*, isn't it?"

"Business makes the world go around," John said happily, and then he was off, talking about his job, something about putting together a portfolio of city bonds, the Dow Jones, the S&P, the Nasdaq.

Kat nodded from time to time. She had her own list of questions that she was tamping down: How did you and Zen meet? What was he like in college? Did he have many girlfriends? If John didn't shut up soon, she might slip and start asking those questions, and if she did that, he might suspect that she had a thing for Zen Delaney, which she did not. She most certainly did not.

John continued to talk. She'd finished her veal piccata and wondered how she could ask him—in a polite, non-bitchy manner—to please, *please* take her back to Oak Lawn Park. She was getting tired. He'd walked her to death. It was time to get the hell out of Dodge.

He ordered another bottle of wine.

Kat had no choice but to stay. Because really and truly, the wine was *excellent*. She'd never had a more expensive, better wine. It was funny how it could happen. She could have a couple of drinks, or perhaps four, and feel tired, then she drank a little more and was ready to conquer the world. Kat felt revved up, ready to go. And John was trying hard to impress her, *wining and dining her.* She giggled. Benson had often tried to wine and dine her, but Benson had been on an allowance from his mother. It was hysterical, a thirty-two-year-old on an *allowance*. Her giggling grew louder.

"What's so funny?" John asked.

"Nothing." Kat put the napkin over her mouth. She needed to get control of herself and realized too late that she was beyond tipsy. Damn it, the wine was *excellent*, and what the hell? She poured herself another glass.

"Shall we order some dessert?" John picked up the menu.

Kat held up her full wine glass. "I'm drinking my dessert."

"What did I tell you?" John said, pleased. "This particular varietal is excellent."

He was killing her. Trying to suppress her laughter brought tears to her eyes. She could only nod.

"So you're leaving the day after tomorrow?" he asked.

That sobered her up a little. Her time was running out; her money was running out. Yet she could not picture herself walking into a bus station (the cheapest way to go) and buying a ticket. She just couldn't picture it. Nor could she imagine putting an ad on Craigslist for a ride (even cheaper). Being in someone else's car put an entirely different spin on traveling across the country. What if the person did turn out to be a felon, transporting drugs across the country? "That was the original plan," she finally managed to say.

"Four days is such a short time for a visit, and I hope you don't mind me asking—I didn't seem to catch it the other night—but who are you in town visiting? I'm gathering that you're not old friends with the Delaneys. If you were, I would have heard about you before." The waiter came to the table, and John ordered the cheesecake and a dessert wine.

Another gulp of wine and sobriety abandoned her completely. "I'm looking for my mother," she said. Too late, she realized that wasn't exactly the way to put it. You couldn't exactly look for a dead person.

John looked confused. His lips were now a dark blood red, like a vampire. "Did she disappear, or are you adopted and looking for your birth mother?"

"Wrong on both counts." Should she tell him? Should she say, "She's dead. The selfish bitch took a nosedive from a 100-foot light tower when she was nine months pregnant with me." It seemed rather mean to ruin this nice man's expensive, excellent dinner. (Dear God, she hoped he wasn't going to expect her to pay half. She hadn't even thought about that.)

"I'm sorry," John said. "I know it's none of my business."

"Are you rich?" Kat asked suddenly, still wondering if he would pay for this dinner and not caring that the question was none of her business.

Instead of being offended, John seemed to like the question. "Well, I do have to say that I've done well, especially considering my age. I had the right mentor, and I was in the right place at the right time. You know how that goes."

"Nope." Kat hiccupped. She had no idea how that went.

Then John proceeded to tell her, not noticing that Kat stared at him with glassy eyes and probably nodded in all the inappropriate places. What she was thinking, as he babbled on, was: Could I fall in love with a rich man, a *real* rich man, not a trust fund baby on an allowance? It would certainly make her life a hell of a lot easier. No, wait. She could simply marry a rich man. Love didn't have to be part of the equation. She saw it all the time in Scottsdale—fat, old, rich men with their twenty-something, blonde, fake-boobed, trophy wives. But even in her alcohol haze, Kat knew that she couldn't marry someone without love, not that she wanted to get married, ever. And she definitely didn't want to get married to Zen Delaney.

By the time the endless dinner—the endless day—was over, Kat didn't particularly care where John took her. So when he said, "I'm afraid I've had a little too much wine to drive you back to Oak Lawn Park. Do you mind if we cab it to my place? I can take a little nap, drink some coffee, sober up, and then drive you back. Is that all right with you?"

If Kat remembered correctly, and that was dubious, they'd left his car in his parking garage, so it didn't sound like a come-on. Plus, he had paid for the expensive meal (making quite the show of pulling out his black American Express card), answering her timid, bated breath, "Would you like me to help with that?" with an "absolutely not." So it didn't seem to make any difference if they went back to his apartment building

"This part of the South Loop is called Printers Row," John said when the cab deposited them at 600 S. Dearborn Street. Annoyingly, he was still playing tour guide and feeding her tidbits of information.

"Good to know," she said, not caring the tiniest bit. She took deep gulps of the night air, trying to clear her brain. It didn't help much.

The revolving door in the front of the building twirled and deposited a person directly in front of them. Kat squinted her eyes and looked up and up. The person was very tall, with striking blonde-white hair piled on its head. Her head. Even though she was very old, with deep wrinkles in her face, and extremely thin, she looked imposing, almost regal. Kat had the absurd, drunken idea that she should curtsy or something.

"What are you looking at?" The woman's voice was deep, husky, a voice coarsened by years of smoking. She lit a long brown cigarette—or was it a cigar?—right then.

"Nothing," Kat stammered. "Sorry." She couldn't stop staring.

The woman stared right back at her with steely blue eyes. "Do I know you?" She took a step forward. She had on a black trench coat and long black boots with three-inch chunky heels, boots that looked worn and hopelessly outdated.

Instinctively, Kat took a step back. "I don't think so. I mean, no, you don't know me."

"You look familiar." She bent down, looking closer, blowing a stream of acrid smoke into Kat's face.

Kat felt a chill run down her spine. The woman, who had done nothing wrong, frightened her. She gave off a faintly medicinal odor, or perhaps it was morgue-like, something akin to formaldehyde? Even creepier was the fact that, for some reason, this woman looked vaguely familiar to her, too. But that was impossible because she had never even been to Chicago before. This imposing, scary woman was a total stranger.

"You definitely look familiar," the woman insisted.

Kat took another step back. "No!"

"Come on," John took hold of her arm, "let's get inside."

When they were safely in the elevator, Kat asked, "Who was that frightening woman?" She had no idea why the woman had spooked her so.

"Just the resident crazy lady," John laughed. "Nothing to worry about. She's all talk and no show. People say she's lived in this building for decades, but I have no idea what apartment she's in. She doesn't socialize much, probably because the HOA has tried to get her evicted numerous times."

"If she's harmless, why would they try to do that?"

"Supposedly, she comes and goes at all hours of the day and night."

"There's nothing wrong with that." Kat could still feel the chill in her spine, and there was absolutely no reason for it.

They had reached John's floor, and John led Kat down the carpeted hallway. "Well, she supposedly has people coming in and going out at all hours of the day and night, too, but I don't know. There are all kinds of rumors about her, but that's all they are—rumors. Really, she's harmless, just the resident crazy lady."

Kat knew that it looked bad, but absolutely nothing had happened. When John dropped her off at the Delaneys' house at seven o'clock the next morning, she hoped that she could sneak up the stairs and pretend that she had been there all night. Nope. The Delaney clan, it would seem, consisted of a bunch of early risers. Early risers with excellent hearing.

Kat would swear that the front door barely made a click when she shut it, but the call from the kitchen was instantaneous. "We're in here." It was Priscilla's voice. "Come join us for breakfast, Kat."

Shit. Could Kat get away with telling Zen's family that she'd gone for an early morning run? No, she wasn't sweaty. A walk, then. Maybe she could tell them she had gone for a walk? Maybe she wouldn't have to tell them anything at all? She could grab a quick cup of coffee and hightail it upstairs to take a shower.

No such luck. In addition to Priscilla, Tanner, and Zen, Lorraine and her girls were there. Did they never eat at their own house? "Sit down, sit down," Priscilla said. "We have Denver omelets this morning." She was already fixing a plate at the stove.

"Good morning," Kat said sheepishly and sat.

"How was your date?" Lorraine, ever perky, asked. "Megan, do not play with your food."

Another thing about this family: It seemed like they told each other *everything*.

"It wasn't a—" Oh, what was the use? It had been a date. "Fine. I saw a lot of Chicago." She hadn't thought she was hungry, but one bite of the omelet, and she was ravenous. It was hard to believe that this woman couldn't make a decent rum cake. Everything else she made was out-of-this-world delicious.

"It must have been pretty good." Zen hadn't looked at Kat since she sat down next to him. "It lasted for almost twenty-four hours."

"Those were the days," Tanner Delaney said. "Sometimes, your mother and I would stay up to see the sunrise. Do you remember, Priscilla?"

"I certainly do," Priscilla said, reaching over to give her husband's hand a fond pat.

"Yes." Kat seized the opening. "That's what we did."

"Uh-huh," Zen said.

"How romantic," Lorraine said, wiping a smear of jelly from Tammy's round pink cheek. "Enjoy it while you can. When you have kids and get up at the crack of dawn, sunrises don't seem so great when you'd rather crawl back into bed."

"That's the thing," Zen said. "Crawling into bed." He finally looked at Kat.

She couldn't read his expression—anger, disappointment? She blushed and shook her head, hoping it sent the message: *I didn't sleep with him.* Zen shrugged. Did he get the message?

"Nothing like a good, firm mattress," Tanner Delaney said. He had dressed this morning. Each day of Kat's stay, he seemed to improve.

"I want one of those sleep number beds," Lorraine said. "I keep bugging Benny about it. I'm hoping he'll surprise me and get one for our anniversary."

"I'm going for a ride." Zen pushed his chair back from the table. "Thanks for breakfast, Mom."

"Excuse me," Kat said. She took her plate to the sink and followed Zen out the back door. "It's not what you think."

He pumped air into the front tire of his bike. "It doesn't matter what I think."

Kat pressed on, desperate to make him understand, desperate to set the record straight. "We had too much to drink at dinner, and he didn't want to drive me home. I seem to be drinking quite a bit these days, and it's not like me. Anyway, John suggested that we go back to his place and nap, but we didn't wake up until this morning. I slept on his couch; he slept in his bed. He wanted me to take the bed in the spare bedroom, but I insisted on the couch..." She was babbling.

"It's fine, Kat." Zen's voice remained neutral.

Did he believe her or not? She needed him to believe her. "Honest," she said weakly.

"Okay, Kat." He put on his helmet and straddled the bike. "Let's move on. Did you get a hold of your birth certificate?"

"Yes!" She, too, wanted to change the subject. She told him about the conversation with Shane and her mother's maiden name.

"Today, we'll pay your family a visit," he said as he clipped his feet into the pedals.

"Really? You're going with me?"

"You don't have a car, and you don't know your way around these neighborhoods like I do," he pointed out.

"I know, but I didn't expect you to help." She'd almost said that she didn't expect him to forgive her, but why? She hadn't done anything wrong. Yet she still felt that, in some way, she had betrayed him. It made no sense.

"Why wouldn't I help?"

She smiled at him—grateful once again—and hoping, hoping that she didn't have green pepper stuck in her teeth, even though Zen seemed to have a knack for catching her at her supreme awfulness, both physically and emotionally. "Thanks, Zen."

"Besides, I don't have anything better to do," he said as he rode off.

So, he giveth, and he taketh away, Kat thought. *The lovely piece of shit.*

18

APRIL-MAY 1981

Melody knew what it was, but she refused to believe it. Her agitation, muscle aches, and profuse sweating were only signs of nerves. On this point, she would have to agree with Marcus. She led a very stressful life, even though Marcus—bland, thoughtful, dutiful Marcus—did not, of course, know the real reason for her increased nervousness. For two weeks after the last episode with that perverse Dr. Desoto, she was on pins and needles. Literally, she felt them pricking all over her body, tiny, quick jabs of pain. Was the doctor going to tell the whole sordid story? Was he going to hire an attorney? What else could he do to hurt her?

Apparently, he was going to do nothing. He avoided Melody and Sylvia like the plague, even turning around and walking in the opposite direction if he saw one of them approaching in the hospital hallway. Then there was the announcement that Dr. Desoto would take a leave of absence. The rumors swirling around in the gossipy world of Mercy Hospital were that Dr. Desoto had a mental breakdown or that he had some other kind of significant health problem. No, said others, that wasn't right. The aging doctor had decided to take his wife of nearly fifty years on a belated Mediterranean cruise. The real reason didn't matter to Melody. What mattered was that the man was suddenly, miraculously *gone*.

"We're in the clear," Sylvia said to Melody soon after the doctor left. "We can relax now."

Melody nodded in agreement. She could put that wretched episode of her life behind her. All was well.

And yet, all was not well; she couldn't relax. Melody's *nerves* made it difficult to do her job. She fumbled with syringes and bandages. She often seemed to be daydreaming and not quite *with it*. At home, she dropped plates and left the tea kettle on the stove's burner, whistling, screaming endlessly until the water had burned off, and the bottom was scorched.

"Baby, kitten, you need to be more careful," Marcus said after he had taken the useless tea kettle out to the trash. "I know you're as worried about Mother as I am, but the doctor said it was only a minor stroke. We need to take it one day at a time. We need to focus."

Evelyn's minor stroke left the right side of her face sagging and flaccid, but it wasn't what concerned Melody. (Evelyn was going downhill rapidly, and Melody knew there would be more strokes. Evelyn was dying. Every single person on the planet was dying, daily.)

One day at a time, that was her concern. She needed something to help her get through one day at a time. She made an appointment with her doctor to refill her prescriptions for Xanax and diazepam. Dr. Bennett, handsome and tall, had been so kind to her when she was recovering from her *still born* baby. He had been so understanding of her pain.

Dr. Bennett was not so kind and understanding now. "I wrote your prescriptions for six months, Melody. Surely, you've had time to recover, to regain your equilibrium. You're young. You have your whole life ahead of you." He gave her a professional smile, closing the folder that contained her medical history.

Melody couldn't tear her eyes from the picture on his desk: Dr. Bennett, with his wife and three children, all blonde, all tall, all smiling. The perfect Aryan family. "I'm only asking you for another couple of months, Dr. Bennett. Something else has come up, something stressful. My mother-in-law is in poor health." Melody dropped her eyes to her lap, ashamed. Once again, she was using poor Evelyn as an excuse.

"I see." Dr. Bennett let the words hang in the air.

Melody hoped he didn't see. She was clasping her hands so hard to keep them from shaking that the effort made her entire body tremble. She felt a mustache of sweat break out on her upper lip. "My husband wants to have another baby," she said, not knowing why, apropos of nothing. She wanted to snatch back the words. They had no relationship as to why she was here on a mission for more drugs.

"Excellent!" Dr. Bennett boomed. "That might be just the ticket, Melody. I wish you luck." He stood up, finished with the appointment, finished with her, problem solved. All a woman needed to be happy was to have a baby. Look at his perfect Aryan wife and children. Weren't they the picture of bliss?

Melody felt the tears pool and blinked rapidly to hold them at bay. She was not going to let this son-of-a-bitch, this *man*, see her cry. (She concentrated on Sylvia's voice in her head: "He's a chauvinist pig, Melody. All men are chauvinist pigs.") She didn't take the hand he extended. All the pig had to do was write out a prescription. Why wouldn't he just write out a lousy, fucking prescription? Her legs ached as she walked to the door; her stomach cramped.

"You're in perfect health, Melody. I bet you get pregnant within the year," he reassured her as she opened the door. "And then you certainly wouldn't want to be on any unnecessary medication. You know as well as I do the number of people who abuse prescription drugs. I don't understand it myself, and I'm sure you don't either …"

Melody closed the door, walked quickly to her car, and vomited.

The symptoms of her withdrawal were becoming more advanced. How could that be? *She, Melody Arnold, was not a drug addict!* All she needed was something to help her function, only for another couple of months. That was all. It was perfectly normal. She had gone through so many major upheavals in her life in the last year. Anyone in her unenviable position would do the same. Anyone.

She stopped at the first gas station she saw and went into the bathroom to rinse out her mouth and splash cold water on her face. Thank God she had vomited outside the car. She didn't need Marcus noticing a putrid smell in his beloved Buick that she would have tried, in vain, to cover with Lysol and perfume. She didn't need Marcus to ask more questions. Marcus always asked questions, probing, concern for her well-being clouding his eyes. He was suffocating her with his misguided, misinformed *concern*. Just the thought of Marcus made her shaking grow more violent. Just the thought of Marcus made her more desperate for the numbness that a tiny tablet of any opioid would provide.

Melody called Sylvia at the filthy phone booth outside the door of the gas station. How many people had handled this greasy phone? How many people had made emergency phone calls from this receiver, breathing into it their desperate pleas and concerns? Months ago, Melody wouldn't have picked up this phone, but that Melody no longer existed. (How quickly life could change—a blink of the eye, a wrong turn, a bad decision, a *still born* baby.)

"I can't stand it," Melody breathed into the phone as soon as Sylvia answered.

"I know what you mean." Sylvia, too, suffered from *nerves*.

"I want to jump out of my skin." Melody hadn't realized it until just then, but she was clawing at the skin of her neck with her left hand, the hand that did not hold the filthy receiver. She itched all over, but the harder she scratched, the more the itch burned. Her skin was on fire, and there was no relief. She needed relief.

"I'm going to make the phone call," Sylvia said. "There's no other way."

"Don't do it," Melody said, but her itching, burning skin was crying: *Please make the call.*

"There's no other way," Sylvia repeated, her wobbly voice coming through the phone from a great distance. "It's my turn. I owe you."

"You don't owe me anything."

Sylvia didn't pursue the matter. After all, by tacit agreement, they never talked about Dr. Demented and the lost supply of drugs. "Maybe I can persuade him to come out to the suburbs, your neck of the woods," Sylvia said. "That sounds safer than meeting him on a dark street in a seedy part of the city, doesn't it?"

Melody didn't know. How could she? She had never done this before. However, she said, "The suburbs probably would be safer."

"That's what I'll do then." Sylvia's wobbly voice grew even thinner.

"I'm going with you." Even though Melody was scared—as she was sure Sylvia was, too—she couldn't let her best friend buy drugs from one of Thelma's ex-dealers alone. They had always dismissed the idea as being too dangerous for them, too low, too seedy. Until now. Until there was no other choice.

"Thank you," Sylvia said gratefully. "We'll go together."

"Yes, together." And Melody put the filthy phone back into its filthy cradle.

Naturally, Marcus was suspicious when Melody gave him another weak excuse, an unbelievable lie: Another nurse had suddenly taken ill—possibly her appendix—and Melody was needed at work immediately.

"It's one o'clock in the morning," Marcus mumbled.

Melody hadn't fallen asleep at all. She had lain rigid, sweating, burning next to her sleeping husband for hours, waiting for Sylvia's call. The drug dealer Sylvia finally contacted (apparently, most of Thelma's drug dealers did not have a permanent address) was the third one Sylvia had slept with, the one with only one attribute. His name was Clyde.

"It's my job." Melody dressed hurriedly in her starched nursing uniform. She would have rather worn black, the incognito color in the movies when stealthy, exciting escapades happened in the middle of the night. But she couldn't. Her husband thought she was going to work, and this was nothing like the movies. There was nothing glamorous about it. Not even close. And she was scared to death.

"I don't like this," Marcus said, his voice still sleep-coated. "Young women should not be driving alone at night."

"Shh, Marcus, go back to sleep."

Melody left quickly, quietly, and met Sylvia in the parking lot of Jewel, as they had arranged. "This is a good place to meet." Melody looked around at the mostly empty parking lot. "It's well-lit."

Sylvia started her lime green Volkswagen Rabbit; her hands shook on the steering wheel. "This is not where we're meeting that scumbag, Clyde. We're going to an abandoned railway yard a few miles from here."

"Why?" Melody said, alarmed. "I like it here. I go grocery shopping all the time at this store. I feel safe here."

"I don't know *why*," Sylvia snapped. She glanced at Melody's startled face. "Sorry. I guess low-life drug dealers like seedy places, even in the suburbs."

"Shit." Melody slumped back on the seat.

"Exactly."

They drove to the designated spot in silence, both young women taut and nervous, with Sylvia occasionally glancing at the directions. They arrived in minutes, too soon. Sylvia parked on a side street and left her lights on. They could see the slumped and rusty rail cars ahead, the overgrown weeds flanking the abandoned tracks, and in the distance, toward the far end of the dilapidated, sorry, dismissed yard, a very tall light tower.

The place was eerie, yet sad, and Melody couldn't take her eyes off the light tower. "So what do we do now? Wait?" she whispered.

"No, we're supposed to meet him at the light tower," Sylvia said glumly. "Shit."

"Do you think there are snakes or rats?" Melody shivered as she looked at the tall overgrown grass. She wished she had worn thigh-high boots, the kind that fishermen wore as they waded into the lake to retrieve their cache of churning, helpless fish caught in nets.

"I think those would be the least of our problems right now, although I guess you could say we are dealing with a *human* snake or rat." Sylvia reached over Melody, fumbled in the glove compartment, and produced a flashlight. "I came prepared. I should have been a girl scout."

"I think that's the boy scouts' motto." Melody still stared at the tower. It seemed so far away.

"Whatever. You might want to take off your hat. You look a little conspicuous."

"And a lime green car is not conspicuous?" Melody took off her hat. She was certainly not dressed appropriately, and that was the least of her worries.

"How badly do we want this?" Sylvia turned to look at Melody, her face earnest in the glow of the dashboard. "We could leave right now and forget the whole thing."

We could do that, Melody thought. *Forget the whole thing.* But her body—itching, searing, sweating—seemed to have other ideas. "We could, but—"

"I know." Sylvia opened the door. "Shit, I know."

They made their way slowly toward the light tower, stumbling over rocks and discarded beer bottles and knotted brambles, occasionally clutching at each other to prevent a fall. *This will be the last time,* Melody told herself. She only needed something to get her through the next month or two. *She was not a drug addict.* She clutched her purse that contained the money that she had again borrowed from Willie. Too late, she realized that she should have brought Marcus' gun. "We should have brought a weapon," she whispered to Sylvia.

"Damn it," Sylvia hissed. Then: "I have this flashlight, though, and it's two against one."

It wasn't two against one. In the flashlight's eerie glow, Melody could make out three dark figures at the base of the light tower. She clutched at Sylvia's elbow, making the flashlight's beam ricochet off the shadows. "We're outnumbered." Her gut instinct told her that she and Sylvia should turn and flee the scene as fast as possible. However, they were so close, and her skin itched, burned.

"They must have already seen us," Sylvia whispered. "It's probably too late to turn back now."

It was. "Syl," someone called, his voice low and urgent. "Over here. Get your beautiful ass over here. Pronto."

Sylvia swallowed so loudly that Melody could hear the gulp. "Let's hold hands," Melody said, reaching for Sylvia's.

Sylvia shook her off. "For god's sake, Melody. I don't know how to go about this, but I'm pretty sure that we should not approach our prospective drug dealers *holding hands.* Get a grip. We need to act professionally in this situation."

Professionalism. Yes, that was the ticket. They needed to act professionally. Melody could do that. She did it all the time at work, no matter how much sympathy and pain she felt for a young girl with blonde ringlets dying of leukemia or a newly engaged victim of a motorcycle crash who had just had both his legs severed. She stood up straighter. This was nothing compared to the suffering she witnessed every day at work. It was a simple trade, an exchange of merchandise for cash. People did it all the time.

Except for the fact that this was illegal.

Except for the fact that the sellers might be carrying guns.

Except for the fact that if the cops somehow found out about this transaction, they could all go to jail.

It was too late to turn back now, and as she and Sylvia made their way toward the base of the light tower, Melody had a strange premonition that she was walking toward her fate, that something irreversible was happening. This overpowering feeling surpassed even her fear of what was about to take place. She had to get a grip on herself, slow her shallow panting. *This is the first and last time I will do anything like this*, she said to herself, forcing herself to believe it. *I will never come here again.*

Clyde leaned against the light tower while the other two huddled nearby. "You never called me back, Syl," he said in a fictitious, hurt tone. "My women always want more than one helping of Clyde." His shaggy, greasy dark hair showed from under his stocking cap. The other two were also wearing stocking caps.

Melody felt like saying, "It's April, you morons. Why are you wearing stocking caps?" But she didn't open her mouth. She couldn't.

"Cut the crap, Clyde," Sylvia said as forcefully as she could, although she couldn't quite disguise the tremor in her voice. "Do you have the goods?"

Clyde laughed, disclosing his yellow, decaying teeth. "Did you hear that, boys? This tall piece of ass thinks we're playing Starsky and Hutch, or some shit like that."

The other two, beefier than Clyde, laughed appreciatively.

Melody wondered if the other two were Clyde's bodyguards. Did drug dealers have bodyguards? Her mouth grew even drier.

"Let's get this over with," Sylvia said. "Give me the stuff. We have the money."

"Turn off that fucking flashlight," Clyde said. "You might as well be sending an SOS to the fucking cops.

"No," Sylvia said, but it came out more like a question. "I don't trust you."

"You don't trust me? You hear that?" Clyde turned to his two companions. "The bitch doesn't know how nice we've been playing here. What do you think about that? Should we start playing a little rougher?"

The two beefy companions moved closer, and Melody could see a long, red, lurid scar down one of the men's cheeks. The other had a smashed face like a bulldog. Not bodyguards. Henchmen. Enforcers.

Sylvia continued to stare at him, frozen with fear and indecision.

"I said," Clyde's voice was low, slow, and deliberate, "turn off that fucking flashlight."

Even though he was scrawny, it seemed to Melody that Clyde suddenly metamorphosed into a menacing figure, a gnome with an evil sneer, a malicious intent. Like a rabid lion, he looked ready to pounce, but Melody knew that he would not be the one inflicting any bodily harm. No, that job would fall to scarface and the bulldog. Melody wrenched the flashlight from Sylvia's hand and turned it off.

"That's better," Clyde said. "At least one of you bitches has some sense."

Melody knew that neither she nor Sylvia had any sense at all. If they did, they wouldn't be in this deserted railway yard in the middle of the night with these men.

"Take their purses," Clyde instructed his goons. "The stupid cunts brought purses."

As Melody's eyes adjusted to the light, she could make out the men dumping their purses on the ground, grabbing the money she and Sylvia had decided to put neatly into envelopes, and then going through their wallets. Melody wondered if they would take everything, and then, absurdly: Did drug dealers take credit cards?

"Let's get a couple of things straight here." Clyde, suddenly, was right in front of them, his sour breath on their faces. "I'm the one in charge. I'm the one doing you bitches a favor. Got it?"

"Yes," Melody said. She wanted to push him away, to get his foulness away from her body, but of course, she did not. She did not want to anger him any further, and she did not, *did not*, want to die in this wretched place.

Sylvia said nothing until Melody elbowed her, hard, in the ribcage. "Yes," she croaked.

"Good." Clyde reached into his inside coat pocket and pulled out a plastic bag. He pressed it against Sylvia's chest and held it there. "I like you, Syl. You're a fantastic fuck—maybe not as good as your old lady when she got good and desperate—but good enough, and remember, I'm doing you a favor. You'll remember that, won't you?"

Melody could see a glistening on Sylvia's cheeks. Was she crying? Melody answered for them both. "We'll remember," she said hurriedly. Sylvia would fall apart any minute, and this awful runt of a man needed to be gone.

"This is the good stuff," Clyde said to Sylvia in a tone that resembled a caress. "In memory of Thelma, huh?" He laughed. "It's a little gift, a favor. Got it?"

"We've got it," Melody said.

"And favors don't come free." He kissed Sylvia forcefully on the mouth, and to his goons said, "Now."

Melody and Sylvia stood stark still and watched them slip into the night. Then Sylvia fell to her knees and vomited. "What have we done?" she cried. "What have we done?"

Once again, Melody and Sylvia had a story, a shared history, an unsavory episode that they didn't talk about. They might allude to it occasionally, but it wasn't to be dwelt on.

The heroin made it easier to forget. Clyde's *little gift* was a bag of white powder. Heroin. Diamorphine. They resisted until the oxycodone pills—what Sylvia had "ordered"—were gone, and it was all that remained. The white powder in a clear cellophane bag.

"We're not addicts," Melody said, that first time, as they sat at Sylvia's kitchen table.

"No, we're not," Sylvia agreed, even as she heated the dissolving powder in a tablespoon over a candle that sat between them.

Even as she watched, mesmerized—how did Sylvia know how to do that?—Melody said, "We're nurses. We're fully in control. It's just that we lead stressful lives."

"That's right," Sylvia said, even as she drew the liquid into a syringe.

"We take opioids, we know what the effects are, and they haven't affected our lives." Melody could not take her eyes off the syringe as the liquid filled the cylinder. For some reason, a childhood song, one she hadn't thought about in years, came to mind: "The itsy bitsy spider climbed up the water spout ..."

"They haven't affected our lives one bit." Sylvia tightened a belt around her upper arm. "We're just going to see what all the fuss is about."

Melody watched the syringe going into Sylvia's bulging vein, mesmerized, hypnotized. "We're just doing research."

"Research." Sylvia's voice already slurred as she handed the syringe to Melody.

Even as Melody tightened the belt around her own arm, and even as she inserted the needle into a vein, she didn't think any harm would come from this new drug experience. Heroin, after all, was just another opioid that blocked the brain's ability to feel pain. Melody needed to escape the pain. It was no big deal.

Melody was wrong. The heroin produced a downer effect that rapidly induced a state of relaxation and euphoria. She had never felt so relaxed, so peaceful! She felt like she was floating on air; she didn't have a care in the world. Marcus, Evelyn, her *still born* baby, all of them melted away. They didn't exist; they had never existed. She wanted the euphoria to go on and on and on ...

Once was not enough.

She needed more. How could they get more of this wonderful drug?

Sylvia flatly refused to contact Clyde again, and Melody didn't blame her. "He wants me to fuck him, and I'm not stooping that low again. We'll have to ask around in my old neighborhood. If Thelma could do it, we can, too."

"Yes," Melody said, excited. It had been three days since their first experience in Sylvia's kitchen, and Melody craved more. It would be easy. She'd practically lived in that neighborhood for her last two years of nursing school; she knew the place.

Not really. Melody didn't know the back alleys, and she didn't know the seedy apartments, with dirty mattresses strewn on the floor and cockroaches the size of mice, the smell of unwashed bodies so foul that she wanted to vomit. But they did score some heroin. She and Sylvia were so damn lucky! Melody just knew that her life was going to be so much better now. She would use the heroin sparingly, of course. She was not an addict. However, on days when she felt the blackness, the walls of her small world closing in upon her, trapping her, suffocating her, she could go into her bathroom, lock the door, and find peace …

Evelyn died in her sleep in the early hours of a Thursday morning, and Marcus cried more tears over her than he had over their dear, dead baby boy. He was inconsolable, and his grief repulsed Melody. In fact, it occurred to her that she was becoming repulsed by everyone's grief. She saw too much of it in her line of work, to the point that she no longer read the paper or watched the news. All of it was too much to bear. Too much.

"It's just the two of us," Marcus said to Melody, clinging to her.

The funeral was over, and everyone had gone home, leaving their house scattered with sandwich crumbs and lipstick-smeared coffee cups. Ma had offered to stay and help clean up, and Melody told her that it was okay, that she could clean up herself. Now she regretted that decision. She needed Ma because she needed a buffer between herself and this clingy, needy man. "I need to clean up, Marcus." Melody tried to extract herself from Marcus' arms.

"Oh, Mellie," Marcus sobbed into her shoulder, "you're all I have now."

You're all I have now. The idea terrified Melody. If she thought Marcus had been suffocating and possessive before, what was he going to be like now? She was saddened by Evelyn's death, certainly, but she was also a little angry at her. Melody had almost gotten up enough courage to ask Marcus for a divorce, but now there was no way she could do it any time soon. Evelyn's death left a big hole in Marcus' life, and it was a hole that he expected Melody to fill. She was stuck, sinking even lower into the quicksand of this marriage, this life she did not wish to live.

"Marcus, I need to clean up. Why don't you go watch TV?" There would be endless, endless nights of TV watching with Marcus. That realization was the one that finally made Melody cry. She'd been dry-eyed at the funeral and the reception after, and once again, everyone mistook her emotional void as bravery. Once again, she had fooled them all.

Especially Marcus. "Oh, dear kitten, you're crying. I know you're as upset about Mother's passing as I am. How selfish of me not to try to comfort you." He smoothed her hair. "We'll muddle through this somehow, together."

Melody cried harder. Together. They would *muddle through together.*

"There, there." Marcus patted her back.

Melody desperately needed to go upstairs and lock herself in the bathroom, but Marcus would ask—as he'd been asking a lot lately—why she spent so much time in the bathroom.

"I'm taking bubble baths," she told him, and she would fill the tub with steaming hot water, just in case he was standing outside the door. Marcus usually stood outside the door.

"To relieve the stress," he had nodded. "Yes, that's good."

"To relieve the stress," she had parroted back. Marcus always, always conceded to *stress*.

"I'm motherless," Marcus said now, still clinging tightly to Melody, smoothing her hair, patting her back. "I suppose I'm an orphan."

Oh, it was too much. Melody wanted to scream, "You are a thirty-five-year-old man, not an orphan. Act like a *man*."

"Let's go to bed," Marcus said. "It's been a long and stressful day."

"It's six o'clock in the evening, Marcus." Her voice was muffled, hoarse; he was smashing her against his chest, suffocating her.

"We don't have to sleep," he said, still smoothing, patting.

She knew he wanted her. She could feel his erection against her belly. Despite his grief, he still wanted her. She'd been avoiding him for weeks now, and although she knew he was confused by this avoidance, he didn't say a word. Marcus tried very hard not to say unkind words to his little flower. It made Melody furious.

"Really, Marcus, I need to clean up this mess."

Neat, fastidious, fussy Marcus said, "Leave it until the morning, baby. It will still be there in the morning."

"No, Marcus, there might be ants." It was highly unlikely. Marcus faithfully sprayed for bugs once a week.

"I suppose we can now take that vacation we've been talking about. Maybe a week in June?"

What was he saying? They had never talked about taking a vacation. It was an unbearable thought. One week. Seven days and nights. Alone. With. Marcus. She would be with him, in his sight, for hours on end. "We'll talk about it another time," she said, muffled against his chest. Was the man never going to let go of her?

"It's just the two of us," Marcus said again.

Like she needed to be reminded. "I'm finding it hard to breathe."

Marcus seemed not to have heard her. "We should make another baby."

Make another baby. As if they could construct a baby out of blocks or clay, or paper, glue, and glitter. A paper baby. A paper doll. "Marcus, I can't ... breathe." Marcus had her arms pinned at her sides, and his arms around her were twin boa constrictors. Trapped, she was trapped. A baby would positively seal her fate. She had already tried to give him a baby—and failed. Wasn't that enough?

Marcus did not loosen his hold. "What do you say, flower? Should we make another baby? Enough time has passed, I think."

"Marcus ... I ... can't ... breathe." He was going to kill her right there and then, smothering her with his love.

"Yes, we'll take a vacation in June," Marcus announced. "We'll make our baby then."

Melody was going to faint. He was depriving her of oxygen. He was waiting for something from her, but what? Weakly, she nodded against his chest.

Then he released her, grabbing for her shoulders and looking earnestly, hopefully in her eyes. "Really, Mellie? Do you mean it?"

Melody took deep, gulping breaths of air. Black dots swam across her vision. She had had this sensation before—the almost fainting, breathlessness, swimming dots—when had that been? Yes, she remembered. The limping man, the morphine, his hands around her neck. The morphine. Had that desperate, ruthless man been addicted to heroin? Yes, that was it. Now she knew it for a certainty. The man had been a heroin addict.

"You have made me so happy, baby. On a day of such sadness, you have made me happy again." He gave her a quick, hard kiss on her lips.

Once again, he stopped her breathing. Marcus would not let her breathe.

"I love you so much, Mellie, so much." His face was wet with new tears.

She took a step back, avoiding another kiss, another stifling, suffocating embrace. Sometime soon, very soon, she would tell him. She would say to him, forcefully: *I am not going to have your baby, ever.* She couldn't do it now, though. She just couldn't, not with his face and his earnest, shiny eyes so close. Those eyes were suffused with love for her, and she couldn't bear it. She looked away.

Marcus, as always, did not seem to notice that Melody had not returned the sentiment. "You are my world, Mellie, my entire world."

She couldn't bear it, not for one second longer. "On second thought, Marcus, I think I'll take a bubble bath. It has been a very *stressful* day."

Melody had never been in a pawn shop before. But this one on a side street in Beverly seemed incredibly shabby, shady, and disturbing, with peeling gray paint, bars on all the windows, and trash—mostly beer bottles—cluttering the entrance. She'd chosen it randomly out of the Yellow Pages, with the only criteria being that it was far enough away from Evergreen Park that Marcus would never find out. Not that Marcus would ever step foot in a pawn shop. However, to be on the safe side, she had chosen Last Chance Pawn Shop miles away from home, even though the name seemed rather ominous.

Also, unfortunately, true. Last chance. She was definitely out of other options. Since she turned over her paycheck to Marcus, she had to ask him if she wanted cash. It wasn't that he wasn't generous—he always gave her what she asked for—but he always wanted to know everything she would spend it on. They had had quite a few of these inane conversations:

"Can I have some money, Marcus?"

"What do you need it for?"

"I'm going to the grocery store like I do every Saturday, Marcus."

"What are you going to buy?"

"Do you want to see my list?" Melody never made a list, but Marcus didn't need to know that.

"Of course not, baby. I'm just interested in everything you do." Marcus would be standing with his hands in his pockets, not yet ready to relinquish the cash.

"I'm going to buy cucumbers and chicken." At this point, Melody would say the first thing that came into her head, anxious to get the money and out of the house.

"What are you going to make with the cucumbers?"

"A salad." Melody would then be tapping her foot, not that Marcus noticed her impatience. Marcus never seemed to notice her impatience, and she didn't even try to hide it.

"That sounds delicious, kitten."

"Can I have the money, Marcus?"

"What about the chicken? Are you going to fry it?"

"I'm going to bake it, Marcus." Melody would have made up her mind by then that she wouldn't buy the chicken or the cucumbers.

"That sounds delicious, too. I'll look forward to it, Mellie."

"Can I have the money now, Marcus?"

"Of course you can have the money, baby. Don't I always give you what you ask for? You just tell me how much you need."

"Forty dollars." Melody would have one hand on her hip, and one held out to cradle the money.

"That much, huh? That seems pretty steep for cucumbers and chicken."

"Cucumbers are out of season, and I'm going to buy a very large chicken."

"Well, I guess that explains things." Then Marcus would pull out the hefty stack of folded bills—kept neatly together by a silver money clip—and slowly count out the exact amount, never less and never more, into Melody's outstretched hand.

If Melody had gone to Marcus on this day and asked for money, he would have inevitably asked, "What do you need it for?" What was she supposed to answer? Obviously, not the truth: "I'm not going to buy cucumbers and chicken, Marcus. As a matter of fact, I'm going to buy heroin. Can I pretty please have the money now?" Fat chance of that happening, although the imagined scene did bring a smile to Melody's lips.

The truth of the matter was that heroin was an extraordinarily expensive habit. Buying any drug off the street was expensive. Melody and Sylvia had been unaware of just how much money drugs could make disappear.

Before they had Thelma's wonderful candy shop, then prescriptions, and then, well, the tawdry affair with that tiny, sadistic man who called himself a doctor. Now they had to spend their own money, and Melody was painfully aware of how indebted she was to Sylvia, who had her own bank account and supplied more money than Melody. It was time for Melody to step up to the plate.

She'd gone to Willie first, even though she still owed him money for both the mythical overtime that had to be explained to Marcus and for that first trip to the light tower. She met him at the neighborhood tavern that all her brothers and Daddy frequented on a payday Friday only after he reassured her that Daddy and Mikey and Frankie were playing in a poker tournament at the Legion. She felt bad that she had to ask Willie for money once again, and she adamantly did not want anyone else in her family to find out about it. She would never in a million years ask her daddy and Ma for money. They'd be lucky if they had a pot to pee in for retirement, and her other two brothers ... Well, they were rather dim and loud and nosy.

Melody reasoned that Willie would not have drunk the entire amount if she got there early enough. However, she wanted him to have had enough to drink to be in a generous mood. She found him quickly on his regular bar stool (all her brothers and Daddy had regular bar stools at O'Brian's, with little brass plaques on the back that had their names engraved on them), but he was past the happy and generous drunk stage and well on his way to the next phase—morose.

The first thing that Willie said to her was, "Women are bad people." He was already slurring.

Not a good sign. Melody slid onto the stool beside him (Mikey's chair). "I'm a woman. Do you think I'm a bad person?" She was trying for a playful tone, but she wasn't in all that good of mood herself. Work had been brutal—two heart attacks and a child who had been hit by a car while riding his bike—and the morphine she had taken a few hours before was starting to wear off. She'd been sweating a lot lately, and she was pretty sure she didn't smell even remotely close to a rose. All she wanted was to get home to her bubble bath.

Willie looked at her with bleary, bloodshot eyes. "Nah, you're my sister. You don't count for nothing."

"Gee, thanks." Melody ordered a glass of water. Her mouth felt as dry as dust.

"I meant Sabrina. She's a bitch. Pretty as a picture but mean as an alley cat. Do you know her?" Behind Willie's beer was a neat row of empty shot glasses.

"I don't know Sabrina, but Willie—"

"You're lucky. Pretty as a picture but mean as an alley cat." Then Willie proceeded to tell Melody all about the girl who had just broken his heart.

Melody tried to listen patiently, but something seemed to be wrong with her hand. It shook when she tried to lift the water glass to her lips. And her heart. It seemed to be beating erratically. She needed her bubble bath, yet she tried to be patient until Willie started to repeat the litany of Sabrina's sins for the third time. "Listen, Willie, I'm sorry about Sabrina, but I was wondering if you could lend me some money. I know I still owe you some, but I'll pay you back as soon as I can, and I wouldn't ask unless it was something important." The words rushed out. Melody desperately needed to get out of the stifling, smoky bar.

"I don't have any money," Willie said mournfully. "Sabrina liked nice things, so I bought her a necklace from J.C Penney's and a watch from Kmart and so many cartons of smokes I lost count. That bitch." A single tear rolled down Willie's cheek and plopped into his beer.

"But your paycheck?" Melody tried.

Willie shook his head slowly, sorrowfully. "All gone. I endorsed it over to Sean here." He nodded toward the round, bald bartender. "I figured I'd be here a while, and I told him to keep them coming. It's one of those nights."

"Surely, there's some left over?" Melody tried again, ashamed at her desperation.

"Sorry, sis. It's a sad, sad world." His head drooped dangerously close to his beer, but then he perked up a little. "I just had an idea. Why don't you ask your husband? He's rich. There you go. You can ask him." For the briefest of moments, Willie seemed pleased with himself.

"Marcus is not rich, Willie."

"Oh," Willie said, his head again drooping, nodding over his beer. "I need another shot, Sean, and get one for my sis."

"No, Willie, I need to go." This wasn't going to work. She would have to come up with another plan. She tried to pick up her water glass again, but her shaking hand slopped water all over the bar.

"You got the DTs, sis?" It was unfortunate that Willie chose that moment to lift his head out of his beer.

"What? No. Oh." She slid off the barstool.

"It's okay, sis. I've been there. Have a drink. It's a sad, sad world." He drank the shot Sean put in front of him. "Women are bad people."

Melody ran out of the bar.

So that left Last Chance Pawn Shop. Melody sat in her car outside the entrance for thirty minutes before gathering the courage to walk in. The inside was a reflection of the outside: grimy, cluttered, forlorn. She barely noticed the collection of desperately discarded possessions—musical instruments, glass cases with watches and jewelry and guns and knives, unmatched furniture, record players—as she walked toward the fat man sitting behind a counter, chewing on a cigar. He, too, was behind bars. To Melody, he looked like a creature at the zoo, a gorilla or a bear.

Melody stopped at his cage and reached into her purse. "How much will you give me for these?" With her shaky, sweaty hand, she handed him Marcus' pearls.

19

APRIL 2012

The newspaper article had stated the town Melody Arnold was from, and they knew her maiden name. With Zen's expert computer and investigative skills, and with the help of the trusty Delany family phone book (older people still tended to have landlines, Zen said), they located three Callahan addresses in nearby Bridgeview: Frances Sr., Frances Jr., and Michael.

"The town they listed in the newspaper is where she lived with her husband," Kat said. "For all we know, her family could have lived miles away, or even in another state."

"Very possible," Zen conceded, "but I grew up on the South Side, too, and for some reason, a lot of us never venture very far out of our childhood neighborhoods."

"You did," she pointed out.

"Different story." Zen did not elaborate. "It's worth a try. At the very least, they might be distant relatives."

One of these days, Kat would find out more about Zen's mysterious stories, but now was not the time or place. "Maybe I should call?" Once again, now that she was close to discovering more about Melody Arnold's past, Kat felt a sense of dread, almost fear.

Zen, Kat was learning, was a man of movement, of action. He could sit and listen with the best of them, but he wanted to *act* when it came time to do something. "You're not going to be in town much longer, Kat. I vote we go and knock on some doors."

Yes, she knew that. She was supposed to leave the next day. Granny Nanny would be expecting her, and the thought of going home to the bungalow in Scottsdale sounded wonderful and warm to Kat. But. There was still so much she didn't know about Melody Arnold. But. There was still so much she didn't know about Lorenzo Delaney.

They decided to start with the patriarch—if he actually was the patriarch, Frances, Sr. Within minutes from the Delaney house, they were sitting in front of 1113 S. Roosevelt Street. It was a brick row house, three stories, tall and narrow, with dormer windows on the top floor and rotting window boxes on the bottom floor. A rusty chain-linked fence surrounded a small yard with more weeds than grass on this sunny April morning, and Kat suspected that it'd had more weeds than grass for quite some time.

Since an older, white-haired man sat on the front stoop, a beer in his hand at ten o'clock in the morning, eyeing them suspiciously, Kat could not afford the luxury of stewing or take the time to gather her courage. If Zen were a man of action, she would show him that she, too, could be a woman of action. She took a deep breath, opened the car door, and walked up the front sidewalk.

"Are you Frances Callahan?" she asked.

The man cocked his head and stared at her, then gulped a swallow of beer. There was something youthful about him. His face was only lightly etched, and his thin wispy white hair still held an orangey tinge. "Do I know you?"

What was going on? For the second time in mere hours, someone who could not have possibly known Kat had asked her this question. "No, I'm Kat Flowers." She held out her hand, but he didn't take it. She decided to get right to the point. "Are you, by any chance, related to a woman named Melody Katherine Callahan, who married a man named Marcus Arnold?" She held her breath. She hadn't heard him come up the walk, but now she realized that Zen was standing right beside her.

"Mellie," the man said, and immediately tears glistened in his bloodshot blue eyes. "She was a good girl. Everyone said she was a disgrace to the family after she did what she did."

Someone had known and loved *Mellie*. This man, obviously drunk at ten o'clock in the morning, had known and loved *Mellie*. Kat swallowed hard. This Mellie could not be the same Melody Arnold, who had climbed up that light tower. This Mellie had a family.

"Mellie committed suicide. Mellie is in hell. Damn Mellie to hell!" He took another gulp of beer.

"And you were related to Mellie, how?" Zen softly asked.

The man, drunk and thrust into the past, into a possible painful memory, seemed not to hear Zen's questions. "Some demon must have possessed her. That's the only thing we could come up with. She had a good job, was married to a good man. I don't know why she was always asking me for money. That last time, I told her I didn't have any, but I did. I should have given her the damn money. It's always about the damn money! That Sabrina was a bitch. Why I married her, I'll never know. I knew she'd leave me, Frankie and Mikey told me she'd leave me like roadkill, and she did."

The man's tears moved Kat. She had no idea who Sabrina, Frankie, and Mikey were, but Mellie's husband, according to this white-haired man, had been a good man. Marcus Arnold had been a *good man*. Once again, her throat constricted, and she couldn't speak. Instinctively, she reached out her hand and put it on the stranger's shoulder. His drunken, Chicago-accented nasal voice sounded croaky and unused, as if he hadn't spoken to anyone for a very long time.

"Everything went to hell after Mellie did what she did. Everything. Frankie and Mikey told me to forget about her, but I never did. They never did either. We all said there was one saving grace, though, and that was that Ma wasn't around to know what she did. It would have broken her heart like it did Pa. Pa died of a broken heart. The doctors all said it was a brain aneurysm, but I know better. If Mellie had been around, she could have fixed him. Mellie was a nurse; she was Daddy's little girl. She knew how to do the hymen hug thing. She saved Ma's life that one time. But not the other. No, Mellie wasn't around the other time."

Out of the disjointed memories that this man was spilling, Kat could only grasp on a few fleeting things at a time. Mellie had been *Daddy's little girl,* so unlike what Kat's upbringing had been like. Melody Katherine Callahan had seemed to have it all. What had gone so terribly wrong?

"And the worst part," the man continued, his glazed, bloodshot eyes locked firmly on the past, "was the—no, maybe it was the best part, I don't know—was the baby girl. Mellie had a baby girl after she was dead! How could that happen, we all asked? How can a dead woman give birth? Was that really Mellie's baby? Did those people at the hospital say that just to make us feel better?"

The old man seemed to have forgotten that Kat and Zen stood before him. "Was it a blessing or a curse? People around here would ask. Was it the work of God or Satan? I would tell them it was a damn blessing after I brought the baby home from the hospital, a damn blessing! People are so damn ignorant, can't think a thought for themselves. The priest tells them to jump, and they ask how high. I tried to hold onto it, I did try, I went to church, but after Mellie's husband took the baby away, I washed my hands of the whole thing." He crushed the empty beer can in his fist and wiped his mouth. The crushing of the aluminum can snapped him out of his reverie. He blinked, pulling the two people standing in front of him into focus.

Zen asked his question again, "And you were related to Mellie, how?"

"I was her brother. I still am her brother. William Callahan." Their faces were starting to come into focus for him. "Who are you? If you're some of those blasted Jehovah's Witness people going door to door, trying to get me to read some shit, you can forget about it." He tried to stand, but his legs gave out, and he landed back down on the stoop with a thump. When Zen offered him a hand, he accepted.

"I'm not a Jehovah's Witness, Mr. Callahan. I'm ..." She should say, *I'm Kat Flowers* again, thank him for his time, and turn around and leave. He might not even want to know anything about this lost baby of Mellie's. It would be easier—it made more sense—to turn around and leave. Kat looked at Zen.

Zen nodded encouragement. Zen, it seemed, was always destined to nod encouragement to Kat.

Kat took hold of William Callahan's hand. "I'm Kat Flowers, but I guess my real name is ..." She had never said it aloud before, had never imagined that she would. "I know it's going to be difficult for you to believe, but I'm ..." She took a deep breath. She didn't need any more encouragement from Zen. "I'm Katrina Arnold, Mellie's daughter."

He insisted that Kat and also Zen call him Uncle Willie. That is, he insisted after he could find his voice, after Zen retrieved him another beer, and after he had finished a litany of: "I'll be damned, I'll be damned, I'll be damned."

"You resemble Mellie some, you know," Uncle Willie said after a closer inspection of Kat's face. "Your hair is a much lighter shade of red, but your eyes. You have Mellie's blue eyes."

Kat, obviously, had not known that. "Do you, by any chance, have a picture of her, Uncle Willie?" She had never used the word *uncle* before. For that matter, she had never used the words *aunt, cousin, grandma,* or *grandpa*. (Years ago, she'd been instructed to call Missy's parents by their first names, Georgina and Pete, and of course, Granny Nanny was Granny Nanny.) Now it was too late for grandma and grandpa. Her uncle had already told her that they both had died, and Kat felt an unexpected pang of regret. It was sheer luck—and Zen—that had brought her here, but she was too late for so many things.

"There must be one somewhere around here," Uncle Willie said. "Let's go in the house and take a look." Again, Zen extended his hand to help him up, and this time Uncle Willie made it into a standing position. "I don't think that Pa burned quite all of them after Mellie did what she did, but I'm not sure. He was in quite a state."

When Kat walked through the door of 1113 S. Roosevelt Street, she almost fainted. She had never fainted before in her life, but her head felt suddenly light, and her vision swam. She was walking into a piece of Melody Arnold's, Melody Katherine Callahan's, *Mellie's* past. The woman had lived in this house, eaten dinner in this house, done her homework, cooked, cleaned, laughed, and loved in this three-story row house. She had been alive. Zen caught Kat's arm before she toppled.

"Breathe," he whispered into her ear.

Kat breathed.

"You'll have to pardon the mess," Uncle Willie said, taking a seat in a cracked leather recliner in the living room, his usual seat judging by the table next to it that was crammed with beer cans, wadded up fast-food paper bags, and the remote control. "I wasn't expecting company." He seemed to have forgotten all about the picture.

The rest of the living room was not cluttered, but a thick layer of dust coated everything. The floral wallpaper, the threadbare rugs scattered over the scuffed hardwood floor, the faded blue velour couch and love seat, all of it looked like it could have been from the 1950s. It reminded Kat—fleetingly, absurdly—of Ralphie's house in the movie *A Christmas Story*. Ralphie had desperately wanted a BB gun for Christmas. (Why was she thinking of movies now? Was her brain so overloaded that she'd snapped all the synapses? She wasn't thinking clearly.)

When Kat and Zen took a seat on the couch, a plume of dust exploded into the air. Melody coughed.

"I'm not much for housekeeping," Uncle Willie apologized. "Ma used to do all the cooking and cleaning around here, and after she passed, we all kind of lost interest. Then Frankie and Mikey got married and moved out, but they dropped in and spent the night whenever they had rows with their wives, which was damn near three or four nights a week. After my three-month marriage to that bitch Sabrina, I moved back home for good. Pa and I did the best that we could. Two old bachelors."

"The house looks fine," Zen said politely.

"Frankie and Mikey?" Kat asked.

"My brothers. Your other two uncles."

She had three uncles! It wasn't too late to meet at least some of her family. "Do I have cousins?"

"Yes, you do, Katrina. Frankie and Mikey each had three. So, six in total. They're a mixed bag, though, I tell you, a mixed bag."

Well, she should fit right in. They couldn't be any more *mixed* than her, a thirty-year-old, unemployed Tilted Kilt waitress whose mother had offed herself by jumping off a 100-foot light tower in an abandoned railway yard. And oh, yes, she had been nine months pregnant at the time. Kat should fit right in with a *mixed bag* of cousins.

"I can't believe you're here, Katrina." Uncle Willie was having a hard time keeping his eyes open. "I'm not dreaming or having a blackout or something, am I?"

"You're not dreaming," Kat said, "and we were certainly lucky to find you."

"I've been right here all along. Why didn't you come looking sooner? Thirty years ago, when Marcus took you away and told me he'd be in touch as soon as he was settled, I believed him. Then days passed, then weeks, then months, then years, and nothing. I didn't have that computer internet thing back then—still don't know how to use one—but I hired a private investigator who ran away with my money and found nothing. Nothing. I thought maybe Marcus had taken you and moved to Mexico. First, Mellie was gone, then you. It was a crying, fucking shame." Uncle Willie didn't bother to wipe the tears from his cheeks.

"I'm sorry," Kat whispered. This poor man, her Uncle Willie, practically reeked of loneliness. Her father had done them both a great disservice, and here she was, apologizing. "We were only six hours away, in Carbondale. My father changed our last name, and he never mentioned my mother's name, not until a few days ago. I didn't know. I didn't know anything. He told me on his deathbed. He's dying of colon cancer."

"There, there, Katrina." He leaned over to pat her hand but was a little too far away to reach. "I didn't mean to make you cry. You're here now."

His compassion made her cry harder. She wasn't crying for her dying father, or dead Melody Arnold, or herself. She cried for her Uncle Willie and his years of futile waiting. She was almost sure that was the cause. Zen handed her a tissue. He must have gone through her purse to find one. Her purse, too, was a mess. She cried harder.

"There, there," Uncle Willie said again. Her weeping was making him uncomfortable. I'm sorry about Marcus. I always thought he was a good man, and oh, did he love Mellie! He gave her a big diamond ring—it was his mother's, I think—and pearls. Real pearls. He was an engineer, you know. He made good money. Over the years, I've often wondered what happened to those pearls. They seemed to disappear. That's neither here nor there now, I guess."

Zen went into the kitchen and got Kat a glass of water. The glass was dubiously clean, a little cloudy, but she drank it.

"Marcus must have had his reasons." Uncle Willie's voice was slow, thoughtful, or drunk. "He must have had some damn good reasons for taking you away and changing your last name, but I'll be damned if I know what they are. Poor man. Colon cancer, you said? Well, I guess we all gotta go sometime. It's going to be one thing or the other." He yawned, and his eyes drooped.

Kat had gotten herself under control. "You're tired, Uncle Willie. We should go, but before we do—the picture?"

"No, no, don't go, Katrina. I'm enjoying your company. I don't get much company. I'm just going to take a little catnap. It's been a long day."

It was eleven o'clock in the morning.

"Do you need some help getting to bed?" Zen, ever polite, ever the gentleman, asked.

"No, no, I'm just going to sleep in my chair here. I do it all the time, like an old man. I'm only fifty-five, but since I retired last year—I was forced to retire—I like my little catnaps."

Kat couldn't prevent the shock from showing on her face. She'd thought he was much older.

"It's a shocker, huh?" Uncle Willie chuckled. "They always said beer made you fat, but I'm telling you, it just makes you *old*." His head started to nod. "I'll tell you what. I'm going to close my eyes for a few seconds. Why don't you look around, see where your mother grew up. This was her home, too, for twenty-two years. If we still have any pictures left of her—Pa kind of went on a rampage, you might say—they'd be in the attic somewhere. Help yourself."

Looking around was precisely what Kat had wanted to do since entering this dated, surreal house, but she hadn't wanted to ask, thinking it would be rude. The last thing she wanted to be to this nice old man, her uncle, was rude. "Are you sure you don't mind?"

"Make yourself at home." Uncle Willie's voice was faint; his eyes finally closed. "Be nosy. I've got nothing to hide."

Mellie had climbed up these same steps. Mellie had walked down this very same hallway. She had touched the same doorknobs and opened the same doors. Unlike the eerie feeling she'd gotten from Mercy Hospital when she'd been thinking along the same lines, the feeling Kat got from this house on 1113 S. Roosevelt Street in Bridgeview was a feeling of disbelief. It was so outdated, so old-fashioned that it was hard to imagine a young woman living here. Her mother lived here in the sixties and seventies, but the house's amenities pre-dated that. The upstairs bathroom had a claw-footed tub. The kitchen sink was as big and round as a washbasin. Very possibly, Kat's grandmother and mother had washed clothes in it. There wasn't a dishwasher, microwave, or dryer. A woman who lived in this house had some work to do.

Everywhere throughout the house, the curtains were drawn. Had it been this dark when Mellie lived here? Surely not. Before tragedy struck, there must have been light, sunshine streaming through the windows. Kat desperately wanted to believe that. She brushed away a cobweb as she opened the last door in the third-floor hallway. She'd already been in what she assumed was the master bedroom and two other bedrooms, one of which was currently Uncle Willie's room, with clothes thrown over the chair and an unmade bed. This last bedroom must have been Mellie's room, but maybe it was no longer a girl's bedroom. Perhaps it had been made into a sewing room or a game room. She stepped inside the dusky room and flipped on the light.

Kat could immediately see that it was still Mellie's room. The twin bed was neatly made up with a white eyelet bedspread. Posters hung on the wall—The Eagles, Fleetwood Mac, James Taylor, Journey, Foreigner—the edges curling and yellowed with age. A vanity sat in one corner with a matching eyelet ruffled skirt, and a white desk placed under the window looked out at the neighbor's brick wall. The pin-pricked bulletin board on one wall—that at one time was probably filled with pictures and teen-aged memorabilia—was empty now. Kat opened the tiny closet: an old wool coat and empty hangers, a couple of boxes filled with high school textbooks (English literature, physics, European history). Despite the posters and the frilly bedspread and vanity skirt, the room seemed strangely impersonal, a motel room where a person would land for a night or two and then leave for other destinations.

Kat knew it was ridiculous to feel disappointed. The person who had occupied this room left it more than thirty years before. But still. She'd expected more, and she still was no closer to finding out what kind of person Mellie Callahan had been. What, exactly, had she been expecting? A ghost? A haunting presence? Perhaps Kat had. She didn't especially believe in the supernatural, but she wouldn't have minded seeing a red-haired ghost sitting at the vanity table, brushing her hair.

"What do you think?" she asked Zen, who had been silently following her during her trek through the house. "There's not anything personal here."

"Well, Kat, she moved out of this room when she got married, right? She probably took everything with her, pictures, scrapbooks, maybe a diary."

As usual, what Zen said made sense. "I know, but it seems like she left without a trace. Don't you think it's rather odd? Don't you still have stuff at your parents' house? I know that Lorraine does." Even though she'd awakened the past four mornings feeling disoriented in Lorraine's room, Kat could feel a presence, a very perky presence. But not here. In a way, this strange, impersonal room reminded her of Benson's condo, decorated by Carmella, with its white sterile walls, rugs, and furniture. That KKK condo, like this room, exuded no personality.

"I've still got tons of stuff at my folks' house. Mom keeps threatening to give it all to Goodwill, but she won't. Memories, and all that kind of thing. Some people are more sentimental than others." Zen stared at the Fleetwood Mac poster. "Stevie Nicks was hot, wasn't she?"

"I don't give a flying fuck about Stevie Nicks," Kat said. So was Zen attracted to blondes? Carrie was a blonde.

Zen held up his hands. "Hey, Kat, I know this is emotional for you, but could you cut out the sailor speak? You're not even drunk."

"Like you never swear?" Had she ever heard him swear? It didn't matter. Whether she had or hadn't, the point was that he didn't need to act like a damn saint all the time.

"You know what, Kat? Sometimes you act like a first-class bitch."

"Well, at least I'm a *first-class* bitch," she retorted. This man, who'd been driving her all over town, saved her in a tornado, rescued her from the train station in Carbondale, and given her a place to stay, was so fucking aggravating.

"Why in the hell are you mad at me?" Zen's voice was heated.

"I don't know!" Damn it all to hell, she started to cry again.

In a second, he crossed Mellie Callahan's room and took her in his arms. "I know this is tough for you."

She let herself relax in his arms. It felt good to be held by him, too good. He'd held onto her in the bathtub in Joplin, Missouri, but this embrace was not the same. No man, it seemed, had ever held her in such a way. "I'm not mad at you," she muffled into his shoulder. "I'm mad at her, at Melody Arnold, at Mellie Callahan, at the woman who refused to be my mother. Why didn't she want me?" There, she had finally said it out loud. Why hadn't her mother wanted her?

"Oh, Kat," he said tenderly, "there are some questions we may never find the answers to." He rubbed her back and smoothed her hair.

She raised her head from his shoulder and looked into his compassionate green/gold eyes. She wanted him to kiss her. It was not an appropriate time or place in Mellie Callahan's childhood bedroom, but she wanted him to kiss her, willed him to kiss her.

Had he sensed it? He hesitated a moment, then pulled back, breaking the embrace. "Should we check the attic? Maybe you'll find what you're looking for there."

So that was that; the moment passed, unfulfilled. Kat told herself it was probably for the best, but it was one more thing she didn't really believe. She wiped her eyes with the back of her hand. "It's worth a try."

He let her lead the way back to the hallway and the pull-down staircase located in the ceiling. Kat couldn't get it down herself because of the warped boards, but Zen gave a firm yank, and the folded stairs came down. They climbed up the rickety ladder.

Once up, they couldn't straighten up under the slanted eaves and hunched over, they picked their way through the eclectic mishmash of junk: old mattresses, broken lamps, a Singer sewing machine, old clothing, old light bulbs. "Why in the world do you think they saved old light bulbs?" Kat asked. She had never seen such a diverse collection of crap.

"As I said earlier, some people are more sentimental than others," Zen answered, picking up a tattered lampshade.

"There's a difference between being sentimental and hoarding a bunch of crap."

"Yeah, this takes sentiment to a whole new level." Zen tripped over a box. He bent down to read the scrawl on the top. "Bingo. This is a box of family scrapbooks."

Once again, Kat allowed herself to dare to hope, and once again, she was disappointed. As they pulled out the first, the second, the third, and the fourth musty book, they were all the same. Every single one of them had gaping holes where pictures of Mellie would have been. There were pictures of three red-headed boys, pictures of a plump, harried-looking woman, usually in an apron, and photos of a short, stout, balding man. Mellie's brothers, mother, and father, but no Mellie.

"Uncle Willie was right," Kat said, studying each picture. "Grandpa Callahan certainly went on a rampage." Although disappointed that there weren't any pictures of Mellie, Kat was still fascinated. These people were her family. Maybe Uncle Willie would let her have a picture or two? She would ask.

"He was thorough," Zen agreed.

Kat flipped slowly through the fourth and final album. This one had more glaring blanks. "He must have taken out Mellie and Marcus' wedding photos, too." A picture on the last page stopped her cold. She couldn't breathe. It was a black and white picture of a small tombstone surrounded by flowers, the tombstone of Marcus Walter Arnold, Jr.

Kat couldn't believe it, was in fact, astounded. She'd had a brother, a brother who would have been about eighteen months older than her. That wasn't exactly true either. That baby had been born months too early; he'd been born dead. Stillborn.

"That cord thing was wrapped around his little neck if I remember correctly." Uncle Willie had awakened from his catnap and was again drinking beer. "It was a damn shame, an accident. We were all pretty broken up about it." He handed the picture back to Kat.

"I'm sure that Mellie was heartbroken?" Kat had never harbored any maternal instincts that she was aware of, but this Mellie would surely have been devastated by the loss of a child, her first, a baby boy. Didn't they have grief counseling for that kind of thing?

"Funny you should ask that," Uncle Willie said. He fumbled around his messy table, looking for something. "Damn it, I wish I could still smoke. That damn doctor. What does he know? A cigarette now and then can't hurt you."

"Why is it funny that I would ask that question?" To Kat, there was nothing funny about it. That poor baby boy and his poor mother. Mellie would have only been twenty-two. Even Kat, who harbored no maternal instincts, thought it was incredibly sad.

"Do either of you have a smoke? I'll pay you a quarter for a smoke. It'd be great if you had a Marlboro." Uncle Willie looked at them wistfully.

"Neither one of us smokes," Zen said.

"Surgeon General, my ass," Uncle Willie sighed.

While Kat was painfully aware that drunken Uncle Willie might not be the most reliable of witnesses or orator of the past, he was all she currently had. "Marcus Walter Arnold, Jr.," she prompted.

"Oh, right. The funeral. I don't remember Mellie crying at the funeral. We were all bawling our eyes out, and she didn't shed a tear. That's what I remember anyway. We all thought she was so brave. I remember Ma kept saying to her, 'Don't worry, Mellie, you can have more children. You're young. You can have lots more babies.'"

Kat was afraid to ask, but she forced herself. "What did Mellie say to that? Do you remember what she said to that?"

Uncle Willie searched in his foggy memory and came up with, "I think she said, 'But I want that baby, that baby boy.' Something along those lines, I think. My memory isn't what it used to be."

Kat had that tight constriction in her throat again. So was that it? Was this the missing piece of the puzzle? Mellie had been so grief-stricken over the loss of her first baby that she didn't want another one so soon after losing him? If Kat looked at it objectively, which was very difficult for her to do since she was that second, unwanted baby, she could find the tiniest glimmer of understanding. A young woman was so grief-stricken about the loss of her first baby that when she got pregnant again soon after, she might have been afraid that she would lose the second one as well. Even though she carried the baby to term, her fear caused her to climb a 100-foot light tower. And jump.

Nope. No. Not even close. There was not even a speck of understanding on Kat's part. Melody Arnold had heard the baby's heartbeat in the hospital. She knew that baby, her second, was alive. What in the hell had been wrong with that dreadful woman? She had come from a family who loved her. According to Uncle Willie, she worked at a meaningful job, married a good man, and yet, as Marcus had put it, she'd *made a choice*.

Some fucking choice.

"She drank a lot of juice after the baby was born dead," Uncle Willie said out of nowhere. She didn't go to work for a while, and she didn't eat much, but she drank a lot of juice when I went over to visit her."

If it had been me, Kat thought, *I would have been loading up that juice with alcohol.* Maybe that's what she had done? Maybe Mellie had been a closet alcoholic! Looking at Uncle Willie now, it seemed like a distinct possibility. Maybe Mellie had been drinking throughout her second pregnancy and thought she'd harmed her baby, that the baby might be deformed in some way. Were they aware of Fetal Alcohol Syndrome back then? Kat was again stretching, speculating, but it was all she had to go on. How could she tactfully—and she had never been particularly tactful—ask Uncle Willie such a question? (*Note to self, Kat: Alcoholism runs in your family. Terrific.*)

Zen to the rescue, again. Now Zen, Zen could be tactful. "Uncle Willie, Kat doesn't know anything about her family. As you know, her father didn't give her much information. Is there anything she should be aware of?

"Like what?" Uncle Willie asked suspiciously.

"Like what they ask you when you go to the doctor's office," Zen said easily. "You know how they make you fill out those incredibly annoying, incredibly long forms before you see the doctor. They ask you all kinds of ridiculous things, like does heart disease run in your family, diabetes, thyroid problems, mental illness, cancer, liver disease, osteoporosis? That type of thing. When Kat goes to the doctor's office, she doesn't know which of those things she should put an X by."

Boy, was he good. Kat liked how he had interspersed the maladies.

Uncle Willie relaxed, smiled. "I hate those damn useless forms! I hate going to the doctor." Even though Uncle Willie had mentioned his father's brain aneurysm, his mother's mysterious death, and drank like a fish and used to smoke, he decided: "No, nothing like that, no sir. Katrina has a clean bill of health, a clean slate. The Callahans are as healthy as horses."

Uncle Willie next insisted that Zen and Kat share a beer with him. "I hate to drink alone."

Right. Uncle Willie had already consumed a six-pack in the short time they'd been there, but Kat felt like she could use a beer, too. Uncle Willie, glad to have an audience, rambled on about such disparate things as his childhood, his ex-wife Sabrina, the bricklayer's union, the local bar, and people in the neighborhood. He didn't seem to notice that Kat and Zen had no idea who he was talking about.

After Kat thought a suitable amount of time had passed—she didn't want to be rude to Uncle Willie, but the house was depressing—she said, "We need to be going, Uncle Willie. Thank you so much for everything." Uncle Willie insisted that she take some pictures with her, and Kat was grateful. They were the only tangible thing she had linking herself to the past.

"You will keep in touch, Katrina, won't you?" Uncle Willie wanted to see them to the door, and even though he was a thin man, he was so drunk that Zen couldn't hoist him up from the cracked leather recliner.

"I will," Kat said, and she meant it. She had his phone number now, and she would regularly call when she got back to Arizona.

She felt emotionally drained yet again, so the one beer had given her a slight buzz. Plus, Uncle Willie was so drunk that she didn't see any harm in asking one last question. "Uncle Willie, why do you think Mellie jumped from that tower?"

"I don't know, Katrina. Maybe a demon possessed her." His eyes started to droop again, and Kat thought he would drift off, but then he straightened up a bit, seeming to remember something. "If anyone would know, it would be Sylvia, her girlfriend, Sylvia. They were tight, I tell you. She was very tall, that Sylvia, and I remember one Thanksgiving she came over, and all of us wanted to ask her for a date, but she thought she was too good for us. Yes, Sylvia might know. She and Mellie were thick as thieves."

"May I help you?" the priest asked. He was in his mid-thirties, his brown hair receding slightly, his brown eyes kind.

Without thinking, Kat gave her stock answer to the question, the one that she always gave to fawning salesgirls at shops in the mall (which was one reason why she no longer went to the mall, all those young, fawning, hopeful girls), "No, thank you. I'm just looking."

"Looking for what?" the priest asked kindly, smiling.

Kat blushed. "Sorry." The priest still stood before her, smiling, and it was his church, so she explained further. "My parents got married in this church. I just wanted to see ..." She had almost added, "what it was all about," but realized that it wouldn't make sense to him. Why would it? It didn't exactly make sense to her. So far, the two places she had visited in Melody Arnold's/Mellie Callahan's life hadn't been especially revelatory. Also, on the way to the church, she and Zen drove past the place where Melody and Marcus used to live. It was now a parking lot that didn't hold any clues either. ("Razed years ago," Uncle Willie had said. "I heard something about mold.") Yet Kat still held out hope that St. Mary's Catholic Cathedral would offer some insight.

And her dead baby brother was buried in the cemetery outside. Uncle Willie had gotten a small, two-minute wind before she and Zen made it out the door of 1113 S. Roosevelt Street and dropped that tidbit of noteworthy news. Her parents had gotten married, and her brother was buried at this church. Kat didn't give the priest this information; she wasn't in confession, after all. Still, she felt a little guilty that she wasn't divulging the entire truth.

"Look around. Take your time," the priest said. "I'll be in the rectory if you have any questions."

She had questions, all right, but none that he could answer. "It's a beautiful church," she said, hoping to sound pious or something like that.

"It is," he agreed cheerfully, and as promised, left her alone.

And it was. *Majestic* was the word that came to Kat's mind. *Cavernous* was the other. The floors and columns placed intermittently down the impossibly long aisle were rose-tinged marble. The Stations of the Cross, in vivid stained glass, were positioned on walls to her left and right, above the rows upon rows of wooden pews. The domed ceiling must have been forty or fifty feet high, and way up ahead at the altar, she could see the enormous wooden cross with the crucified, porcelain Lord. There was something decidedly Renaissance about it. Whoever designed this church must have been a big fan of the Italian Renaissance. The only reason Kat knew this was because she had taken an art history course in college. She'd never been to Italy; she'd never been anywhere. Maybe getting a passport sometime down the road wasn't such a bad idea, not that she would give Zen the satisfaction of knowing he was right about one more thing.

Zen offered to come inside with her, but she'd declined. He'd certainly done enough to help her, but it wasn't that. She needed to be alone. In the car on the short drive to the church, which they could easily have walked to, they hadn't talked much. Kat just wasn't up to more speculation and off-hand guesses about Mellie's life. She just couldn't, and he seemed to sense that. "I'll go get some gas," he'd said.

"Good idea." It seemed a lifetime ago that Kat had worried about such mundane, trivial, everyday things as getting gas, or going to the grocery store, or picking up dry cleaning. A lifetime ago. She was supposed to go home tomorrow and begin those things all over again, as if nothing had ever happened, as if she still did not know anything at all about Melody Arnold.

She could not go back, not yet. She had to find this Sylvia Hammond and talk to her in person, this woman who had been Mellie's close friend. Unbelievably, after a little prompting, Uncle Willie had come up with her last name during his brief two-minute second wind. But Kat could not impose on the Delaneys anymore, and Zen was moving into John's apartment.

She also needed to go back to Carbondale. She had promised Shane— and her father. She needed to see him one last time.

Marcus had stood at the end of this impossibly long aisle, waiting for his bride, his hands clasped in front of him. Mellie would have stood where Kat did now, her arm linked with her father's, her face veiled. It would have been difficult to see the expression on the waiting groom's face from this distance. The pipe organ would have boomed out the wedding march, and the congregation would have stood, looking at Mellie, anticipating the bridal procession. Kat, standing here now, could hear the music, feel the eyes upon her. For no discernible reason, she felt nervous, and her hands, clutching an imaginary bouquet, were clammy.

Without really thinking about it, Kat began to slowly walk down the aisle, retracing the same steps that Mellie would have taken to join her groom. Had she been a glowing, happy bride, or had she been filled with apprehension and misgiving? It seemed to Kat that it took an infinite number of steps to reach the altar, plenty of time for a young woman with misgivings to change her mind, unlink her arm from her father's, and run out of the church. But Mellie hadn't done that. Instead, she had placed one foot in front of the other and made it to the end, to the man she'd promised to marry. And she had married that man in front of family, friends, and God in this massive, majestic church.

By the time Kat reached the altar where the groom, wedding party, and priest would have been waiting, she was sweating heavily, and her heart pounded. Mellie's father would have handed over Mellie to Marcus, and he would have taken her arm. They would have walked up to stand in front of the priest, who would have been towering over them on the top step, ready with the authority to pronounce them husband and wife, ready with the authority to join them together for eternity.

Kat could see it all before her as if it were happening at this exact moment: the long ago, young couple exchanging vows, exchanging rings, the lifting of the bridal veil, the perfunctory kiss, the tears on Mellie's face. The tears on Mellie's face. Kat could see them clearly. Were they tears of joy, of bridal rapture? No, they were not.

Panicked, Kat turned and ran out of the church as Mellie Callahan had not thirty years before. She burst through the heavy wooden doors and plopped down on the top concrete step, gasping for air. When her heart finally quieted, and she could speak, she said aloud, "I am not psychic, and I absolutely do not have any supernatural powers. I couldn't have seen what I just thought I saw." She shook her head. "Impossible!" she said adamantly. She had not seen the reluctant, young, red-headed bride and the over-eager, bespectacled groom. She had not seen the tears on Mellie's face.

Yet she had. For some reason, she had. "Why didn't you *run?*" Kat cried out, rocking back and forth on the step, clutching her stomach. A young woman pushing a baby stroller on the sidewalk below gave Kat a startled stare and walked faster.

"Because you were pregnant," Kat whispered. "You married Marcus Arnold because you were pregnant, and you were a good Catholic girl. That was it, wasn't it? There was no fairy tale, no promise of happily ever after. Not even in the beginning."

Then the baby had been stillborn. And then a few short months later, Mellie had gotten pregnant again. That's why she couldn't run. No, Mellie Callahan didn't *run*. Melody Arnold *jumped*.

Kat put her hands over her eyes. "Jesus," she whispered.

"You're in the right place, young lady. Are you here for choir practice? I hope you're a soprano. Betty Lou has a nasty case of laryngitis. Are you her replacement?"

Kat took her hands from her eyes and saw a white-haired lady, her arms laden with sheet music. The organist, perhaps? She cleared her throat. "No, I'm not here for choir practice. I'm not a soprano; I can barely carry a tune." Kat got shakily to her feet. "I'm sorry."

"Not to worry, dear." The white-haired organist looked at her oddly. "Are you all right?"

"Yes, I'm fine," Kat said, even though she wasn't, even though she still had to make a stop at the cemetery and visit the grave of a baby boy, her brother.

"The priest is here if you need to talk."

"I'll keep that in mind." Kat stood up and quickly ran down the stairs. She wished the little white-haired organist had been Granny Nanny. If so, Kat would have folded herself into her arms and cried her eyes out. However, the organist wasn't Granny Nanny, and Granny Nanny wasn't here because Gran, in her infinite wisdom, knew that Kat had to confront her past alone, no matter how painful it was. And damn it, it was painful.

She could hear the organ music from the small, neatly tended cemetery adjacent to the church, some hymn that Kat couldn't quite remember. Except for today, she hadn't been inside a church in years, but the hymn comforted her as she carefully picked her way through the gravestones. A few had flowers; most did not on this early spring afternoon. Marcus Walter Arnold Jr.'s—beloved son, b. October 2, 1980, d. October 2, 1980— did not. The small tombstone was placed next to a larger one: Evelyn Parsons Arnold—beloved mother, b. December 4, 1914, d. April 29, 1981.

Marcus' mother? It must be her father's mother, her grandmother. Two members of her family were buried here, side by side, flowerless, and Kat had not known them, both dead before she was born.

The poor, barren graves. Flowerless, they looked abandoned, unloved, forgotten. Why hadn't she brought flowers? It didn't matter that Kat hadn't known about her baby brother until two hours before or that she had not known about her grandmother's grave until now. These people, her family, needed flowers. Casual observers strolling by should know that these two people were remembered. Kat quickly left the cemetery and walked down the sidewalk with a sense of urgency until she came to a yard with a white picket fence. Just inside, rose bushes lined the path to the door. Not caring that she was trespassing and not caring who caught her, Kat unlatched the gate and grabbed two handfuls of roses. The thorns bit into her skin and drew blood. Kat didn't even feel the thorny pain or notice the blood dripping from her hands.

She returned to the cemetery and fell to her knees between the two graves. Carefully, she placed a bunch of roses on each one. "I will not forget you," she said. "Now that I know you existed, I will not forget."

Then Kat cried. She cried more over these two unknown relatives, grandmother and brother, than she had ever cried over anything or anybody before, including her lost mother and father.

It was not time to cry over Marcus and Melody Arnold. Not yet.

20

JUNE-JULY 1981

The money that Melody got for Marcus' pearls from the gorilla man at the Last Chance Pawn Shop was enough to hold Melody and Sylvia over for a while. If they were careful and used oxycodone sparingly and heroin even more sparingly, they could last for a couple of months without worry.

"Maybe we should make a schedule or keep a chart of when we use our little helpers," Sylvia suggested. "It's probably a good idea to try to regulate ourselves, right? After all, we're nurses. We're used to writing down on a chart every time a patient takes medication."

This suggestion came about after Melody and Sylvia barely escaped what they considered a close call. They'd just finished one of their rare shifts together, and it had been a dreadful doozy of a day. A family of eight had gotten their VW van stuck on a railroad track when they ignored the flashing lights at the crossing. The train, unable to stop in time, crumpled the vehicle like a tin can. After hours of trying to save the three who had survived, the prognoses for their continued survival seemed bleak. One of them, the youngest daughter, had lost the bottom half of her face.

In a desperate effort to get the image of the little girl out of her mind, Melody suggested that they powder their noses—their old code word—in the bathroom of the nurses' lounge. Sylvia, equally devastated by the trauma, had readily agreed. Automatically, just like old times, they crammed together in one stall while Sylvia searched through her bag.

Just their luck. That nosy, awful Linda walked in. "Who's in there?" her shrill voice asked. "Are there two of you in there? What's going on?"

Quickly, Melody hopped up on the stool and crouched there, leaving only Sylvia's legs showing through the bottom of the door. Linda was the biggest gossip at Mercy, and it was hard telling what her deviously fertile imagination would come up with to explain two nurses in the same stall. She might come up with the idea that Melody and Sylvia were lesbian lovers, but who knew? Enough rumors were swirling around about drug theft since Dr. Adams, that promising asshole of a neurosurgeon, had been caught stealing Quaaludes from the pharmacy, dismissed from his job, and now faced possible legal action. His career was in ruins, and the gossipy world of this hospital thrived on *ruination*.

"What are you talking about, Linda? It's only me, Sylvia."

"I saw four legs just a minute ago," Linda said uncertainly.

"Nonsense," Sylvia said. "It's been a rough shift. Everyone's tired."

"But I thought I saw—"

"For god's sake!" Sylvia barked with convincing mortification. "Can't a woman take a crap in peace?" She flushed the stool.

"Oh, well, sure, sorry," Linda said. "It has been a long and difficult shift. That poor little girl. I must be seeing things."

"Yes, you are." Sylvia flushed the stool again for good measure.

To be on the safe side, Sylvia waited for five minutes after Linda scurried away to leave the stall. Melody waited for five more before she walked out of the bathroom.

Now Melody was driving Sylvia into the city. Marcus, she knew, would be displeased that she was late in getting home. Since Evelyn's death, he had become even more attentive to Melody's comings and goings.

"It's not a bad idea to keep a chart," Melody said slowly to Sylvia, "but I don't want to leave anything lying around that Marcus might find." Melody also—and she didn't dare say this to her dearest friend—preferred not to know how often she took a little helper or a bubble bath. She told herself that she only took her little helpers when she really needed them, even as she suspected that the times she really needed them were becoming more frequent. Melody had a reason for that. She and Marcus were having difficulty finding the right balance in their marriage now that it was only the two of them. Yes, there was definitely a reason.

"Good point." Sylvia fiddled with her More cigarette because Melody couldn't let her smoke in Marcus' Buick. "We wouldn't want Mr. Righteous to find out. Besides, it's not like we're drug addicts or anything. We're just recreational ... people.

"Right." Melody knew that Sylvia was reluctant to say, *users*. It implied the wrong kind of thing, the wrong message of who they were. She understood and agreed. However, and it was another thing she didn't dare say to her dearest friend, her attitude toward their little helpers was not that they were recreational but that they were *necessary*.

"Are you sure you can't get out of it?" Sylvia then said.

Melody felt her heart sink and groaned. "I've tried everything I can think of to get out of it, but I can't." And she had. She'd told Marcus she was scheduled to work overtime that week, that Ma needed her to help put on the screen windows, that she sunburned so quickly that she wouldn't enjoy the trip. All exaggerated fibs, but Marcus had held firm. "He put down a deposit on the room, and to Marcus, that means this vacation is written in stone."

"Cheapskate." Sylvia pretended to puff on the unlit cigarette.

"And I told you, I promised him I'd go on the night of Evelyn's funeral."

"Under duress. Marcus was crushing you to death."

Melody always told Sylvia everything. Almost everything.

"Killing you softly with his hugs." Sylvia sang to the tune of "Killing Me Softly with His Song."

"Can we drop the subject?" Sylvia's observation hit a little too close to home.

"I'm sorry. Me and my big mouth." But Sylvia didn't sound sorry at all. After a few moments, sensing Melody's discomfort, she added, "It's just that I'm going to miss you."

"I'm going to miss you, too." Melody didn't want to go on this trip to Wisconsin Lake. In fact, she dreaded it with every ounce of her being. Five whole days alone with Marcus with no escapes, no work, no made-up errands, no trips to visit Ma. Just the two of them. What was she going to do? Marcus wanted to *make* another baby. The paper doll baby. Melody would not let that happen. She'd made an appointment with a doctor (not the Aryan Dr. Bennett, who wouldn't even refill her prescriptions) to get a script for the pill. Marcus had wanted to go with her because she'd told him it was a routine check-up. So Melody ended up canceling the appointment. Then everyday life got in the way—and she and Marcus hadn't had sex for weeks, no worries there—and for the second time in her adult life, Melody had not followed through on getting the pill.

Melody refused to believe it was an omen. It was not an omen.

She would feign menstrual cramps, or migraines, or flu-like symptoms to avoid sleeping with her husband. He would not force her to have sex with him. Marcus would never do that, force her. He might look longingly at her or resignedly sigh, but he would not force his baby, his sweetheart, his kitten, his little flower, to have sex.

They pulled up in front of Sylvia's apartment building. "Oh, I almost forgot." Sylvia started to dig in her cavernous, messy purse. "I have a going-away present for you." She pulled out a bag from Kmart. "Sorry, I didn't have time to wrap it."

"You didn't have to do that, Syl." Melody was touched, as she always was when anybody, except Marcus, did something nice for her.

"Yes, I did," Sylvia said.

Melody pulled out a strand of imitation pearls and looked questioningly at Sylvia.

"He's going to take you out for at least one nice dinner," Sylvia explained. "And when he does, he's going to want you to wear the pearls. I know these are pretty cheap-looking, but let's hope he doesn't notice." She smiled her broad, red-lipped smile.

"You're the best, Syl! I hadn't even thought about that, but you are absolutely right. Marcus would want me to wear the pearls." She gave Sylvia a fierce hug. What would she ever do without such a wonderful friend?

Sylvia hugged her back, equally hard, and just before she got out of the car, she asked, "What are you going to do about ... you know. Five days is a long time."

"I don't know." It was perhaps the most pressing thing on her mind about the whole vacation, even more so than Marcus' baby-making plan, which she could avoid. Unlike their house, which had plenty of rooms to hide in, Melody would be confined in a small motel room with Marcus for five long days. How was she going to keep Marcus from finding out that she needed a *little help* now and then?

Marcus' choice of Wisconsin Lake as their vacation destination was further proof to Melody that her husband did not know her at all. Yes, the 10,000-acre lake was pristine and beautiful. (Every species of fish in Wisconsin inhabited the lake, Marcus told her proudly, for some unknown reason). And the one-bedroom cottage he'd rented at Burhop's Lakeside Lodge, located between Merrimac and Lodi in Central Wisconsin, was furnished with a full kitchen and bathroom with a shower. There was an outdoor shaded area with a grill, picnic table, and fire pit. ("All we needed to bring were towels, dishtowels, food, and a spirit to have fun!" Marcus explained happily.) Yes, it was beautiful, lovely, just perfect, Melody agreed dutifully, if somewhat sullenly.

What she really felt but didn't say was, "It's so rustic, Marcus. I feel like I'm in the middle of nowhere. Plus, I have never boated or fished, and I don't know how to swim that well. And I turn red as a beet in the sun! I'm a city girl. What in the hell were you thinking?"

However, her most pressing concern was the secret she could also never voice to Marcus: *How could she take a bubble bath if there was no tub?*

"This place is everything the brochure said it would be," Marcus said as he unpacked. "There is so much to do here, and they say the sunsets are spectacular!"

And no television, Melody noticed as she looked around the room, panicked. What was Marcus planning to do every evening to occupy his time? Melody had only one guess, one sure guess—*make* a baby. Five minutes in the room, and Melody could feel the walls close in, suffocating her.

"What do you want to do first?" Marcus finished unpacking and clapped his hands together, as happy as a child. "There's a free ferry at Merrimac, Devil's Lake State Park, Parfrey's Glen, House on the Rock, or the Mid-Continent Railway Museum," Marcus read from the brochure. "Or we could go hiking or swimming, or rent a boat. The possibilities are endless!"

Melody took deep breaths to keep the panic under control. Her only hope would be to keep Marcus so busy during the day that he fell immediately asleep each night, exhausted. Then she could quietly creep into the bathroom.

Marcus strode across the small room and took Melody in his arms. "What a wonderful way to celebrate our first anniversary!"

Melody had completely forgotten that their first anniversary was the day after tomorrow. "Our first anniversary. Wow." She had been married to this man for an entire year, and they were still, for the most part, strangers. Wow.

"I know!" Marcus said, with this rare, boundless enthusiasm. "Can you believe it?"

"No, Marcus, I can't." Who was this man?

"Let's go for a swim."

"I think I'd like to take a nap." Melody could close the drapes, take an Oxy, and settle into the darkness. That would kill a few hours.

Marcus grinned and blushed. "I like that idea, too. Very much."

Oh, dear God, what had she been thinking? "On second thought, I think a swim is a better idea," she said quickly. "Who wants to take a nap when we have beautiful Wisconsin Lake—inhabited by every species of fish in the state—right outside our cabin door?"

"That's my little kitten," Marcus said with an actual grin. Melody had never seen Marcus *grin*. "I knew you'd love it here!"

Who *was* this man?

While Marcus bobbed happily in the water, Melody sat under an umbrella on the shore in her demure, black, one-piece swimming suit, slathered in sun lotion, sipping from a thermos of vodka and orange juice. (Marcus had packed towels; she had packed vodka.) Out in the open air and sunshine, away from their airless house, she studied her husband objectively. He was lean and very white in his striped trunks, but he had a decent build: adequately broad shoulders on his smallish frame, no fat on his stomach, a practically hairless chest, nicely shaped legs. Without his glasses, his creased trousers, and his pressed white shirt with a pocket full of pens, he looked much younger than his thirty-five years, almost boyish. Would other women find this man attractive? Very possibly. It was the first time she'd ever thought of such a thing.

Maybe—probably not, but *maybe*—she had been judging him too harshly over the last year. Did he love her too much? Yes. But he didn't know her for what she really was: a terrible person. She'd known that something was wrong with their baby, and she didn't do anything. She relied on her little helpers to make it through the days. She'd done things that no self-respecting woman would do to obtain those helpers; she was a fraud, and she knew it. Perhaps it was her guilt that kept her from returning his love.

Perhaps she had never really given him a chance.

Nonsense. It was, of course, nonsense. The heat must be making Melody light-headed to be thinking such thoughts. Or perhaps she was drunk on vodka or high on the morphine she'd taken in the bathroom while she changed into her swimming suit. Whatever. Right now, in this place, Marcus Arnold did not seem like such a bad guy.

Melody was off the hook that first night, for it was Marcus who got seriously sunburned. He was already starting to blister when they finished an early dinner at the lodge. The pressure of his light cotton shirt on those blisters caused him great pain.

"I'm sorry, baby," he moaned as she pressed cool towels against his blistered shoulders, then applied soothing aloe lotion. "I should have known better." Melody still came prepared. Along with the vodka and her helpers, she'd packed a first aid kit.

"Shh, Marcus, it's okay." He was in such pain that he didn't notice her shaking hands. When he finally fell into a restless sleep, Melody tiptoed to the bathroom and found her own relief.

On the second day, it rained and rained. Marcus still suffered from his sunburn, and Melody tended to him. She liked this role. After all, she was a trained nurse, a professional, and it was what she did best. It was pleasant, this role reversal. For once, she was the one in charge, and Marcus was suitably grateful. "Thank you, Mellie," he kept saying. "Thank you, my little flower." If Marcus could be like this all the time, Melody thought that maybe they could make this marriage work.

However, after about the thousandth "thank you" and the thousandth endearment (baby, kitten, flower, honey, sweetheart), Melody's nerves started to fray. "Why do you call me such silly things?" She'd wanted to ask him this question for quite some time, and now that he was docile, in pain, she felt like she could.

Marcus seemed surprised. "Why, they're only my pet names for you, baby."

"I'm not your pet, and I'm not your baby."

"Sure you are."

"No, I'm not." She applied the lotion to his oozing blisters with more force than necessary.

Marcus winced. "Ouch!" He reached up and grabbed her hands.

By this time, Melody's nerves were so frayed that she could not control the trembling in her hands or her body. "Don't you respect me, Marcus?"

"What has respect got to do with it?"

"Everything."

"Why, honey, you're shaking like a leaf." Marcus changed the subject. Marcus was an expert at changing the subject.

"It's chilly in here." Melody hoped he didn't see the sweat glistening on her forehead or the patches under her armpits. She hadn't taken a single little helper in hours because Marcus kept watching her. Marcus was always watching her.

"Put on a sweater, baby. I don't want you catching a cold."

He hadn't heard a word she said. "I'm going to take a hot shower." The rest of the night, she sipped vodka and cranberry juice and pretended to read the romance novel she brought along. She fell asleep on the uncomfortable chair.

Marcus woke her up the next morning with a kiss on her forehead. "You are some nurse, kitten. I'm raring to go! Happy anniversary!"

At first, through the fog of her hangover, Melody had no idea where she was. And who was this strange man standing before her? "I don't—" she began.

He knelt beside her. "You're even beautiful when you wake up, flower. I am so lucky to have you."

Have you. What did that mean?

"Get dressed," he said, smoothing back her hair. "We'll have breakfast at the lodge, and then we'll go visit the railroad museum. I made reservations for tonight at a top-notch restaurant the brochure recommended. We'll have steaks and champagne, the whole kit and kaboodle!"

Melody struggled to get up. "I need to take a shower first."

"You took one last night, baby, don't you remember?"

Oh, yes, she remembered now. She'd taken a pill, and then there was all that vodka. She was in Wisconsin, with Marcus, but she wasn't quite sure how or why. "I need—"

Marcus laughed gaily. "My wife," he said to the room, "is very clean. She spends a lot of time bathing!"

Did he suspect something? Melody felt a sudden and deep chill of dread. She had to get herself together. Marcus could never find out what she did in the bathroom. It was only temporary, after all, just until she felt better. She only needed help until she *felt better*.

Somehow, Melody managed to get dressed under Marcus' watchful eye. Somehow, she made it through the breakfast and then the railroad museum. She let this man, her husband, lead her like a horse with blinders on through the events he'd scheduled for the day, their first anniversary.

"You're wearing your pearls, aren't you, Mellie?" Marcus asked as they dressed for dinner.

"Yes, Marcus, I'm wearing the pearls," Melody called from the bathroom as she struggled with the clasp and then turned to the mirror. Involuntarily, she gasped. Was it the poor light in this room? For all the time that Melody spent in the bathroom, she rarely looked at herself, and now she knew why. She looked like a shadow of her former self. Her skin was so pale that even her freckles were pale, and that made the dark circles under her eyes and her cheekbones more pronounced. How much weight had she lost? But it was her eyes that frightened her the most. The blue looked washed out, hollow.

How could Marcus not notice the change in her appearance?

Because Marcus did not really *see* her. Marcus only saw the image of her that he had created, his pet, his baby, his child bride.

"I need to do something," Melody said to her ghastly reflection. She needed to get her act together. She could not go on with this double, secret life. This marriage to Marcus could not go on as it had before. She would have to try harder. Even though she was exhausted, spent, she would have to try harder, but how? She used to be a good girl, a good person. How had she done that? She would have to remember, or at the very least, she must pretend to remember.

Melody wiped the tears from her hollow eyes and went to dinner with her husband to celebrate their first anniversary, wearing the cheap imitation pearls, hoping that Marcus wouldn't notice. Luckily, in the dim light of the restaurant, he did not. She smiled when she was supposed to and responded to his questions when she was supposed to. She let him order her too much food: seafood bisque, spinach salad, sirloin steak, garlic mashed potatoes, steamed vegetables, fruit, chocolate cake that the wait staff brought out with a lit red candle, singing for them. She could tell that all this made her husband very happy. She smiled more. She was *trying*.

She and Marcus made love that night. It was what she was supposed to do, and it was fine. As always, Marcus was very tender, and when he told her he loved her—he loved her so much!—over and over again, Melody murmured a response that he interpreted as her reciprocated love.

She still tried the next day, too. She didn't take any little helpers before the wretched boat ride that had her heaving over the side. Marcus felt terrible. "I didn't know that you got seasick, my lovely little flower. I am so sorry." She was not seasick. Her body was revolting against the lack of help, against the lack of sustenance.

Melody tried. With all her might, she tried. She and Marcus made love again that night, and after, as she lay restless, sweating, trembling, crying next to her loving husband, she thought: *Just one more time. That's all I need, just one more dose.*

She crept out of bed, searched through her suitcase for the little cellophane bag with its white powder, the syringe, the silver tablespoon, a shoelace, and a lighter, and went into the bathroom. Quietly, oh so quietly, she shut the door and turned on the light. "Just one more time," she whispered. "That's all I need."

Melody sat on the closed stool, her upper arm tied off with the shoelace and the syringe poised, searching for a vein, when the bathroom door opened.

"What are you doing?" Marcus cried. "Dear God, baby, what are you *doing?*"

"You told him it was a B-12 shot?" Sylvia was incredulous.

"Yes, I told him that just before our vacation, I had been diagnosed as anemic, but I hadn't wanted to worry him." Melody had never been more frightened in her life than when she saw Marcus standing in the bathroom doorway. His green eyes were wide behind the thick lenses of his glasses, and he, too, seemed genuinely frightened. "Dear God, baby, what are you *doing?*" he had asked again in a horrified voice.

"And he bought that? You had your arm tied off, and he truly believed that you were taking a B-12 shot? Unbelievable." Sylvia shook her head in amazement and lit another cigarette. On this nighttime journey into the city, it was her turn to drive. These necessary treks to Chicago's underbelly made them both incredibly nervous, and Sylvia was chain-smoking.

On that night two weeks before in the cabin, pure adrenaline had taken over Melody's next actions, as it often did when the most acute trauma cases came into the ER. She didn't remember exactly how she quickly untied her arm and put the tools of the trade into a bag, but she did remember murmuring to Marcus, soothing him, leading him back to bed. "Nothing to worry about ... anemic ... just a monthly B-12 shot ... nothing to worry about ... shh ... go back to sleep."

"I guess it's not entirely unbelievable. Marcus is a very trusting person, after all." Once again, Melody had lied to him. She had told so many lies to Marcus during the last year that she couldn't begin to keep track of them all, and she was always afraid that she would trip herself up, contradict herself. It was like living on the edge of a cliff.

"Or maybe Marcus is a complete idiot," Sylvia said. "Thank God."

Melody shifted uncomfortably in her seat. "Marcus is not an idiot."

"Sorry." Sylvia didn't sound sorry at all, as usual.

No, her husband was not an idiot. The thought made Melody uneasy, and she wasn't going to tell Sylvia about the latest episode that should have aroused his suspicion. It was too shameful, and she could hardly bear to think about it herself. But what else could she do? Sylvia still contributed more than her share of money to their purchases, and although Sylvia never said a word about this unequal partnership, Melody felt guilty. Truthfully, it was Marcus' fault. He made her hand over her paycheck, just so she would have no cash of her own, no freedom. He left her no other choice.

Immediately after their return from their "honeymoon," as Marcus liked to call it, things returned to normal. Their boring, drab, rote existence carried on in that airless house. They ate their meals, they washed dishes together, Marcus scoured the sink twice with Comet, and then they watched television, endless hours of television. Marcus' laughter at inane sitcoms and his sobbing during corny dramas were enough to make anyone crazy. It was summer, yet they stayed cooped up in that dark house as if they were prisoners in a cold Siberia.

It was small wonder, Melody rationalized, that her vow to *get her act together* was short-lived. The boyish exuberance that Marcus had displayed on their vacation quickly became a distant memory, and Melody wondered if she'd only imagined Marcus clapping his hands and grinning and frolicking in the water. He was once again his unexciting, chained-to-routine self. The familiar panicked darkness fell over Melody, the walls felt like they were closing in on her, and she desperately wanted to numb her mind from her mind-numbing life. Bubble baths were again a top priority.

This meant that she needed money.

This meant that Marcus left her no other choice: Evelyn's jewelry.

Yes, Melody felt guilty. She was flooded with guilt the first time she took a sapphire and ruby pendant out of the jewelry box that still sat on the dresser in Evelyn's room. (Everything in the room was just as it had been when Evelyn was alive. Her clothes still hung in the closet, the bed pillows plumped. Marcus was not yet ready to "go through" Evelyn's things, he said.) Melody thought that Marcus probably had no idea what was in his mother's jewelry box. Most men wouldn't know what was in their wife's jewelry box, let alone their mother's. It was all Marcus' fault, Melody tried to convince herself as she left Last Chance Pawn Shop, trying to hold back her tears. If he would just let her keep her own money, she wouldn't have to do this.

"It doesn't take much time to go through money and drugs," Melody said to Sylvia.

"You can say that again." Sylvia nodded sadly.

The second item she took out of Evelyn's jewelry box was an ivory cameo hat pin. No one wore hats anymore, and Melody had never seen Evelyn wear this piece. It would never be missed.

But oh, yes, Melody felt guilty. She was flooded with guilt when the caged gorilla man at Last Chance Pawn Shop said, "This here is an antique, looks like a family heirloom. You sure you want to hand this over?"

It was too late to back down, too late to make another decision. Melody and Sylvia were going into the city in two days. "How much?" she said.

The very next evening, sitting in front of the television watching *Magnum, P.I.*, Marcus casually—oh, so casually—asked, "Have you been wearing some of Mother's jewelry?"

The question jolted Melody out of her morphine-induced trance, and her heart started to pound. "Why, yes, in fact. I borrowed a couple of pieces to wear to work." Melody never wore jewelry at work, especially not the gaudy diamond and emerald and ruby ring that Marcus had made such a production of presenting her with at Thanksgiving. Did he even know that?

"Oh, that's nice," Marcus said distractedly. "Mother would have been pleased." He was engrossed right then with Thomas Magnum and T.C. flying in a helicopter somewhere over Hawaii. Then, the dreaded commercial and Marcus' attention fully focused on Melody. "Why didn't you put the sapphire and ruby pendant and ivory cameo hat pin back?"

Oh, dear God, Marcus knew exactly what his mother had in her jewelry box. Of course. How could Melody have been so stupid? Her thumping heart grew louder. She was sure he could hear it; it was deafening.

"I … they're at the jeweler's getting cleaned." Lies upon lies upon lies. Neverending lies, impossible to stop once she started.

"Really?" Marcus raised an eyebrow.

"Yes, the silver chain on the pendant was a little tarnished, and I thought … Well, I thought I might as well get them both cleaned. I was already there, at the jeweler's, you know, so why not both?" How long was he going to keep staring at her, letting her fumble on? "They're such lovely pieces," she added lamely.

"Yes," he said, "they are." Thankfully, the commercial ended, and Marcus' attention was again riveted to the TV.

Melody tried to put that exchange with Marcus out of her mind, along with the more pressing problem. The jewelry was gone, pawned, and probably in someone else's possession. She would not get the pieces back, and what lie could she use to explain that? But now in the car with Sylvia, as they approached their worst destination yet, her nerves in tatters, Melody had the unthinkable apprehension that Marcus was not merely suspicious. No, Marcus knew *everything*.

"Impossible," she said aloud. She'd been careful, discreet. Marcus was not only trusting but also somewhat oblivious of the real world, of *life*. Her mind, in desperate need of a fix, was playing tricks on her.

"Not impossible," Sylvia said, her voice high-pitched with worry, "just stupid. What in the hell are we doing here?"

"Getting supplies," Melody said automatically. That's what they always said on these increasingly dangerous missions when they needed reassurance. They were *getting supplies*.

"We are in fucking Cabrini-Green, the worst project in Chicago. People get killed when they take out the trash."

It was true. Cabrini-Green had the worst reputation in Chicago for violence, and they were driving slowly past the compound of run-down apartment buildings. Many of the windows were boarded over, and the hard-packed dirt yard was strewn with trash. On this warm summer night, plenty of people strolled about, looking for something to do—all young, all black, all male.

Melody wasn't sure if the young men looked menacing or simply bored. "I don't mean to be a racist or anything, but—" Melody reached up and locked her door and rolled up the window.

Sylvia did the same. "We're supposed to ask for Jamal." Sylvia dropped the cigarette she was trying to light.

"Where do you get this information?" Melody asked. They were starting to draw attention. A few of the young men stared openly at Sylvia's lime green car with disdainful interest.

"Don't ask."

"Fine. I didn't want to know anyway." Melody really didn't. The subject of Sylvia's connections, most relating back to poor Thelma, was another thing they didn't discuss. The list of things they didn't talk about had snowballed, about on pace with the mountain of lies necessary to keep their double life a secret.

One of the young men, who wore a baggy sweatshirt, reached into his pants pocket. "Do you think he has a gun?" Sylvia's voice was high-pitched.

"Yes, he has a gun." Melody would bet her life on it.

"We desperately need to get some supplies," Sylvia said. "I'm totally out."

"Me, too."

"I guess the question is, how desperate are we?"

Melody was very desperate. After the Marcus episode, she felt like she hung onto the edge of the cliff with only her fingernails. "Surely, Jamal is expecting us. Maybe that's Jamal reaching into his pants pocket? Maybe he's reaching for our supplies?"

It didn't matter whether the hooded young man was Jamal. He did indeed pull out a gun, pointed it up in the air, and fired.

It was a warning, and Sylvia treated it as such. She threw the car into drive and stomped on the gas, running red lights all the way to Compton Street. Instinctively, Sylvia would always drive back to Thelma's old apartment.

As terrified as Melody had been at Cabrini-Green, her disappointment was even more acute. They hadn't gotten their supplies, and she needed something, anything. She didn't have to tell Sylvia that.

"The word on the street," Sylvia said as if she'd been using that kind of language all her life, "is that there was a sweep in this neighborhood a couple of days ago. A lot of arrests. That's why we were at Cabrini-Green." Sylvia's hands were fluttering like birds. "I'm going to have to swallow my pride—and probably a lot more than that—and contact Clyde."

Melody didn't want to feel it, but she did. A small surge of hope. Yes, Clyde would be the answer to all their problems. However, she owed it to Sylvia to say, "You don't have to do that, Syl." Secretly, though, she was thinking, *please!*

Sylvia acted like she hadn't heard Melody. "I know where he's been hanging out lately, this dive bar on Clayborn Street. Don't ask me how I know."

Melody didn't. "Let's go."

Melody had always thought that the bar her daddy and brothers frequented defined tacky, but O'Brian's didn't hold a candle to this bar, the Runaround. From the outside, it looked like the ramshackle corrugated tin building was collapsing, falling in on itself in despair. The whole neighborhood, one that Melody had never been in before, was a poster for despondency, with boarded-up windows, graffiti-covered walls and doors, and rusted automobiles lining the street, tireless. "I'm beginning to think that Cabrini-Green isn't the worst neighborhood in Chicago," Melody said. Although it was hot out, she shivered.

"I'm going to throw up." Sylvia opened the car door and retched into the gutter. "Nerves," she said when she finished. "I'm suffering from nerves."

"I know just how you feel." Melody could only stare at the desolate bar. And Melody did know exactly how Sylvia felt. When there was too much time between the little helpers, she, too, suffered horribly from *nerves*.

"Let's get this over with." Sylvia popped a Certs into her mouth.

Melody had half hoped that Sylvia would offer to go in by herself. No such luck, and of course, that wouldn't have been fair. "We'll make it quick, slip in and out," she said as she got out of the car. She and Sylvia were in this together. They were a team, a dynamic duo. A dynamic duo getting supplies in possibly the worst neighborhood on the South Side of Chicago.

Nurses in search of heroin.

The bar was smoky and dark, which was expected, but it also had a very rank smell: urine, sweat, or perhaps, disease. Men occupied the stools and booths, but there were a few women, women with bleached hair, too much makeup, and too short skirts. Melody supposed they were prostitutes, but she didn't care. Then Melody's shivering grew more pronounced as she definitively recognized the smell. The place smelled like a decaying corpse, like death.

"Look what the cat dragged in," Clyde called from the farthest booth in the back. He had his two bodyguards or henchmen or whatever they were with him—scarface and bulldog. "Didn't I tell you? They always come back to old Clyde."

So much for slipping in and out of this bar undetected. However, Melody was with a six-foot-tall platinum blonde. Of course they would be noticed. She followed Sylvia to the table.

Sylvia began, "We want to—"

"I know what you want," Clyde said. His hair was so greasy it looked like he had washed it in salad oil.

"We have money." Clyde seemed to notice her for the first time, and Melody's shivering became uncontrollable.

"Naturally." Clyde took a long drink of his beer. "Yes, I always know what my clients want, but then you aren't really my clients, are you? You went behind old Clyde's back, didn't you? Believe me, I know everything that goes on in this town."

Sylvia also shivered badly. "I'm sorry, Clyde. It won't happen again. Do you have anything?"

"Now she apologizes," Clyde said to his goons, who laughed on cue. "Syl, here, dissed me, and now she wants to apologize. What do you make of that?"

All of them knew that Clyde held all the cards in this game. What was he going to make them do? Did he want them to beg? Would she stoop that low? Unfortunately, Melody knew the sorry answer to that sorry question.

As did Sylvia. "What do you want, Clyde?"

"I don't take kindly to people dissing me, Syl." Clyde then took his time lighting a cigar, making them wait, making them squirm.

"I said I was sorry, Clyde. Anything you want." Sweat glistened on Sylvia's face.

"I told you before. Favors don't come cheap." Clyde blew a thick stream of smoke.

"Please," Melody said softly.

Again, Clyde stared at her, considering.

Melody held his gaze. "Please," she said again.

Clyde came to a decision. "Okay, I guess you could say I'm a forgiving man." He pointed his bony finger at Melody. "I want her."

Clyde was not such a bad guy. He let Melody shoot the smack first. "It looks like you could use it," he said, not unkindly.

Melody, shivering and close to vomiting, urgently needed it. They were in the back room of the Runaround. A filthy mattress was on the floor, and Melody would swear that she saw a rat run across it. "How much?" she asked.

"This one's on me." Clyde prepared the shot.

"Is that needle sterile?" Melody could not help but ask, even though at that point, she no longer cared. She wanted that needle in her vein.

Clyde only laughed. "Come here."

Melody went to him. And Melody was so very, very grateful for that essential rush of euphoria, the warm flushing of her skin, the dry mouth, and the feeling of having heavy arms and legs.

Clyde wasn't such a bad guy after all.

He waited until Melody was *on the nod*, in an alternately wakeful and drowsy state, before he undressed her on the filthy mattress in the back room of the Runaround and climbed on top of her.

She had never had sex when she was on heroin. It was a vague thought, as was this: *I am a heroin sex virgin.* God knew that she'd never had sex with Marcus when she was high. She always waited until she'd come down some before she crept into bed beside her sleeping, snoring husband.

She might have fallen asleep; she didn't feel a thing. She didn't remember anything; she refused to remember anything.

"It was supposed to be me," Sylvia cried on the way home. "Damn it, Mel, it was supposed to be me!"

"It doesn't matter," Melody said, still drowsy. "We got the supplies."

"We're never going to stoop this low again." Sylvia thumped her hands on the steering wheel.

Sylvia needs a shot, Melody thought.

"I mean it."

"We always say that." Yet it seemed that they continued to stoop lower and lower. Melody's head lolled against the headrest.

"Well, this time I *really* mean it."

"Okay." But Melody knew that there would be a next time and a next time and a next. Unless they quit. And Melody did not want to quit. She wanted this feeling to go on forever and ever. Amen.

A little while later, Sylvia asked softly, "He didn't hurt you, did he? I'll kill him with my bare hands if he so much as hurt a single hair on your head."

"He didn't hurt my hair." Melody was not quite sure what Syl was talking about.

"If I remember correctly, and I always remember correctly, he wasn't that bad in the sack," Sylvia mused aloud.

"It wasn't a sack," Melody said. "It was a mattress."

"Go to sleep." Sylvia reached over and patted Melody's hand. "You're spending the night at my place. We can't let Marcus see you like this."

"Who?" Melody could not keep her eyes open.

"We won't mention this again."

Melody didn't answer. She was asleep.

So the Runaround incident became one more thing to put on Melody and Sylvia's Do Not Talk About It List. If they didn't talk about it, it never happened. That was what they chose to believe.

21

APRIL 2012

Kat was supposed to leave today. She wanted to; she didn't want to. Zen had thoughtfully—or did he just want to get rid of her?—checked the bus schedule and volunteered to take her to the Greyhound station. He probably did want to get rid of her, and she really couldn't blame him. In the short time he had known her, if she wasn't being a first-rate, raving bitch, she was freeloading off him and his incredibly nice, nosy family, or she was crying her eyes out. He probably thought she was the most fucked up loser he had ever met.

She probably was.

If she left, she would have no time to redeem herself.

If she left, she would not have time to find and meet the mysterious Sylvia Hammond, the person who Kat had convinced herself held all the answers.

Kat was now almost positive that Mellie had gotten knocked up and married Marcus out of a sense of duty, not love. Also, she had probably suffered from either a severe case of post-partum depression, or more likely, a profound sense of grief over the death of her baby boy. Then before she had had a chance to recover fully, she'd gotten pregnant again. Sure, all those things would make even a normally happy person a little wacky, but delusional and suicidal? There had to be more going on in Melody Arnold's mind to spur her to climb that light tower. Crucial pieces of the puzzle were still missing.

Kat turned off the hot water and stepped out of the shower, still undecided about what she should do next. As of this moment, there was only one thing she was sure of. She needed to call Granny Nanny. Gran had called three times but hadn't left a message, which was unlike her. Usually, she left long rambling messages that were cut off in the middle when the time had elapsed, messages that went something like: "Katrina, dear, I'm in the produce section of Fry's. I decided to stop in after my shooting lesson at the gun club. I had Dan this time. Did you know he's a retired FBI agent? I realized I had a small amount of you know what in my purse, which made me a little nervous during the lesson, but the nice man certainly did not want to see inside my purse. Anyway, I decided I was hungry for beet salad, so I stopped in here, but now I'm thinking along the lines of a cucumber salad, even though the cucumbers are not on sale. I was wondering if you—beep!"

Shit! A sudden panic seized Kat. What if Granny Nanny and Mr. Williams had been arrested? What if they'd already gone to the assisted living center and been caught trying to sell pot? It was a far-fetched possibility, but still. So many far-fetched things had happened in the last few days—so many cosmic bitch slaps that Kat had lost count—and it was unlike Granny Nanny not to leave a message. Kat dressed quickly. Her phone was in Lorraine's bedroom, and she needed to get to her phone.

Kat had forgotten to bring in her brush, so she opened the cabinet under the sink to look for one. Priscilla, unlike Granny Nanny, was not a one-product woman. The array of face creams was impressive: Neutrogena, Roc, Estee Lauder, Garnier, Oil of Olay. Kat wondered which one actually did the trick. Priscilla did have great skin. Hurriedly, Kat moved aside a box of tampons, still searching for a brush or comb.

Tampons. Shit!

Kat sat down hard on the floor. This panic attack was paralyzing. Her periods had always been regular, and this one should have started three days ago. She'd even packed tampons in her long-lost suitcase in preparation. When was the last time she had sex? El Chorro. The last time had been after she'd had dinner with Benson at El Chorro to celebrate her birthday. That was a couple of weeks ago, and Kat barely remembered it because it had been so boring. It had been so boring that she might have even fallen asleep. Had Benson used a condom? They had sex so infrequently that Kat hadn't bothered to pick up her pill prescription, thinking that she might as well save the thirty bucks.

Shit!

"I need to get a grip," Kat said to the box of tampons she clutched in her shaking hand. "I've been under a lot of stress during the last couple of weeks. That's all it is. Stress. I could not get pregnant during sex that boring."

"Of course you could," the tampon box seemed to say.

"I refuse to be pregnant with that pretty man's baby," Kat said back, then threw the box viciously into the cabinet.

She was being ridiculous; it was not possible. Carmella would be the imaginary child's grandmother. Inconceivable. Benson would be a *daddy*. Out of the question. She, who had no maternal instincts whatsoever, would be a ... She couldn't even think the word.

Had Melody Arnold had these same thoughts?

It was very possible.

"But I have no intention of jumping off a 100-foot light tower," Kat said, getting slowly to her feet. "Even if it's true—and it is *not*—I wouldn't do what she did. I would *never* make that choice!"

There was a knock on the bathroom door. "Are you about ready to go?" Of course, it was Zen.

Screw the brush. The man had perfect timing when it came to seeing her at her worst. She might as well give him one last thrill. Kat opened the door. "Almost," she said, clawing at her wet, tangled hair with her fingers.

"Quite the lively conversation you were having with yourself." Zen smiled, looking perfect in his blue jeans and t-shirt. Of course.

How much had he heard? "Were you eavesdropping?" Kat's question didn't have the tone of indignation she had hoped for.

"Not my style."

"Good." It was all she could think of to say as she stared into his green/gold eyes. She realized with sudden clarity that she was going to miss this man very much, too much. "Good," she said again, not moving.

Zen cleared his throat. "John's waiting downstairs. I packed my stuff in his car already, and we thought we'd drop you off at the Greyhound station on our way into the city. Kill two birds with one stone, I guess. I hope you don't mind."

"Why would I mind?" She did mind. She wanted just a few more minutes alone with him before she left. She wanted to thank him for all he had done for her, and she wanted ... Well, she wasn't sure what she wanted.

Zen cleared his throat again. "Okay, then. I'd offer to carry your suitcase down to the car for you, but—"

"Right. Kind of funny, huh? For someone with a lot of baggage. I don't even have a suitcase. I have a Target plastic bag."

Zen stared at her just as intently as she stared at him. "I'm going to miss you, Kat."

"Me, too," she said quietly. *Just kiss me,* she thought.

Once again, Zen backed away. "I'll meet you at the car."

Another lost moment, the last one. "I'll say goodbye to your folks, and then we can be on our way." She squeezed by him before he could see that her eyes were shining with tears.

Kat forgot all about calling Granny Nanny and a missed period that was definitely due to stress. She stuffed her few clothes into the bag and then went to say good-bye to Priscilla and Tanner Delaney—and Lorraine and Benny and Megan and Tammy and Phillip and Janet and their three boys. It was more emotional than Kat would have thought. She would sincerely miss these kind people, along with Priscilla's cooking. She would pay them back for everything they had done for her, someday, some way.

"Come back and see us any time," Priscilla said.

"If you're ever in Arizona, you have to give me a call," Kat said, hugging her.

Tanner Delaney hugged her next. "It was a pleasure."

"Thank you for everything." Then Kat quickly left before she could burst into tears again. She'd cried more in the past few days than she had in her lifetime.

Kat sat in the backseat, and John and Zen sat in the front on the way to the Greyhound station. She had very little to offer to their conversation. It would be nice to be home, and it would be wonderful to see Granny Nanny, but once again, Kat felt like a failure. She had learned some things about Melody and Marcus Arnold, but it didn't feel like enough. She would try to contact Sylvia Hammond from Arizona, but it wasn't the same as meeting her in person, the woman who had been best friends with Mellie Callahan.

They pulled up to the Greyhound station, and all three got out of the car. "Are you sure you have to go? I wish I had the chance to show you more of the city," John said.

He'd said this when she first got in the car, and she gave him the same answer as she had then. "I'd love to see more of the city, but I guess it's for the best if I go home. I have just enough money to cover the bus ticket."

"It's been quite the experience." Zen held out his hand.

Kat just stared at it. After all they had been through together, he was only going to shake her hand?

"I know this sounds off the wall," John said, "but if it's only money you're worried about, my buddy's catering company that Zen's working for tonight is short another person. I know you work in business, but—"

"I'll take it." Just like that, Kat decided, and it didn't take much thought at all. She was not done here, not by a long shot. Instinctively, she knew that. She had too much unfinished business that needed to be taken care of, one way or the other.

"You know, it's not a bad idea," Zen said. "Kat told me she had some experience in the restaurant business." He was smiling broadly, and then he winked at her.

If he said anything about the Tilted Kilt, she would have to kill him.

"Great!" John clapped his hands together. "It's settled then. You can stay at my place for a couple of days in the spare bedroom, and Zen can have the couch." He threw his arm around Zen's shoulders. "You don't mind, do you, buddy?"

"I don't mind at all." Zen was still smiling.

"I really don't think that the service industry is your true calling," Zen said, hours later, after their shift ended. The event had been a private party in the new Modern Wing of the Art Institute, and they'd spent the last four hours passing hors d'oeuvres and glasses of champagne and picking up used paper plates and napkins.

"Nope." Kat unfastened the ridiculous black bow tie they had been forced to wear, again wondering why servers were always coerced into wearing such ridiculous outfits. This catering company insisted on black pants, white tuxedo shirts, and bow ties. "I guess I might as well tell you that I got fired from Tilted Kilt. I was going to quit, but the manager beat me to the punch. How pathetic is that?"

Zen politely chose not to comment on the *pathetic* part. "You only dropped that tray of champagne because the big guy with the mustache wasn't looking where he was going." Zen, too, had ripped off his bow tie and stuffed it in his pocket.

"That's an overly kind excuse for my ineptitude, but I'll take it." The night had grown chilly, and Kat wrapped her thin jacket more tightly around her. "However, how do you explain the second tray of champagne I dropped?"

"You tripped?" Zen offered.

"I'll take that, too." Although she hadn't tripped. She'd been so intent both times on balancing the fragile flutes (so much less sturdy than beer mugs) that she hadn't paid attention to where she was going. The first time she ran into mustache man, he had been very kind about the champagne dripping down the front of his tux. The second time she ran into a woman who was definitely not happy with champagne dripping down the front of her expensive silver gown. Of course, there was a mess of shattered glass on the floor both times that Kat had to clean up, her face flaming.

"They should have used plastic cups," Zen said as they rounded the corner to Wabash Avenue. Overhead, a train rumbled loudly on the El.

"Yeah, right. A glitzy event like that should use red Solo cups for the champagne. Let's face it, Zen. I'm a klutz." She was so cold that her teeth chattered. Was it possible that all those years in Arizona had thinned her blood?

"Okay," Zen agreed, "you're a klutz."

Kat wished he hadn't so readily agreed, even if it did happen to be true. So now, in addition to the times she'd been a bitch and a blubbering crybaby around him, she could pencil in *klutz*. It was a good thing she wasn't interviewing to be his girlfriend. What a staggering resume she had presented him with so far.

"But a gorgeous one," Zen added, taking hold of her arm. "Hey, you're shivering. Let's duck into Miller's Pub and get you warmed up. I could use a few beers myself."

It was past midnight, but the Chicago landmark—decorated with signed celebrity photographs from famous patrons through the years—was crowded. They managed to find two empty stools at the far end of the bar. Zen ordered them each a beer with a whiskey chaser.

Romantic, it was not. Finally, Kat had some time alone with Zen when they weren't trying to solve the riddle of Melody Arnold, and he didn't have Carrie hanging all over him, and they were in a crowded bar where a person had to shout to be heard. The older man sitting next to Kat accidentally elbowed her in the ribs.

"Shit!" Kat said.

"Watch it, buddy," Zen said to the man, who shrugged. "Move over closer to me." Zen pulled her stool so close to his that their thighs touched.

Kat could feel the heat of his skin through his clothes. She was no longer cold. Nope. The heat from his body seemed to spread through hers. It just figured that her body would behave like a Benedict Arnold. He had shown absolutely no romantic interest in her, yet her body responded to even an innocent touch from him. The man who'd elbowed Kat left, but she didn't move her stool away from Zen.

They each had two more beers and two more shots as many of the other patrons started to put on their coats and leave. Instead of dwelling on her own thoughts as she had been doing for days—the puzzle of Melody Arnold, the fact that she still hadn't called Granny Nanny, her period that was late due to stress—Kat stayed focused on the man she sat next to. Intensely aware of his every movement, she had the definite feeling that something was bothering him. For days he had been kind to her, helped her, yet she knew so little about him. She might as well add *self-involved* and *selfish* to her staggeringly unimpressive resume.

Zen seemed in no hurry to leave and go to John's apartment either, so Kat waited until more patrons left, and the din in the room had reached a reasonable volume to ask, "Is something bothering you, Zen?" He seemed to be drinking faster than the other couple of times they'd had drinks together, and embarrassingly, she was having no trouble keeping up with him.

"Maybe," he said.

Maybe the reason she didn't know very much about this man was that he volunteered so little information about himself. However, she wasn't going to ask the question she was dying to ask. She would say that he didn't have to tell her if he didn't want to, that it was none of her business. But then she asked the question anyway. "Did you and Carrie have some kind of disagreement?"

"No, Carrie and I did not have some kind of disagreement, Kat. Carrie and I are friends. That's all. Friends." Zen motioned to the bartender for another round.

Well, now she could add the word *juvenile* to that resume. Why had she asked a nosy question that made her sound like she was in junior high?

She might as well have slipped him a note like they had done in her eighth grade English class, notes sent to boys that followed along the lines of: So and so likes you. Do you like her? "Sorry," she said. "I didn't mean to pry."

Zen ran his hands through his wavy, slightly too long, sandy hair. "I'm sorry. I didn't mean to snap at you."

He thought that was snapping at her? Boy, she could give him a lesson or two about *snapping* at people. "It's okay. If you don't want to talk about it, you don't have to talk about it. We'll just get drunk. It would seem as if it's in my genes." She still hadn't moved away from his thigh, although three empty stools stood next to her now. Unfortunately, Zen didn't seem to notice.

Zen stared at the row of whiskey bottles lined up on the shelf behind the bar. "It would have been her birthday today. She would have been four," he said slowly.

Kat waited. For some reason, she knew he was talking about his former job at CPS. What was it he had said in the car on the way out? He had worked at CPS for a while and then got *burned out?*

"She was a very pretty little girl. I mean, extraordinarily pretty, with curly blonde hair and blue eyes. She was so proud that she could hula hoop."

"That is pretty impressive for a three-year-old." Zen looked at her like she was interrupting, and Kat vowed to herself that she was going to shut the fuck up from here on out. If Zen was finally going to open up to her, she would force herself to be patient. She owed him that—and so much more.

"Her name was Crystal Miller, and she came from a middle-class family. Both parents worked, and everything seemed as it should. Then her father lost his job, then the mother, and then they lost their house. It was like three strikes, and they were out." Zen took a big swig of beer. "I shouldn't be telling you this. It's in the past, right? Why dwell on the past?"

"I think you're talking to the right person here, Zen. What have I been doing for the last few days?" Kat subtly moved even closer.

"It's different, though. You had no control over what your mother did. I did have some control, and I blew it."

Kat patiently waited for him to continue.

Zen shook his head. "I've been trying not to think about this all day. I don't want to think about it, but you drink a couple of beers, and you know."

"I'm sure it wasn't your fault." Kat knew that she had no real idea what she was talking about, and furthermore, she realized she was rather lousy at comforting someone. Should she put her hand on his arm? It's what she wanted to do, so she did.

Zen leaned into her. "It was one of the neighbors in the apartment building that they had moved into after they lost their house who called CPS. She was an older lady, the nosy type, and she was convinced that something fishy was going on. The little girl, Crystal, she said, was left outside alone all day long. There was a funny smell coming from the apartment, and she was convinced that both the parents were on drugs. I was assigned to the case, and on my first visit, I honestly didn't see anything wrong. We dealt with nosy neighbors all the time at CPS, and the Millers' apartment was neat and clean. And then Crystal showed me how she could hula hoop, and then she showed me how well she could color. 'In the lines, and everything!' she told me. Mrs. Miller, of course, was appalled by my visit. 'We've just had a little run of bad luck,' she said. 'We'll be back on our feet in no time. I don't know what Mrs. Grayson is talking about.'

"I took Crystal aside and asked her the usual questions. Things like: What do you eat for breakfast? What time do you go to bed? What games do you like to play? Every answer she gave me seemed to point to a normal childhood. Plus, she seemed like such a happy little girl. And as I said before, the apartment was neat and clean, and God knows I had seen so much worse. I left thinking that Mrs. Grayson was simply a nosy neighbor with too much time on her hands.

"On my follow-up visit, things had changed. I could sense it, but I couldn't put my finger on it. The apartment was still relatively neat, although not as clean as before, and Mrs. Miller couldn't quite look me in the eye, even as she kept assuring me that everything was fine. She had lost weight, and she hadn't washed her hair. Strange things to notice, I know, but it was part of the job. Crystal's hair, too, looked like it needed to be washed and combed. However, you can't remove a child from a home because her hair is tangled and dirty. She showed me how she had gotten even better at hula hooping, still all smiles and seemingly happy.

"And that time Mr. Miller was there, dressed in a suit. He'd just gotten back from a job interview, he said; he was sure he would be hired. And then he said to me, 'Can't you see that we're a happy family? Don't you people at CPS have better things to do than bother people who are trying hard to get their lives back in order? Why don't you go try to help the families who have *real* problems?'

"I left, feeling embarrassed, but also slightly uneasy. I felt that there was something not right about the situation, but as I said, I couldn't put my finger on it. The case was closed, as far as CPS was concerned. There was nothing more I was supposed to do.

"But a couple of weeks later, I did go back. It wasn't an official visit, but I was in the neighborhood—okay, I wasn't in the neighborhood, but I just had a feeling that I should drive by and check things out." Zen stopped and turned on his stool to face Kat. He had tears in his green/gold eyes. "There had been a fire. The Millers' apartment was gutted."

"An accident," Kat said. "Older apartment buildings have faulty wiring." Kat desperately wanted that little blonde-haired girl to be okay.

"It wasn't an accident." The tears were spilling down Zen's cheeks now. "That bastard—Mr. Miller—shot his wife and daughter and set the apartment on fire. Then the chicken shit ran. They still haven't caught him. Why didn't I stop him? Why didn't I save that beautiful little girl? I should have done more."

Kat put her arms around Zen, and he cried. She knew it wouldn't do any good to tell him that it wasn't his fault, which it wasn't, and she also knew a thing or two about feeling guilty over things that were beyond your control. She let him cry in her arms in the now deserted bar and hoped that she was offering him some comfort.

It was the very least she could do.

The next morning Kat woke up on John's couch entwined in Zen's arms. She didn't remember much of the stumble home and certainly didn't remember why she was here on the couch instead of in the spare bedroom. Had Zen kissed her before they passed out on the couch? *That* she wished she could remember. Under normal circumstances, she would have been happy to be in this man's arms, but she could taste her breath. It was vile. These hungover awakenings were becoming a very unsavory pattern in her life lately, and she would have to stop it. She shifted slightly on the couch. Could she gently extract herself, scoot into the bathroom to brush her teeth, and return before he awakened?

No such luck.

"What have we here?" John was dressed in a gray suit and had his briefcase in hand. He didn't look pleased.

And why should he be pleased? He'd been gracious enough to open his home to an old friend and a relative stranger, and now he had two derelicts asleep on his *excellent* Ethan Allen couch. Kat shifted uneasily.

Zen stirred and groaned. "Black coffee," he said, "and a dozen Tylenol."

Kat stiffly righted herself to a sitting position. "I'm sorry, John." She tried to think fast, but it wasn't easy with the throbbing in her head. She and Zen had a couple more drinks after he told her his story, and he'd said that he'd never shared that story with anyone before. Even in her drunkenness, and even now, Kat felt touched. She would keep his confidence. "I had an awful night at work last night, and we stopped for a couple of drinks."

"So I heard," John said. "The catering company doesn't want you back, Kat."

"I would be surprised if they did." What in the hell did she care anyway? It was an overdue, unacknowledged fact. She was a terrible waitress—incompetent, impolite, rude, surly, snide … The list went on and on. She would have to find a new, better job as soon as she got home, or she really might have to sell her eggs to some infertile couple.

Her eggs. Shit. Her no-show period. Shit. What if she was pregnant? And she had been drinking heavily. It was her turn to groan.

"It wasn't her fault," Zen said. "We were in a crowd of well-dressed people with no sense of personal space."

"Right." John looked at first Zen, then Kat. He seemed to come to a decision. "I won't be home until late. I have a date." He turned abruptly and left.

"I think we pissed him off," Kat said.

"He thinks I'm invading his territory," Zen answered.

"I'm not his territory."

"Good."

Now, what did that mean? Before she could ask him—should she ask him?—Zen said, "You can use the bathroom first."

Was he just his usual gentlemanly self, or could he smell her vile breath? "Sure thing." In the bathroom, Kat hurriedly peed and brushed her teeth. She pulled her hair into a neater ponytail, and all the time, her mind raced. Her period still hadn't come, but if she ignored that for the time being, maybe the nagging fear would go away. The more pressing concern was that she had pissed off John. She doubted that he wanted to show her more of the city now, so she didn't have much time left in his apartment. Which meant that she needed to find Sylvia Hammond, fast. On the other hand, Zen had finally opened up to her, and she wanted more time with him.

"Can I take you out to breakfast?" she asked him when she came out of the bathroom. She hoped he wouldn't mind ordering from the value menu at McDonald's.

"Sorry, Kat, but I'm meeting with my adviser at the law school this morning." Zen got up from the couch and stretched.

Even hungover and in rumpled clothes, he looked good. It was a damn shame. "I could meet you for lunch." Kat hoped she didn't sound desperate, but she probably did.

"That might work." He smiled. "Can I give you a call later?"

"Sure." Then to try to salvage a little bit of pride, she added, "We should leave it open-ended. Something might come up in my search for Sylvia Hammond. You never know."

"You never know," he agreed.

After he left the apartment, Kat said aloud, "I have to get a grip. It is romantic suicide to lust after a man who is not remotely interested in you, you stupid bitch." Really, what did she care if he wanted to have lunch with her or not? She had more important things to worry about.

She didn't want to think about those things.

She dialed Granny Nanny's number, praying that she would answer. Kat had so much to tell her, and it seemed like it had been weeks since she'd heard her gran's voice. And now that she was alone in a stranger's apartment in a strange city—something she should probably be getting used to by now—she felt something akin to *abandoned*. It was ridiculous to feel that way; Kat had always prided herself on being strong and independent. She didn't take shit from anyone. Just ask any employer who had been misguided enough to hire her. So she must simply be exhausted from the emotional roller coaster of the past few days. That had to be it.

Just as Kat was about to give up hope, Granny Nanny answered. "Hello, Katrina, dear."

"Gran!" Kat felt faint with relief. "You aren't in jail!"

"Why in the world would I be in prison, dear? I'm not a felon."

"I'm not thinking clearly these days." Boy, was that an understatement. It was more like life had turned her upside down and shaken everything out of her pockets.

"I'm having a hard time hearing you, dear. These casinos have lousy reception."

Casinos? "Where in the hell are you, Gran?"

"Vegas. At Caesar's Palace. It's quite the place, Katrina, quite grand. You should see our room! It turns out that Nathan is a bit of what you call a *whale*."

"Who in the hell is Nathan?" Had Granny Nanny completely lost her mind in Kat's absence?

"Nathan is Mr. Williams, dear. Even old people have first names."

"Let me get this straight. You went to Vegas with Mr. Williams."

"That's right, dear, and he's a bit of a *whale*. He's quite the poker player. We've been up all night long!"

"I thought that you and Mr. Williams were going to sell pot to seniors in assisted living facilities?"

"We haven't given up on that idea, dear. We're working on it."

The crafty old woman moved at the speed of light. Also, she now had an accomplice. Double trouble. "Wow, Gran, you've certainly been busy while I've been gone." Kat was happy that Granny Nanny had found something to occupy her time in her absence, but still. Hadn't the sweet old lady missed her at all?

Even over the phone, Gran could still read her mind. "Of course, I miss you terribly, dear. I'm going to find a bar and order a scotch. Did you know that you could drink all day and all night here? And the drinks are free! Then you can bring me up to date on your adventure."

"Are you drunk, Granny Nanny?" In all the years she had known Granny Nanny, Kat had never seen her drunk.

"Not yet, dear."

Then Kat got it. Vegas. Nathan. Up all night. Granny Nanny was possibly drunk. "Did you and Mr. Williams *elope?*"

"Heavens no, dear! Why would I want to go and get married at my age?"

Finally, the opening Kat had been waiting for. "And what age is that, Gran?"

Even tipsy, Granny Nanny wasn't going to divulge her age. "I found a bar, dear. Fill me in on your adventure."

So Kat brought her up to date. She told Granny Nanny about Mellie Callahan's family, Marcus Walter Arnold, Jr., and the surreal visit to the church. Kat told her about the non-date with John and that she was staying at his apartment in the city, along with Zen.

The crafty old woman. "How are you getting along with that nice young man? I liked him the first moment I laid eyes on him."

"He's been ... more than helpful."

"How much *more*?"

"It's not a romantic relationship," Kat said hurriedly. "He's been helping with research. He's much better at investigating than I am, and he's driven me places. I really liked his family, and he has this ex-girlfriend, and he ..." She needed to stop babbling. "I mean, we're friends, kind of. I mean, maybe we're friends."

"I see," Granny Nanny said.

Damn. The crafty old lady probably did. Quickly, Kat changed the subject. "Oh, and Uncle Willie told me about this woman who was Mellie Callahan's best friend. My next step is to try to find this woman, this Sylvia Hammond."

Gran's gasp was audible over the phone. "What did you say the name was, dear?"

"Sylvia Hammond."

"Dear Lord." Gran gave another gasp.

Kat's heart quickened. What was going on? "Are you okay, Gran? Are you having a heart attack or something? For god's sake, tell the bartender you need an ambulance!"

"Calm down, Katrina, dear. I am not having a heart attack. You took me by surprise, that's all. My, my, the world is such a small place. However, that would certainly explain the phone call."

Kat took deep breaths to try to get her racing heart under control. "Okay, Gran, you're not having a heart attack, thank God, but damn it, you better not be getting senile on me. I have no fucking idea what you're talking about."

"I think your language skills have deteriorated somewhat since you left Arizona," Granny Nanny said.

"Gran!"

"It makes sense to me now," Gran continued. "My, my. I don't think I ever told you this, Katrina, but I had a half-sister, Thelma Tebrow. After my father divorced my mother, he left Arizona. We weren't sure where he went at first, but then somehow, my mother found out that he had moved to Illinois and remarried and had another daughter. This was years later, you understand. Thelma would have been quite a bit younger than I was. I never met her. More years passed, and I heard she had married a man named Hammond, had a son who died in Vietnam, and had a daughter, Sylvia."

Kat was incredulous. "Sylvia Hammond is your *niece*?"

"It would seem so, dear, but of course, there could be more than one Sylvia Hammond, and if she still has the last name Hammond, it would seem that she never married, or she could have married and not changed her name."

"Sylvia Hammond is your *niece*?" That was a cosmic bitch slap to end all cosmic bitch slaps. Could Kat's life story get any more screwed up?

"I never met her either, but it certainly does explain the phone call I got on the morning I found you at the bus station."

"What phone call?" Kat whispered. Her throat had gone dry.

"The caller didn't identify herself. She had a deep voice, though. I do remember that. I remember wondering if the woman smoked. Her voice had that raspy quality that heavy smokers have."

"Gran!"

"I'm getting there, Katrina, dear. The woman with the deep voice said that there would be a sixteen-year-old girl at the bus station, arriving at 2:10 in the afternoon. The girl had run away from home, and she would need a safe place to stay. Then she hung up."

"I don't understand." Kat could not wrap her mind around what her gran was telling her.

"I didn't understand either, but as it so happened, I was going to the bus station anyway because I had promised to take my friend Verna. She was going to Boise to visit her nephew, as you know."

"Gran!"

"I'm getting there, Katrina, dear. And then I saw you. You looked so lost, just sitting

there with a crust of bread in your hands and your battered suitcase at your feet. It took me about thirty seconds to think of you as my own granddaughter, and I forgot about the phone call. The phone call didn't matter. I would have taken you home with me no matter what. The rest, as they say, is history."

"Do you think it was Sylvia Hammond who made the phone call?" Kat's mind was reeling. "But that doesn't make sense. How would she know that I had run away? I'd never even met her!"

"The caller didn't identify herself, dear," Gran reminded. "However, I suppose it could have been Sylvia Hammond. Since she had been Mellie's best friend, your father would have known her. Perhaps he found out which bus you were on, and perhaps he knew that Sylvia had a relative in Arizona?"

Could that be possible? Could her father have actually tried to protect his runaway daughter? Of all the inexplicable things she had found out in the past few days, this possibility won first prize. "That really seems like a long shot," Kat said.

"Life is mysterious," Granny Nanny said knowingly, "and stranger things have happened."

22

AUGUST-SEPTEMBER 1981

It had been an omen. Melody had known that all along, yet she'd chosen to ignore it. For the second time, she had canceled a doctor's appointment to get the pill. Why had she done that? Every woman in the whole damn world between the ages of eighteen and forty was on the pill—except for her. And she was, of course, pregnant. Again. At the age of twenty-three, she was pregnant for the third time, and for the third time, after taking an at-home pregnancy test, she cried.

Naturally, she phoned Sylvia first. "Just call me Fertile Myrtle."

"How about if I just call you stupid?" was Sylvia's reply.

Melody sobbed into the phone. She still clutched the little test tube that had the unmistakable round donut in the bottom, undeniable proof of what she'd already known. Her period was weeks late, and Melody was never late. But she'd tried to convince herself it was because she was under so much *stress*. Was living with Marcus starting to rub off on her? It was a *distressing* thought.

Sylvia relented. "You know you have a choice."

"No, I don't," Melody wailed into the phone.

"Don't pull that Catholic guilt trip shit on me. Get an abortion, and don't tell Marcus. He'll never find out."

For once, Sylvia did not understand where Melody was coming from. *I've already killed two babies* were words she wanted to say but couldn't. What chance did this tiny third embryo have? Melody was convinced that her body had failed her baby boy and would probably fail this baby, too. But if this baby did live, had she already damaged it with her little helpers? She'd seen addicts give birth to addicted babies and wondered how those women could do that to their children. Why hadn't they simply stopped? Her case was not quite the same, though. She was *not* an addict.

"I'll go with you," Sylvia said now. "I'll even make the appointment."

Melody did not want to have another *still born* baby. She could not go through that pain again. In fact, she still relived the pain of losing her baby boy every single, lousy day.

"What's your work schedule for next week?" Sylvia asked.

But what if she was capable of having a healthy child? What if it had been a fluke of nature, as the doctor said. What if it hadn't been her fault? Of course, she would have to stop taking her little helpers, and the thought terrified her. How would she get through each day?

"Wednesday looks good for me," Sylvia said.

And if she had a healthy baby, she would be tied to Marcus forever. Perhaps that was the most terrifying fact of all.

"Melody," Sylvia said impatiently, "are you still there, or am I talking to myself?"

"Wednesday sounds good." Wednesday was six days away. Melody would have time to think about this decision more rationally than she could right this moment. "Marcus is due home any second, and I need to start dinner."

"Barefoot and pregnant," Sylvia said when Melody hung up the phone.

Melody had just finished burying the test tube and pregnancy test box at the bottom of the trash can when Marcus walked into the kitchen. The sight of him made Melody freeze, not because she'd almost been caught doing something behind Marcus' back once again, but because of the look on his face. Always very pale, Marcus looked positively gray. In addition to his briefcase, he had a manila envelope in his hand.

"Are you ill, Marcus?" Melody had never seen her husband look like this. Something must be very wrong.

He seemed to be looking at her but not actually seeing her. As if he was in a trance, he walked through the kitchen and into the living room. He fell heavily into his recliner and covered his face with his hands.

Melody followed him into the living room with a growing sense of dread. "Do you want me to make you a cup of tea, Marcus?" Melody never made Marcus tea, but now that she had followed him into this room, she realized it was a mistake. With sudden clarity, she just *knew* that this had to do with her. What was in the ominous manila envelope?

Marcus groaned. "How could you, Melody?"

Melody. Something was terribly wrong. "I'll go get you that cup of tea." Melody started to back slowly out of the room.

"I shouldn't have done it." Marcus still had his hands over his face. His voice was muffled.

"That tea—" But Melody was rooted to the spot, unable to move.

"I was worried about you. That was all. A young woman going out at night, it's a dangerous situation."

"What did you do?" Melody whispered, her heart pounding painfully in her chest. She already knew.

"I hired a private investigator."

"Oh, God." Melody's chest felt like it would explode. Weeks before, she remembered he had made a rare joke about hiring one, but Melody thought he would never do it, that he had been enamored with one of his favorite TV shows, *Magnum, P.I.* But Marcus had done it. What had Marcus' private investigator found out?

Marcus dropped his hands, and Melody could clearly see his tear-stained face. "I trusted you, Melody."

"How long?" She should be indignant that her husband would do such a thing, but what she felt was a terrifying, paralyzing fear. What did he know?

"Right after we got back from our honeymoon."

So she had been followed for two months. Oh, the things she had done in those months! The trips to the pawnshop, the trips into the city to get supplies. "What's in the envelope?" she whispered.

"Proof." Marcus still held the incriminating envelope in his hand, and now he undid the gold clasp and dumped its contents on the floor.

There were pictures of those trips into the city, but the one that made Melody's knees buckle was of the Runaround. Surely, the investigator had not followed her inside. Surely, he had not been in that rat-infested backroom. She was on her knees, but she did not reach out to touch the poisonous pictures.

"Where are your pearls, Melody?"

Melody could only shake her head.

"You stole Mother's jewelry," Marcus said, and then came the barrage, his anger exploding. "You abuse drugs! You are a liar! You are a whore!"

"No," she said, even though what he said was true. Melody shook her head. "No."

"I married a lying, filthy whore!"

I'm so sorry. But Melody couldn't get the words out. She deserved to be berated with the sorry, ugly truth.

Then abruptly, Marcus was on his feet. "I want a divorce!"

Melody was stunned. Perhaps she shouldn't have been, but she was. For her entire marriage, she had longed for this very thing, but now it only added to her paralyzing fear. The words tumbled out of this fear. "I'm pregnant."

Marcus stopped his tirade. He was breathless. "Is it mine?"

The floodgates opened for the second time that day, and Melody was sobbing uncontrollably, on the floor, on her knees. "Yes, Marcus, it's yours. Of course it's yours."

As it turned out, there were worse things than being smothered by Marcus' love. When that love was cloaked in suspicion, it became even more suffocating.

After he lifted her off the floor that terrible night, Marcus said he wanted to know everything. "I have to know the extent of the problem if I'm going to help you, Mellie."

Just like that, after she blurted out that she was pregnant, she was *Mellie* again.

"It doesn't matter now, Marcus. I'm pregnant. I'm not going to do those things anymore." Just like that, she would have to break the cycle of her habit, and just like that, getting an abortion was no longer an option.

"I am a forgiving man," Marcus said. "Obviously, I am a forgiving man. However, I want to know every single detail. I need to know what to forgive you for, don't I?" He took out every single picture from the wretched manila envelope and asked her to explain what she'd been doing in that place and time.

Melody tried her best to answer the questions. What else did she have to lose? The jig was up; she had been caught. Moreover, she was going to have to pay the steep price. Obviously, she didn't tell Marcus everything. She certainly didn't tell him about Dr. Demented or Clyde, and she didn't tell him the extent of her use or how many different drugs she had taken. Her use of drugs had only been recreational, she told him. Her job was very *stressful*. This, naturally, Marcus could sympathize with.

At the end of that tearful, anxious night, they ascended the stairs to their bedroom. Marcus had his hand on her shoulder. "I'm sorry I called you a whore, baby. I know you would never do anything like that. I let my emotions get the better of me."

So Marcus did not know *everything*.

"Trust must be the basis of our relationship. Don't you agree, kitten?"

Melody was so exhausted that she would have agreed to anything. "Yes, Marcus."

"That's my girl. We'll muddle through this together like we always do."

"Yes, Marcus."

"No more going out alone, flower. From now on, when you work the night shift, I'll drive you to and from work."

"Yes, Marcus."

"We're going to have a baby, honey."

"Yes, Marcus."

In a way, it was a relief to have her double life exposed. For that night, it was a relief.

However, when Melody woke up the next morning, she discovered that Marcus had found her little helpers—all of them—and flushed them down the toilet. She was going to quit, sure she was, for the sake of the baby, but when Melody discovered what he had done, she panicked. "What have you done, Marcus?" She absolutely could not do this cold turkey. She wasn't ready.

"Out of sight, out of mind," Marcus said, almost cheerfully.

Oh, if it were only that easy. Marcus didn't have a clue as to what was about to happen, but Melody did. Already, she felt achy, particularly in her back and legs, and an hour later, she vomited.

"Baby, you have morning sickness!" Marcus seemed to be very pleased about this.

"I guess so." Melody was on her knees in front of the toilet. It was better if Marcus thought her withdrawal symptoms were signs of morning sickness, but how would she explain diarrhea, aches and pains, fever, insomnia, and anxiety over the next five to seven days? Yes, he knew that she had taken some recreational opioids, but he was never going to know the extent of what she had actually done. Melody could not let that happen. She was too ashamed.

She was just going to have to tough it out. "I think I'm going to call in sick," she said to Marcus once she had crawled back in bed, sweating profusely. Marcus had brought her toast and tea. Would he never learn? "I'm a coffee drinker, Marcus. You know that."

"Caffeine is not good for the baby. This is herbal tea."

Oh, yes, the baby. What was this withdrawal going to do to the baby? Once again, her body was betraying her. It was paying off the debt of all those euphoric feelings, all those wonderful, blissful highs. Those wonderful, blissful highs had only been a temporary loan.

"I am going to take such good care of you, flower, you and the baby. The past is behind us." He stood beside the bed, smiling.

Melody wanted him to stop hovering. Her nose started to run uncontrollably. "Please go to work, Marcus. I'll be fine."

When he finally went to work, Melody knew she was not going to be fine. It had only been a couple of hours, but Melody felt like she wanted to die. On top of that, most of all, she had a strong craving to take more heroin. If Marcus hadn't disposed of everything she had, would she have taken more, despite the baby? Melody started to cry. She was so weak, so very, very weak.

When Melody could raise her head from the sweat-drenched pillow, she called Sylvia. "This is so bad, Syl." She told her how Marcus had hired a private investigator and flushed all her helpers down the toilet.

"It just figures he would do something like that," Sylvia said. "Now, he's got you completely under his control."

At that moment, Melody did not give a flying fuck about Marcus' control issues. "All I want is one more syringe. I could do this if I had one more."

"What you need," Sylvia said, "is methadone. I can get you some."

Yes, methadone, a synthetic opioid. That wouldn't hurt the baby, would it? That could get her through. "God bless you, Syl."

When Sylvia dropped off the methadone two hours later, Melody said, "I'm a weak person, Syl. It's a terrible discovery to know that you're weak."

"You're not weak, Mel. Marcus blindsided you." Sylvia, one of the most competent nurses—if not *the* most competent nurse—at Mercy Hospital, looked decidedly uncomfortable at the sight of Melody.

"I'm a fright." Melody had seen withdrawal patients many times in the ER, but she had no idea that it would feel this dreadful.

"Yeah, you look like shit." Sylvia seemed to make up her mind about something. She sat down on the edge of the bed. "I should go through this with you."

"You don't have to. You're not the one who's pregnant." But Melody was touched that Sylvia would be willing to do that. Once again, as always, Sylvia had come through for her.

"Thank God for that." Sylvia picked up Melody's hand and started stroking it. "It's getting to be too much, though. I'm not sure when we did it, but we seemed to have crossed over the line at some point."

"The Runaround," Melody said.

"Yes." Sylvia was silent for a long time, staring out the window. "I'm going to do this with you. I've decided. It's too dangerous."

"It's not fun anymore." Melody's aching, nauseous body was proof of that.

"Right, it's not fun anymore."

"It used to be fun back in our research days."

"I think the research is over, Mel."

"It's not like we became addicts or anything." Melody ached in every joint of her body. Even her nerves seemed to be sore.

"Of course not. We were never addicts," Sylvia said decisively.

Melody knew she'd read it somewhere, and she finally found the passage she was looking for in the box that contained her textbooks in the attic. She hadn't been back up into this barren, lonely attic since the day she had brought Marcus' crib down, the day she had lost her mother-in-law. The memory gave Melody chills. These days, everything gave Melody chills or anxiety. She had been clean for four weeks now. What in the hell was going on?

She found her answer and read: "Post-Acute Withdrawal Syndrome (PAWS) refers to withdrawal symptoms that continue to bother you after the acute initial detoxification of drugs has taken place. Post-Acute Withdrawal Syndrome may last for weeks or months, sometimes even a few years after quitting. Post-Acute Withdrawal Syndrome often includes symptoms such as confusion, sleep problems, anxiety, and depression. How severe and long-lasting the Post-Acute Withdrawal Syndrome symptoms become depend upon how much stress you're under, and how much physical and psychological damage was caused by the drug and addiction."

Then there was this gem: "Post-Acute Withdrawal Syndrome puts people at greater risk of relapse if the person does not receive adequate support."

And then there was the icing on the cake, the medical example: "Ben's post-acute withdrawal syndrome included symptoms of anxiety and sleep problems, which lasted for two years after he quit heroin."

Melody didn't need to read anymore. "This is just terrific, isn't it?" she said to the barren, dusty room. "Ben and I might be in the same boat." Two years! Melody didn't think she could tolerate it for two more years. Why couldn't she be more like Sylvia, who didn't seem to have any more problems after the initial detox? If anything, Melody suspected that Sylvia had taken far more drugs than she had. Perhaps it was because Sylvia did not have Marcus peering over her shoulder or standing outside the bathroom door or waiting in the car for her after work. Marcus was always hovering around, waiting. For what? Did he think that his precious flower would relapse if he relaxed his vigilance for one second?

Probably, and Melody had to admit that it was a distinct possibility. At times her cravings were so intense that she wanted to rush out of the house, jump into the car, and drive into the city. Damn the consequences! She would find Clyde ...

So far, she had not done that. Instead, she did take bubble baths now. Lots and lots of fragrant, steaming bubble baths. She brought in a radio and listened to songs that reminded her of better, happier times and places. The hot water soothed her aching body. In the tub, she could escape Marcus for a good hour. In the tub, she could cry.

What was wrong with her? Why couldn't she just be happy? Weren't normal people happy, at least some of the time? *What in the hell was wrong with her?*

She had suggested to Marcus that perhaps she should go back on Xanax.

"You're perfectly fine, Mellie. Everyone gets a little down now and then. You'll snap out of it. Besides, the baby—"

Yes, the baby. Amazingly, it was the baby that had become the impetus for her to continue, one sober step at a time. She was only eleven weeks along, and she hardly dared to get her hopes up, but maybe this time, if she were very, very careful, the baby would be fine. If she tried her best to be a good wife to Marcus, maybe God would give her a healthy child. Maybe that had been the problem with her first baby? Had her baby boy somehow sensed that he would not be born and brought home to the arms of a loving couple?

Such ridiculous thoughts she was having lately with the double whammy of hormones and PAWS! If only she could get a decent night's sleep. Melody was so tired, but she couldn't get more than an hour or two of sleep at a time. She would wake up suddenly, sweating, heart pounding, and every time, she would have no idea where she was. And inevitably, the craving would start. If she could only shoot up one more time!

Marcus had actually given her an out, and she had refused! "I want a divorce!" he had said.

Why hadn't she said, "I want a divorce, too!"

What had possessed her to say instead, "I'm pregnant."

Melody had gone over and over that scene in her head and come up with an answer: *fear*. If she divorced Marcus, she would no longer have a home, furniture, a car, or a pot to pee in. She didn't have any credit score, and she had no idea how much money was in their joint checking account. Was it even a joint checking account, or was it in Marcus' name only? How much did they pay for mortgage and utilities? Melody didn't even open the mail. She'd allowed Marcus to take care of all these things, and now she was completely in the dark.

Plus, if she divorced Marcus, she would become a huge disappointment to Ma, Daddy, and her brothers. They didn't get divorced in the Callahan family. No, they *stuck it out*. They all thought Marcus was such a jewel. He was a good provider, handsome, and he had taken care of his ailing mother until the day she died. He didn't run around with other women, and he didn't drink. Therefore, if Melody divorced him, it would have to be her fault. Marcus was perfect; Melody was a failure.

So Melody tried. She tried very hard, and it wasn't easy. When a person was sober, she saw everything in black and white—mostly black. There was no graying around the edges, no blurring of right and wrong, and no escape.

"Do you think this is how people live?" she had asked Marcus a couple of nights before, during a commercial, naturally. Melody felt like she could literally climb the walls.

"What do you mean, pumpkin?"

Pumpkin. Another new pet name. "Do you think that people just get up in the morning, eat breakfast, go to work, come home, eat dinner, wash dishes, and then watch television?"

"Why, yes, I do," Marcus said.

Melody tried again. "Don't you ever feel like something is missing?"

"What would that be?" Marcus seemed genuinely puzzled.

"Excitement, Marcus. I'm talking about excitement." Melody wanted to scream out of frustrated boredom.

"Why, kitten, you're all the excitement I need." Marcus' program was back on.

Melody shed a few tears then, but Marcus was too engrossed in his program to notice. She had to face facts. Her husband didn't have a clue, and neither did she.

They were supposed to go to that Sunday dinner at 1113 S. Roosevelt. In fact, Marcus adamantly wanted to go. "I could sure use some of Ma's roast beef." He rubbed his hands together.

Melody wanted to say yet again, "She's not your ma, she's *mine*." Instead, she said, "You always say that her roast beef is too grisly." Melody was trying to figure out what to wear. Her jeans and most of her slacks were too tight around her waist now.

"I think I mentioned once that it was a little fatty. I didn't say *grisly*."

"And you always get upset when Frankie, Mikey, and Willie drink too much."

"They do drink too much," he said.

"I know, but you don't have to mention it every single time."

"I won't mention it today." He had already dressed in brown trousers and a white button-down shirt.

She would have to wear a dress. She was only eleven weeks pregnant, but nothing fit. Was that a good sign?

Marcus looked at his watch. "Uh, baby, we're running late."

"Ma will wait dinner for us if we're late." They were not running late. Dinner was at noon, it was twenty till now, and Ma and Daddy only lived five minutes away.

Marcus began to pace. "I don't want Ma to think we're being disrespectful by being late."

"She won't think we're being disrespectful." The first dress she tried on had horizontal stripes. It made her look liked a striped cow. Why had she ever bought that dress in the first place? It must have been on sale.

"Everybody's going to be there, right? Your whole family?"

"It's Sunday dinner, Marcus. It's mandatory." Well, they'd been mandatory for her until she got married. She used to resent that family ritual, but for the life of her, she couldn't now remember why. She and Marcus rarely went to Ma and Daddy's house for Sunday dinner—or at any time, for that matter. She didn't know the reason for that either. It was another pattern they had fallen into early in their marriage, the *not going*.

"Good," Marcus said. "That's good."

"Why is it good?" Melody asked absentmindedly. She decided to wear her gray dress. However, when she pulled it over her head and smoothed down the skirt, she noticed the big stain. That's right. She'd spilled red wine on it the last time she wore it, the night of their "honeymoon" dinner. She hadn't forgotten to take it to the dry cleaners; she had forgotten to get rid of it. She never wanted to wear this dress again. She took it off and threw it on the bed with the rest of the unsuitable clothing.

"What was wrong with that one?" Marcus looked at his watch again.

"Didn't you see the big stain on the front?" Melody had convinced herself that this was one of Marcus' problems. He couldn't see what was right in front of his eyes.

"No, it looked fine to me."

Melody sighed and took another dress, navy with a white collar, from the closet. She hadn't worn this dress in ages, and she knew why when she put it on. It made her look like Little Orphan Annie. Had she always had such terrible taste in clothes?

"What was wrong with that one?"

Melody stood with her hands on her already thickening hips. She could feel how the flesh was starting to overhang the rubber waistband of the half-slip. And her breasts felt too full for her bra. "You know, Marcus," she said with exaggerated patience, even though Marcus never seemed to notice the exaggeration. "This whole process would go a lot faster if you weren't standing there critiquing and talking."

Instead of leaving, Marcus strode to the closet and picked out a short, skin-tight black tube dress that Melody used to wear out to the clubs during her and Sylvia's days of research. Remembering those days made Melody feel an acute longing, something akin to homesickness. Those days were gone for good.

"Wear this," he said.

"You've got to be kidding. It's too tight and too short. I'm a matron now, remember?" Yes, that's what she was: a twenty-three-year-old fucking *matron*.

"Look, Mellie," a note of pleading crept into Marcus's voice, "could you just put something, anything on so that we can get going?"

"Why are you so anxious to go to Ma's for Sunday dinner?" Maybe she should have been suspicious earlier. Marcus wasn't acting like himself.

"You know I love your family, kitten."

That was utter nonsense, pure bullshit. Melody always suspected that Marcus thought her family was a little too low-class for his taste. "Marcus, what's the real reason?"

Marcus busied himself by pulling out dress after dress from the closet. "I thought I'd make our big announcement today."

She should have known that he had something up his sleeve. "We've discussed this, Marcus. I want to wait until I'm at least twelve weeks along before we tell them." Melody felt like it was a safety net. If they didn't tell people about the baby until way past the first trimester, it was a good omen. They had told her parents way too early the last time.

"But you're close to that now."

"Not yet," she said to Marcus.

"Fine. Not yet." Marcus held out a genuinely awful flowered dress.

Melody knew how this would go. They'd get there, and as they were all eating, Marcus would stand up, tap his spoon on his water glass to get everyone's attention, and then make the grand announcement that they were pregnant once again. It would be a repeat of his performance last Thanksgiving, and it would be unbearable.

"I'm not going," she said, pulling on her pajama bottoms.

"But—" Marcus still held out the genuinely awful flowered dress like some kind of offering.

"Go on. You can go by yourself."

"I'm not going without you, Mellie."

"Fine. Then both of us won't go." It was so like her husband to ruin something she looked forward to. So like him. However, she was not going to give him the satisfaction of making his grand announcement. It was too soon.

Melody called home. "Ma, I'm sorry, but we can't come today. I'm not feeling well." She hated telling this lie to Ma, but it was only a little white lie, a baby fib. She would explain it all a few weeks from now, and Ma would be so thrilled with the baby news that she wouldn't even remember this missed Sunday dinner.

"Oh, Mellie. Well, I am disappointed, but I understand." Melody could hear her turn on the mixer to mash the potatoes. "It's been too long, Mellie. I don't feel like I ever get to see you anymore."

Melody felt a pang of guilt. She had been avoiding Ma. First, the detox, plus the pregnancy, then she'd tried to relearn how to live life without any little helpers. Ma knew her too well. If she'd seen Melody during these weeks, she would know that something was up. "I'll come and visit next week, Ma, I promise." Melody rushed off the phone, not wanting to blurt out an announcement herself.

Marcus and Melody were eating lunch (apples and bologna and cheese sandwiches because she wanted him to suffer) when the phone rang less than an hour later. The phone was nearer to Marcus, but Melody jumped up to answer it, hoping it was Sylvia and that she would relieve some of the monotony of the long day ahead.

The person on the phone was crying, and Melody could hear a lot of static or background noise. "Who is this? Please calm down," she said in her professional nurse's voice. "I can't understand what you're saying."

"Oh, Mellie!"

She could finally make out the voice. It was Willie.

"Why didn't you come?"

"Please calm down, Willie, and tell me what the problem is." Melody suspected that he was drunk, sloppily drunk over that Sabrina girl again.

"It's Ma, Mellie!" Willie sobbed.

Melody's panic blossomed quickly. "Put her on the phone, Willie."

"No, she can't. You don't understand. Ma choked on the roast beef, Mellie. Ma choked again! She swallowed down the wrong tube!"

Dark spots floated across Melody's vision. "Dear God."

"You weren't here to save her, Mellie, like before. You weren't here to do that hymen thing. Why didn't you come to Sunday dinner?"

"Ma …" And then, Melody's world went black.

23

APRIL 2012

Strange things kept happening. After her phone call with Granny Nanny, Kat restlessly paced around John's apartment. She should find the nearest CVS and buy a pregnancy test. She should google Sylvia Hammond, see where she lived, and find her. However, Kat didn't want to do either of those things. If she didn't take a pregnancy test, she could still convince herself that she wasn't pregnant. If she could locate Sylvia, her research would be over, and she would need to go back to Arizona. And that would leave unfinished business with Zen, even if the unfinished business turned out to be one-sided or all in her mind.

Kat vetoed the pregnancy test (*she did not want to know*), which left Sylvia. Uncle Willie had said he was pretty sure that Sylvia still lived in the area. "That tall girl loved this town," he had said, "and her mother is buried here. I don't think Sylvia would leave her mother." However, given that Uncle Willie might not be the most reliable source, Sylvia might have moved to Los Angeles or Moscow or Venice. Kat gave herself a couple of minutes to fantasize about a trip to Venice with Zen, who would naturally insist on going with her. In her fantasy, Zen said, "I want to go to Venice with you, Kat. We're a team, aren't we? I've fallen in love with you. What could be more romantic than a trip to Venice with the woman I love?"

Kat's laughter snapped her out of her daydream. It was such a ridiculous fantasy that she had to laugh. Zen would never say anything like that. Boy, she was truly starting to lose it. She needed to focus. Keep busy. Keep moving. Find out, once and for all, what had provoked Melody Arnold to climb determinedly up that 100-foot light tower and jump.

What came up in the census record that Kat pulled up stunned her. It just couldn't be. She quickly searched the apartment for John's mail and found a small pile on the hallway table. Unbelievable. Sylvia Hammond lived at 600 S. Dearborn. John lived at 600 S. Dearborn. Sylvia Hammond lived in *this very building*.

Kat looked up at the ceiling. "What in the hell is going on here, God? All these freaky coincidences are starting to make me nervous. Maybe Zen was right, and I can't take a joke, but *really*?"

Zen had answered her ad on Craigslist, Zen, whose father happened to be one of the EMTs at the scene of Melody Arnold's death and Kat's birth. Zen's family happened to live not far from where Mellie Callahan grew up. Sylvia Hammond, Mellie's best friend, just happened to be Granny Nanny's half-niece, and she also happened to live in the very same building as one of Zen's college buddies where Melody Arnold's daughter happened to be mooching a stay.

"Okay, God, you have an amazing sense of humor, or else Melody Arnold is trying to tell me something from the grave. Which one is it?"

God didn't give an immediate answer.

But what if Melody Arnold was trying to tell her something from the grave? The thought spooked Kat. She didn't believe in ghosts or the supernatural, not really, but a lot of weird stuff seemed to be going on. Kat paced furiously around the apartment. She needed to get out of this place and clear her head. She needed time to sort through the jumble of thoughts playing cat and mouse in her overloaded brain.

Maybe she was going crazy?

Had Melody Arnold gone crazy and then jumped off the light tower?

Was it possible for a person's brain to just *snap*?

"I've got to get out of here," Kat said as she grabbed her coat and purse. "I'm talking to tampon boxes and God. It's downright unhealthy."

Kat's phone rang while she waited for the elevator. It was Zen. "I'm sorry, but I can't make lunch, Kat. Something came up."

Well, that was a poor, general excuse if she ever heard one. "Fine," she said curtly.

"Really, something has come up. My—"

"I said that it's *fine*, Zen."

"Are you okay? You sound a little odd."

Kat almost said, "I sound odd because I'm going a little crazy, and I might be pregnant." Instead, she said, "Sylvia Hammond lives in John's building."

"Holy shit."

Kat took some satisfaction in the fact that she had finally gotten the saintly Lorenzo Delaney to swear. "Holy shit," she agreed. The elevator came, and she hung up.

Down in the lobby, a tall woman with white/blonde hair was arguing with the bald security guy who sat behind the front desk. It was the same lady Kat had seen on the night of her non-date with John. The resident crazy lady. She had on the same outdated black boots and black trench coat.

"Milton, if the person is on my permanent list, you have to send him up. You're not supposed to be running a prison here."

"I'm not going to send up a person who is clearly high on something. He could be a danger to the other tenants," Milton said stubbornly. It was obvious that he'd said this before.

"Gerard is as harmless as a kitten, Milt baby. You know that." The resident crazy lady started to rummage in her huge purse. "All he wants to do is crash at my place."

"The Transportation Building is not a flophouse," Milton said.

The resident crazy lady found her cigarettes and pulled one out of the crumpled pack. "I've lived here since before you were born, Milt baby. I've seen you guys come and go, and I could get you fired. I've been down this road a time or two."

"Don't you dare light that cigarette. This has been a nonsmoking building for years."

"Damn shame, too. I sure do miss the damn eighties." The resident crazy lady lit a cigarette and deliberately blew smoke in the security guard's face.

"You cut that out, Sylvia!"

Sylvia. Kat stopped in her tracks. She'd planned on tiptoeing past quietly, but now she froze. There weren't that many women named Sylvia hanging around, and Uncle Willie had said that Mellie's friend was tall. He hadn't been exaggerating. With her boots on, this woman was well over six feet tall. And scary. This woman, Sylvia Hammond, was scary as hell. If Kat could only get her feet to move, she would skip the elevator and run up the seven flights of stairs to John's apartment. But she couldn't. Terror glued her feet to the ground, just as it had when she couldn't take that one step out of the plane to skydive. Now, as then, she was petrified to take the leap.

"Damn no-smoking rules! Where's a girl supposed to find an ashtray?" Sylvia furiously smoked as ashes rained on the floor.

"Put that out now, Sylvia." The top of Milton's bald head was red as a tomato.

"Hand me your Coke can," Sylvia said.

Milton didn't seem to know what to do next.

"Hand me the damn Coke can," Sylvia barked.

Milton handed it to her. "Why do you always have to cause so much trouble, Sylvia?"

"I don't like to *play nice*, Milt baby. It bores me." Sylvia dropped the smoldering cigarette into Milton's Coke can.

"Hey! I just opened that can."

"So shoot me."

"You know that the security team here doesn't carry guns."

"Then you're not making this place very secure, are you?" Sylvia slammed her heavy purse on the desk, which made Milton flinch.

Kat, watching, flinched involuntarily.

"So get this straight, Milt baby. The next time Gerard or anyone else on my permanent guest list walks through this door, let him up. I don't give a rat's ass what time of day or night it is. *Let him up.*" Sylvia picked up her purse and turned around.

Kat wished that she could sink through the floor or magically disappear. She would have preferred to be anywhere else but in this small lobby with this imposing woman whom Kat had convinced herself knew all the answers to her questions about Melody Arnold.

"What are you looking at?" Sylvia boomed. Sylvia did not talk in a normal voice. Sylvia barked.

"Nothing. I'm sorry. I was just walking by," Kat stuttered.

"Do I know you? You look familiar." Sylvia stomped closer.

Kat still couldn't move. In the daylight, Kat could see that the woman wasn't as old as she'd thought the first time she saw her. Although her face was lined, she wore makeup, including bright red lipstick. "No," she whispered.

"Oh, right. You're that rude girl from the other night. Tell me, *sweetheart*, do you always stare at strangers?"

Kat could only shake her head. If this woman would just go away, Kat would never bother her again, never ask her the questions she so desperately wanted to have answered.

"Take my advice. Stop it!" Sylvia turned to go, then turned back. "But you do look familiar. I never forget a face. Even though you're a rude girl, tell me your name. It's going to bother the hell out of me for the rest of the day if I can't place your face."

"Kat Flowers," Kat managed to get out.

"Doesn't ring a bell. What the hell." Sylvia turned to go once again.

This was her only chance. Even though the woman was rude and imposing and terrifying, she probably knew more about Melody Arnold than anyone else, and if she left now, Kat didn't know if she would ever find the courage to knock on her door. "Melody Arnold," she whispered.

Sylvia heard and whipped around. "Oh, my God!" she barked.

Here she was, sitting in the apartment of the woman who had been Mellie Callahan's best friend. In the lobby, Sylvia had barked, "Come with me!" After cowering for a second or two, Kat somehow managed to move her feet and follow Sylvia to the elevator, where they rode up silently to the eleventh floor. Once in the apartment, Sylvia barked, "Sit!" And Kat planted herself in the nearest chair while Sylvia busied herself in the galley kitchen. The apartment was neat, a one-bedroom, but the furniture, old and threadbare, looked as if it had been there for a long, long time. Mellie had visited this apartment, possibly sat in this very chair. It had probably looked pretty much the same all those years ago.

Sylvia came out of the kitchen carrying two glasses and thrust one in Kat's hand. "Screwdriver," she said and settled in on the adjoining couch. She stared at Kat before she asked, "So, how do you know about Melody Arnold? I'm pretty sure I know the answer but tell me anyway."

The screwdriver was strong—two-parts vodka and one-part orange juice—and Kat was glad. She hoped it would take the edge off her nervousness. Sylvia didn't look nearly as menacing now that she had taken off her boots and was sitting down, but Kat remained scared of her. God forbid she should ask the wrong question. Sylvia would bite her head off. "I don't know her. That's why I'm here."

"You're her daughter," Sylvia stated and nodded. "I'll be damned. What in the hell took you so long? With all the internet crap, it's not that hard these days."

"My father didn't tell me what my mother's name was until a few days ago."

Sylvia nodded again. "That Marcus. He always was a controlling son of a bitch."

Uncle Willie thought Marcus was a good man. Evidently, Sylvia was not a member of the fan club. "He moved us to Carbondale and changed our last name," Kat said. The strong drink gave her courage. Although still nervous, she could get through this.

Sylvia snorted. "That figures. The son of a bitch."

"I ran away to Arizona when I was sixteen, and Granny Nanny found me in the bus station—"

"That part of the story I know," Sylvia interrupted. "You call her Granny Nanny? Cute. I've never personally met the woman."

"Did you make the phone call on that day? I just found out about that this morning."

Sylvia lit a More cigarette. "I'm not going to ask you if you mind if I smoke because I don't give a rat's ass if you do or you don't. And it's my apartment." She inhaled deeply. "Yes, I made that phone call. After Marcus—and I hadn't heard from the son of a bitch in sixteen years—called and said that he knew you were on a bus to Arizona and remembered that I had an aunt in Arizona and wanted *my help*, after all that time."

"Marcus called you?"

"Yeah, talk about a blast from the past. He sounded frantic."

"Marcus was frantic?" Over her? It was going to take Kat some time to digest that information. All these years, she thought he hadn't cared, but maybe he had, a little.

"Would you quit interrupting me?" Sylvia said.

"Sorry."

"Anyway, I found the phone number in some old papers of Thelma's and made the call. I didn't do it for him; I did it for Mel.

"Thelma and Mel?" Kat needed to slow down on her drink. After waiting for information for so long, she didn't want to miss anything, and Sylvia was piling it on thick.

"My mother and your mother." Sylvia took a deep drag and coughed.

"She wasn't my mother," Kat said.

"You can say that again," Sylvia agreed. Then she seemed to want to change the subject. "So, how is old Marcus now?"

"He's dying of colon cancer."

"We're all dying."

"Are you always this morbid?" Shit, why had she said that? It had just slipped out before Kat could stop it. Had Sylvia put truth serum in the drinks?

But Sylvia laughed. "Well, Kat, when you see the types of things I've seen, you tend to think darker thoughts than most people. When Mel and I were nurses, we saw all kinds of shit, and then later …" Sylvia lit another cigarette from the butt of her first. "I don't suppose you've ever seen a man with his wife's dildo stuck so far up his ass that you needed to take an X-ray to locate it, and when you did, you could see that the damn thing was still vibrating."

"Can't say that I have." One thing was loud and clear to Kat: Sylvia Hammond was not a warm and fuzzy person. Why had Melody Arnold been best friends with this woman?

"I didn't use to be this *morbid*." Sylvia looked pointedly at Kat. "I work with addicts, trying to get them off the streets. I was up all last night, and if I seem a little *morbid*, that's too bad."

Kat blushed, but damn it, she refused to apologize again. Why hadn't Sylvia tried to find her? If her best friend Paula had left a motherless child, would Kat step in and be there for the kid? The answer was … Well, she was going to have to give Sylvia a break on that one. Besides, who would want Sylvia as a substitute aunt? Not her.

Sylvia still stared at her, and it started to make Kat mad. The woman really didn't give a *rat's ass* about being nice, so Kat might as well get to the point. "Why did Melody Arnold, when she was about to give birth, climb up a 100-foot light tower in an abandoned railway yard and jump?"

Sylvia cocked her head. "Do you always cut right to the chase?"

"Having to wait thirty years to find out something, *anything* about your mother is not exactly cutting to the chase."

"The son of a bitch didn't tell you anything?"

"As I said before, I didn't even know her name!" Kat felt dangerously close to crying, and she wasn't sure why. "Was Melody depressed? Was she on drugs? Did she and Marcus have an unhappy marriage?"

Sylvia held her hand up. "Whoa! We're going to need more screwdrivers." When she got back from the kitchen with their glasses refilled, she said, "Mel was a good person and a good nurse. I'm a tough old broad, but even I don't like to think about the light tower. I prefer to remember her as my best friend. We were there for each other through good times and bad." Sylvia sat back down. "We met on the first day of nursing school at Resurrection University. I never had a friend like her before, and I've never had a friend like her since."

"Did Melody love my father?" The second drink was even stronger than the first, and Kat felt grateful because it was happening again. Every time she got close to finding out information about Melody Arnold, her throat tightened, and a growing sense of dread filled her chest.

"Are you married, Kat?"

"No."

"Me either. That's one mistake I didn't make." Sylvia lit another cigarette, even though the room was so full of smoke that it looked like a fog had rolled in. "So, due to our lack of experience, I don't think we're in any position to judge what makes a happy marriage."

Kat was not going to let Sylvia cop out on her. "Did she love him?" she asked again.

"She grew to depend upon him, and he *doted* on her."

"But you didn't like him."

"I couldn't stand the son of a bitch, and he couldn't stand me."

Kat wondered if Mellie had felt like the rope in a tug of war between her husband and best friend. It would have been a difficult position to be in. Then, too, Mellie hadn't been in love with her husband, but her staunchly Catholic family had liked him very much, so divorce would have been a last-ditch option.

"Did she marry him because she was pregnant?"

"You can do the math, can't you?"

Kat had tried to do the math, but it wasn't conclusive because the baby boy had been prematurely stillborn. However, she was going to take Sylvia's response as a *yes*.

"She wasn't thrilled when she got pregnant again, was she?"

"No, not at first."

Kat was surprised at how much Sylvia's answer hurt. She had suspected this, but it was painful to hear it said out loud from someone who had been there.

Sylvia saw the look on Kat's face. "But once she got used to the idea, she did. She thought that you would be the answer to all her problems."

"What were the problems?" Kat leaned forward; she felt dizzy.

Sylvia let out a raspy sigh. "Look, Kat, I've been up all night. I'm exhausted, and trying to exhume the past exhausts me further."

"I've waited thirty years, Sylvia." *Please, God,* Kat thought, *don't let her stop now, not when I'm this close.*

"Some things are better left unsaid," Sylvia said in a surprisingly quiet voice. "I'm not going to tell you everything. Mel and I kept our secrets."

"Just throw me some crumbs, Sylvia." Kat noticed for the first time how tired Sylvia's bloodshot eyes did look.

"Would you like to see a picture of your mother?"

Staring into the eyes of Mellie Callahan was like staring into her own. Uncle Willie had been right. Kat did have her mother's blue eyes, and her hair was a much lighter shade of red. Mellie Callahan looked like the quintessential Irish girl—curly dark red hair, cornflower blue eyes, fair skin, and freckles. She wasn't overtly beautiful, but she was certainly cute. However, that was not what struck Kat the most. "She looks so young." Sylvia said the picture had been taken at a party when they were in their senior year of nursing school.

Sylvia nodded. "We would have been twenty-one, I guess, but Mel always looked younger than her age, probably because she was such a little thing, five-three. We look like Mutt and Jeff, don't we?"

Kat couldn't stop staring at the picture. Not only did Mellie look young, but she looked *hopeful.* Then, not even three years later, she was dead because she had chosen to jump off a 100-foot light tower. Uncle Willie's far-fetched theory that she had been possessed didn't seem so off the chart of possibility now.

"I have fantasized about what she looked like for my entire life," Kat said slowly. "Seeing what she actually looked like is eerie." And disconcerting. This girl was so *young*.

"Not what you expected?" Sylvia coughed as she lit yet another More.

"When I was a little girl, I imagined that she looked like Linda Evans on *Dynasty*. Marcus and I always watched that show."

Sylvia snorted. "Marcus and his damn TV."

Kat finally looked up from the picture. "I just can't get over how young she looks."

"We were deep into our research phase then. We worked hard in school, but in our free time, we liked to cut loose."

"Mellie liked to party?"

"We were college students. What did you do in college? Did you go to college?"

"Yes, I went to college, Sylvia, and I did the usual things. I drank my fair share of beer, naturally." Kat had no intention of sharing the fact that it was after college, in her slightly slutty twenties, when she reached the apex of her so-called wildness, which wasn't that wild, in her opinion.

"Exactly," Sylvia said.

"What do you mean by 'research phase'?"

Sylvia considered the question. She had fixed them each another screwdriver, but Sylvia showed no signs of intoxication. "Did you smoke pot in college?"

"I tried it a couple of times, but it didn't do much for me." Kat, on the other hand, was feeling slightly tipsy, and her nervousness was gone. Funny, but she was starting to like cranky old Sylvia. "Are you trying to tell me that Mellie was a pothead? Not that I care, by the way. Personally, I feel like marijuana should be legally bought and sold. Granny Nanny likes the occasional joint."

"What about prescription drugs—Oxy, Vicodin, Percocet, Valium, Xanax? Did you try any of those?" Sylvia looked at her intently.

"Hell, no. And for the record, I didn't sniff glue or drop acid either. Jesus, Sylvia, why are you so nosy?" The woman worked with drug addicts. Maybe she asked these questions out of habit? Cranky old Sylvia, with her ruthless stare, was starting to make Kat feel uneasy again.

"Do you know anything about drug addiction, Kat?"

"Listen, Sylvia, I'm not one of your patients or clients or whatever you call the derelicts you pick up on the streets. I've seen movies about addicts, and *that's it*. I might be drinking a little too much lately—why do you keep plying me with screwdrivers?—but I have no interest in drugs. Why would a person want to go and mess up her life with drugs? My life is enough of a mess as it is. Right before I got out here, I got fired from Tilted Kilt. Can you believe that shit?" She had to face it; she was pretty drunk by now. Damn. She should ask Sylvia if she could have the picture and then leave. She might never know why her mother jumped from that light tower, but at least she knew what the suicidal bitch looked like.

"So, you get another job." Sylvia shrugged.

"So, you get another job," Kat mimicked.

"You're a hothead, aren't you?" Sylvia seemed unperturbed by Kat's outburst. "Mel would have liked you."

That statement utterly deflated Kat. She sagged into the chair, drunk and exhausted. "What is it you're not telling me?"

"What I'm *trying* to tell you," Sylvia corrected. "You keep derailing the train of conversation."

"Sorry," Kat muttered.

"No, you're not, and I don't give a rat's ass about you being *sorry*. What I'm *trying* to tell you is that people make mistakes, and people make poor choices. Some choices are much worse than others, and the consequences are more severe."

"I can vouch for that," Kat said.

Sylvia sighed. "Look, Kat, I'm tired. I'm going to get some sleep, but I'd like you to come with me tonight when I make my rounds."

"I think I'll take a pass on rounding up the derelicts."

"No, you're not going to do that, and I'll tell you why. Your mother was one of those derelicts, Kat. Your mother, Melody Callahan Arnold, was an addict, which is one of the reasons why she jumped off that light tower."

24

DECEMBER 1981 - MARCH 1982

Melody thought about guilt in two ways. It could pile up on you until you felt like you were drowning in mud, or it could suck you down into its quicksand maws. Either way, you couldn't breathe, couldn't move, and you were trapped. Either way, the pressure built in your chest, your lungs, your heart. Either way, you had the overpowering urge to close your eyes, let it overpower you, and suck you in. And then you could give in. Surrender. Stop. Concede defeat.

If only she had gone to Sunday dinner, she could have saved Ma.
If only she had not fought with Marcus, she could have saved Ma.
If only she had found something to wear, she could have saved Ma.
There were too many *if onlys*, and Ma was dead.

Of course, the consuming emotion she felt might have been *grief*. It shared many of the same qualities as guilt. Perhaps they were cousins? Perhaps they were twins, Siamese twins, joined at the hip? You couldn't have one without the other. They were a package deal.

"You're going to have a strong urge to use again," Sylvia said. "Look what happened to me after Thelma. To say that I was a shipwreck is putting it mildly."

"You're wrong, Sylvia. I don't have a strong urge to use again. I have an overwhelming urge to use again."

"You're right," Sylvia agreed. "Every day is a struggle."

"Every day is an epic battle." Melody still suffered from PAWS, and her symptoms hadn't gotten any better. She wasn't sleeping well, and she felt anxious all the time. "If I wasn't pregnant—"

"But you are," Sylvia said firmly. "We've seen babies born to addicts." She and Melody didn't directly call themselves addicts. They had a silent understanding that it could be acknowledged but not vocalized.

"That might be the only thing that's stopping me."

"That, and the fact that you've already fallen in love with this baby."

"Yes." It was true. The baby had started to kick a few weeks after Ma died, and he or she hadn't stopped since. Each thump was a reminder to Melody, the baby seeming to say, "I'm here! Don't forget about me!"

"One day at a time."

"One foot in front of the other." Melody took a deep, shaky breath. "I don't know what I'd do without these pep talks from you, Syl. You've helped me get through the hell of the past three months."

"Ditto," Sylvia said. "Are you ready to go in now?"

They stood in the front yard of her parents' house. Marcus had gone in before with the two hampers of food that Melody had prepared, but she needed a little more time before she went in. "Do you suppose Daddy and the boys are going to plant Ma's flowers in the spring?" Melody pointed at the window boxes on the front porch.

"Hell, no, but we can do it. I don't know a damn thing about planting flowers, but you tell me what to do, and I'll do it."

"This is going to be awful." Melody felt a clenching in her stomach, then the baby kicked, making his or her presence known. At her sixteen-week ultrasound, the technician had asked if she wanted to know the sex of the baby. Melody decided that she didn't want to know. She couldn't explain why she didn't want to know. She just didn't.

Melody hadn't been inside the house since the day of the funeral. On Thanksgiving, she had asked—no, she had begged—for a shift at the hospital. She wasn't ready to face a holiday without her ma, not yet. And now it was Christmas, and she still didn't feel like she was ready. When she went in, and when Ma was not in the kitchen in her reindeer apron, her face flushed from the heat of the stove, when Melody didn't smell the ham and the pies, it was going to be real. Again. Sometimes Melody could pretend that it hadn't happened, that it had all been a terrible mistake. If she worked long enough hours, she could occasionally get her mind to shut off. Sometimes.

"I don't mean to rush you, Mel, but it's cold out here. I'm freezing my ass off, and I really would hate to lose it. It's one of my best *assets*." Sylvia stomped out the third cigarette she had smoked while standing in the yard.

"It smells like snow."

"The longer we wait, the drunker they're going to be," Sylvia pointed out.

That was very true. Melody took a deep breath. "Okay, I'm ready." She wasn't ready, but she had no choice. Daddy and her brothers knew she was standing in the yard.

Willie chose that moment to open the door. "Mellie, we're getting hungry in here!"

"I wonder what they're eating now that Ma isn't around to wait on them?" Melody muttered under her breath.

She soon found out. TV dinners, lots of TV dinners.

"And chicken potpies," Frankie said glumly.

It was as Sylvia and Melody had predicted; all the Callahan men were drunk, depressingly drunk. Melody couldn't blame them. If she weren't pregnant, she would join right in. She'd brought a Christmas tablecloth covered in smiling Santas, but it didn't do one iota to lighten the gloom. Without Ma around, no Christmas tree stood in the front window, and no garland circled the stocking-less mantel. Even though they were all ostensibly grownups, Ma had still insisted on putting up the red felt stockings with all of her children's names written in glitter. And Christmas carols didn't blast from the stereo. Without Ma around, the place looked and smelled differently. It was dirty, with no underlying scent of pine-scented Lysol.

Without Ma around, the home had no heart.

Melody would never be as good of a mother as her ma. She realized that suddenly, and the tears she'd been holding back all day threatened to spill down her cheeks.

Marcus, of course, was not drunk. Instead, he seemed to be in a jolly mood, as he was most of the time these days. Melody tried so hard not to resent him for this. She tried not to resent him for the fact that he now knew where she was every second of the day and night. Marcus was a very happy man. "I brought the ultrasound picture of the baby," he said now when the Christmas non-revelers fell into another gloomy silence. "Would you look at that?" He placed the photo on the table, inordinately proud.

Sylvia, who was trying valiantly to catch up with the Callahan men in the drinking department, rolled her eyes. If possible, the relationship between her and Marcus had grown even more strained in the last few weeks. One night, as Marcus pulled up to collect Melody from work, Sylvia had hissed, "I don't know if he thinks he's your fucking chaperone, or if he's stalking you. Jesus, Mel."

Marcus had told Daddy and her brothers that she was pregnant at Ma's funeral. At Ma's *funeral*. Still, Melody didn't say anything. No, she tried very hard to be who she was supposed to be. She tried very hard to *keep it all together*.

Willie picked up the photo. "I don't see anything." He passed it on to Frankie and Mikey. "Do you see a baby in this picture?"

"Nope," Frankie said.

"It looks like a cave," Mikey said.

"Dad, do you see anything?" Mikey passed the photo on to Frank, Sr.

Poor Daddy. Melody could cry just looking at him. He'd spent most of the meal quietly sipping his beer and staring into space. Before they sat down at the table, Willie had pulled Melody aside and whispered, "He's a lost soul without her, Mellie. It about breaks my heart in two."

Melody knew all about lost souls and hearts breaking in two. "He'll get better in time," she said to Willie, not believing it for a second.

"What am I looking at?" Daddy's voice slurred. He dropped the photo on the table.

"An imaginary baby," Frankie said.

"You moron." Sylvia snatched up the picture. "The baby isn't imaginary." She glanced at Melody to see how she had taken the remark and saw that she had placed her hands protectively over her stomach. "Your sister is six months pregnant. Can't you see that? This was taken at sixteen weeks, so obviously, the baby was a tad smaller then. The peanut shape is the baby." Sylvia traced the image with the tip of her long red nail.

Marcus placed his hands over Melody's. "We've got quite the kicker here."

"I like babies," Willie said. "They smell good."

After that, the silence descended again until Mikey broke it. "I miss Ma."

That woke up Daddy. "Damn it!" He pushed himself up from the chair. "Your mother should be here with us! Where is that woman? That's what I want to know." Sweat bathed his face, and he swayed unsteadily.

His family stared at him with wide eyes. Had Daddy lost it, or was he just roaring drunk? Melody prayed that he wouldn't have a heart attack.

"Where is that woman?" Daddy roared. He looked at everyone accusingly.

"Uh, Dad," Frank said, "Ma passed. You know that."

"Passed *what?*" Daddy shouted.

Frank looked miserable as he said, "Passed *away*, Dad."

"No, damn it, *no!*"

Sylvia was beside him. "Mr. Callahan, why don't you sit down? Melody, why don't you go get your daddy a glass of water and a cool compress?"

Melody couldn't move. Her father's eyes had settled on her, and they were pinning her to her seat. She knew what he was going to say before he said it.

"You," Daddy pointed his calloused finger. "You were supposed to be at that Sunday dinner. Damn it, why didn't you come to that Sunday dinner?"

"Daddy, I—"

"You saved her before, and you could have saved her again. Why didn't you come, Mellie?"

"We couldn't remember how to do that hymen thing," Mikey said. Frankie and Willie echoed: "We couldn't remember."

The tears flooded down Melody's cheeks. "I should have come, Daddy. I'm so sorry." The weight in her chest pressed down so hard that she could hardly breathe.

Daddy sank into his chair and buried his face in his hands. The wracking sobs shook his entire body. "Claudia," he sobbed. "Mellie."

Her brothers were crying, too, and even though they didn't look directly at her, Melody could feel their accusation. They all blamed her for Ma's death, and why shouldn't they? It was her fault, all her fault. She was a trained professional, and she hadn't done her job. She was a member of this family, and she hadn't shown up. She hadn't been in the right place at the right time. She hadn't been where she was *supposed* to have been.

"I'm the reason she didn't come," Marcus said. "I had to ... I ... uh ..."

Marcus was a terrible liar, and his attempt was totally futile. Her daddy and brothers knew whose fault it was. Hers.

"It was an accident." Sylvia patted Daddy's back and looked at Melody. Her eyes said it all: *This is what you should be doing, comforting your father.*

But Melody couldn't. "I'm so sorry, Daddy," she cried and ran from the house, somehow knowing that she would never return.

Marcus did not understand why Melody couldn't stop crying. Marcus did not understand anything about her. "The baby is fine. *Thriving* is what Dr. Crowley said at our last appointment," Marcus said. Marcus had gone to every single doctor's appointment with her. Of course. "Nothing is going to go wrong this time, kitten. We've got everything under control."

Did he honestly think that? Couldn't he see that she was positively *not under control*? She still had trouble sleeping, and when she did, on occasion, manage to fall into a troubled sleep, she had nightmares, vivid nightmares about her baby boy, and Ma calling out to her for help, and in each dream, she wasn't able to reach them. She wasn't able to move. Her legs would be like concrete pillars, and her vision was cloudy. She could hear them, but she couldn't force herself to move, couldn't open her eyes. She could not help them and could not save them.

She had dreams about this baby, too. In one dream, it was a baby girl, a pretty baby with golden-red hair, and Melody was happy, so happy. She had done it this time! She took the baby to Mercy to show her off. "Look at my beautiful baby girl," she said to all the nurses, and it took her a while to notice they all looked at her strangely. "What's wrong?" she would ask as the panic started to build, but they all turned away. When she finally looked down at the pink-clad bundle in her arms, she screamed. She wasn't holding a healthy baby girl. No, she was holding a paper doll that stared up at her with lifeless blue eyes.

She would wake up screaming from that one, and Marcus would inevitably say, "It's just the hormones, kitten. Our baby is fine. He or she is *thriving*."

However, the dreams that really made Melody think she was losing her mind were when she dreamed she was using again. She could see the track marks on her arms as the needle went into a vein. She could feel the euphoria, feel the blissful high as her arms and legs grew heavy. Then, she would come down off the high in the dream and not know where she was. Sometimes, she was in a rat-infested apartment with dirty mattresses on the floor. Sometimes, she would be in her bathroom, and sometimes, she would be on the cold ground under the light tower where she and Sylvia had bought drugs for the first time. Then, in all the dreams, she would remember she was pregnant. She had used while she was pregnant. *She had killed her baby.*

And again, she would wake up screaming. And again, Marcus would say, "It's just the hormones, kitten. Our baby is fine. He or she is *thriving*."

He didn't have a clue that she would wake up craving the drug. At those moments, her body *ached* for the drug. In those moments, when she was not fully awake and in the grips of terror, she would sell her soul to the devil for one more high. It was a devastating thought, and it was true.

Small wonder that she cried all the time.

"I think I need to see a therapist," she finally broke down and said to Marcus when they did the dishes one evening. "I have these horrible nightmares, and I'm anxious all the time. If I could talk to a professional, I might feel better."

"Oh, my little flower," Marcus said indulgently, putting his arms around her. "It's just the hormones. You're fine. I'm sure it's normal to be anxious after what we went through last time." Marcus let the water drain from the sink and picked up his canister of Comet. "Besides, why would you need a therapist when you have me to talk to?" He sprinkled Round One of Comet into the sink. "And you know that I think that psycho-babble is a bunch of nonsense."

"It's not nonsense, Marcus. It's a respected medical field."

Marcus finished Comet Round One and began Comet Round Two. "You have me," he said firmly.

Maybe he had a point. Maybe it was the hormones acting on top of the PAWS symptoms, and maybe after the baby was born, everything would be all right, and she would feel better. She would have a child to care for, someone who needed her. She would feel normal. She would be *cured*. Was that even possible? Melody honestly didn't know anymore.

Marcus had the bright idea that a little retail therapy would be just what the doctor ordered. In a way, it was sweet of him to try to cheer her up, but in another way, it was typical Marcus. "Why don't you go into the city and buy something pretty?" he said, handing her some folded bills.

"I'm eight months pregnant, Marcus. I'm not really in the mood to try on clothes." She had gained thirty-five pounds with this baby, and on a five-foot, three-inch woman, it looked huge. She waddled when she walked, her ankles were swollen, and she had hemorrhoids. She had all the classic symptoms of pregnancy, in addition to her non-classic symptoms of withdrawal. Now, on some nights, she didn't fall asleep at all.

"How about a hat?" he said, smiling.

She had to smile back. "A scarf might still fit."

"You know that you look beautiful to me."

"You can say that a hundred more times, and I'm still not going to believe it." At this late stage of her pregnancy, Melody appreciated the compliments, but it did help support her theory that Marcus didn't really *see* her.

"You'll be home to start dinner?"

Typical Marcus. He was magnanimously giving her money and a little freedom—and then setting limits. "Sure, unless someone's looking to pick up an eight-months-pregnant baby whale." She might as well go, even though she wasn't in the mood to shop. It would be good to get out of the house on this dreary February day. "On second thought, I think I will go." She got her black wool coat out of the hall closet and put it on. It was useless to try to button it over the mound of her belly.

"See you at five," Marcus said as she went out the door.

She wandered aimlessly around Marshall Field's, but nothing caught her eye. She hadn't even bothered to look at the folded bills Marcus had given her. It couldn't be more than twenty or thirty dollars, the usual amount he allowed her. Besides, shopping was no fun without Sylvia, and Melody wondered if she was at her apartment. She hadn't seen much of Sylvia since that awful Christmas dinner, and Melody had a sickening feeling in the pit of her stomach. Sylvia might be disgusted with her for not comforting her father and not standing up for herself in front of her family. It had been Sylvia's constant mantra for years: "You need to stand up for yourself, Mel. Most of the people in this world like nothing better than doormats, and we are not doormats." Stand up to Marcus. Stand up to the doctors at work who didn't act like they respected nurses. Stand up to this and that and this and that. Sylvia had an endless list of people who should be *stood up to*.

Sylvia had denied that she was mad at Melody ("We've never even had a minor tiff, Mel"), although she couldn't help but add that she thought Melody should have told her father and brothers that it was *not her fault* that Claudia choked on a piece of grisly roast beef. "I have a new man in my life, Mel," Sylvia said then. "His name is Ted, and we get along together fabulously. Believe it or not—and I can hardly believe it myself—but I think I might be falling in love."

"That's great, Syl." Melody tried to suppress the flare of jealousy that immediately went off after this bit of news. The jealousy was twofold. First, she knew that Sylvia wouldn't have as much time to spend with her, and second, she envied the feeling that she had never experienced. What did it feel like to *fall in love*?

Melody saw Sylvia a couple of times since that exchange, and both times, Sylvia talked about Ted, Ted, Ted. Ted was a successful stockbroker on LaSalle Street. Ted came from a well-respected family on the North Shore. Ted took her out for expensive dinners. Ted was incredible in bed. Ted, Ted, Ted.

Melody missed her terribly, and she suddenly, desperately needed a dose of her best friend. Maybe Sylvia was home? Since Melody hadn't talked to her in a while, she didn't know what Sylvia's work schedule was this week, but there was a possibility that she was home. Melody clung to that possibility. After all the weeks of crying, she needed Sylvia to make her feel better, to make her feel *alive* and not like she was performing an anxious sleepwalk (if only she could sleep!) through her boring life with Marcus. Sylvia had to be home.

Melody called from a payphone outside the women's restroom. The phone rang hollowly until the sixth ring when Sylvia finally picked up. "Hello?" Her voice sounded groggy.

"Oh, Syl, did I wake you?" Melody nervously twisted the metal cord. Why would she suddenly be nervous talking to her best friend? It made no sense.

"No, Mel."

"Can I come over? I'm at Marshall Field's, so I could be at your place in ten minutes."

"There was a long pause before Sylvia said, "Now is not a good time, Mel."

"I'll only stay for a few minutes." The cord was so tight around Melody's fingers that they were turning red.

Another long pause. "It's not a good time, Mel."

"Are you sick?" Sylvia's voice sounded odd, but then Melody had another thought. "Is Ted there? It's okay if he is. I'd like to meet him." She didn't particularly want to meet this dashing mystery man—she knew it would be difficult to hide her jealousy—but she needed to see her best friend. For the past two months, Melody felt as if she'd been hanging onto her life and sanity by a mere thread. She needed Sylvia to make her feel better, to reassure her that she was not losing her mind.

To that, Sylvia didn't reply.

"Please, Syl. It's been too long since I've seen you. I miss you. I need you. Please." Melody didn't care that she was begging her best friend to see her. Sylvia was probably disgusted with her, the ultimate doormat, and Melody didn't blame her. But she couldn't go on without Sylvia. It was unthinkable, and Melody had to remedy this situation. She would buy Sylvia a quick gift, a scarf, as a peace offering, and she would apologize for not being stronger, for not being as strong as Sylvia.

"Mel—"

"I'll be there in ten minutes." Melody hung up the phone. She had made up her mind. Sylvia had to see her, and that's all there was to it. She'd already lost so much, and she wasn't going to lose her best friend.

Ten minutes later, she knocked on Sylvia's door. The doorman knew her, and she was on Sylvia's permanent guest list, so there was no need for him to buzz Sylvia on the intercom. "I'm here, Syl," Melody said as she knocked and knocked. "I'm here." In her hurry to get to the apartment, she'd forgotten to buy Sylvia a scarf.

Sylvia finally opened the door and stood before Mel in a stained bathrobe, her platinum hair snarled around her face, the dark circles under her bloodshot eyes almost black against her pale skin. "Ta-da," Sylvia said, not smiling.

"Oh, no." Melody's heart felt like it plummeted to her feet. From the way Sylvia looked, Melody had no doubt as to what she'd been doing.

"Oh, yes," Sylvia said.

"Why? Did you break up with Ted? You should have called me. I would've helped you through it, just like we help each other through everything."

"There is no Ted."

"No Ted?" Melody followed Sylvia into the living room where the evidence was indisputable; it was magnetic.

"No Ted." Sylvia flopped on the couch and reached for a glass.

That confused Melody. It wasn't like Sylvia to make up a boyfriend. She wasn't the type to have a perfect imaginary man that she could brag about to all the other nurses.

"There was a man who said his name was Ted and who said he was a stockbroker and who said a mountain of shit. But his name, as it turned out, wasn't Ted. His name was Maury."

"Why would someone lie about all that?" Melody asked as she eyed the syringe. Then she knew. "He was a junkie."

"Bingo," Sylvia said.

"And he's a friend of Clyde's."

"You have hit the jackpot, my friend." Sylvia poured vodka into her glass with shaking hands.

"Clyde set you up." The world of an addict was a treacherous place. Although Melody hadn't been part of that world for an extended length of time, she knew enough. Clyde probably still held a grudge against Sylvia, and Maury probably owed Clyde money, and in Clyde's devious dealer mind, he probably thought he had the perfect solution.

"I don't do things half-assed," Sylvia said bitterly. "I didn't just fall off the wagon. I *jumped*."

Melody still could not take her eyes off the needle. She could remember the high so vividly. She remembered the euphoria, and best of all, she remembered that when she was high, she didn't think about all the crap in her life. It just melted away.

She forced herself to tear her eyes away from the laden coffee table (the syringe, the white powder, the candle) and look at Sylvia. "I still wish you would have told me. I would have done anything I could to help."

"No, I don't do things half-assed," Sylvia continued. "No, sir. A man who calls himself Ted tells me he loves me. He's mad about me, he tells me. And oh, by the way, incidentally, he occasionally does the recreational drug here and there. No big deal, right? No big deal, I tell him. I used to dabble myself." Sylvia lit a cigarette, even though another one was still smoldering in the ashtray. "I thought I loved him, Mel."

"Sylvia, don't beat yourself up."

"I'm an excellent judge of human nature. Have you noticed, Mel? An excellent judge." Then Sylvia broke down in sobs. "I am so ashamed, Mellie, so ashamed. That's why I couldn't tell you."

Melody put her arm around Sylvia's broad shoulders. "People make mistakes," she said, knowing it sounded lame and hollow, even if it was the painful, honest truth.

"I'm an idiot," Sylvia sobbed. "I saw what drugs did to poor Thelma, and I'm a nurse. I should fucking know better!"

"How long have you been using?" Melody asked when Sylvia's sobs finally quieted.

"Six weeks."

"When did you find out what this Ted—Maury—was up to?"

"Two weeks ago."

Melody nodded; she understood.

"Yeah." Sylvia had calmed down enough to reach for her glass. "I'm back."

"Does it feel the same?" The baby kicked, but it didn't tamp down Melody's growing craving. If she got high one more time, everything would be okay. She would be able to cope. She would be a better, happier person. She was far enough along in her pregnancy that it couldn't hurt the baby. Just one more time, that's all she needed.

"Don't go there, Mel."

"How did it feel?" Melody persisted.

"It feels the same. You feel terrific, and then you feel like shit. You feel terrific, and then you feel like shit. Same old Merry-Go-Round."

Melody couldn't help herself. She could not. She fingered the syringe.

"You're pregnant, Mel."

"Just one more time. That's all I need. It won't hurt the baby."

"Please don't do this, honey. It's tempting, I know. Look at me. I failed the test, but you don't have to." Sylvia, too, stared at the drug paraphernalia. "You know how hard it is to quit once you get started. You know how hard it is."

"One time won't hurt anything. One more time before I become a mother." Melody's heart thumped in her chest with excitement. She knew she could handle this. She had been waiting for this.

"I don't have enough for both of us, Mel, and as you know, this is an expensive habit. I'm short on cash until next payday."

Melody's disappointment was acute before she remembered. "Marcus gave me some money to go shopping. It's probably not much, though." She dug through her purse and pulled out the folded bills.

"Holy shit," Sylvia said as she watched Melody count the bills.

"Two hundred." Melody's face was flushed. "Marcus gave me *two hundred dollars*. It must be a sign, Syl." They stared at each other.

"Make the phone call," Melody said.

Once was not enough. That was the damnedest thing of all. Once was never enough.

Once was too much.

For two weeks, Melody went to Sylvia's apartment as often as Marcus let her out of his sight. She didn't dare bring anything into the house, and once again, she was living a double life built on lies. It was all so very wrong, yet Melody couldn't stop herself. *Tomorrow, I will quit*, she told herself. *I do not have enough drugs in my system to hurt the baby*, she told herself, even though the baby wasn't kicking as much as before.

"That's natural," Dr. Crowley said at her last checkup. "The baby is running out of room."

"That's funny," Melody said. "The baby's running out of room, and I'm running out of time."

Dr. Crowley laughed. "The baby will be here soon enough. Be patient, Melody."

That wasn't what she'd meant.

And then Sylvia got arrested. She wasn't buying drugs on the street or anything sordid like that, she told Melody after Clyde—of all people—bailed her out. ("I couldn't call you, Mel. I didn't want to get you in trouble," Sylvia explained.) No, the cops had come to her apartment out of the blue. Someone had tipped them off.

"It might have been your doorman," Melody said. The doorman at the Transportation Building seemed like the suspicious type.

"It might have been Marcus," Sylvia replied.

Had it been Marcus? Oh, dear God, did Marcus suspect something? The paranoia was paralyzing, and the withdrawal was agonizing. Melody couldn't keep any food down, and her baby wasn't getting any nutrients.

It was funny. She was more frightened of the withdrawal hurting the baby than she'd been about the heroin hurting the baby.

"I'm taking you to the doctor," Marcus said.

Melody could smell his concern. In fact, all her senses were heightened these days, and she couldn't sleep at all. "It's just the flu, Marcus. Everything will be all right."

She did not believe that everything was going to be all right. Something was dreadfully wrong. Her body, once again, was betraying her. No, that wasn't quite right. She had betrayed her body. She had betrayed her baby.

It was better not to say anything to anyone.

Marcus would not leave her bedside. "Really, Marcus, everything will be all right," Melody said wearily.

"Okay, flower, if you say so."

Poor unsuspecting Marcus—he didn't have a clue. Or did he? Had he tipped off the police about Sylvia? Did Marcus now know *everything*?

Oh, God.

The baby was not kicking as much as he or she had before.

She had used heroin seven times while she was pregnant.

Oh, dear God.

25

APRIL 2012

Kat could only stare at Sylvia. A couple of days before, she and Zen had suggested drugs as a possible motive for Melody Arnold's leap off the light tower, but they had quickly dismissed it as too far-fetched to be a possibility. Yet now her best friend, thirty years after the fact, was telling Melody's daughter that her mother had been a drug *addict*.

"Are you fucking kidding me?" Kat said.

"Would I fucking *kid* about a thing like that?"

"How … why?" Kat wished, too late, that she had not had so much to drink. The orange juice soured in her stomach. "She was a nurse!"

"And a damn good one, too," Sylvia agreed.

Kat looked down at the picture she still held in her hand. The red-headed, freckled, smiling young woman looked wholesome and innocent. To Kat, she looked like someone who was the exact opposite of what a drug addict would look like—not that she had ever met any drug addicts. "She's too all-American to be a drug addict," Kat said as if that settled things.

Sylvia snorted. "We come in all sizes and shapes and from all ethnic and economic backgrounds."

"We?" What was Sylvia trying to say? Kat wished she had declined the two or three strong screwdrivers.

"Yes. *We*." Sylvia opened a new pack of Mores. "At the time, we didn't call ourselves addicts, but we were."

"What were you addicted to?" Kat looked at the picture again. This woman, this Mellie, looked like she wouldn't take anything stronger than an aspirin.

"Opioids were our drugs of choice. Then, eventually, heroin."

Kat looked at Sylvia, her eyes wide. *"Heroin?"* She stared at the picture of Mellie. It was unbelievable. "You guys didn't mess around, did you?"

Sylvia snorted again. "I guess you could say that." She finished her drink and yawned. "I have to get some sleep, Kat. We'll go check on my *derelicts* later tonight." She stood up and stretched like it was the most natural thing in the world to tell the daughter of your former best friend that her mother had been addicted to heroin.

"Wait a minute, Sylvia, please." Kat didn't know what question to ask first. Had Melody Arnold used heroin when she was pregnant? Had she been high when she jumped? How had she gotten out of the hospital? Why did she think her baby was dead? She settled on this: "Did Marcus know?"

"He found out about it the first time when he hired a private investigator. The second time, I told him after Mel—"

"She took heroin when she was pregnant with me!" Kat interrupted, outraged. "What I'm getting out of this whole thing is that Melody Arnold was a selfish bitch!"

Sylvia crossed to Kat's chair in one long, swift stride. Looming over her, she said in a deadly calm voice, "That is the last thing your mother was, Kat."

Kat shrank back in her chair. She was positive that Sylvia wanted to slap her. She was also positive that despite Sylvia's age, she could probably kick Kat's ass. "What am I supposed to think?" Then, damn it, she began to cry. Again.

Sylvia sighed wearily, returned to the couch, sat, and lit another cigarette. "You don't hold your liquor very well, do you?" She exhaled a long plume of smoke from her nostrils. "It's surprising, considering your relatives. All the Callahan men could drink like thirsty camels."

For some inexplicable reason, Kat wanted to say to Sylvia, "I think I might be pregnant, and here I am, drinking like a Callahan man and obviously not doing it very well. I'm no better than Melody Arnold. I'm no better than Mellie. *I'm no better than my mother.*" The thought made her cry harder.

Sylvia waited, and the silence grew.

Finally, when Kat could speak, she said, "I'm sorry, Sylvia. I'm not having a very good day, and that's the understatement of the decade. I've only known about ... my mother ... for five days, and in addition to not holding my liquor well, I don't seem to handle shock very well either. For thirty years, I thought my mother died in childbirth, and then I discover that she takes a nosedive off a 100-foot light tower, which I somehow, against her will, survived."

Sylvia stared at the burning tip of her long, brown cigarette. "I thought it was a miracle, a goddamn miracle."

"I guess with odds like that in my favor, I should buy lottery tickets more often," Kat said.

Sylvia ignored her, as she should, and continued. "Your surviving that fall could be called many things: bizarre, unbelievable, a defiance of fate, luck. I don't know. I've never been religious. And God knows that I should have been because of the horrendous things I've seen in this world, but I thought that you were a miracle."

Kat highly doubted that Sylvia Hammond still thought of her as a miracle. Miracles didn't get falling-down-drunk this early in the day.

Sylvia went on. "I was in shock, as we all were. Everyone always wants an explanation for everything that happens, and sometimes, there is just no explanation. Sometimes, life can be a bitch, right?"

"Sometimes," Kat said quietly. She didn't want to point out that sometimes it could be not so bad. Sometimes, it could be all right. (If Granny Nanny were here, she would probably add something pithy right about now, something like you could always make lemonade out of lemons. Dear Gran. She insisted on seeing the cloud's silver lining, the pot of gold at the end of the rainbow, the light at the end of the tunnel. Dear Gran.)

"Her family didn't even have a funeral for her. The word was that they were too ashamed, damn them. They should have had a funeral for Mellie. Instead, they went on and on about how she'd disgraced the family and would burn in hell." Sylvia swiped at a single tear that ran down her cheek. "Damn them."

"Marcus didn't want a funeral either?"

"Marcus was too torn up to be any use to anyone. The son of a bitch." Sylvia stared into her glass as if she could see the future, or the past, inside the melting ice cubes. "A couple of days after it happened, I got the idea that I should take the baby and raise her as my own. I don't know where I got that idea. I would have been a lousy mother, but still, the idea took hold. And grew. I started thinking that Mel would have made a will, and in the will, would have made me the baby's guardian. It didn't make any sense, but I wasn't thinking clearly at the time. I couldn't believe that my best friend was gone."

Kat didn't know what to say to that. So Sylvia had wanted to step in and do something for Mellie's baby. Kat swallowed, hard. Sylvia had cared. It was hard to believe that this tough old broad could ever feel emotion, but she had.

Sylvia's voice sounded detached, yet there was an underlying sadness, and she seemed to have forgotten that Kat, the baby, was sitting across from her. "I went to Marcus and demanded that he give the baby to me. What a raging idiot I was, thinking that he would just hand over the infant. 'It's what Mellie would have wanted,' I said to him. 'It's probably in her will.' But big surprise. Mellie didn't have a will. What twenty-four-year-old has a will? At twenty-four, you think you'll live forever. Marcus and the baby disappeared shortly after that. Gone without a trace, as they say. The son of a bitch."

"Did you try to find the baby?" Kat whispered.

"No, I did not."

Kat couldn't blame her. Being a working single mother in the early eighties would probably have been even more difficult than it was now, and Kat had worked with enough office assistants and servers to know that it was damn hard. The point was that Sylvia had tried. She had cared.

Sylvia seemed to snap out of her trance. She slammed the glass on the coffee table so hard that ice cubes went flying. "What I did was go on a binge. If Mellie was no longer there to be my best friend, then heroin would take her place. I quit the job that I loved and made scoring my top priority. You'd be surprised how much time and effort it takes to keep the high going. It's a full-time job, Kat, a full-time job." Sylvia's voice continued to rise. "How low do you think you can go, Mel? I've got to tell you, we had no idea how low you can go. The depths of depravity. That's what I liked to call it at the time. The depths of depravity. And the bitch of it was that I didn't give a flying fuck! You were dead, and I was pissed."

The force of Sylvia's rage made Kat cower deeper into her chair. "I'm not Mel."

"Damn it! I know you're not Mel! I'm not senile yet." Sylvia rolled up the sleeve of her black blouse. "Look at this. This is the result of a five-year binge."

Kat stared at what looked like a group of bruises running in succession up Sylvia's arm, and she could see the bruised looking, puckered, scarred skin. She shivered.

"And this." Sylvia rolled up her other sleeve. "And this." She pulled off her sock to show her ankle. "Yep, all courtesy of my best friend, dope, smack, H, heron, dust, shit. What a great buddy he turned out to be. I watched drugs kill Thelma, but did I care? Hell, no. Like mother, like daughter."

Kat willed herself not to vomit. The sour orange juice was at the back of her throat. "Did Melody's arms look like that?"

Sylvia puffed furiously on her cigarette. "No, I had more time to practice. Maybe Mel lucked out."

"Oh, God," Kat gasped.

"I didn't mean that. I've thought it too many times, but I don't mean it, not anymore." She stubbed out the cigarette. "Go home, Kat. I'm exhausted. I'll see you tonight."

Kat didn't argue; she left.

Like mother, like daughter. It was the first thought that came into Kat's mind when she awoke at five in the afternoon from her three-hour nap. She was disoriented and groggy from the screwdriver-induced slumber, yet the thought rang out clear as a bell: *Like mother, like daughter.* Could it be possible to be like a woman you had never even met? Did genetics play that strong of a role in a person's makeup?

"I am not like her," Kat said to the room. "I would never in a million years think of committing suicide."

Yet the circumstances that had driven Melody Arnold to take such a drastic measure were becoming somewhat clearer. She had gotten married to the wrong man because she was pregnant and thought it was the right thing to do, then she had lost that baby and fallen into a deep depression. Plus, her job as an ER nurse had to have been traumatic at times. Plus—and this was the big one to Kat—she had dabbled in drugs that led to full-blown heroin addiction. Really, the woman had been a train wreck.

"Like I'm so perfect," Kat said to the room. "I can't keep a decent job, and I get involved with the wrong men, including a pretty boy gigolo who was pimped out by his mother. On top of that, I might be pregnant with his child, and I refuse to acknowledge it. I'm a real prize, all right."

But she would still never do what Melody Arnold had done.

"If I'm pregnant, I will get an abortion." There, she had said it out loud. And she didn't like the sound of it, not one bit. It would be just one more cop-out in a long list of cop-outs. It would be the *crème de la crème* of cop-outs. She would be judging the fate of another human being.

Oh, my God. She would be just like Melody Arnold.

Kat got quickly out of bed, her heart pounding. She was nothing like Melody Arnold. She was not that desperate.

Desperate. Perhaps that was the key to Melody Arnold.

Before she could go any farther with that train of thought, Kat heard the front door open and close. Zen. She needed to see Zen.

"Hard day?" Zen asked when he saw her.

Kat glanced at herself in the hall mirror. Her crinkled cheek looked like it had been run over by a tractor tire. Typical. "Melody Arnold was a drug addict," she said.

"It's unfortunate but true. Some nurses get addicted to drugs. They have ready access, and the job is stressful."

"I'm talking heroin here."

"Wow."

"Yeah, wow," she echoed. That pretty much summed it up. Why would she expect Zen to be outraged or something along those lines? It wasn't his alleged mother they were talking about here. But then again, she had expected more from him than a *wow*.

"I'm guessing that you talked to Sylvia Hammond?" Zen took off his jacket and threw it over a chair.

"Yes, it turns out that she's the woman the people in this building call the resident crazy lady, but she's not crazy. Well, maybe she is a little."

Zen plopped down on the couch and ran his fingers through his sandy hair. He looked tired. "So I guess you found out the reason why Melody Arnold jumped from the tower," he said distractedly. He picked up the paper folded on the coffee table.

"Are you okay?" Kat went and sat beside him on the couch, even though he hadn't invited her. He was probably sick and tired of all the drama she had brought into his life ever since he made the innocent decision to share a ride with her across the country. She didn't blame him. However, a tiny bit of sympathy would be nice right now.

"I'm just tired. Late night and all, as you know."

Kat plowed ahead. "I think drug addiction was part of the reason she jumped, but I don't think it's the only reason. The paper said she thought the baby was dead, even though she heard its heartbeat through a stethoscope. I think that something else was going on in her head. Maybe she was delusional, or going through withdrawal, or something like that."

"Maybe," Zen said.

Zen, who had been so supportive during the last week, was giving her nothing right now. There had to be a reason he seemed so distracted. "Tell me what's wrong, Zen. I can be a good listener."

"Can you?" he smiled a little.

"Not really, but I can try."

"Can't a guy who had a late night and woke up with a hangover just be tired?"

It was a reasonable question, but Kat still said, "No."

Zen put the paper down, sighing. "Okay, you win. Again. I just found out how much in debt I'll be after three years of law school. I've been walking around the city, wondering if it's the right thing to do."

"Everyone takes out student loans these days. It's pretty much become a fact of life, and the interest rates are low." Kat had only finished paying off her debt a couple of years before.

"And the reason I couldn't meet you for lunch was that I met Mom and Pops at his doctor's office. They think there might be another blockage. He might need more surgery."

"Oh, no! He looked like he was getting stronger every day when we were there." Kat felt genuinely distressed. Tanner Delaney was such a nice man—solid, responsible, a good husband and father—and he had saved many lives, including hers. It didn't seem fair.

"Do you mind, Kat?" Zen pointed at a chair. "You smell like an ashtray."

"Sorry. Sylvia chain-smoked for the three hours I was there. I didn't think to change." Kat blushed and changed seats, even though she didn't want to leave his side. She sniffed a strand of hair. He was right; she stank.

"I guess you'll be going home soon," Zen said.

Zen's voice was matter-of-fact, and Kat couldn't read his face. Was he happy to see her leave? Sad? She couldn't tell. "I guess." She felt like crying. She would miss this man terribly, and she might as well admit it. She was falling in love with him. It wasn't reasonable for her to fall in love with him, but true to form, she had gone and done it anyway.

"I'll miss you," she said.

"Same here."

Same here? She could just shake him. Couldn't he at least say the words, *I'll miss you?* Was that asking for too much? "Good to know."

"Well," he said.

"Well." Kat looked at him. The man had saved her from choking on a Big Mac.

"I'm really tired."

"You look tired." The man had saved her from a tornado.

"I think I'll take a nap."

"That sounds like a good idea." The man had helped her find the answer to so many questions.

"You might want to watch TV out here. Do you mind if I use your bed?"

Kat didn't mind at all. "Do you mind if I join you?"

Kat couldn't believe she had said the words aloud. She absolutely needed to start filtering her thoughts before she blurted them out. She blushed a deeper shade of red.

"Pardon?" Zen looked startled. He cocked his head to the side and stared at her.

Who said *pardon* anymore? It was so old-fashioned. It was so Zen. "I, uh …" How was she going to get out of this awkward situation? "Uh …"

"Did you just ask if you could join me? In bed?"

Kat squirmed under his direct gaze. Only one thing was sure right now: Zen was not exactly jumping up and down with joy at the prospect. "I might have said something along those lines." Kat wished that the floor would open up and swallow her.

"Do you want to sleep with me?"

"It was a joke. Haha." Kat wondered if it was possible to die from embarrassment. Why did his beautiful eyes stare at her so earnestly? If there had been a blanket handy, Kat would have put it over her head.

"I see," Zen said, "a joke."

Only it wasn't a joke. Kat did want to sleep with him. She wanted him to hold her like he had in Mellie's bedroom. She wanted him to kiss her. Most of all, she wanted to feel safe in his arms, and she knew that she would.

"Are you in the habit of asking men to sleep with you as a joke?" Zen still wasn't smiling.

Her embarrassment started to blend into annoyance. It wouldn't be the end of the world if they had sex. They were two consenting adults, after all. Why was he making such a big deal out of her suggesting it? "No, I'm not in the habit of asking men to sleep with me. In fact, this is a first for me."

"I'm flattered," he said.

"Oh, don't be!" she snapped. Her anger grew. Zen acted like a thirty-four-year-old prude. He didn't want to have sex with her? Fine. But for once, he wasn't acting like a gentleman. A gentleman wouldn't sit here and grill her. A gentleman would act like he hadn't heard her.

"Why do you want to sleep with me?" Zen was now in his earnest listening pose. He leaned forward, his forearms resting on his thighs.

"Oh, God!" Kat exploded. "Why are you making a federal case out of this? It's a perfectly natural act between a man and a woman. It was just a suggestion. I didn't mean anything by it. Let's forget the whole thing."

"I'm not in the habit of having casual sex," Zen said.

"Well, bully for you! Aren't you the perfect Boy Scout? They should put your picture on a poster for abstinence."

"How about you?"

"No!" He looked like he expected more, so Kat, needlessly, continued. "I mean, not anymore. My slightly slutty twenties are well behind me." Oh, God, why had she told him *that*?

"I'd like to know more about your slightly slutty twenties."

"It's none of your business," she said hotly.

"If I'm going to sleep with someone, I think it's important to know that person's sexual history." Zen cleared his throat.

"Are you for real?" Kat's voice rose. "The next thing I know, you'll be asking me to take an AIDS test."

"That would probably be a good idea." Zen's mouth twitched.

Kat saw it. "Are you *teasing* me again?"

"Nope. I don't joke about sex, unlike some people in this room."

There it was again. "Lorenzo Delaney, for a saint, you can be a real jerk."

"I thought I was a boy scout."

"What you are is an asshole."

Zen grinned. "I really would like to hear more about your slightly slutty twenties. I'm intrigued."

"Forget it!" Boy, had this conversation deteriorated rapidly. Once again, her mouth had gotten her into hot water. Was she ever going to learn?

"Define *slightly* slutty." Zen was clearly enjoying himself. He settled back on the couch, his arms outstretched and draped over the top.

"Why do you like to rile me up like this?" Kat knew that her face was now flaming.

"It's very entertaining."

"I've had enough!" She got up from her chair. She would go into the spare bedroom and slam the door, hard. Zen could forget about his nap.

Zen jumped to his feet and grabbed Kat's arm before she could rush past. "Hey, I meant it when I said I was flattered." He wasn't smiling now.

"Let go of my arm!" She tried to wrench it out of his grasp, but she couldn't. He was holding her tightly, but it didn't hurt.

"I didn't know that you had those kinds of feelings for me." He looked at her intently with those beautiful green/gold eyes.

"Who said that I did?" But Kat had run out of steam. When he looked at her like that, she felt like she was drowning.

"We've been through a lot together in the past week. I think you're beautiful, and I like your spunk."

Spunk. It was so old-fashioned. It was so Zen.

"I'm going to miss you when you leave."

His face was so close that Kat could see how long his sandy lashes were. *Kiss me*, she thought. *Ask me to stay*. Zen leaned even closer, and Kat closed her eyes.

Her phone rang. It was on the coffee table, but she wouldn't answer it. It could ring forever. She was not going to let this moment slip away.

Zen finally picked up the ringing phone. "You should probably answer this, Kat. It's your brother calling."

Kat could only stare at the ringing phone. If Shane was calling her, it could only mean one thing. Her father was dead.

She didn't want it to be true. Had Marcus been a distant father to her? Most definitely. Had he been a lousy father? Not necessarily. That's what she'd started to realize. During the revelations in the past days, it had become increasingly clear to her that he had loved Mellie Callahan, a troubled young woman who had plummeted from a 100-foot light tower to try to kill herself and their baby. It was an understatement to say that that tragedy could undoubtedly change a man's outlook on life and love and leave an irreparable emotional scar. Taking his baby away from people who knew the story and changing their last name so that no one could find them might not have been the best choice in that horrible situation. But maybe, just maybe, he had done it to escape from the past in the only way he thought possible. Maybe, just maybe, he had done it to protect his daughter.

Kat took a deep, shaky breath and took the phone from Zen. "Hi, Shane."

"I'm sorry to bother you, Kat, but there's something you should know," Kat's younger brother said.

"He's dead, isn't he?"

"Who's dead?"

"Marcus. I'm sorry, Shane. I know how much you loved him." Now, she would never have a chance to tell her father that she'd gotten a glimmer of understanding of what he had been through. Now, she would never get a chance to apologize for being a cocky, sassy teenager. So her father hadn't exactly been a saint? Well, she hadn't been sainthood material either, not even close.

"You don't need to talk about Dad in the past tense just yet, Kat."

Kat had been so sure that her father was dead that it took a moment for her to figure out what Shane was saying about a man named Dad and *past tense*. "Do you mean that he's not dead?"

"I wish you'd stop saying that." Shane's voice sounded mildly irritated. "Gee, whiz. I'm calling with some good news. Dad rallied a bit, and we brought him home from the hospital. It's where he wants to be. Home. I thought you should know."

Kat's relief so overwhelmed her that her knees buckled. Zen caught her, just as he had too many times in the short period he had known her. "That's great, Shane. I mean I—" Kat didn't know what she meant. The emotional turmoil of the last week was thoroughly getting to her. She needed time to process all this new information. She needed time to accept the fact that the fairy tale she had conjured of her dead mother was a myth, and she needed time to come to terms with why her father had chosen to cloak his grief in such a cold and aloof façade.

"He wants to see you," Shane said next.

Kat dropped her phone. "Shit!" She scrambled to the floor and reached for it under the coffee table on her hands and knees. "Are you still there, Shane?"

"What was that?" he asked.

Kat didn't think he needed to know exactly how much of a klutz his older sister was. "Say it again, Shane."

"What was that?" he asked, perplexed.

"No, before that."

"Oh, he wants to see you."

After thirty years, her father *wanted* to see her. Kat couldn't believe it. "He *asked* to see me?"

"Well, duh, Kat. You are his daughter."

Shane and Cody would never understand that their father had been entirely different with how he raised them, the sons of a woman who had the guts to stick it out, unlike her mother, who hadn't. Kat wondered if he'd looked at her every day and been forced to think of Mellie Callahan. Had Kat been a constant reminder to him of his pain in losing his wife—and *how* he had lost his wife? Probably so. It had been an unfair situation for both of them. However, he had known. She had not.

"When do you think you can come, Kat? I would say, the sooner, the better."

"I'll be there tomorrow," she said quickly.

"Great. I'll let Dad know."

Kat continued to stare at her phone after Shane hung up. She was getting a second chance to talk to her father, and she was scared shitless. There were still so many things she wanted to say to him, so many things she wanted to ask. But she'd lost the list of twenty-two questions that she'd brought with her from Arizona. They'd been on the seat of her Mazda when it was stolen, and she could no longer remember, exactly, what she'd planned to ask her father on that day. It didn't matter. This time she wasn't going to prepare any questions. She would just let her father talk—if he wanted to.

"I'll borrow my mom's car," Zen said then.

"Thank you." Would she ever be able to repay his kindness? Even though she very much wanted him to go with her on this trip, she would have hesitated to ask him. It seemed like too much of an imposition, yet Zen had volunteered before she even had to ask.

It was so Zen.

26

MARCH 22, 1982

Melody was past the worst of her withdrawal symptoms when the first contractions started at 12:20 a.m. on March 22. The contractions were mild, but she felt sure that they weren't Braxton-Hicks contractions, which she had been having for the last ten days. They were the real thing. But after all the weeks of longing for this day, Melody now felt filled with dread. She wasn't ready to be a mother. She wasn't worthy of being a mother. She would never be as good a mother as Ma.

Just the week before, Melody had asked Dr. Crowley if she could deliver the baby at St. Matthew rather than Mercy. "Of course, Melody, I understand completely. You're going to want some privacy during the birth of your baby."

That was not it at all. Melody wanted a different hospital because, after the baby's birth, everyone would know. Everyone would know what she had done to her baby, and everyone would know who she truly was. She was not a competent, professional nurse. She was an addict who had used during her pregnancy. Everyone would know her shame and the truth: She was a terrible person; she was a baby killer.

"This is going to be the happiest day of our lives!" Marcus said as he picked up the gray duffel bag that Melody had packed days before. "Our baby is going to be born today!"

Melody did not want to go to the hospital just yet. "My contractions are too far apart. We have time, Marcus."

"I think we should go now, Mellie. I know that nothing is going to go wrong, sweetheart, but just to make sure, I insist that we go now." He had already put on his coat and hat.

Melody did not want to go to the hospital at all. When she got to the hospital, it would be the beginning of the end, and everyone would discover her shameful secret. The baby would have no heartbeat. "Really, Marcus—"

"You finish getting dressed, and I'll go warm up the car."

When he left, Melody went into the bathroom and vomited, and then she sank to the cold linoleum floor and cried. After two weeks of withdrawal symptoms spent lying in bed, which was the entirety of her maternity leave, she had had plenty of time—way too much time—to think of all the mistakes she'd made. What had she done to her baby? After failing her baby boy and Ma, she should have been a stronger person, but she hadn't been. She was weak. She should have learned her lesson, but she had not. So far, as a student of life, she had been a dismal failure.

Marcus knocked politely on the bathroom door. (Marcus was always knocking on the bathroom door. Marcus gave her no privacy.) "Baby, are you all right? The car is all nice and toasty to take our baby to the hospital."

Melody splashed cold water on her face. "Just a minute," she called to Marcus. To her reflection, she hissed, "What have you done?"

"Are you all right?" Marcus asked from the other side of the door.

Melody wanted to scream: *No, I am not all right!* But it was too late for that. She opened the door.

Marcus had her coat in his hands, and Marcus—because Marcus never really saw her—did not notice Melody's red eyes. "The happiest day of our lives," he said again.

In the car, her husband could not stop jabbering. "All these months, and we've never talked about baby names! What are your thoughts, kitten? If it's a girl, I think we should name her Evelyn after my mother. Yes, that would be a good name for our daughter."

Melody breathed through a mild contraction—they were still too far apart to be intense—before she said, "What about my mother? What about the name Claudia?" It was funny. No, it was hysterical. Why hadn't they talked about baby names before? Wasn't that what normal parents-to-be did?

"I think Evelyn," Marcus said firmly.

"Katrina." The name just came to her, and Melody liked the sound of it.

"What kind of name is that? It doesn't have any family history." Marcus, overly careful, drove ten miles under the speed limit.

"Good. Katrina can make her own history." Oh, God, was it already too late for that? Too late, too late for everything.

"That's nonsense, pumpkin. The baby needs a good, strong family name. Be reasonable. Evelyn is the best choice. I know it's your hormones talking, and you aren't thinking properly."

Melody couldn't take it anymore. "Would you shut the fuck up!"

In his surprise, Marcus slammed on the brakes, and the car behind them, which had narrowly avoided plowing into them, honked. Marcus clutched the wheel tightly. "I can't believe you just said that to me, Mellie. A wife is not supposed to say that to her husband. We are on the way to the hospital on the happiest day of our lives!"

"Marcus, shut the fuck up!"

Marcus pulled the car to the curb and turned to Melody. "What is wrong with you, Mellie?"

"Damn it, Marcus, I'm in labor. Am I supposed to be the life of the party?" She could see the concern in his eyes from the light of the dashboard, and she started to cry again.

"Yes, I'm sure that being in labor is very stressful, but that's not it, is it?"

"Would you please just drive?" Now Melody wanted to get to the hospital. She desperately needed to get away from those green, staring, probing eyes.

"I let you go to Sylvia's house," he began.

"Leave Sylvia out of it, Marcus." Melody had to turn away.

"Look at me, baby."

"Would you just fucking *drive*?" Marcus was no fool. In all probability, Marcus knew everything and was trying to trap her in her web of lies. Marcus, in all likelihood, had tipped off the police about the drugs in Sylvia's apartment.

"I know," Marcus said quietly.

Oh, God. *Marcus knew.* No, Marcus couldn't possibly know because the baby wasn't born yet. Then, *everyone* would know that she had used heroin and harmed her baby, that she was an unfit mother, an unworthy person, that something was horribly wrong with her.

"Please look at me, flower."

Melody was caught; Marcus had her trapped. She had no other choice but to turn to him.

He took her hands. "I know that I love you more than you love me."

Melody was too stunned to say anything. The statement was so far off the mark from what she'd expected him to say that she couldn't respond.

"I've known it from the very beginning, Mellie," Marcus continued. "I attributed it to the fact that you were young, twelve years younger than me, and the first baby was a surprise, and then when he—"

"I don't think we should talk about this now, Marcus." She did not want to hear a recap of all the sadness that had happened in their short life together, and it was painful to listen to the sorrow in her husband's voice. He had grieved, too. She'd witnessed his grief, but he had moved forward. She had not.

"And then when Evelyn died," Marcus took off his glasses and wiped at his eyes before continuing, "I knew we could muddle through. Together, we could become stronger, and you would grow to love me more."

"Please, Marcus." She wanted to put her hands over her ears to make him stop.

"I've done everything I know how to do to earn your love, Mellie." Marcus had so many tears now that he reached into his shirt's breast pocket and took out his monogrammed handkerchief. Monogrammed handkerchiefs had been Melody's Christmas gift to him. *That was all*, yet Marcus carried one with him every single day.

"Oh, Marcus." It was unbearable.

"Do you love me, Mellie?"

There it was, out in the open. Melody had tried so hard to be a good wife in the last months before her relapse. She had *honestly tried*. He was a good man—her family thought he was a good man—so why did she so willfully resist him? Because she did not love him. The silence went on for so long that Melody had to drop her eyes.

Marcus finally cleared his throat and straightened his shoulders. He started the Buick. "I need to get you to the hospital. Everything is going to be fine when the baby arrives. Let's go have our baby, Mellie."

She'd checked into the hospital at 1:00 a.m., and hours later, Melody lay drenched in sweat, utterly exhausted. Her cervix was not dilating as it should, and her water had not yet broken. One OB nurse summed it up perfectly when she said, "Mrs. Arnold, I think we have a failure to progress situation here."

Yes, Melody thought, *That's me in a nutshell—a failure to progress.*
Another nurse helpfully suggested that perhaps Melody had false labor.
Yes, Melody thought, *My labor is false.*
But why did it hurt so damn much? She'd refused any drugs, which made Marcus beam. "My wife's a real trooper," he said to the nurses. "Have you ever seen a woman in labor be this brave before?"

After all these hours, Melody suspected that this situation was actually called prodromal labor. From all of her pre-delivery reading, Melody had gathered that prodromal labor was difficult to define. For some women, this phase of labor could last for a day or two. For other women, it could last for weeks. During prodromal labor, the types, intensity, and regularity of the contractions varied widely. In Melody's case, she experienced time-able, regular labor contractions that would reach regular intervals and then fade apart and die down.

Melody also knew the cause of this type of labor could be that the baby was not in an optimal position, and her body was trying to help it get into a more favorable position for birth. Or it could be that her cervix was posterior, and the contractions helped the baby ease to a better position. Another possibility could be that she was effacing, which was just as critical as dilation. Or the final and most probable option: She could be very slowly dilating.

In the back of her mind, Melody knew all these things. She was a nurse, after all.

However, she was not a textbook case. Oh, no. In her case, she was failing to progress because she had harmed her baby. The baby did not want to be born to a mother like her. That was the reason.

Melody was utterly exhausted. After weeks of insomnia and fitful sleep, Melody didn't have the stamina to continue, yet the contractions would start again, and Melody would think: *Finally, it's happening. The truth will be born.* Then the contractions would fade apart and then die down. It had been going on for hours. This physical and emotional roller coaster would never end.

Marcus kept telling her that she was a trooper as he fed her ice chips. "I'm so proud of you, flower."

"You look tired, Marcus. Why don't you go home and get some rest? This might take a while." She wanted to be alone. She was bone-tired and wanted to close her eyes and have everything gone, done, finished. Yet when she closed her eyes, the contractions would start again, the roller coaster climbing and dropping.

"I don't want to miss a thing."

"Oh, Marcus," she said sadly. He had no idea what was about to happen.

When Dr. Crowley finally arrived at ten o'clock, he examined Melody. "Six centimeters," he said.

"Is that all?" Melody wanted to cry. No, wait. She'd already been crying.

Dr. Crowley patted her shoulder. "Every woman's labor is different. Things are progressing normally."

Melody knew he was lying to her.

"How are you holding up?" he asked.

"She's a trooper," Marcus said.

"I'm very, very tired." Melody could not begin to put into words how she felt—weary beyond tired, yet still filled with fear and dread.

"You're young and strong," Dr. Crowley said. "When this is over, you won't even remember the pain, and you'll have a bundle of joy to take home. We'll give it another couple of hours, and then we'll talk about inducing or a C-section."

Melody knew he was lying to her. She would live with this pain for the rest of her life. She had caused the suffering.

"I think there's something wrong with the baby." She could not keep up the pretense much longer.

"Now, Melody, we've been through this. What happened to your first baby was an anomaly."

Melody wanted to scream: *He was not an anomaly. He was still born.* But she had no energy to scream. She didn't even have enough energy to cry anymore.

"Everything in this pregnancy has gone extremely well." Dr. Crowley patted her shoulder again.

"This baby has been thriving," Marcus added.

Melody said to both of them, "I think the baby is dead."

Marcus gasped. "Mellie, honey, don't be ridiculous. The baby is fine."

"Now, now, Mellie." Dr. Crowley took the stethoscope from around his neck. "I just heard his heartbeat. It's your turn." He placed the earpieces in her ears and placed the silver disc on her belly. "Do you hear that? That's the sound of a good, strong heartbeat."

Melody knew he was lying to her. She didn't hear a thing.

Marcus listened next. "I hear it," he said, relieved. "That is the sound of a good, strong heartbeat, Mellie."

Marcus always told her lies.

"I can bring in a monitor," Dr. Crowley said.

"That won't be necessary." What was the point? Her baby was dead. She was going to have another *still born* baby because she had killed another child. It had been in her power not to put that needle in her vein, but she did it anyway. Then she'd done it again and again and again.

She did not deserve to live.

The next round of contractions began, accelerated, and stopped. Melody wasn't surprised. This baby was never going to be born.

She did not deserve to live. Melody kept coming back to that thought, that truth.

Melody must have dozed off after that last round of contractions—her dream-thoughts churning in her mind—and when she opened her eyes, Sylvia stood by the bed. For the first and only time in her life, Melody wasn't happy to see her. "What are you doing here?"

"Marcus called. I came as soon as I got off work."

"Marcus called?" That, too, was a first.

"He said you were under a lot of *stress*." Sylvia smiled. "I'd say that's putting labor mildly, wouldn't you?"

"I'm a failure to progress," Melody said.

"Or it could be prodromal labor." Sylvia was a very competent nurse. "Well, I guess the good news is that the baby is going to come out sooner or later, one way or the other." She pulled up a chair next to the bed. "Marcus is in the cafeteria, getting something to eat. He said he'd give us some time together, alone. Immediately, I smelled a fish in Denmark. What in the hell is going on, Mel?"

"My baby is dead, Syl. My body does not want to give birth to a dead baby." Melody's voice was emotionless.

"Complete and total bullshit! Marcus said you heard the baby's heartbeat through Dr. Crowley's stethoscope.

So it had come to this. Sylvia and Marcus were talking about her behind her back. Even her best friend could betray her. "I didn't hear a heartbeat," Melody said.

Sylvia studied her for a few moments. "I'm going to tell the doctor that I think he should induce you. This has gone on long enough. Where are those slutty-looking OB nurses? I tell you, Mel, if I were an OB-GYN, I'd have those babies out, pronto."

"Don't you understand, Syl? This baby is not going to be born."

Sylvia studied Melody again, assessing. "What drugs have they given you?"

"I haven't taken anything."

"So that's it. You're delirious from prolonged pain."

"No, that's not it." Melody shook her head sadly. "I've made up my mind."

"You're talking crazy shit, Mel, and frankly, you're scaring me a little bit. Besides, why would you pass up drugs if people are *handing* them out? I'll go get you some." Sylvia started to rise, but Melody grasped her hand with surprising strength for a woman who had been in labor for so long.

"Don't you understand, Syl?" Melody asked again. "That's the whole problem."

"Why do you keep asking me if I understand?" Sylvia said irritably. "And what's the whole problem?"

"Drugs."

Sylvia sat back down. "You need to cut this out, Mel. The odds are stacked strongly in your favor that your baby is going to be healthy."

"I shouldn't have used at all when I was pregnant."

Sylvia didn't say anything.

"But it's more than that," Melody continued. "I can't live with them, and I can't live without them. When I don't use drugs, the world is such a bleak and dreary place that I don't see the purpose of getting up in the morning, and when I do use, well, the world becomes a tangled web of lies and secrecy. What's the point?"

"What's the point of *what*, Mel? Your crazy talk is starting to give me a headache, and I absolutely think I should go get you some—"

"What's the point in living?" Melody interrupted.

"Jesus, Mellie! I've seen women acting in all sorts of odd ways when they're in labor, but you really take the cake. Just take some drugs, have the damn kid, and get on with it!" Sylvia dug frantically through her large purse. "I don't know why you can't smoke in hospitals anymore. Damn it!"

"After I give birth to my second dead baby, I'll start to use again. I know I will." Melody tried to make Sylvia understand, but Sylvia wasn't listening to her. Had Sylvia ever really listened to her? Had anyone ever really listened to her? Certainly not Marcus, who would rather sit in front of the blasted television instead of participating in the real world. Wait a minute. Ma had listened to her. But Ma was dead because Melody hadn't gone to Sunday dinner. Poor dead Ma.

"I'm going to repeat this." Sylvia's voice was heated. "Take some drugs, have the damn kid, and get on with it! If you still feel depressed after the baby is born, see a therapist, or get a prescription for Xanax. You are not going to use again, and I'm not going to use again. Jesus, Mel, if I wasn't your best friend, I'd slap some sense into you. Literally. I feel like hitting someone right now."

Sylvia, her best friend, was *not listening*, but Melody kept going. "I think the beginning of the end was when we went to the light tower to buy drugs for the first time from Clyde. That's when it started to feel dirty, when we actually had to buy the drugs."

"You don't think the tawdry business with Dr. Demented was dirty?"

"Dr. Who?"

"The sadistic pervert."

"Stop! If we don't talk about it, it never happened." The memory was always there, lurking behind a closed door, but Melody refused to open that door. Too much humiliation would rain down on her if she opened that flimsy door.

"Sorry," Sylvia said, "you're right." She took Melody's hand. "Look, I know I'm acting like a bitch today, but I'm concerned about your mental health right now. You need to have this baby."

"My baby is dead."

Sylvia sighed dramatically. "When was your last contraction? You haven't had one since I've been here."

"The roller coaster has temporarily stopped. It does that."

"I'm not even going to ask you what that means." Sylvia sighed again and looked at her watch. "I wish I could stay until the baby was born, but unfortunately, I can't. I have my damn court appearance today. My lawyer thinks I'll get off with a fine since it's my first offense, so hopefully, it won't take long. I'll come directly back to the hospital from the courthouse." Sylvia stood up. "Promise me you'll have that baby out by the time I get back."

"I think it's pretty clear that I have no control over this situation." *I don't have control over my life*, Melody thought.

"I'm going to talk to the doctor on the way out," Sylvia said. "It's time to induce or prep you for a C-section."

"I'm a failure to progress, Syl."

Sylvia shook her head and gave Melody a worried look. "Bye, Mel, and don't worry, it'll all be over soon." And then she left.

Melody supposed that it was now out of the question to call Sylvia back and ask her for a ride. Despite what anyone said to her, she knew that she needed to get out of this hospital. Everyone in this place lied to her. She alone knew that her baby was not going to be born—not now, not ever.

Her baby was dead, and it was all Melody's fault.

27

APRIL 2012

Kat and Zen did not talk much on the six-hour drive south to Carbondale. At this point, Kat didn't think there was anything left to say. When Zen suggested that the logical thing to do was to pack up her few belongings in the plastic Target bag and put it in the car's trunk, Kat obeyed. Zen was the logical one. He pointed out that it would probably be cheaper for her to catch the bus from Carbondale back to Arizona and that it would also cut time off of the long trip.

"Don't you think that makes sense?" he'd asked that morning.

"Are you trying to get rid of me?" she'd tried to tease back. She quickly left the room before Zen could answer, and before he could see the hurt in her eyes. It hadn't occurred to her to leave. After all, she wasn't known for her logic, and Zen should know that by now. Plus, she didn't want to leave. She and Zen needed to clear the air about what, if anything, was going on between them. However, it was a distinct possibility that it was just her that needed to clear the air. Zen seemed to have no doubts that she should return to Arizona alone. But then again, it could be that Zen was only being his uber-polite self. She simply could not read the man.

She should have forced him to have sex with her.

As soon as this thought passed through her head on the long ride south, she knew she was on the verge of losing it. She didn't even know how a woman would go about *forcing* a man to have sex with her. Her jangled nerves were getting the better of her. She was nervous to see her father and agitated that she was leaving Chicago without knowing the entire story about why Melody Arnold jumped off of that 100-foot light tower. And Kat was convinced that Sylvia had held something back. She and Zen left Chicago at six o'clock that morning, and Kat hadn't had a chance to say good-bye to Sylvia. That, too, added to Kat's mounting nervousness.

And there was this: Kat *needed* to see the light tower that Melody Arnold climbed up and plummeted off. If the structure still existed, Kat wanted to see it with her own eyes. It would be painful, but Kat knew it was something she had to do to find some peace or understanding of Melody Arnold.

It was a long drive, but to Kat, it seemed like they pulled up in front of her childhood home all too soon. "It could use a coat of paint," she said. The brilliant early spring sunshine only accentuated the shabbiness of the house. Kat wanted to cry.

"So, this is where you grew up." Zen gazed at the house.

"That's debatable. Some would say that I'm still in the process." Kat felt the now all-too-familiar feeling of her throat tightening. It was difficult to breathe or swallow.

Zen turned to look at her and took her hand. "It's going to be fine. You're going to be fine," he said quietly. "He's your dad, and he wants to see you."

"Let's drive around the block." Kat did not want to go inside that house. Memories leaked out the windows of that house.

"They might have already seen the car," Zen reasonably pointed out.

"Quick! Maybe it's not too late." But it was too late for so many things.

"You're stalling."

"You bet your ass, I'm stalling."

"There's nothing to be afraid of."

"There are a *million* fucking things to be afraid of." And there were. Soon, Kat would be confronting her past and facing her father now knowing what her mother had done. What could she say to him that could correct or mitigate the mistakes of the past? Was it his job or hers? Why had Melody Arnold jumped off that damn light tower?

"I think we've been spotted," Zen said as Cody stepped onto the front porch, waving.

"Crap."

"We don't have to stay long. Just give me a signal, and I'll say that my mom needs her car back at a certain time."

"What kind of signal?" Timidly, Kat waved back at her brother.

"How about that annoyingly cute eye-rolling thing you do?"

"I don't roll my eyes." Kat was almost sure that she didn't do that.
"Yes, you do. All the time."
Kat rolled her eyes.
"That's it." Zen smiled.
The situation began to get uncomfortable, with Cody's waving becoming more and more frantic. "Okay. Fine. Let's go in."
"You sound like this is a combat mission."
"In a way, Zen, it is." Zen, with his seemingly perfect family, would never understand.

They got out of the car and went up to the porch. Cody gave Kat a bone-crushing hug. "I'm glad to see you, Kat. Where's your car?"

There was no need to create any additional drama in this situation by rambling on about her stolen car. "It's in the shop."

"You brought your boyfriend," Cody said happily.

"He's not my—"

"Lorenzo Delaney." Zen stuck out his hand to shake Cody's. "My friends call me Zen."

"Okay," Cody said. "Everyone's in the living room. We waited to have lunch until you showed up. Mom made a spam loaf."

"God," Kat muttered under her breath. She remembered the inedible spam loaf of which Missy was unduly proud. During Kat's teenaged years, she convinced herself that her family was the only one in the entire world who actually ate spam.

Cody heard her. "It's even better now, Kat. Mom puts oregano in it." To Zen, he said, "It totally sucks, but we all pretend that we like it. You might call it an acquired taste."

"Everyone included Missy, Shane, Shane's girlfriend, Danica, and her two-year-old daughter, Penny. Just seeing the cute, chubby little girl, dressed for some reason in a pink leotard and tutu, made Kat want to run in the other direction. Her period still hadn't started, and she had been too preoccupied to notice it until now.

"Oh, you brought a friend!" Missy said brightly. She had on another shapeless housedress, green this time. "I wasn't expecting a *friend*. Danica, we need to set another place at the table."

"Please don't go to any trouble, Missy." Kat had been in this house for approximately two seconds and felt claustrophobic. "You don't need to feed us." She would see her father and leave as quickly as possible. That was it.

"Nonsense," Missy said with a little too much force. "Marcus is taking a nap, and I went to the trouble of fixing a meal. You'll eat."

"I'm kind of hungry," Zen said with his charming smile.

Kat rolled her eyes at him.

He shook his head back.

She hadn't meant to give him the signal so soon; she hadn't realized she was doing it at all. Maybe she did do it all the time, and if so, she needed to put it on her growing list of self-improvement items. "Sure, Missy, we'll eat."

"You're in for a real treat," Shane said after he hugged her.

"Some things never change." Kat looked at the brother who so resembled their father, yet was nothing like him. Both Shane and Cody seemed like decent, kind people, despite Marcus, and getting to know her brothers had become something that she honestly wanted to do. It was not too late for that.

The spam loaf, predictably, was awful, the mashed potatoes ("real, not from a box," as Missy pointed out) lumpy, the scalloped corn soupy, and Kat couldn't identify the other green casserole as belonging to any food group. Still, she tried to eat without grimacing. Her arguments with Missy over her notoriously bad meals were a thing of the past, and Kat did not want to relive that scenario. She did not want a repeat performance of the Hawaiian meatballs dinner.

"This is delicious," Zen said.

Kat rolled her eyes.

Zen winked at her and took a second helping of the spam loaf.

They made ordinary family chitchat throughout the meal, talking about the weather, Shane and Cody's schools and jobs, Danica's new clerk position at Walgreens, Penny's play dates, and Missy's plans to put in a vegetable garden this spring. (Kat had to fight to hold her tongue on that one. Missy had talked about putting in a vegetable garden back when Kat lived here. And she never, in the end, got around to planting a single seed.) The one thing that they didn't talk about was the man lying in the back bedroom.

Thirty minutes later, when they were finally done with the meal, Zen said, "Do you need help with the dishes, Missy?"

Naturally, he would offer to help. Damn it. He'd joined right in on the conversation as if he belonged there. It was Kat who had been the most uncomfortable as she sat in the barely used dining room of her childhood home. It was clear that Missy had made an effort to make the meal special. A tablecloth covered the table, and she had used her "good" china, but Kat still felt uneasy, on guard for Missy's attack. It didn't come.

"Katrina can help me clean up," Missy said.

Oh, no. The last thing Kat wanted to do was be alone with Missy. However, she plastered a pleasant look on her face and began gathering dishes. "Sure, Missy."

Missy had smiled brightly throughout the dinner, but as soon as they were alone in the kitchen, her face sagged. "This is so hard." She reached for a paper towel and dabbed at her eyes.

"I'm sorry." Kat did feel sorry for her step-mother, who daily watched her husband die. Then, for the life of her, she couldn't think of anything to say as she watched the woman cry. She turned away and started to load the dishwasher.

"You need to rinse the dishes first, Katrina," Missy sniffled.

Kat turned on the faucet and started rinsing.

"Sometimes, I get so mad that I feel like I could throw things," Missy said. "Why do good men have to die young?"

Kat had no answer to that question, nor did she feel like pointing out that sixty-six was not exactly young. Nor did she question Missy's assessment of Marcus as a good man. To her, he had been a good husband and a loving father to her sons.

"You broke his heart when you ran away, Katrina. You know that, don't you?"

Then Kat turned around. "Why didn't my father try to find me?"

Missy seemed surprised by the question. "Try to find you? Why? He knew where you were."

Kat felt dangerously close to tears herself. "I mean, why didn't he come and get me?"

Missy looked at her with sad eyes. "Because I asked him not to. It wasn't the right thing to do. I know that now, but you were so stubborn and sassy. The house was so much quieter without you. Truthfully, Katrina, you just plain wore me out."

Kat didn't know if her falling tears were caused by Missy's revelation that her father had wanted to come and get her or if they were caused by Missy's revelation that she was the one who had prevented Marcus from doing so. "That's no excuse, Missy, and you know it! I was a *teenager.*"

"And I was only twenty-eight, with two small children to care for. You have no idea how hard it was for me," Missy said quietly.

"But he was my *father*." Kat couldn't prevent the pleading note in her voice, even though it was much too late to plead her case in front of Missy. It was fourteen years too late, fourteen years when she had felt rejected by her father, fourteen years filled with a painful rage.

"People make mistakes."

"For all those years, I thought my father didn't care." Did Missy not recognize the full implications of what she had done?

"I was wrong," Missy said.

Kat could only stare at her, speechless. This was, she knew, the closest she would ever get to an apology from Missy, and she was right.

"Your boyfriend is delightful." Missy gently pushed Kat away from the sink and took over the abandoned rinsing.

"He's not my boy—"

"Good-looking and nice."

"He's not my boy—"

"I think he's a keeper," Missy said.

And that was that.

Marcus' bedroom was as dark and antiseptic as before, but now, Kat didn't want to identify an underlying odor. She instinctively knew what it was, but she was not going to give death a name. She hadn't noticed it during her previous short visit, but someone—probably one of his sons—had mounted a flat-screen TV to the wall facing the bed. It was on, with the volume muted. Her father must still love his television shows. To Kat, it was both comforting and unbearably sad.

Missy hadn't joined her for this visit. All she'd said to Kat after they finished the dishes was, "Whenever you're ready."

Kat was never going to be ready for this, her final visit with her father. He looked so diminished under the quilt, more like a child than a man. She approached the metal hospital bed quietly. If he was asleep, she decided that she wasn't going to wake him. She would hold his hand and kiss his cheek and leave. Maybe that would be enough for her to take away. Not a list of questions or recriminations or wailings about all the should-have-beens. Just a touch.

She took her father's hand, and his eyelids fluttered open. "Katrina." Again, his voice sounded scratchy, unused, forgotten.

"Daddy," she said. She could not recall ever calling him that before, but it just popped out: *Daddy*.

"So you know," he said simply.

"Yes."

Her father closed his eyes. "It was a hell of a thing for her to do. It was a hell of a choice."

"It sure was," Kat said.

"She was my little flower," her father said.

So that was why he had changed their last name to Flowers? Kat wanted to ask, but she didn't. She was going to let her father say what he wanted to say, no more than that.

He opened his eyes again, and Kat could see that they looked clouded with pain. "I now know the benefits of drugs. I can say that." He managed a weak smile.

Kat couldn't remember the last time she had seen her father smile. Kat smiled back through the tears that had started once again. Damn it. She was becoming such a crybaby, and she could do nothing to control it. What she had really learned during the past week was that she couldn't control *anything*.

"Marry someone you love," her father said, "but make sure that that person loves you back."

Kat nodded. She was trying not to grip his hand too hard; she was trying not to hurt him.

"I did the best that I could." Her father's voice sounded like it was fading.

Kat's throat was so tight that she couldn't speak at all. She could only nod again. He probably had done the best that he could, even if she'd thought it wasn't enough. She could have been wrong all these years, or maybe she did expect more from people than they were willing to give.

"Before, I said that I couldn't forgive her for what she had done, but I have now. I must now. I can't go to my grave without forgiving her."

"Don't say that," Kat managed to get out.

The look her father gave her was so sad that Kat felt like her heart was breaking in two. She had to force herself not to look away, to keep staring into her father's pain-filled hazel eyes.

He was silent for a long time before he said the last words he would ever say to his daughter. "And you need to forgive her, too, Katrina. You need to forgive her." He closed his eyes.

Kat stood holding his hand for many minutes longer, but Marcus had said all that he was willing to say. It would have to be enough.

Kat and Zen were nearing the bus station when her phone rang. She almost didn't answer it. Kat didn't recognize the number, and she was utterly exhausted, both physically and emotionally. She hoped that she would sleep all the way to Arizona when she got on the bus, but that probably wasn't going to happen. Everything that she'd discovered about her mother and father in the past days kept running through her head like an endless film loop. She still felt like there was at least one more missing piece to the mystery of Melody Arnold's tragic leap. How could she forgive the woman, as her father wished, if she did not know the entire story?

Then there was Zen. He'd hugged her when she emerged from her father's room, and they'd left quickly after her promise to her brothers to keep in touch (and she was going to keep that promise). Now he was sitting right next to her, possibly for the last time, and Kat knew she should say something, but that *something* was giving her trouble. Obviously, she would have to thank him profusely once again, but it probably wasn't a good idea to say something like: "Thank you so much for everything, Zen. You're a terrific person, and I hope we can stay in touch. P.S. I think I've fallen in love with you. Bye." Kat reached into her purse and picked up the phone.

"You bailed on me last night," a voice barked. Sylvia.

"How did you get my phone number?" Kat didn't remember giving it to her the previous afternoon, although she didn't have any doubt that Sylvia could be pretty crafty. After all, Granny Nanny was her aunt.

"That pompous prick gave it to me when I knocked on your door this morning. Have you ever noticed how he overuses the word *excellent?* The pompous prick."

Kat quickly explained about the unexpected trip to Carbondale. "Right now, I'm pulling up to the bus station. It's time to go home." She looked over at Zen. *Just say you want me to stay*, she willed him, to no avail. He pulled deftly into a parking space.

"Why in the hell do you think it's time to go home? You and I have some unfinished business." Sylvia coughed at the other end of the line.

Kat sat up straighter. It's exactly what she'd been thinking, too. "What do you mean?"

"I've decided to trust you," Sylvia said.

"Gee, thanks." Kat could not keep the note of sarcasm out of her voice.

"Not so fast, young lady. I've decided to trust you with *some* information, not everything. Some things will always be just between Mel and me, and that's the way it's going to be."

"What kind of information?"

"How long will it take you to get back to Chicago?"

"What *kind* of information, Sylvia?" Kat could hear Sylvia exhale and knew she was exhaling a thick plume of smoke.

"Don't be a pain in my ass, Kat."

"Look, Sylvia, I'll give you my address, and you can send me whatever it is that you think I need to know." Zen turned off the ignition and stared at her. Sylvia talked so loudly that Kat was sure Zen could hear every word.

"First of all, I want to show you some places. I can't very well send that kind of information through the mail, can I?"

The light tower. Sylvia could show her the light tower. The prospect terrified Kat, but if she was ever going to get a sense of closure about the pregnant woman who climbed up that tower, she would have to see it. "Is the light tower still there?"

"Jesus," Sylvia said.

"Is it?" Kat persisted.

"Unfortunately, yes."

"She could email you the pictures," Zen suggested.

Did he want her to leave that badly? Kat wondered.

"Who in the hell said that?"

"Zen. He's here in the car with me." Kat wasn't sure if she had mentioned Zen to Sylvia yesterday. Those damn screwdrivers.

"Tell him to shut the fuck up," Sylvia said.

"I'm pretty sure he can hear you." Kat looked over at Zen, who nodded and smiled.

"Good," Sylvia said. "Shut the fuck up, Zen. So how long will it take you to get back to Chicago?"

Kat felt torn. The thing she wanted the most was to have more time in Chicago. On some level, she knew that her business there wasn't quite finished, yet she had been such a real pain in the ass to Zen, his family, and one of his best friends. She was pretty sure she'd worn out her welcome at John's apartment. "I would love to, Sylvia, but I don't have a place to stay."

"I'm sure John wouldn't mind," Zen interjected.

"Hey, Zen person, you don't listen very well, do you? You are not a part of this conversation. *Capiche?* You would stay with me, of course," Sylvia said with finality.

Briefly, Kat wondered if a person could die of second-hand smoke after a night or two in Sylvia's apartment. "I don't know—"

"There's more information I want to share with you, too," Sylvia interrupted.

"Are you trying to bribe me?" Kat meant it as a joke. However, she didn't need to be bribed.

"Just forget it," Sylvia snapped. "You said you wanted to know more about your mother, and I'm giving you the opportunity. If you don't want to take it, fine."

"I can be there in six hours," Kat said quickly. "Thanks for the offer, Sylvia. Really."

"That's more like it. We can start tonight."

Zen started the car and pulled out of the Greyhound station's parking lot. Kat couldn't read the expression on his face.

"Okay," Kat agreed, and then remembered. "Hey, Sylvia, what's the other information?"

"It can wait until you get here."

"Look, Sylvia, I've waited my entire life, and right now, I'm sick and tired of surprises. I don't want to have to dwell on this for another six hours."

Sylvia hesitated, coughed. "True enough," she said. She paused again. "I have the note."

"What note?" Kat felt like her brain had been so overstimulated in the last few days that she didn't grasp things that she should.

Another pause. "I didn't give it to the police. I didn't think it was any of their damn business."

Kat's recognition dawned. "Oh," she gasped.

"Yes," Sylvia said, "I have your mother's suicide note."

28

MARCH 22, 1982

Melody had to get out of this hospital *now*. There was no reason to be here because she was not going to have this baby. Her baby was dead. If, after hours, days, and weeks of labor, this baby finally arrived *still born* and horribly deformed, Melody knew that the nurses would whisk it away. They would put her new dead baby in the morgue, just as they had done with her poor baby boy. Then, as they had done with her poor baby boy, they would bury it in a box in the cold, dark earth. Melody could not let that happen. She would not let that happen again.

Marcus came into the room. "How are we doing here, pumpkin? Have we made any progress?"

What did he mean by *we*? There was no *we*. Now there was just her and her poor dead baby. "I'm a failure to progress," she said dully.

"Now, now, Mellie, the baby will come when he or she is ready to come."

Marcus always told her lies.

She hadn't had a single contraction in over an hour.

"Do you want some more ice chips," Marcus asked as he reached for the container.

She didn't want any damn ice chips! But instead of saying this, she would have to be nice to him to throw him off the track. "I'd rather have a gin and tonic," she said.

Marcus chuckled. "That's my little flower. Even under the stress of her labor, she still has a sense of humor."

Marcus talked about her in the third person, as if she wasn't even there. Marcus had never really *looked* at her.

"It's quite a sight around here," Marcus said conversationally. "The place is crawling with pregnant women. Every room is filled with a woman having a baby, and they're even walking up and down the halls."

Bless him! For once, he had given her something of value. "How many women are walking in the halls?"

"I don't know. Three or four? Why are they doing that?"

Damn him! Marcus hadn't listened to her and pushed an ice chip through her clenched lips. He never listened to her! And he didn't see her smoldering glare. "Sometimes, it helps the labor along."

"Do you think we should give it a try?" he asked, excited. "We could be part of the pregnant parade!"

She'd tried so hard to be a good wife to this man and failed at that, too. It was not his fault that she didn't love him. It was not her fault that he loved her too much. "I suppose we could give it a try." She could blend in with all the pregnant women, and no one would suspect what she was up to.

"I'll help you out of bed. Where's your bag? You packed a robe, didn't you? Some of the women ... Well, they really should be wearing robes. Unmentionable parts are showing."

"At this point, Marcus, most of the women are beyond modesty." Where had he put her coat? She would need her coat.

Marcus located her bag and pawed through it. "You didn't bring a robe, pumpkin!" he said, genuinely chagrined. "Do they have one you could borrow around here? Surely, they have extra robes in a hospital?"

"You know what, Marcus? I'm kind of cold. We could use my coat as a robe."

"It is rather cold in here," he agreed. "Instead of a robe, I guess your coat would work." He'd hung it up in the small closet and now laid it over the chair by the bed.

She would need her purse. "Is my purse in the closet, too?"

Marcus chuckled. "Why do you need a purse, Mellie? You're not going to the supermarket. Do you want to put on lipstick, too?"

Think fast, she told herself. "I think I have a tube of ChapStick in there. My lips are so dry, Marcus."

"Oh, baby. Of course. I'll go to the nurse's station and get it. I had them put it in the safe."

It was a good thing she'd asked. Who puts a purse in a hospital safe? "Why did you do that, Marcus?" she asked evenly.

"You can never be too careful, kitten," he said and went to retrieve the purse.

Melody knew that her time would run out eventually. Eventually, another futile contraction would begin. Eventually, Marcus would catch on. She had to get Marcus out of this room, away from her. That was going to be the hardest part of all. How could she keep devoted, excited Marcus distracted? She was going to need at least an hour, maybe more if her contractions started again.

Television.

Marcus returned with her purse, and for a second, Melody could not remember what she had asked for. She looked at him blankly. "I'm not sure what I—"

"Poor baby," Marcus said. "You're tired, aren't you? I'll find the ChapStick for you."

Bless him! He had given her another out. "You know what, Marcus? I'm really tired. Maybe we should take our little walk later?"

Disappointed, Marcus said, "But don't you think we should do everything we can to help this baby be born?"

Poor Marcus. He didn't have a clue; he never had.

"Marcus, *honey*, I need a little nap before the next contraction. You want me to be strong, don't you?"

It was one of the few endearments she had given him during their marriage, and he beamed. "I'll sit right here."

That was not going to happen. "Someone told me there's a television in the expectant fathers' waiting room. Isn't *Jeopardy* on at this time of day? You could go and watch one of your favorite programs while I nap."

"I don't know ..." Marcus was clearly torn.

"The nurse will come and get you if anything starts to happen. I promise."

Marcus didn't look convinced.

"I promise, Marcus. Please. I need a little rest. It'll be okay." That wasn't true. Adrenaline kicked in now that she knew what she had to do. And now that Melody knew how she would be with her baby, she was determined. She hadn't taken any drugs; drugs hadn't dulled her senses. On the contrary, they now felt like they were on high alert.

"Is it nearby?"

"Just down the hall." Melody had no idea where the room was, but she counted on Marcus' infatuation with television to keep him looking until he found it.

"Okay, flower," he finally said, reluctantly. "You're positive they'll come and get me if the baby starts to come?"

"I promise, Marcus. Now let me get some rest."

Those were the last words Melody Arnold said to her husband.

As she sat up on the bed, Melody thought it was good that the slutty OB nurses were inattentive to a woman who was a *failure to progress*. And then, of course, one of the inattentive nurses stuck her head into the room. "How are we doing in here?" she asked. "Any progress yet?"

Such a stupid nurse. Had she not figured out that the baby was dead? Melody forced herself to smile. She must play the game. "Not yet. I think I'll be sticking around for a while. Who knows? I might set a world record for the longest labor in the world."

"Now, now, honey," the nurse said distractedly, "the baby will come in due time."

She was a liar, too. They were all liars.

"I'll send Dr. Crowley to check on you when he has the time," the lying nurse said. I tell you, I've been working this ward for five years, and I've never seen anything like it. Women are having babies right and left around here. I've never seen it so busy."

"Don't worry about me. Nothing exciting is happening in this room." And then, just to be sure she had enough time, Melody thought she should cover her tracks a little more thoroughly. "I think I might take a stroll down the hall. Maybe I can make something happen then."

"Good idea." The nurse hurriedly moved away.

As quickly as she could, Melody put on her coat, tucking her purse inside, under her arm. She was desperate to get out of this hospital, desperate to obliterate her own failures, and desperate to do the only thing she knew she could do to save this baby from the same fate that her poor baby boy had suffered. This baby was not going to be *still born*.

But she had no shoes! Where had Marcus put her shoes? She searched the tiny closet. The loafers she had worn to the hospital—the only pair that would fit over her swollen feet—weren't there. Where had Marcus put her shoes? Had he put them in the safe, too? The realization came swiftly. Marcus knew that she was planning to escape, once and for all. Her husband had stolen her shoes!

Melody's heart pounded. She didn't have much time, but she must not panic. *She must not panic.* She still had her gray duffel bag in which she had packed some slippers, and she had packed some stationery and her rosary beads. She hadn't said the rosary since she married Marcus. However, she had packed them at the last minute because Ma would have wanted her to have her rosary beads, the ones she'd received from Ma and Daddy at her first communion so long ago, before Marcus, before *still born* babies, before she had fallen into the black hole.

There was a commotion in the hall. A wheeled gurney carried a moaning, screeching woman. The gurney whizzed by Melody's room with the woman shouting, "This hurts so bad! Why didn't anyone tell me it would hurt this bad?" Then as they disappeared around a corner: "Get this thing out of me!" Nurses and orderlies followed, and Melody could hear: "Breach birth. Complications."

It was a sign from God; this was her chance. She must *move*. Melody turned in the opposite direction from the one they had wheeled the woman. The other strolling pregnant women seemed to have scattered back to their rooms because of the commotion, deserting the hallway. Quickly, quickly, Melody walked to the end of the hall, where there must be an elevator. There was! God had given her another sign.

But wait. There was the sign God wanted her to see: STAIRS. Yes, that was what she would do. She would take the stairs. The elevator might be crowded, or worse yet, Marcus might be in the elevator. He would force her to go back to her bed. He would force her to play this through to the bitter, awful end. She couldn't risk it.

She pushed through the doors to the empty, echoing stairwell. What floor was she on? She thought it might be the fourth or fifth, but it didn't matter. She would take the stairs down. She couldn't risk going through the lobby. People would wonder why a pregnant woman was going out instead of checking herself in to deliver her baby (because they would not know that her baby was dead). And Marcus might be there! It was very possible that Marcus would be lurking in the lobby. If the lobby had a TV, Marcus might be lurking there, watching and waiting.

Melody, breathless when she reached the bottom of the stairs, pushed open another door. She was in a basement hallway, dimly lit. If this hospital was anything like Mercy—and all hospitals were the same, weren't they?—there would be storage space down here, perhaps some clerical workers' offices, perhaps the cafeteria. She hoped the cafeteria wasn't down here, filled with too many people futilely eating to escape disease and death. No, wait a minute. She did hope the cafeteria was down here because then there would have to be a delivery entrance. But she couldn't walk through the room. They might already be looking for her. And it was very possible that Marcus might be waiting for her there.

Then she remembered. Thank God, she remembered. After the awful scene in the car when Marcus asked her if she loved him, she had been so distraught that she'd almost forgotten they had parked the car in an underground parking garage: 3A Red. They'd taken one elevator up and walked through a door—it had to have been this very basement!—and ridden another elevator up to the maternity ward. She had to find that door.

She looked at her watch. It had only taken a minute or so to get to the basement, but time was not on her side. She must move quickly. She must *will* her feet to carry her heavy body. In the distance, she heard voices, and she moved toward them. She made a left into the next hallway and saw people up ahead. Immediately, she turned around and retreated to the doorway at the bottom of the stairs. It was too risky.

Think, she told herself. The seconds ticked loudly in her head. Of course! She must go back up one flight of stairs to the first floor. The first floor must have an emergency exit door. Melody knew that Mercy had an emergency exit on the first-floor stairwell. They had practiced emergency evacuations through that door, and this hospital would not be different. In case of fire, patients must have a means of exit. She hauled herself up the stairs, one step at a time. She had to conserve her energy. She couldn't lose faith.

And God was on her side. He would guide her every step of the way. There was the promised emergency exit door within her reach. She pushed through it, praying that there wasn't an alarm on the door, or if there was, that some careless janitor had disengaged it. (Why would there be an alarm? Hospitals were not prisons—or were they?)

No alarm, and the door swung open. And Melody walked, walking away from St. Matthew Hospital into a dreary, ugly, windy day.

And God watched over her.

29

APRIL 2012

Zen insisted on walking Kat to Sylvia's door. "You don't have to do this," Kat said. "The building is safe, and it's not like I have a lot of luggage or anything." However, she was touched. Maybe he was as reluctant to say good-night as she was? Maybe he was actually, finally going to kiss her?

No such luck.

"I want to meet this Sylvia. She sounds like quite a character." Zen knocked on the door.

"Oh," Kat said, trying to hide her disappointment. What, exactly, was she expecting? On the long car ride back, Kat had not gathered her courage and asked Zen how he felt about her. It would have been the perfect opportunity, but ultimately, she couldn't do it, and she knew why. If she confessed how she was starting to feel about him, and he said that he didn't feel the same way, she would be beyond embarrassed. And God knew that she had been embarrassed in front of him too many times to count. She would be beyond disappointed; she would cry. Again.

"It's open," Sylvia called from inside.

They opened the door to find Sylvia, dressed in her black trench coat and clunky boots, packing a big satchel with bottles of methadone piled on the coffee table. She looked up. "Who are you?" she said to Zen.

"This is Zen," Kat quickly said. "He's the one who drove me to Carbondale and who's been helping me all this week."

"What the hell kind of name is Zen?" Sylvia barked.

"It's a nickname," Zen said easily, flashing his charming smile.

"Yin and yang, Zen and zang," Sylvia sniffed. She looked him up and down. "You're rather attractive, though."

"Thanks," Zen said.

It was Kat who was embarrassed at Sylvia's frank, predatory appraisal. "Sylvia!"

"What's your problem, Kat? I've had more men than I care to count, and none of them turned out to be worth a damn. However, it was always more pleasant if the man of the hour was reasonably attractive." She looked Zen up and down again. "Not bad at all."

For some reason, Kat felt the need to explain the situation to Sylvia. "Zen is not my boyfriend."

It was Kat's turn to get the assessing gaze from Sylvia. "Why the hell not?" she barked.

Kat blushed.

"We don't know each other that well," Zen offered smoothly.

What was he talking about? He didn't think he knew her? In Kat's opinion, Zen probably knew her better than anyone—with the exception of Granny Nanny, of course. She rolled her eyes. Damn it, she did do it all the time.

Zen must have thought that the eye-rolling was still their signal. "I'd better be going." He backed toward the door.

"What's your hurry?" Sylvia lit a cigarette, coughing.

"Yeah, Zen, what's your hurry?" Kat said. Was he that anxious to be rid of her?

Zen stopped in his tracks, and for once, he seemed to be at a loss for words.

Her packing done, Sylvia leaned back in her chair, still staring at the two of them, still assessing. "I smell sexual tension in the air."

"Jesus, Sylvia." Kat blushed a deeper shade of red.

"And believe me," Sylvia continued, unperturbed, "I am an expert at smelling sexual tension. An expert. I'm a regular hound dog when it comes to sexual tension."

"You really know how to make a person feel at home, don't you, Sylvia?" Kat muttered.

"I call them like I see them, Kat. Always have and always will."

"You've got to admire that." Zen's smile had returned.

Kat rolled her eyes. Zen could be such a kiss-ass.

"Not really. My mouth has always gotten me in trouble." Then Sylvia said, "You blush just like your mother, Kat. Mel could blush as the drop of a hat."

Seeing an opportunity to change the subject, Kat said, "Could I see the … note?" She didn't know why, but she couldn't bring herself to say the word *suicide*.

"In due time." Sylvia gathered her bag. "Right now, I've got rounds to make." She strode toward the door, opened it, and called over her shoulder: "Are you coming, Kat?"

Kat did not want to do this. She'd had enough for one day. But would Sylvia allow her to see her mother's note if she didn't? "Do I have a choice?"

"You always have a choice. You just need to make the *right* one."

"Am I supposed to come along, too?" Zen asked.

"Do you have a gun?" Sylvia cocked her head.

"No, and isn't it illegal to carry a weapon in Chicago?"

Sylvia laughed. "You've got to be kidding me! Do you know how easy it is for a drug kingpin to get a gun in Chicago?"

Now Kat really didn't want to go.

"Do you know martial arts, Mr. Yin Yang Zen Zang?"

"Sorry, no. But I ran track in high school."

Sylvia considered and made her decision. "Then you are absolutely no use to us. Come on, Kat." She was out the door.

"I don't think you should do this," Zen said to Kat. "It sounds dangerous."

"I'm pretty sure—I hope—she's exaggerating." However, Kat wasn't sure.

"Come *on*, Kat," Sylvia called from the hallway.

Kat gave Zen one more look and followed Sylvia.

"Who did you say you worked for?" Kat asked as Sylvia drove an old battered VW van to their first stop. Blankets, cases of bottled water, boxes of crackers and condoms, and other assorted paraphernalia filled the two back seats.

"I didn't." Sylvia darted in and out of the lanes of traffic on Dearborn Street.

Kat was no longer worried about drug kingpins and weapons. She worried that Sylvia would crash into a bus. "Do you think you could slow down a little?"

Sylvia ignored that suggestion. "I guess you could say that I'm a one-woman nonprofit organization."

"You do this by yourself?" Kat thought Sylvia was employed to do this, but it didn't look like that was the case.

"Yep." Sylvia parked in front of a dilapidated apartment building.

"Why?"

"I do it because I used to be a drug addict and because I think the resources available to get people off drugs are woefully inadequate. I supply methadone when I have it. To people on the streets, I give blankets and water. Mostly, I just listen." Sylvia stared at the apartment building.

"That's rather noble of you." Kat knew people in Arizona who volunteered at soup kitchens and who were Big Sisters and that sort of thing, but to put yourself in danger night after night seemed like it went way beyond simple volunteering. It was, in fact, noble.

"Noble my ass." For once, Sylvia didn't bark. She turned to Kat, and she had tears in her eyes. "The real reason I do it is because of your mother."

Kat felt her throat tighten up. Somehow, she knew what Sylvia was going to say next.

"I was the one who introduced Mellie to drugs. It started here, in this apartment building where I lived with Thelma. We thought it was innocent fun to try all of Thelma's opioids. We called it our *research*."

"But you were nurses!"

"Nurses aren't saints, Kat. It's funny. At first, Mellie acted like she thought they were, too. At one point, during nursing school, I accused her of thinking that nurses were too high and mighty to shit." Sylvia gave a small smile. "I still miss Mellie. I miss her every day. Even though I know how the story turns out, I still think of those days as the best of my life."

Kat felt the anger begin to simmer. If it had not been for Sylvia, her mother might still be alive. "How can you say that? A woman jumped off a 100-foot light tower because of your *innocent fun!*"

"Maybe," Sylvia said quietly.

"*Maybe?*" Kat couldn't keep her voice from rising.

"There were other factors involved."

"Such as *what?* That's what I've been trying to find out, Sylvia!"

"Depression, desperation, delusions. Take your pick. Looking back on it now, it seems obvious that Mellie should have seen a therapist after her baby boy was stillborn. Although back then, it wasn't as common as it is now."

"What do you mean by *delusions?*" Sylvia was never going to tell her everything—Kat knew that—and she also knew that it was probably for the best. But Sylvia offered information now, and Kat better calm down and listen, even though it was hard. When Sylvia talked about Mellie, Mellie became a real person to Kat, a living, breathing person. A young woman with her whole life ahead of her. A young woman who had been introduced to drugs and had a genetic or emotional disposition to become addicted.

"The last time I saw her in the hospital, she was talking crazy shit."

"She thought the baby was dead."

Sylvia looked at her closely. "Yes, Kat, she thought you were dead."

Kat shivered, not because it was chilly outside, which it was, but because it was still hard to reconcile herself to the cold, hard facts. She had been the baby in Melody Arnold's womb when she climbed up that light tower. She, Kat, had been the one who survived the leap. Against impossible odds, she had survived, cushioned only by the amniotic sac. Frankly, it was unbelievable.

"Mel had been in prodromal labor—labor which starts and stops, sometimes for days—and she was exhausted. I think the prolonged pain, combined with her exhaustion—and I know that she hadn't slept well for months—might have contributed to her delusions. But then again, I'm not a psychiatrist or a psychologist, so I can't say with any absolute certainty."

"If you thought she was talking crazy shit, why did you leave her?"

It started to rain, and Sylvia stared at the drops running down the windshield for a long time before she answered. "That's another regret I have to live with every day of my life. I had a definite uneasy feeling about the whole thing. That damn OB-GYN took his sweet time. I know that the maternity ward was exceptionally busy that day, but that didn't excuse the son of a bitch for not inducing Mel or prepping her for a C-section. And then Mel with that crazy talk about her baby being dead ..." Sylvia lit a cigarette with shaking hands. "I left because I had a court date for my first arrest."

Kat wanted to ask her how many times she'd been arrested, but it seemed irrelevant. "I suppose that's a good reason."

"No," Sylvia said, "it was not." She smoked quickly, furiously, inhaling deeply and exhaling long streams of smoke.

Despite herself, Kat coughed.

"If it bothers you, roll down a damn window. I'm not putting it out."

Kat inched down the window and didn't dare complain to Sylvia that rain pelted her right shoulder. Sylvia was finally telling her things she needed to know. She waited, but Sylvia seemed lost in thought.

Finally, Sylvia said, "I should have stayed."

"You didn't know."

"I should have known. I was Mel's best friend, damn it!"

"How can you possibly know that your pregnant best friend is going to climb up a 100-foot light tower and jump?"

Sylvia didn't say anything.

"Right, Sylvia? How could you possibly have known that?"

"Fucking drugs," Sylvia said and lit another cigarette off the smoldering butt of her first.

When Sylvia finished her second furiously smoked cigarette, Kat decided to ask one more question. It was time to get to the point. After thirty years, it was more than time to ask what she'd been anguishing about ever since she read the newspaper article. "Do you think she jumped because she didn't want me? Was that part of the reason? Be honest with me. I can take it." However, Kat held her breath.

"No," Sylvia barked.

"No, *what*?" No, her mother didn't want her, or no, that was not the reason she jumped?

"No, you were not the reason, nor part of the reason, why your mother jumped off that tower." Sylvia opened the car door. "We've wasted enough time. It's time for you to meet Juanita. Juanita struggles with meth addiction."

Sylvia was done answering questions.

And Kat was done asking.

It was a long night. Kat didn't know how Sylvia did it. She watched in amazement as a fifty-four-year-old woman flitted from place to place, from the apartment on Compton Street to a neighborhood in Rosewood, and then to lower, lower Wacker Drive where the homeless men and women huddled beneath plastic garbage bags and pieces of cardboard. It was that dark and dank place, with people clustered against the concrete pilings alongside the road that got to Kat the most. Many of these people, Sylvia explained, had been reduced to begging on the streets during the day. Many of these people, in addition to substance abuse, also had a mental illness. Many of these people—most of these people, Sylvia stressed—had been cut off or abandoned by their families. Forgotten.

Everywhere she went, Sylvia was known and expected.

Everywhere she went, Sylvia dispensed the methadone, water, blankets, condoms, and crackers.

Everywhere she went, Sylvia dispensed compassion.

"How're you doing, Gretchen?" Sylvia asked one gray-haired, toothless woman of indeterminate age who was lucky enough to have a man's coat as a blanket. "Did you get that sprained ankle examined at the free clinic on Washington Street? I told Dr. Grunner to expect you."

"Doctors scare me, Miss Sylvia. Besides, what doctor wants to look at a ragged piece like me?" Gretchen asked sorrowfully. "I don't smell too good."

"Nonsense," Sylvia said. "He's a wonderful doctor and a very nice man. If you're afraid to go, I'll go with you."

"That would be nice, Miss Sylvia," Gretchen shyly said as she took a water bottle.

"I'll pick you up on Tuesday." Sylvia gently patted her arm.

Gretchen was not the only one that Sylvia offered to help. As she passed among the men and women, Sylvia made notes on who had gotten arrested, who had gone on a bender, and who had died.

Kat, trailing along behind her, wondered, *Who is this woman?* Sylvia could act like such a bitch to so-called respectable society, but she was like a dark angel to these homeless, lost, and abandoned citizens. Kat felt ashamed of herself for calling them derelicts. And she was ashamed that her first impulse was still to shrink away from these people—from their smell, their dirty clothes and mismatched shoes, their possible volatility, and their need.

Was she that white and middle-class?

Yes.

What, exactly, was Sylvia trying to show her? Melody Arnold had never been homeless. Melody, in fact, had been deeply loved.

After they roamed the cavernous underground street for close to two hours, Sylvia approached a young black man, possibly in his early thirties, obviously zoned out on something. "Have you seen Belinda this evening, Devon?"

Devon stared at her with bloodshot, vacant eyes.

Sylvia took him by the shoulders and gently shook him. "Devon, where's Belinda?"

He could only shrug and shake his head mournfully.

"It's all right, Devon. I'll find her myself."

"Who's Belinda?" Kat asked as she picked up her pace to follow Sylvia's brisk walk down the street.

"She's a special case. I want you to meet her. I'm not going home until I find her."

How did this fifty-four-year-old woman do this night after night? Kat was cold, tired, and hungry. Did she sympathize with the men and women Sylvia had introduced her to this evening? Yes. Did she want to go back to the apartment? Yes, yes, and yes.

"If she's not here, we'll check the hospitals."

Kat knew that they would. Sylvia was on a mission, and Sylvia, Kat had come to understand during the long night, would not be deterred by mere mortal discomforts such as food and sleep. Despite Sylvia's brazen and outspoken nature, she was an amazing woman. She must have been one hell of a nurse.

"There she is," Sylvia said after thirty more minutes of searching. She walked even more quickly toward a small figure huddled next to a concrete pillar, alone.

As they came closer, Kat could see that Belinda was a young woman in her early twenties. Even though her blonde hair was dirty and matted, she was a strikingly pretty woman, and she shook uncontrollably.

Sylvia knelt and put a blanket around Belinda's shoulders. "Bad night?" she asked.

Belinda's teeth chattered. "I tried to be good."

"I know you did, honey," Sylvia soothed.

"It's so hard."

"Yes, it is." Sylvia put her arm around the shivering young woman.

"Gaston won't let me see my baby." Belinda started to cry. "Why won't he let me see my baby? I'm a good mother. You know that, Sylvia, don't you?"

"I know you're a good mother, honey."

"Not even court-supervised visits anymore."

Sylvia produced a tissue. "He wants you to get clean, Belinda."

"I've tried."

"You have to keep trying," Sylvia said.

"I want to go home." Instead of using the tissue to dry her eyes, Belinda tore it into shreds.

"I'll take you home." Sylvia took the shredded tissue from Belinda's nervous, plucking fingers and gave her another one.

"I can't go home!" Belinda cried, panicked. "Gaston would know everything!"

"There, there," Sylvia calmed. "We won't tell your husband."

As she watched Sylvia soothe the young woman, Kat was struck by how intimate the exchange was. Sylvia had obviously done this many times before.

"Gaston wants to send me back to rehab, but I can't go back there. It doesn't work for me. I'm too far gone." Belinda cried harder as she shredded the second tissue.

Sylvia handed her a third. "No, you're not, Belinda. You have to keep trying."

"But I can't! It's hopeless."

"No, it's not." Sylvia let Belinda sob into her shoulder for minutes before she said, "I'll take you to your sister's house, okay?"

"I try, and I try, and I try, but I'm so tired of trying."

"How many times have you—" Kat stopped when Sylvia shook her head vigorously at her.

"There, there," Sylvia soothed again. To Kat, she said, "Would you help me get her up?"

Kat took hold of Belinda's other shoulder. The tiny woman weighed practically nothing, and Kat was pretty sure that Sylvia could carry the girl all by herself.

"Who are you?" Belinda seemed to notice Kat for the first time.

"She's my friend," Sylvia said.

"You won't tell Gaston, will you? Then he'll know everything." Belinda looked frightened.

"I won't tell Gaston," Kat promised. It seemed of paramount importance to reassure the poor woman.

However, by the time they had made the long walk back to the car, she knew why Sylvia needed her assistance. Belinda seemed to *wake up* during the walk, and three different times she tried to break from their grasp and run. "I will not be kidnapped!" she screamed. "You are taking me against my will!"

Sylvia kept up a reassuring patter, and when they finally put her in the backseat of the van, Belinda collapsed into a heaving, sobbing mess. "I'm so sorry," she kept repeating. "I'm so sorry."

Kat wasn't sure if she was apologizing to them, to Gaston, or to the world at large. Probably all three.

After they deposited Belinda at her sister's, who'd sighed resignedly before ushering the still sobbing young woman into the house, they were finally on their way home. Kat was bone-tired after the long and stressful day: the trip to Carbondale, the revelation from Missy, the short but meaningful visit with her father, the missed opportunity with Zen, and then the long night with Sylvia. Yet she was strangely alert. So much had happened in the last twenty-four hours, and it was all starting to sink in.

"The poor woman," Kat said. It was hard to get the image of Belinda out of her mind. What had gone so terribly wrong in her life that it caused her descent into the hell of addiction? "How many times has she been in rehab?"

"Four," Sylvia said as she sped through the deserted streets. "And she's been hospitalized for attempted suicide three. She's twenty-five and has a one-year-old son."

"You would think that she would know better." Kat was sympathetic to poor Belinda, but still.

"Sober, yes. Addicted, no," Sylvia said succinctly.

"Was her life so terrible?"

"On the surface, no. Belinda is married to an up and coming hedge fund manager, and she had a promising career as a computer programmer."

"Geez, I don't get it." Kat didn't. If anyone should be taking drugs, it was her. Currently, her life pretty much sucked, but she wasn't even tempted. Granted, she'd been drinking too much during the past week, and on top of that, she might be … She wasn't even going to go there. She couldn't.

"There's nothing to *get*," Sylvia said. "Addiction is an equal opportunity employer."

"But she has a baby!"

"Are you dense, Kat? What I've been trying to tell you—over and over again—is that addiction can happen to anyone, and until you've been there, you have no idea how fucking hard it is to get the fucking monkey off your back."

"What fucking monkey?" Kat asked, exasperated.

Sighing, Sylvia dodged a garbage truck and started singing in a throaty, off-key voice:

> Hey dad, you been smacking da H again, quit it bitch, you have a monkey on
> Your back
> But the morphine eased the pain,
> And the grass grew round his brain,
> And gave him all the confidence he lacked.
> With a Purple Heart and a monkey on his back.
> There's a hole in daddy's arm where all the money goes.

A hole in daddy's arm. In her case, Kat thought, it would be *a hole in Mommy's arm where all the money goes*. Involuntarily, she shivered. Melody Arnold, her mother, shot up heroin and couldn't stop. She couldn't get the monkey off her back. She'd been twenty-four years old when she died.

"John Prine," Sylvia said, "a song called 'Sam Stone.'"

Kat listened to John Prine on the Sirius Outlaw Country station, but she'd never heard this particular song before. Even sung in Sylvia's tuneless voice, the lyrics would haunt her: *morphine eased the pain; grass grew round his brain.*

Sylvia pulled into the parking garage. "The song pretty much sums it up, I think."

"How did you manage to quit?" Kat got out of the van, suddenly dead tired and completely wiped out.

"It took years." Sylvia again led the way, her clunky black boots echoing in the parking garage. "I threw away my career, relationships, and almost my health. Finally, I just got pissed enough at myself to quit. It still wasn't easy."

"You're one of the strong ones who could wrestle the monkey from your back." Kat didn't doubt that for a minute.

"I wouldn't say that." They entered the building, and Sylvia pushed the elevator button.

"And Mellie wasn't." There, Kat had to say it. If Mellie had been strong enough, wouldn't she still be here today?

"Mellie was strong enough."

Kat waited for further explanation, but Sylvia seemed to be finished. Under the harsh hallway fluorescent lights, Sylvia looked every bit her age and tired. They rode the elevator in silence, and it wasn't until Sylvia unlocked her door that Kat found the courage to say, "You're still her loyal friend."

"Yes," Sylvia said simply.

Kat helped Sylvia make up the couch, but her overly tired mind still churned. *And gave her all the confidence she lacked.* Her poor, young mother. Kat looked at Sylvia. "How awful," she said.

Sylvia nodded. "Now you're starting to get the picture."

Kat slept until noon, and when she awoke, Sylvia was gone. Was the woman superhuman? Did she not need sleep? Any way she looked at it, Kat concluded that Sylvia was a woman with a mission. She didn't appear to have a regular job. Instead, she spent her nights helping people on the streets.

Where did she get her money? Not only did she not seem to need any sleep, but she also seemed to survive on thin air. Maybe there was an entire network of recovering addicts who helped each other out, a kind of Underground Railroad? Whatever. Kat had a feeling that she was never going to find the answers to those questions. Sylvia would never tell her, and Kat was never going to ask. It was finally becoming clear to Kat that some people would rather not have information pried out of them. They would prefer to divulge it in their own sweet time.

Kat took a quick, hot shower and went into the galley kitchen to find something for breakfast. No such luck. Apparently, the woman didn't eat either. What Sylvia had left, however, was a note explaining that the orange juice was in the fridge, and the vodka was in the upper left cabinet above the sink. "The breakfast of champions," the note said. "Help yourself."

Kat poured herself some orange juice. She would not start drinking again at this time of day. She carried the glass into the living room, with its worn-out furniture, shag carpeting, and an old TV that still sported rabbit ears. It seemed as if time had frozen in this room, this room that Mellie had probably visited many times. Kat could almost see the red-headed, freckled girl sitting in the burnt orange chair next to the couch. Had they taken drugs in this room?

Probably.

Kat had an uneasy feeling in the pit of her stomach, staring at the ghost-less chair. Everything hit too close to home. She'd come searching for her mother's past, and what she'd discovered had been so far from the fairy tale she'd conjured. In her wildest dreams, she would never have come up with this version of events. She had thought, naively, that learning about her mother would help her finally know herself.

Boy, she'd had no idea, none whatsoever.

It was too much to take in all at once.

And she might be pregnant.

Kat didn't want to be alone with her thoughts. Plus, the urge to snoop became overpowering. Did Sylvia have more pictures? Did Sylvia have Mellie's diary, if one existed? Where in the hell was the note Mellie wrote? Why hadn't Sylvia left *that* note on the kitchen table?

Vodka. Kat heard the vodka calling her name. "It's five o'clock somewhere," she said to the room that was still stuck in the eighties, stuck in the past. "London is five hours ahead. Hell, it's 5:00 in London." Kat walked back to the kitchen and filled a glass with ice and a generous slug of vodka.

She was turning into an alcoholic.

She was falling in love with the wrong man at the wrong time, once again.

She might be pregnant.

She was becoming completely unhinged, just like Melody Arnold.

"I need to call Granny Nanny, like *yesterday*," Kat said. The fact that she was talking to herself again frightened her even more. She searched through her purse for her phone. Dead as a doornail. Starting to panic, Kat looked around the room. Judging from everything else in this room, Sylvia must have …

Kat saw it—a landline. Yes. She punched in Granny Nanny's number. If Gran didn't answer, she didn't know what she'd do.

Gran answered. "If this is a telemarketer, you are wasting your time. I'm sure you're a lovely person, and I know you're only making minimum wage, and you should be thankful you have a job at all in this economy. However, I am not interested in any products at this time. Oh, well, if you are offering a good deal on Noxzema, I would not be averse to listening to your little spiel."

Kat's relief was so great that she sank heavily into the burnt orange chair. "It's me, Gran. I'm calling from Sylvia Hammond's phone. That's why you didn't recognize the number."

Granny Nanny chuckled. "I thought you were a telemarketer! Katrina, dear, how are you?"

"I'm … I'm …" Kat thought she'd spill her guts to Granny Nanny as she always did, but now she found that the words wouldn't come. She didn't want to tell Gran that in addition to jumping off a 100-foot light tower, Melody Arnold was also a heroin junkie. Was she too ashamed? At this point, Kat honestly didn't know. "I'm fine."

"How's the case going? Have you made any new discoveries?" Gran's voice sounded far away, and it cut in and out.

"Where are you, Gran? I can't hear you very well."

"Mr. Williams and I are on the train. We caught it in Williams, and we're on the way to the Grand Canyon. It's rather touristy, but there are these young cowboys who are quite handsome. Speaking of young men, how's Lorenzo?"

The crafty, noisy old lady never, ever missed a beat. Kat started to feel better already. Just hearing Granny Nanny's comforting voice could do that to her. "He's fine, too." Then, to change the subject, Kat said, "But you were just in Vegas."

"Yes, dear, and now we're on our way to the Grand Canyon."

"Are you and Mr. Williams on speed or something?" What was up with the two of them? They acted like a couple of teenagers. Then a crushing thought descended, making her feel physically ill. Perhaps it was *she* who had been holding back Granny Nanny all these years? Perhaps her neediness had been more of a shackle to Granny Nanny? If that had been the case, Kat would use everything in her power to change that situation. She would make sure that it never happened again.

Granny Nanny chuckled gaily once more. "Of course not, Katrina. However," and Gran lowered her voice so that it was barely audible, "Mr. Williams does take Cialis."

"I'm ... I'm very happy for you," Katrina stuttered. She definitely didn't need to know that fact. However, Kat was genuinely happy that someone she knew was having sex. It certainly wasn't her, thanks to Zen.

"I am very happy," Gran concurred.

Kat's stomach turned somersaults, so she decided she might as well verbalize what she was thinking. "Look, Gran, if I was the one who held you back all those years, I'm so sorry. I never meant to."

"What complete and utter nonsense, Katrina!" Gran quickly said. "You have been a joy to me. You didn't give me a chance to finish. What I was going to say next was: I would be even happier if you were here, too."

Kat's relief brought tears to her eyes. "Thanks, Gran. I love you, too. I should be home in two or three days."

"What's wrong, dear?"

The woman knew her so well. "Nothing, Gran."

"Katrina," the crafty old woman said firmly.

"Gran, I'm fine. It's just been an emotional week." It would take days, weeks, maybe even years to try to come to terms with everything that Kat had learned about Marcus and Melody Arnold.

"I would imagine so, dear, but you're a strong young woman. You know that, don't you?"

Strong was the last thing Kat felt at this point. "Sure, Gran."

"You're using Sylvia's phone?" Really, nothing got past the woman.

"I'm staying with her. She's quite a remarkable woman."

"That's so good to know ..." Gran's voice became fainter. "And you, too, Katrina dear, are a remarkable woman ..."

The connection was lost, but Kat had gotten what she needed from Granny Nanny. Bless her crafty, lovely heart.

Kat figured that the least she could do for Sylvia was buy her a few groceries at the CVS on the corner. The woman was so busy that she probably didn't have time to shop, and Kat was pretty sure that she hadn't quite maxed out her credit card. At least, she hoped that she had a few bucks left on it. When she returned to Arizona, one of her first priorities would be to get a decent job, maybe two, that allowed her to pay back all the people who had helped her in Chicago.

Kat turned into the next aisle of the drug store, on her way to the front cashier. Her stomach rumbled, and she walked quickly, not noticing what aisle she was walking through. Then she saw it out of the corner of her eye, the row of home pregnancy tests. She stopped in her tracks. *Shit.* The boxes waited, taunting her. Should she buy one or not? Without her quite realizing what it was doing, her right hand reached out to the nearest box, snatched it off the shelf, and dropped it in the cart.

There. It was done.

Two people were in line in front of her, and Kat waited impatiently. It was so tempting to wrestle open the bag of Fritos and take a handful. It wasn't stealing if she was going to pay for it, right? However, when she saw people do that kind of thing in the grocery store, she thought it showed a lack of self-control and always wondered why they couldn't wait for five more minutes. To distract herself, she thumbed through a copy of the *National Enquirer*. She jumped when she felt the tap on her shoulder.

"Inquiring minds want to know?" It was Zen, looking good in a Bulls t-shirt and stylishly ripped jeans. Naturally.

"What are you doing here?" she asked, startled.

"Same thing as you." He nodded toward her cart. "Buying some groceries."

Her cart. The pregnancy test was right on top, and Kat didn't want Zen to see it. It was none of his business, and there probably wasn't anything between them except for what she'd conjured up in her own murky imagination, but she still didn't want him to see it. Too many questions to answer. Too many mistakes to quote. Quickly, she dropped the tabloid paper on top of it. "What a coincidence," she laughed shakily.

"Not really. This is the closest place to buy anything resembling groceries in the neighborhood. So, how'd it go last night? Glad to see you're still in one piece, not missing any limbs, no bullet holes to be found." He smiled. "Seriously, I'm glad to see you're all right." He reached over and patted her hand that clutched the cart.

His touch sent a hot jolt through her body, the damn Benedict Arnold. Kat flushed, and to cover her fluster, she rapidly started to tell him about the previous night while unloading her groceries onto the conveyor belt. She kept eye contact with him the entire time, trying to distract him from what she put on the belt. She lifted the pregnancy test to the belt under the National Enquirer.

Kat breathed a sigh of relief. The check-out boy had put everything safely in a bag, and Zen hadn't seemed to be paying attention to her purchases. She handed the check-out boy her credit card. "Do you have any plans for this afternoon?" she asked Zen.

"As a matter of fact, I don't."

"I think it's time to take a trip out to the light tower." She hadn't consciously been thinking along those lines, but with sudden clarity, she knew that was what she would have to do.

"Are you sure?" Zen frowned.

"It's time." She couldn't prolong the inevitable any longer, nor did she want to. If she was ever going to get any closure, she had to see the tower that Melody Arnold had jumped from.

"Uh, ma'am?" The check-out boy cleared his throat.

"It's miss."

"Okay, miss, do you have another credit card? This one has been declined."

"Do you need to shout?" It seemed to Kat that he had used an overly loud voice for the situation. It might be her imagination, but she would swear that people turned to stare.

The check-out boy crossed his arms. "Do you have another card?"

Kat had other credit cards, but they were all maxed out as well. And of course, Zen would have to be there as a witness to her embarrassment. It just figured. "No, I don't. You'll have to take some items off and try the card again."

"I can help." Zen handed the boy his MasterCard.

"No, you can't, Zen." Kat snatched the card out of the boy's hand—she was really starting to dislike that young kid—and handed it back to Zen. Zen was low on cash, too, and about to start law school. She couldn't let him bail her out one more time.

"Fine," the surly kid said, and he dumped the contents of her bag back onto the conveyor belt. "What about this?" He held up the blue and white box of the pregnancy test.

"Why don't you just wave it in the air so the entire store can see?" Kat snapped. She didn't dare look at Zen. "Take it off the bill."

The people in the line behind her did not hide their impatience during the humiliating process. Kat returned the box of strawberry pop tarts, microwave popcorn, frozen pizza, the pint of cookie dough ice cream, and the National Enquirer as well. All she had left was a bag of Fritos and a can of chicken noodle soup. So much for trying to pay Sylvia back.

"I'll see you later," Kat said to Zen as she grabbed the bag of her meager purchases. All she wanted to do was flee the scene and Zen. Why was it that she was always at her worst when she was around him? Was it because she so desperately wanted him to like her? How very, very pathetic.

"No, wait for me. We'll drop this stuff off and then go catch a train out to the light tower."

Was he still willing to go with her? Good God, he was a nice person.

"It's not what you think," Kat said when they were on the sidewalk. It was, of course, exactly what it looked like. A woman bought a pregnancy test because she thought she might be knocked up. A woman didn't buy one for a science project, for pete's sake.

"How do you know what I think?" The day was overcast and cold, with a bitter wind coming off Lake Michigan. Zen turned up the collar of his jacket.

Well, that pretty much summed things up. "That's just it. I don't know what you're thinking." It was the truth.

"Besides," he said. "It's none of my business."

"I suppose not." Yet Kat hoped that he would care enough to ask what was going on. At the very least, wouldn't he be curious?

They were in John's apartment, and Kat microwaved the soup before Zen finally asked, "So, who's the father?"

"First of all, I'm pretty sure I'm not pregnant. It's just been a stressful, out-of-the-ordinary type of week, to put it mildly." Kat poured the hot soup into two bowls. "And secondly, I absolutely refuse to be pregnant with Benson's child. I *refuse.*"

Zen sat down at the table. A smile twitched at his lips. "I'm no expert, but I don't think it works that way. You can't simply *refuse* to be pregnant."

"Well, that's what I'm doing." Kat found a box of crackers in the cabinet and joined Zen at the table.

"Tell me about Benson."

Kat rolled her eyes. "Our recent breakup was the most non-dramatic breakup in the history of breakups."

Zen rolled his eyes.

Kat laughed. "That truly is an irritating habit, isn't it? I have to quit doing it. However, in this case, it's the truth. We lived together for a year, and in retrospect, I don't think we even liked each other all that much." She then gave Zen the Cliff Notes version about pretty boy Benson and his allowance, Carmella and the KKK apartment, and finally, about finding out about Benson's golf "lessons."

Kat talked through their lunch and continued talking as they walked toward the train. Zen, as she already knew, was a good listener and didn't interrupt. Kat was amazed at how good—how freeing—it felt to talk about Benson and the fizzled out end of their so-called relationship.

When she finished, Zen said, "If you don't mind my saying, pretty boy Benson sounds like a freeloading, lazy Mama's boy."

"You speak the truth, my good man. You speak the truth."

They stood on the platform at the southbound station, waiting for their train. Zen had thoughtfully provided her with one of his warmer jackets, along with some gloves and a scarf. It was only in the lower forties, but Kat thought it was freezing. Maybe this wasn't such a good idea after all on this dreary, windy day, but she was with Zen, and she knew he would, once again, help her through this.

"I don't think he was good enough for you," Zen said now. The train rumbled in the distance.

Kat looked up at his kind green/gold eyes. "Thank you."

It was one of the nicest things anyone had ever said to her.

30

MARCH 22, 1982

Melody walked one block south of the hospital and stood on a corner, trying to hail a cab. She'd done this quite a few times with Sylvia during their research days when, on the nights they didn't go home with dates and had too much to drink and too much nose powdering, they realized that they'd missed the last train back to Thelma's apartment.

Poor, poor Thelma. She died with a needle sticking out of her arm. That was not going to happen to Melody. Oh, she knew the temptation all too well. She had fallen into the temptation of Satan. She had been his willing partner, and she would not let that happen again. She would guarantee that never happened again.

A cab went by with its light on—occupied. Another slowed, but when the grizzled cabbie saw Melody, he shook his head and passed on by. Time was of the essence, and Melody stepped farther off the curb, into the street, and started to wave frantically. She was getting cold, and her stomach started to cramp. *Please,* she willed.

And God listened. The next taxi slowed and stopped. Gratefully, Melody opened the door and got in.

"You're in luck, lady," the young driver said. "The hospital is just back a block."

To Melody, he looked like he couldn't be more than sixteen, and it wasn't his picture on the permit displayed on the dashboard. "How old are you?" she asked, not that she cared. The important thing was that he would take her where she wanted to go.

"I'm seventeen, ma'am. I have a valid driver's license and everything." The top of his ears turned pink, and Melody could see the glint of his braces.

"That's not your picture on the permit," she said, not that she cared. The boy was going to take her where she wanted to go.

"There's no need to grill me, ma'am. Do you want me to take you back to the hospital, or not?" His blush crept down his cheeks to his neck.

"No, I don't."

"I don't understand, ma'am—"

"I don't like it when people call me *ma'am*," Melody interrupted. "I'm only twenty-four." She felt the start of another useless contraction and grabbed her stomach, stifling a moan.

"Please don't have that baby in the car, lady. I wouldn't know what to do. And my brother would kill me if you messed up his car." He wore a panicked expression on his face.

"Don't worry. I'm not going to have this baby in your car." She didn't bother to explain that she wasn't going to have this baby anywhere, ever. "Why are you driving your brother's cab?" she asked, not that she cared.

"I'm not supposed to tell." His right eyelid twitched with nervousness.

Melody knew he thought she was some crazy lady. So be it. However, she needed him to drive the damn car. She tried to act reasonably. "It's okay. I don't need to know your business, and you don't need to know mine. Agreed?"

The kid couldn't keep his mouth shut. "My brother's back is acting up, and he couldn't afford to take a night off. He's got an autistic kid, and you know, that kind of thing is super expensive. So I offered to help him out. I was only trying to do something nice for my brother, but if anyone ever found out, we could be in a shitload of trouble. He might lose his license, and I don't know what would happen to me. Do you think I could go to jail?"

"I don't know," Melody panted. "You're a minor. I don't think so, though." The contraction wound down.

"I'm thinking this is a really bad idea," the kid said.

"Look, you can drive this car, can't you?" Oh, God, another contraction started. She needed to get this kid to *move*. What if they had already noticed that she'd left the hospital? What if Marcus was walking the streets, looking for her? He could be here any second. He would know that she was in this cab.

"Sure, I can drive this car! My brother wouldn't have entrusted me if I wasn't a safe driver."

"Of course, you're a good driver. I can tell that," Melody said. "And I'll tell you another thing. I promise I won't ever tell anyone about this, not a soul—if you drive this car to where I want to go."

The kid looked doubtful.

"I promise." Melody raised the two fingers on her right hand. "Scout's honor."

"I used to be a boy scout," the kid said.

"That doesn't surprise me at all."

The kid made a decision and turned around. "Where to, lady?"

"Do you know where the abandoned railway yard is at on 96th Avenue and Blue Line Road?"

"Sure, I used to take my BB gun there and shoot at old beer bottles."

Did she have to spell it out? "Take me there, please," she panted. The contraction was cresting.

"Are you sure?"

"I'm positive."

"You're the boss."

"Could you please hurry?" Time was of the essence. She was running out of time.

"Your wish is my command," he said grandly and started to drive.

He didn't say another word as he drove Melody through the streets of Oak Lawn Park and then Chatham, and Melody was relieved that she didn't have another contraction. Since the baby would never be born, the contractions were unnecessary, utterly hopeless. This poor baby was not going to be *still born*. Melody would not allow it.

However, when they got to the overgrown and dismal railway yard at a little past four o'clock, the kid's nervousness returned. "Are you sure about this, lady? It's kind of a cold and windy day for a picnic if that's what you're planning to do."

"I'm sure." Melody gave him all the money in her purse. Then, to reassure him, she added, "Remember, I promise I won't ever tell anyone about this."

"You're a nice lady," he said.

Melody would never know that, as it turned out, the kid could keep his mouth shut. Even when he found out what the nice lady had done the next day, he didn't tell anyone about the taxi ride to the abandoned railway yard. He never told a soul.

She was almost there. Twice, she had stumbled over twisted weeds. Twice, she had fallen but had gotten back up. It took a great deal of effort to heave herself off the cold ground and plunge herself forward into the icy wind, but she had done it. She knew what she had to do, and nothing was going to stop her. All she had to do was keep her eyes trained on the light tower and put one foot in front of the other.

Melody's mind did not register the ugliness of the abandoned railway yard. She didn't notice the burned-out old cars, the trash, the rusty tracks, or the mice that scurried before her. She kept her eyes on the light tower, the tall, imposing structure, the scene where she'd first bought illegal drugs. It had been the beginning of the end then, but she hadn't known. Now she knew. Now she knew where evil originated. If she had not bought those drugs, she would not have killed her baby. Yes, she knew that now.

And she was going to pay the ultimate price.

Finally, she reached the large, round structure, her journey almost complete. All she had to do was climb up the ladder that snaked to the very top. She sat her duffel bag down next to the tower's base and reached for the first rung. She climbed up one, two, three rungs, and then her foot slipped. The slippers were not going to work. She climbed down and took them off. She was ready to begin again.

She had another contraction, and Melody fell to her hands and knees. This one was bad, the worst one so far. Why did they keep coming? There was no use for them; they accomplished nothing. Her dead baby was not coming out of her womb. She was not going to be *still born* like her brother.

She.

Melody suddenly knew that the baby was a girl. Her daughter, Katrina.

As the contraction reached its crest and then ebbed away, Melody cried. She cried for her poor choices, lost children, lost mother, lost life. Drenched in blame, Melody cried for all the things she had destroyed. There were so many things she could have done differently, and now it was too late. Too late.

Time was of the essence; time was running out.

Everything began and ended at this light tower.

Melody reached into the duffel bag for a tissue. She would wipe her eyes and then begin again. She would finish her journey. This one thing in her life she was going to do right. Her hand felt the stationery as she searched for the tissue. She paused. She should write a note, shouldn't she? Isn't that what people did? Wasn't that the right thing to do? She should write a message to Sylvia.

Sylvia. She would miss Sylvia, her best friend, her confidant, her partner in crime. She loved Sylvia like a sister, and the thought of that made Melody start to cry again. Sylvia would miss her, but Sylvia would understand. Sylvia, better than anyone, would understand. She would know why this had to be done.

Melody started to write but heard a noise and looked up. Was it Marcus? Had he found her? Her heart began to pound. He would make her go back to the hospital, and then everyone would know her shameful secrets. And the baby girl would be *still born*, just like her poor brother. Melody could not let that happen!

A feral cat came out of the weeds about ten feet away from Melody and slouched toward her, hissing. Melody scrambled to her feet. Was this another sign from God? Was he telling her she was out of time? No, no, God would not send a feral cat. It must be the work of the devil! Melody screamed and threw a rock at the animal. The cat, still hissing, turned and ran back into the weeds.

"Oh, dear God," Melody said. She trembled, and her heart still raced. Yet she knew what she had to do. This one thing in her life she was going to do right.

She reached up for a rung and began again. Her galloping heart propelled her forward. She moved as quickly as she could, but she was careful, oh so careful. She did not want to fall; she would not fall. Adrenaline coursed through her veins; she was strong. She must reach the top, and she would. It was the most important thing she would ever do.

She was almost at the top when she heard a siren. Marcus. He had found her, as she knew he would. But it was too late. She was almost at the top. Almost there ...

Marcus was running toward the tower, yelling something she could not hear. But it was too late. She reached the dome top and hoisted herself up into a crouching position. It was windy up here and slippery. She had made it! It was so beautiful that Melody started to cry again. She could see for miles and miles. On top of the light tower, she could finally see things clearly. Up here, she could forget her past and see the future. Up here, she knew that her baby was safe, with her.

She stood up slowly and extended her arms. Slowly, she leaned forward.

Yes, up here, she could see her future.

And it was lovely.

31

APRIL 2012

The walk from the train station to the abandoned railway yard was less than a half-mile. Kat wished it was longer. Much, much longer. As they drew closer, closer to the scene of Melody Arnold's fatal leap, Kat's anxiety mounted. She pulled Zen's jacket more tightly to her body, but it offered little protection against the wind. It was April in Chicago, but it felt like winter to Kat. She was freezing.

Zen noticed and put his arm around her shoulders. "Chilly day," he said.

"I remember your dad saying that March 22, 1982, was a windy day, too." Her birthday. Kat nestled against Zen's side, but she still felt cold. It was only an eerie coincidence that this day was also windy. That was all it was: an eerie coincidence.

All too soon, they were at the abandoned railway yard. They stopped at the edge of the overgrown lot filled with rusty old railway cars, trash, and twisted weeds. To Kat, it looked like a bleak sea of garbage. It had to be one of the most depressing places she had ever seen. She looked up and to the west and could barely make out a tall, round structure: the 100-foot light tower. Her heart clenched painfully in her chest.

"You don't have to do this," Zen, by her side, said quietly.

"Yes, I do." She took Zen's hand for added courage as they started to make their way through the thick weeds and brambles. Kat stubbed her toe, hard, against something metal. "Oh!" The pain brought tears to her eyes.

"Watch out for the tracks," Zen said, too late.

"How could a woman in labor do this?" Kat said after she got her breath back, and they started walking again. The brambles snagged at her legs and ankles, trying to pull her down.

"It probably wasn't this overgrown thirty years ago."

"Still," Kat said. "How?"

"Yeah, it would have still been tough."

Kat's legs felt heavy as they made their way toward the light tower, and she kept her head down, concentrating on every step, every step that Melody Arnold had taken on her last day on earth. She had to have been driven by some compulsion or some delusion.

Melody Arnold had thought her baby was dead, and she'd already given birth to one stillborn baby. She must have felt that she couldn't live through that pain again, so she had escaped from the hospital, arrived here somehow, and then determinedly kept walking through this horrible field of weeds to get to the light tower. She had a hospital bag with her. Melody Arnold had packed for her final journey.

Kat and Zen finally reached the clearing at the base of the light tower. Kat looked up. It was so much higher than she'd imagined. How in the world could a pregnant woman climb all the way to the top? *Sheer will.* That's what Officer Simpson had said, and Kat had to believe that it was true. Melody Arnold had climbed this 100-foot tower through *sheer will.* "Dear God," she said.

"Unbelievable," Zen said.

Suddenly, Kat had to *know* what Melody Arnold had felt. She had not planned on this—not at all—but she walked to the ladder and grabbed a rung. She hoisted herself up to the first rung, then the second, then the third. The wind rocked against her body.

"What are you doing?" Zen said, alarmed. He was directly below her.

"I want to know what it feels like to be on the top of that tower." She moved up another rung and could feel the adrenaline as it started to course through her body.

"I can't let you do this, Kat. It's not safe. I can see that some of the rungs are almost rusted through." He tugged at her leg.

Kat moved up another rung.

"Look, if you're going to do this, I'm going to have to follow you up. And I don't want to! I, for one, do not have a death wish."

A death wish. That was it. Melody Arnold had a death wish, and in an extraordinary way, it sounded lovely: a death *wish*.

"What about the baby?" Zen yelled.

"She thought the baby was dead." Kat moved up another rung.

"Damn it, Kat! I'm talking about *your* baby." Zen climbed onto the first rung of the ladder.

"I'm not pregnant! I can't even afford to buy a pregnancy test!" The wind got stronger, and she had to yell to be heard, to make him understand.

"Look at me, Kat!" Zen yelled.

Kat wanted to keep going. She was barely ten feet off the ground. Melody Arnold had made it all the way to the top.

But just as quickly as it had come, the adrenaline vanished. The feeling of power vanished, and Kat's arms ached from holding on so tightly. She twisted, ever so slightly on the rung, and looked down at Zen. She felt dizzy. "What am I doing?"

"Something incredibly stupid."

"I'm afraid of heights," she said, focusing on Zen. She couldn't bear to look down. What had possessed her to start climbing this damn tower? Was it the same thing that had possessed Melody Arnold?

But she was not her mother.

A strong gust of wind almost caused her to lose her grip. "Shit!" she yelled. "Please get me down from here!"

"Easy does it." Zen climbed up right behind her. "We'll take it nice and slow, one step at a time."

Shakily, with Zen piggy-backing her down, they made it to the ground. Kat's heart beat furiously. "I don't know what came over me. I just had this sudden urge to climb the tower, which is insane. As I said, I'm afraid of heights." She looked up, up, up to the top of the tower.

That's when Kat saw it: The woman crouched on the top, her red hair flying loose in the wind, her coat billowing open to reveal the large mound of her stomach. Slowly, the woman stood up. Slowly, she extended her arms and leaned forward. Her mother was smiling.

"No!" Kat screamed and collapsed into Zen's arms.

"I could see her up there," Kat said when she had finally composed herself. She still nestled in Zen's arms. "It looked like she was getting ready to fly."

Minutes before, it had seemed so real, but now when Kat looked up, all she saw was the top of the light tower, empty. Her mother had vanished. It was as eerie and disturbing as the scene that had played out before her in the church. That, too, had seemed so real. "Do you think I saw her ghost?"

"I don't know." Zen rubbed her back. "You've been through a lot in the last week. Maybe you only saw what you've imagined ever since you read Pops' newspaper article."

He didn't understand. Kat had spent the last week willing herself *not* to imagine the scene. Since reading the article, she had tried not to focus on the actual physical nature of her pregnant mother climbing up this very tower and then jumping off. Instead, Kat had focused on her anger at Melody Arnold. But now she was here, and there was no denying what had taken place at this tower in the desolate, abandoned railway yard. It had happened. Melody Arnold, her mother, had jumped to her death.

With a smile on her face.

Kat shuddered. "It's so horrible."

"It is," Zen agreed. "However, you survived. It's pretty much what I would call a miracle."

Tanner Delaney and Sylvia had said the same thing, and perhaps it was true. What were the odds of a baby surviving a fall like that? A baby. *Her.* It was so hard for her to reconcile herself to that fact. She was the baby who had survived a 100-foot leap off a light tower in an abandoned railway yard. She was the fucking miracle.

She would never wholly fathom why her mother had done it. As Kat had come to understand, Melody Arnold had been in an unhappy marriage, suffered from depression after losing her first baby, and then turned to drugs and full-blown addiction. What was it Sylvia had said? Oh, yes, depression, desperation, delusions. That explained many things, but still, Kat could not fathom anyone's desire to kill herself. She just couldn't. It wasn't in her nature. Yet she was going to have to come to terms with the past. She had no other choice. Her father had asked her to forgive her mother.

She looked up into Zen's compassionate eyes and thought: *What the hell.* She was tired of waiting. She leaned into him and kissed him.

"Hey," Zen said when they parted some seconds later.

"I've wanted to do that for days now." Kat closed her eyes and took a deep breath. I think I'm falling in love with you." There, she'd said it. For better or for worse, it was out in the open.

"I don't know what to say."

"How about something along the lines of *ditto*?" Kat opened her eyes. The look in his eyes wasn't warm and fuzzy. Kat would have to say that the word for it was *concern*.

Zen looked away for a moment and then returned his gaze to Kat. "I like you, too, Kat, a lot, and I'd be lying if I didn't say that I've wanted to kiss you on more than one occasion."

"Then, why didn't you?" Kat had a gut feeling that she wasn't going to like where this was going.

"I know from experience that when people are in highly emotional or vulnerable states, their thinking can become confused. What they think they feel at one moment might not be true the next week, or even the next day. You've had a life-altering week, Kat."

It was Kat's turn to look away. His voice was so kind that it hurt. "And you've been a big part of that week, Zen. Thank you." Maybe he was right, but she didn't think so. She knew what she felt, and even if Zen did not reciprocate the feeling, Kat was not sorry that she'd told him that she might be falling in love with him.

"It's been an honor," he said sincerely.

It was so Zen.

"Well ... good." Kat didn't know what else to say, and for once, she was glad when her blasted phone rang.

It was Sylvia. "Are you at the light tower?" she barked.

How did she know that? But then again, she was related to Granny Nanny. Maybe all women in that family were clairvoyant. "I am," Kat said.

"Did you find the bag?"

"What bag?"

Zen, of course, could hear her loud voice perfectly, and he raised his eyebrows.

"Don't be dense, Kat. The bag your mother took with her to the hospital. I told Ronnie precisely where to put it. That pinhead. He's about as dependable as a teabag, but I flatly refuse to go to that awful place. It's supposed to be on the south side of the tower, leaning against the base. That's where I found it thirty years ago after I got the call—after what happened. No one seemed to have noticed it, so I snatched it up, hid it under my coat, and took it home. I've had it ever since."

"Why did you do that, Sylvia?" Kat asked, although she already knew.

"I wanted to make sure that there wasn't anything in there that would change people's opinion about Mel."

"Do you mean drugs?"

"Anything that would change people's opinion about Mel," Sylvia said firmly.

"Was there anything incriminating?" Kat asked hesitantly. For some reason, she desperately hoped that there wasn't, even all these years after the fact.

"Of course not." Sylvia coughed.

Kat walked around the tower, and there it was, a faded gray duffel bag. "I see it."

"I left the contents exactly as I found them. The bag is yours now, Kat."

As Kat drew closer, she could see that the bag had a name tag—Melody Arnold. Her heart seized up.

Sylvia's parting words before the line went dead were, "Your mother was a good person, Kat. And a damn fine nurse."

The wind suddenly died down, and it was weirdly quiet. Kat knelt and slowly unzipped the bag with trembling hands. She could feel Zen's presence behind her, and it comforted her.

What was she hoping for? She had no idea.

On top of the clothing in the bag was a box of opened stationery, and next to it, a crumpled note. Kat felt like she moved in slow motion as she reached for the note and carefully unfolded the ivory sheet. The writing was very faint, looking as if the pen had almost run out of ink, and it was small, barely discernible. Kat bent her head to make out the words.

There were only two: *I'm sorry.*

And that was when Kat Flowers finally cried for Melody Arnold, the poor, young, desperate woman who had climbed up and jumped from a 100-foot light tower in an abandoned railway yard. She cried for Marcus, too, the husband whose love could not save her, and she cried for herself, the motherless, clueless child. But mostly, she grieved for Mellie Callahan Arnold.

Her mother.

EPILOGUE

MARCH 22, 2013

When Kat looked back at the fateful week when she had tried to piece together the story of her mother's life and her spectacular decision to end it by jumping off a 100-foot light tower, the sequence of events still possessed a surreal quality. And during the last eventful year, Kat had spent hours and hours thinking about it. The discoveries had been devastating, yet as more time passed, they had also been liberating. Her meltdown at the base of the light tower, after she'd read her mother's scant suicide note, had been the beginning, releasing years of pent-up rage and frustration that she hadn't known she'd been keeping bottled up inside. She'd been so emotionally exhausted afterward that Zen had to carry her out of the railway yard. Kat still didn't know how he had managed that feat. She must have felt like dead weight to him, but he had done it.

It was so Zen.

They'd caught a taxi back to Sylvia's place, where Sylvia was waiting with a bottle of vodka. "Fuck the orange juice," she'd said. "This calls for straight hooch."

Sylvia didn't go on her rounds that night. Instead, she put an old vinyl record of Eric Clapton on her ancient record player. "This was one of Mel's favorites." Sylvia poured drinks all around. "It's about time we had a memorial service for Mellie." She raised her glass. "To Mellie, a damn good person, and a damn good nurse."

They toasted, and then the three of them drank themselves into oblivion the rest of the evening.

The next day, Zen borrowed Sylvia's van and drove Kat to the bus station. They were both so hungover that they were practically mute. So there were no big promises to keep in touch, as she and Sylvia had done repeatedly the previous night after a tearful Sylvia had given Kat a box of pictures of her mother. However, it seemed to be understood that she and Zen would also stay in touch.

"Be safe." Zen gave her a quick hug.

Kat kissed him on his cheek. "Adios, amigo," she said as she boarded the bus. She slept the entire way to Arizona, and when she arrived, Granny Nanny was waiting for her at the bus station once again. Dear, dear Gran.

They stopped at Walgreens on the way home because Gran was running low on Noxzema, with only two jars left in her stash. When Kat added an EPT kit to Gran's cart, saying, "I'll pay you back as soon as I can," Gran didn't act like it was anything out of the ordinary. "I'm sure you will, dear," she said.

When Kat got home, she peed on the stick, and her heart nose-dived. It was now an indisputable fact. She came out of the bathroom, brandishing the stick. Granny Nanny and Mr. Williams were enjoying a shot of scotch at the kitchen table. "No more of that for me for about eight months," she said. "I can't believe that Benson is going to be a father."

"At least you know that the baby will be pretty, dear," Gran said helpfully, smiling.

"My daughter-in-law has a crib in her attic," dapper Mr. Williams said.

Did they not get the gravity of the situation? However, they both looked so happy, just sitting there, enjoying each other's company, that Kat would not cause a scene. She was not going to do that anymore. "I'm not going to tell Benson." She had suddenly decided it. Somehow or other, she would handle this herself. It was her responsibility, and she was going to be responsible.

"I'm sure you'll do the right thing, dear."

Kat was glad that someone had confidence in her dubious abilities. But Granny Nanny always had. Kat had an overwhelming desire to call Zen and tell him the news. What would he say? Probably something like, "Congratulations." What would he think? Probably something like, "Whew! Dodged a bullet *there*."

She didn't call Zen. For one short week, she'd depended upon him. She'd depended upon him *too much*. She wouldn't do that again. A man needed some room to breathe, after all, even the uber-polite Mr. Lorenzo Delaney.

As it turned out, she didn't get a chance to tell or not tell anyone. A month later, she miscarried. She'd just started to get used to the idea. In fact, the idea grew on her daily. She wasn't getting any younger, and although she'd always been rather repulsed by the very idea of babies, she found her attention drawn to women wheeling strollers in the grocery store and Pamper and Gerber commercials on TV. She worried, though, about how much she had been drinking in Chicago. Could that have harmed the fetus in any way? She researched this on the internet, and she knew that the odds were in her favor. However, she still worried.

As Melody Arnold must have worried. Kat would certainly never condone the fact that her mother had shot up heroin while she was pregnant. But Melody had, and then she had to live with that shameful, awful secret. However, Kat would have to say that she had a better understanding of some of what her mother felt during her pregnancy. The guilt could make you a little crazy.

Not that she was like her mother.

In the future, if anyone ever asked her about her mother and how she died, Kat's answer was going to be the same as it had always been: "My mother died in childbirth." It was true, sort of.

Kat was on her way to yet another job interview when the cramping started. This one was a sales rep for a pharmaceutical company, a position she had zero interest in. Anything having to do with hospitals or medicine unnerved her. (She definitely had not inherited that from Melody Arnold.) Sweet Mr. Williams—he wanted her to call him Nathan, but she just couldn't do it—had called in a favor from a friend of a friend or something like that, and Kat felt obliged to go. Her money situation was grimmer than grim, and with a baby on the way, she would take anything, even this job that would have her in doctors' offices every working day. So be it.

She'd felt some minor cramps since she woke up, but she'd read that this was normal during early pregnancy. However, when the cramping became severe, and she felt the sticky wetness between her legs, she realized this was *not normal*. She turned Gran's car around and sped home, on the verge of panic. This couldn't be normal. She was a healthy woman; her doctor had said so at her first appointment. As Dr. Sheila Carston had said, "It looks like everything is good to go."

It wasn't good to go. The fact was confirmed when Gran took her to the ER. An ultrasound revealed that it was all over. No more baby. It happened so fast that it caught Kat completely off guard, and when they returned home, she felt strangely empty. And then she felt sad, extremely sad. What if this was her one chance to have a baby? Even if she thought she wasn't ready, she would have been prepared by the time the baby arrived. Was it because of the drinking she had done in Chicago? Was that the cause of the miscarriage? Maybe losing the baby was all her fault.

Yes, oh yes, the guilt could make you a little crazy.

Not that she was like her mother. Or was she?

Sometimes, luck does just fall into your lap. Literally. Kat sat at Starbucks, not drinking coffee. She couldn't afford it, but she'd felt an overwhelming desire to get out of the house. Granny Nanny and Mr. Williams were in Gran's bedroom doing God knew what. (Kat refused to think about it.) She half-heartedly surfed the internet for job openings, and at the same time, was making a list of how much money she owed to too many people. It was quite depressing. She decided to take a restroom break and pushed her chair back from the table.

The next thing she knew, a venti latte landed in her lap, soaking her jeans. "Shit!" she cried, jumping up. "What the hell?"

"I apologize!" a woman's voice said. "I tripped. These damn stiletto boots looked so great in Victoria's Secret catalog, but they're hell to walk in. Don't ever order boots from Victoria's Secret catalog."

"Not planning on it," Kat snapped.

"It's a good thing that it was an iced latte." The woman was large and wore a flowing leopard-print caftan. Her frosted hair was in a perfect pageboy. "Otherwise, I would have burned you."

"Lucky me." Kat swiped at her jeans with a meager paper napkin. Great. Now she would have to go home and change.

"The least I can do is buy you a cup of coffee."

Kat would love a cup of coffee. She'd been practically salivating at the smell ever since she walked in the door. Instead of politely saying that it wasn't necessary, she said, "Actually, that would be very nice." Then her stomach growled loudly.

The woman had a broad smile. "And a scone."

"Maybe a blueberry muffin instead?" If the lady was buying, Kat figured she might as well get what she liked.

"Done," the woman said.

She bought herself one as well and ended up sitting down with Kat. Rea was warm and chatty, and Kat liked her instantly. She owned a corporate event planning business, had never been married ("Don't need it!" she proclaimed.), and loved dirty martinis. And then she asked the dreaded question, "So what do you do, Kat?"

Kat shifted uncomfortably. "I'm between jobs right now."

"Interesting," Rea said.

"How so?" To Kat, being unemployed was embarrassing, nerve-wracking, and wretched. Being broke sucked.

"I have an opening. One of my girls' husbands got transferred, and she had to quit. Would you be interested?"

"Yes!" Kat said immediately.

Rea laughed. "Enthusiasm is a must for the job."

"Let me get this straight. You plan corporate parties for a living?" It sounded like a dream job to Kat.

Rea laughed again. "Well, there's more to it than that. We plan all kinds of events for large and small groups: desert jeep rides, cowboy cookouts, trips to Sedona, themed dinners, yadda, yadda, yadda. We do site inspections with prospective clients, write proposals, book bands and entertainment, yadda, yadda, yadda. It's not all linens and flower arrangements and choosing dinner entrees."

Could this woman be serious? Had the cosmic bitch slaps finally come to an end? Before she got her hopes up too high, Kat thought that she should mention an important fact. "I don't have any experience." *Please,* Kat thought, *don't ask me for a resume.* Her for-shit resume could sink the deal.

"I'd train you."

"You'd be willing to do that?" Kat held her breath. It sounded a hell of a lot more exciting than any job she'd ever had before. She wouldn't be cooped up in an office or a restaurant. For once, she would be doing something creative.

Rea shrugged her shoulders expansively. "Of course."

Kat felt like she had to say it. "But you don't even know me."

"In my business, you have to be a good judge of character, and I can learn more about a person in ten minutes than most people can in a year. Plus, I'm the best in the business in this town. I'm not bragging. It's true. I'll personally train you. However, I do have to tell you that the hours, especially during peak season—October to May—can be very long. You'd be working a lot of nights."

"I would love the opportunity." Kat would work harder than any employee Rea had ever had. She would.

"When can you start?"

"How about now?"

Rea had not been kidding about the long hours, but Kat didn't mind at all. She loved the fast-paced business and how she had to think on her feet all the time. The pay was decent, not earth-shattering, but Kat didn't mind that either. She caught onto the business quickly and got promoted after the first month. Kat even liked all the people in the office—all women. Finally, she didn't dread going to work. Finally, she felt like she was doing something important.

Finally, she had a career.

When Kat got the news that Marcus had died, she was out on a date, her first date since she left Chicago. Strangely, she felt that she was being unfaithful to Zen. Well, that was just stupid. They were not and had never been a couple. She and Zen frequently emailed, though, chatting mostly about day-to-day stuff, his law classes, her exciting new job, and never did they mention if they were dating other people. Kat was very happy to learn that Tanner Delaney had not needed a second open-heart surgery, and Zen seemed genuinely sorry to hear that she had lost her baby. He'd been polite enough not to bring up the subject—she had. And in telling him, some of her sadness had lifted. He could still do that to her.

Kat met Thomas Mahoney when she accidentally ran over his foot in the parking lot at Fry's grocery store. Admittedly, she'd been talking on her phone to a vendor for her upcoming event when she backed out of her parking space, but so had he. She heard a yelp and a pounding on the rear fender of her brand new red Mazda (the insurance money had finally come in) and slammed on the brakes, heart pounding.

She jumped out of her car. "Are you hurt?" He wasn't bleeding, and he wasn't lying on the ground mangled, so maybe he was just being an asshole. A handsome asshole. He was tall, with a neatly groomed blonde ponytail. From the look of the biceps peeking out of his black t-shirt, he worked out.

"Have you ever heard of a rearview mirror?" He didn't sound all that angry.

"Is it your habit to go around pounding on people's cars for no reason?" He looked perfectly okay to Kat.

"No, it's not. I only pound on a woman's back fender when she runs over my foot."

"Oh, my God," she said, looking down at his black boots. "Which one?"

"The one with the tire tread," he said, starting to smile.

"Can you walk on it?"

"Don't know."

"Should I take you to the emergency room?" Kat thought that this was just great. She had barely started to get on her feet and pay people back, and now this. However, it was the right thing to do. She had, obviously, run over his left foot.

He took a tentative step. "I think it's fine."

"Maybe you should get an X-ray just to be sure?" Kat didn't know how many tons a car weighed, but surely it was enough to do some damage.

Thomas took a few more steps and then came back to Kat. "I'm pretty sure it's fine. These boots are indestructible."

"Is there anything at all I can do for you?" She would be late for her next appointment if this guy didn't shit or get off the pot. She was very sorry that she had run over his foot, but as he said, he seemed fine.

"How about dinner?" His smile was not nearly as charming as Zen's, but it could be a close second—maybe.

"Excuse me?" He didn't look homeless, but you never knew.

"Can I take you out for dinner?"

She had run over his foot, and now he was asking her out? Granny Nanny and Rea would be jumping up and down and shouting *yes!* for her right about now. They both thought it was high time that Kat started to date again, but Kat still couldn't get the thought of Zen out of her mind. She knew it was ridiculous, but she couldn't help it. However, she had run over this good-looking guy's foot, and he was nice enough to ask her out.

Maybe it was time to move on. "How about if I take *you* out for dinner?" she said. "It seems like the least I can do."

Their dinner at Voltaire was going pretty well. Thomas had worn a sports jacket for the occasion and picked out a decent bottle of wine for their meal. He talked easily about his job as a contractor, which explained the heavy steel-toed boots that had saved his foot from being crushed by her car. When he said he played in a heavy metal band on the weekends called Alien Kingdom, which explained the ponytail, Kat even managed to keep from rolling her eyes and saying what popped into her mind: "You've got to be kidding. Are you seventeen?"

She tried to give him a chance. So she listened attentively and smiled and did all the crap she was supposed to do on a first date. However, it was already clear to her that there wasn't going to be any *zing* with this perfectly nice man, not ever.

Because this perfectly nice man was not Zen.

Her phone rang, and when she fished it out of her purse, she saw that it was Shane. She'd kept her promise to stay in touch with her brothers and called them once a week, as she did with Sylvia and Uncle Willie. They were all planning a visit to Arizona in the unspecified future, and Kat was saving money for plane tickets.

So it wasn't unusual that her brother would call. She had just talked to him two days before, and he'd told her that Marcus was "hanging in there." Marcus had surprised everyone by "hanging in there" for all these months. On two occasions, Kat spoke to him, short conversations that never tapped the surface of their feelings, and needless to say, they never, ever mentioned Melody Arnold. Yet Kat derived a sense of comfort from the banal, cordial communication, the "How are you feeling?" and "What's the weather like there?" and "Did you see the latest episode of *Criminal Minds*?" They were both loyal fans of the show, and Kat relished this small connection.

"What's up, bro?" she playfully said while mouthing to Thomas, "My brother."

Silence. Then, in a thick voice, Shane said, "It's Dad. He's passed."

"No," Kat said. The room seemed to grow silent around her. She'd thought that she'd prepared herself for this awful, inevitable news, but now it felt like the world was standing still. "No," she said again as she felt her throat tighten.

"Yes," Shane said. "I'm sorry to be the one to tell you, Kat."

"When?" she whispered. As if that mattered.

"A couple of hours ago."

Her father had been dead while she sat here, eating dinner, not knowing. She should have known. She should have instinctively felt his leaving, and she should have been there by his side. She was having trouble breathing.

Thomas looked alarmed. His eyes darted around the restaurant.

"I'll catch the next plane out." Kat realized that she had never been to a funeral before. How odd, she thought randomly, that her father's funeral would be her first. How terrifying.

"There's no need, Kat." Shane started to cry. "There's not going to be a funeral or a memorial service. Dad said that people have those to comfort the living, not the dead. We're honoring his wishes."

Her father was not going to have a funeral. Melody Arnold hadn't had a funeral either. They were two lost souls.

That was when Kat lost it again. The first time, she had been alone in front of her brother's and grandmother's graves. The second time, she had been with Zen at the base of the light tower where her mother had taken her tragic leap. For this third and final time, as she cried for her father and what they had lost, she was in the middle of a crowded Italian restaurant, in front of a pony-tailed heavy metal rocker and dozens of other strangers.

And Zen was not there to carry her out.

"What time is your appointment, dear? Shouldn't you be hurrying along?"

The crafty old lady was up to something. Kat just knew it. "Are you trying to get rid of me, Granny Nanny?" Her skydiving lesson wasn't for another two hours, and the old woman knew it. She was definitely up to something.

"Of course I'm not trying to get rid of you, Katrina." Gran opened the stove and took out the carrot cake she'd baked for Kat's birthday. "This is your home, too." Granny Nanny had a surprisingly sharp tone to her voice.

It was a sore subject for her. She still seemed upset by the fact that Kat was moving into an apartment the following week. She would room with Terry, a girl from work who had become a friend during the last few months. Kat, too, had mixed feelings about leaving the house she'd lived in for the last fifteen years (minus the year with pretty boy Benson O'Shea, who in the long run, didn't count). She would miss her gran terribly, but she had Mr. Williams now. Their pot business was thriving—old people were apparently potheads—and she and Mr. Williams were taking a Mediterranean cruise in June.

"I'm only moving two blocks away," Kat reminded her. "I'm thirty-one years old, as of today, and I think it's time, don't you?" Oddly, turning thirty-one was not nearly as traumatic as turning thirty, and Kat was okay with it. To celebrate, she was going to conquer her fear of heights and skydive again. She was still terrified, but she would try one more time.

"I'm going to miss you, dear." Gran's blue eyes shone.

Kat got up from the table and hugged her. "Don't be silly," she said gently. "I'll stop by every day."

"I know, Katrina." Gran nodded her head against Kat's shoulder.

"How about a shot of scotch?"

"That's a good idea, dear."

Kat got down the Glen Livet bottle and two glasses and set them at the usual places on the kitchen table. She poured. "Now spill, Gran. I know you've got something up your sleeve."

"Not a thing, dear." She didn't look Kat in the eye.

Kat was pretty sure she knew what was going on. "I told you I don't want a surprise party or any hullabaloo. You haven't gone and done anything like that, have you?"

"Well, Katrina, you gave me a surprise party for my last birthday. Fair is fair, don't you think?"

It had been a great party if Kat said so herself. All the neighbors had come. "I had an ulterior motive," she said. "I was trying to get you to finally admit how old you are."

"Age is just a number, dear."

Kat rolled her eyes.

"And it didn't work, did it?" Gran smiled craftily.

"No, damn it, it didn't work." Every time someone had asked Granny Nanny what birthday she was celebrating, she had deftly changed the subject. The lovely, crafty old woman.

Gran looked at the clock on the wall. "Shouldn't you be going?"

"Not until you tell me what's going on. I hate surprises." Kat had certainly had enough of them the last year. "Really, I do."

The doorbell rang. "I'll get it." Granny Nanny was on her feet in a flash. She was awfully spry for someone her age, whatever that was.

"Oh, no, you don't." Gran had been a little too quick on the uptake. Something was definitely up, and it had to do with whoever was at the front door. It was probably a delivery of some kind. Granny Nanny had recently taken a very big shine to Amazon.com, so it was probably Kat's birthday present.

Even though Gran was spry, Kat had no trouble beating her to the door. "Ta-da!" she said as she flung it open. She stared, speechless. "Oh!" she finally managed.

It was Zen, and he was smiling broadly. "Happy birthday."

Kat was too stunned to speak or move. He looked even better than she remembered. His hair was a little longer, and then those green/gold eyes ...

"Surprise!" Granny Nanny called out gaily.

"I can't believe you're here." Just the sight of him made Kat's heart beat faster. With this man, there was definite *zing*.

"Nothing could keep me away," he said.

"What? How? Who? Granny Nanny!" Kat turned to her. The spry, crafty, lovely old lady practically danced with joy.

"Go on." Gran gave her a gentle push.

And she was in Zen's arms, which felt so right. She didn't know if Gran had somehow set this up or if Zen had been complicit. She didn't care. "I've missed you so much," she said. Kat was *not* going to cry, not this time.

"I've missed you, too, Kat, more than I've ever missed anybody." He kissed her.

"It's about time," Granny Nanny said.

"I have so much to tell you," Kat said. She was dizzy from the kiss, and it felt marvelous.

"Not now," Gran said. "You'll be late for your skydiving lesson."

"Are you still here?" Just her luck to get the instructor who had witnessed her embarrassing failure the year before.

"Of course I'm still here," Soul Patch said. "I own the business."

"Good to know," Kat said.

"Are you going to make the jump this year?"

Damn it. Naturally, Soul Patch would remember. "I'm going to give it my best shot." The plane ascended, and Kat tried not to look out the window as they went higher, higher. She felt sick to her stomach but also exhilarated. Zen had come with her; he was waiting down below in the hangar. She hadn't asked him to come up with her, and he hadn't offered. They both knew this was something she had to do alone—with a little help from Soul Patch.

"Are you ready?" Soul Patch moved toward the open, gaping door.

She had to follow, and there she was, standing on the precipice.

It was a beautiful early spring day, just like the year before. The blue, cloudless sky looked like the backdrop in a movie set. But Kat was not the same person she'd been the year before. During the past twelve months, Kat hadn't had the recurring dream of a weightless flight that gave her a feeling of peace, an inner serenity that she did not have in real life.

Because she now knew that she had made one leap before, in the womb of the doomed Melody Arnold.

She had been the miracle born out of a tragic leap.

"We're coming over our mark," Soul Patch said.

Without a doubt, Soul Patch was the most annoying man on earth. "Just give me a second, okay?" Kat closed her eyes and took deep breaths. Maybe, knowing what she now knew, this wasn't such a great idea. She was still afraid of heights, and perhaps, if she sought inner peace and serenity, she would be better off taking up yoga.

"We need to jump now," he said.

"I need a minute or two of silence, do you mind?"

Soul Patch sighed. "Circle back," he said to the pilot.

Kat opened her eyes and made the mistake of looking down at the ground. Immediately, she closed them again, feeling dizzy.

How had Melody Arnold felt when she was on top of that tower? Kat had pictured it so vividly when she was in the railway yard with Zen, when she'd looked up and seen the pregnant young woman crouching on the slippery top of the tower, the wind buffeting her. Then the woman stood, extended her arms, and leaned forward. She'd been smiling when she became weightless, free, flying.

"Get ready," Soul Patch said.

Kat would never be ready. But she *had* to be ready. This jump wasn't at all like what her mother had done. Kat wore a parachute, and it would open.

She was in such a better place in her life than just a year before. She had a career, would soon move into her own place, and she knew more about her past, her mother, and her father. For better or for worse, she knew. Best of all, she had Zen waiting for her down below. She had no idea what would become of them. He was finishing his first year of law school in Chicago, and she lived and worked in Arizona. Would they have some long-distance relationship? Would they be friends? Would they be lovers? Would they be both?

Only time would tell.

"Five seconds," Soul Patch said. He reached for her hand, ready to buckle them together.

Kat opened her eyes. It was a beautiful day, the sky a pure, piercing blue. Everything would work out as it should; she would put her faith in that.

"Three, two, one …"

Kat took a deep breath. She knew she could do this if she would only take that first step.

"Now!"

Kat took that first step.

And then she was flying.

TO MY READERS:

Thank you for reading *The Light Tower*. I have completed seven additional novels, each a distinct and interesting story with great characters. If you liked *The Light Tower*, I believe you would like my other novels as well, and of course, I would love for you to read them.

Please visit the Library page on my website at LaurieLisa.com for more details on each of the other completed novels and their upcoming release on Amazon:

- *The Wine Club*
- *Across the Street*
- *Hollister McClane*
- *"star-cross'd lovers"*
- *David's Women*
- *Family Mythology*
- *Queen of Hearts*

You can also join my Reader's List at LaurieLisa.com to receive updates on the pre-orders and release dates for my novels. Feel free to make personal requests to me directly or ask questions about my books.

I look forward to hearing from you!
Laurie.

Manufactured by Amazon.ca
Bolton, ON